Regent's Mercy

Regent's Mercy

Alyson J. Bowles

Mariposa Sources

Contents

Prologue

The man smiled gently as he watched the young woman gently lay her infant in the crib. She hovered for a moment to make sure the baby settled, then turned as she buttoned her top back up. "Sorry about that. The doctors say it's normal for some babies to be fussy. But…"

The man in the forgettable suit smiled broadly now, "Your baby isn't normal."

April looked back and down at the sleeping M'Kylo. "He is to me. I just wish his father could see him."

"Yes, well, that is actually the purpose of my visit." April's mouth flickered with a hopeful smile as she returned to join him at the small dining table in the corner of her quarters. "Dr. Odem says you've been the most vocal about reuniting with your…mate?"

"Yes, his name is Pouduit; he was my Proctor on the ship."

Forgettable Suit Man scribbled something on his notepad. "I'll be blunt, April. The doctor also tells me the others have intimidated you into not telling us everything you know."

"They all know the same thing," she said with a low, shaking voice. He watched April blink rapidly as she glanced over at M'Kylo's crib.

There was no way she could prove it, but April was certain it was not a coincidence that two members of Michelle's clique had ended up in the same lifeboat as she. Both pregnant themselves, they had been a nearly oppressive presence even as the lifeboat began its maneuvers to enter the atmosphere.

Katie and Chrissie had been very quick to impress upon April that it was in her and her baby's interest to be as ignorant as the rest. April was the only Hybrid outside of Michelle's circle who knew who she was to the Ceruleans, and they had been quite effective at ensuring April's compliance. To the point that somehow Chrissie had ensured April's room was bookended between her and Katie.

And the walls were paper thin.

However, as if reading her thoughts, her guest said, "All of the others are downstairs watching a movie. We are alone and secure." Forgettable Suit Man watched as April closed her mouth and focused on the table. He continued, "What if I told you I could ensure M'kylo gets to meet his father as soon as possible?"

"H-how?" April felt her heart swell with the idea of seeing Pouduit again. "They told us there's been no communication from the ships."

Forgettable Suit Man pulled a photo from his inside breast pocket and slid it across the table. April looked down at it to see a familiar face. It was Michelle holding Arya, and judging by the background; it was from a video aboard the *Rising Star.*

"That photo is a still from a video that popped up on the internet about two weeks ago. Someone is trying to bury it but it is starting to spread. It's only a matter of time before it goes viral." Forgettable Suit Man used a single narrow finger to slide the picture back to him and then return it to his inside breast pocket.

"The Ceruleans want her. They've offered a ten-billion-dollar reward for her and the baby girl to be returned to them. We know who she is. We know she was instrumental in the destruction of the alien ship. We don't know why she's the only one of you with spots on the left side and a baby girl or why the Ceruleans want her back so badly."

He waited until April looked up and locked his eyes on hers. "Why is she special? Why is there a vault of silence around her?"

April spread her fingers across the table as if trying to press out wrinkles in the laminate while she thought. "I want you to get me and my son out of here. They've threatened to hurt him if I say anything. He's not safe."

"How long will it take you to pack your things?"

Chrissie was only outside because the pregnancy sickness had snuck up on her, and getting outside was faster than going to the bathroom. Her Marine escort stood silently at a discreet distance as she rinsed her mouth out with the bottle of water he had handed her, and spit. Although she knew all too well it would be a while before the vomit's sour taste faded.

As she leaned her head back for a breath of night air, she saw April briskly moving across the parking lot with a man guiding her with a firm hand at her lower back. When she saw M'kylo's head resting on her shoulder, alarm bells set off in Chrissie's head.

"April!" Chrissie yelled at the girl's back. "April, where are you going!?" April stiffened but kept moving toward a large, dark sedan with government plates. Chrissie felt a lead ball forming in her stomach. "Don't do this!"

Chrissie went to step off the sidewalk when she felt a strong hand clasp her arm. "Sorry miss, but you aren't allowed to leave the grounds without special permission, remember?"

Chrissie whirled on him, "Then where the fuck is she going?"

The Marine looked Chrissie dead in the eyes as the car's engine burst into life, "Where is who going, miss?"

She turned back in time to see the car's taillights turn out of the parking lot and head toward the base's main gate. "Fuck."

Chapter One

This was how she had begun every morning since coming to live with her mate on Cerul. She still remembered being transported from the ship to the exact location where she now stood. How her future mate had let her take in the breathtaking view of the lush forest-covered hills stretching away to the horizon, giving her time to center herself before gently calling her name.

Nicole remembered how the Proctors aboard the *Rising Star* had warned them they would all be unlocked as they were transported to meet their future mates. She had seen others aboard the ship go through the *Phage* and had accepted the inevitability of what it meant for her. She thought she had been ready. Only to discover the sensation of falling instantly in love was not something one could ever prepare for.

That was why she stood on the balcony every morning, looking out at the vast ocean of rolling green while her feet warmed on the clay tiles heated by the sun.

And then there was her favorite part.

Nicole returned to the present as she heard the patter of little feet on those same sun-warmed tiles just before small arms wrapped around her legs, and the collision of a small body almost knocked her over. Nicole smiled as she looked down to see Brylie's bright blue eyes looking back up at her. "Good morning, my son. Did you sleep well?" she asked in Cerulean. He had his father's eyes, Cerulean eyes, but he certainly favored Nicole's fair skin and Nordic blonde hair.

"I dreamed last night," the little boy said excitedly. Nicole's smile brightened, and she turned away from the balcony rail and lowered herself down so she was looking at the child in the eyes.

In English, she said, "Oh? Tell me." She gently rubbed her thumb over his faint brow ridges. A simple show of affection often used with Cerulean children.

Brylie easily followed his mother into the second language, "I dreamed that I got to go on Popa's ship and we traveled far away and I got to meet a princess!"

"A princess, huh?" She widened her eyes in surprise.

He nodded sagely, "Uh-huh, just like in the stories you tell me before bed!"

"And what did you and this princess do in your dream?"

Brylie scrunched up his face, "Nothing! She was little and wouldn't talk."

Nicole mimicked her son's face in confusion. "Littler than you? Then how did you know she was a Princess if she wouldn't tell you?"

Brylie looked away from his mother as his voice took on a tone of wonder, "That was the fun part, Mopa. She told me in my head but like with pictures. And she told me you knew *her*, Mopa!" He looked back at her suddenly excitedly, "Why didn't you tell me you knew a queen, Mopa?"

Nicole was quiet for several blinks as she took in her son's earnest expression. He was earnest. This wasn't one of his fantastical stories or his imagination at play. She finally opened her mouth to respond, only to sense her mate approaching from inside the house. "Good morning, P'alta," she called out, letting Brylie know he needed to switch back to his first language. Speaking English was furiously frowned upon on the home planet.

Nicole stood and turned toward the open glass doors that led onto the balcony. He stepped out with a broad smile, which Nicole did not return. "Good morning, Popa!" Brylie bleated as he skittered across the clay tiles to wrap himself around his father's legs.

P'alta grunted as he scooped the boy up into his arms. In Human years, the child was just over a year old, but physically and to hear him speak, the boy easily could have been six years old. "And a good morning to you, Brylie!" P'alta's deep voice vibrated across the balcony and through Nicole's chest. She bit the inside of her cheek in response. He looked at Nicole, who remained near the balcony rail, "Good morning, Nicolette. Did you sleep well?"

"Well enough," Nicole jutted her chin, "Is she still here?"

"Zouma will be leaving after breakfast; come join us. Please." P'alta turned and carried Brylie back into the house. With a hard sigh, Nicole followed them. She used the distance to calm and center herself before stepping through the doors. Brylie's chipper voice was greeting Zouma as Nicole made her way across the great room toward the dining area.

"Good morning, Nicole."

It took the usual amount of effort not to cut her eyes at the older female and instead force a smile that did not reach her eyes. "Morning, Zouma." The female was rail-thin, with sunken eyes the color of sunset. Zouma's lips had once been full but had thinned once the condition had fully settled on her. Her dark brown hair hung loose and lifeless about her narrow shoulders. Most Cerulean females wore their hair this way to hide the lack of spots on either shoulder. She had pale skin that had become too fragile to spend time exposed to Cerul's twin suns. Sallow and mottled, she often wore clothing covering her neck to ankle to prevent her condition from advancing.

Condition.

It had no official name. To do so, P'alta had once said, would be to give it power over those it claimed. It wasn't openly talked about, but not ignored either. An open secret. In her time on Cerul, she had, however, heard and seen enough to know that it was not a great mystery where the *Condition* had come from. Just not exactly what that cause was. *This* was not an open secret and one that bowas closely guarded. As usual, the Cerulean penchant for guarding information prevented Nicole from finding out.

Zouma appeared soon after Nicole had become pregnant with Brylie. Nicole had screamed and yelled and cursed. *It wasn't fair;* she had protested. After everything Nicole had gone through, being stolen from

Earth, DNA altered to become part Cerulean and female, forced to learn a whole new language and society to go with it...to seal the bond between her and P'alta. Only to have *her* show up when Nicole had already served her purpose.

Nicole had given herself wholly over to P'alta by that time. The *Phage* had hit like a ton of bricks, and P'alta still proudly wore the scar she had given him beneath his right eye during the *Quoy*. She could still remember feeling the bond snap into place as they had mated for the first time and had come to cherish that moment. Sure, it wasn't the ideal scenario for how a boy named Louis had planned his life, but a night of violence and lust had allowed Nicole to embrace the new one. She had given herself to him, submitted completely to him, and her new place in the Cerulean culture. Nicole had accepted it all, but for Zouma's presence, and it was what could have been an idyllic life.

Colonel P'alta Bi'ltun commanded his own ship in the fleet and had been a close second to taking command of the *Rising Star* for the final years of its mission. As such, there were many formal functions he was expected to attend when his ship was in dock. Even as sickly as she appeared, Nicole groused, Zouma was the one P'alta took to state functions and dinner parties. She was the one he doted on even though Nicole had given him the son he proudly crowed about at every chance.

For her part, Zouma tried to be at least friendly with Nicole. This only worsened things as Nicole desperately wanted to hate the older female. Nicole spent much of her time with other Humans brought to Cerul and knew she wasn't the only one who'd been given the role of mistress. She was, however, the only one that didn't have to submit to her mate's *First Wife,* as the humans had taken to calling the Cerulean females their mates had kept or added. No, Zouma tried very hard to ensure Nicole didn't feel seconded by her. She was fond of Brylie and spoke to him like an elder aunt, always careful not to step on Nicole's parenting toes.

"Did you sleep well?" Zouma asked, her smile unfaltering.

Nicole blinked to clear her thoughts and stepped around the table to take her seat. "Well enough, you?" Maybe it was cruel to ask. Nicole knew they weren't having sex as Zouma couldn't handle the stress on her body.

Hell, they weren't even bonded like she was with P'alta. That made the situation worse when Nicole thought about it. Sometimes it was tough not to think of herself as just some sex doll P'alta used to feed his needs.

The female's smile faltered slightly, "Well enough, I suppose."

Nicole sat and ordered an American breakfast for herself and a bowl of oatmeal with brown sugar for Brylie using the holographic console in the middle of the table. She had tried mightily to adapt to Cerulean-style food, but it had never taken. And Brylie preferred oatmeal over anything else in the mornings. Which he showed by diving into the bowl with a spoon as soon as it materialized in front of him. P'alta was just reaching toward the display when the communicator he wore on his wrist started beeping.

He looked down in mild confusion. It was a direct link to his ship, *Star's Feint,* but normally they went through the global comms system to communicate. It chirped again, and Brylie's inquisitive nature kicked in. "Are you going to answer that, Popa?"

P'alta grunted and tapped the device. "Yes, Major Milkas?"

A young voice came back, filling the room as if he stood beside the table, "Sir, we just received... Sir, are you alone?"

"No, I am with my family having breakfast," P'alta said as his eyes flicked between Nicole, Zouma, and finally resting on Brylie. "What could be so important so early, Milkas?"

There was a long pause. Then finally, "Sir, we just received a short message from the *Folded Fist.* They and the entire fleet have been forced to land on the Human planet."

Nicole's fork hovered halfway to her open mouth as P'alta's eyes snapped to hers. "What of the *Rising Star*?" He asked, still holding Nicole's gaze.

"The distress buoy is broadcasting, sir. We believe the ship to have been destroyed as we have been unable to establish contact...with any ships of the transport fleet." Nicole's hand slowly lowered back to the plate as if weighed down by the fork she still held. "The Regents and Commander Et'Kuraul are currently unaccounted for."

Zouma covered her mouth in shock as P'alta surged from his seat and twisted away from the table. "That makes me the most senior in command, correct?" He asked as he strode across the great room toward the bedrooms.

"Correct, sir."

"Signal the fleet to make ready for an immediate departure. Every ship, save for system defense, must be ready to jump within the hour. Send a shuttle down to collect me." P'alta signaled for the door to close behind him as he entered the shared bedroom with Zouma.

"The shuttle is launching as we speak, sir. However..."

P'alta looked up through the ceiling as if he could see clear to the *Star's Feint* orbiting overhead. "Out with it, Major! Now is not the time!"

"Sir, the distress buoy did not signal via subspace, nor was it encrypted. It broadcasted through the old communications buoys."

Colonel Bi'ltun had been heading for the closet to change into his uniform but froze mid-step as his blood chilled and dread filled his gut like boiling acid. In a near whisper, he said, "Notify the outposts, Major Milkas. Notify the outposts and signal the *Regent's Mercy* to get underway. They are to meet us at the border. I'm transferring my flag."

P'alta stood in the middle of the bedroom and scanned the furniture, the unmade bed, the small pile of toys Brylie had left on the floor, and the sunlight streaming through the blinds to cast its rays on the thick gray carpet. His mouth had become as dry as the Zidmaas Desert while his heart thudded slowly, almost painfully in his chest. "C-carry out my orders, Milkas. And do it whisper quiet. We do not want to start a panic."

"At once, sir. The shuttle has just left the dock."

P'alta turned at the sound of the bedroom doors opening to see Nicole walking in. Her jaw was set, letting him know he was about to lose an argument. Zouma's presence was the only argument he'd won since they had mated. Still... "Absolutely not, Nicole." She remained silent but kept her hard gaze fixed on him, her golden eyes boring in with enough force P'alta could nearly feel it. "It is not allowed. Once you step foot on Cerul you cannot leave. You know this." Nicole raised her chin in silent challenge. "Who will stay and watch over Zouma?"

Blood rushed up Nicole's neck and filled her face with anger. P'alta knew he had gone too far; Nicole kept no secrets about Zouma. "I will not stay here and play as her nurse. I will not." She wasn't yelling, but her voice conveyed the same energy. Her feet slid into a fighting stance, and her hands fisted at her sides. He'd already lost this fight. Nicole was as immovable as a boulder once she took that posture.

"That is not what I meant-"

"Yes, it was, P'alta. You are taking me and Brylie with you."

"It is not allowed, Nicole. You-"

"Have I resisted?"

"No-"

"Have I been difficult?"

P'alta blanched. Aside from her issue with Zouma, Nicolette had been a model mate and mother. She had adapted to the ways of her new home and even helped others who were still struggling with the adjustment. His shoulders fell, "No, Nicolette, you have been a blessing in my life. But what about, Zouma? I cannot leave her here unattended. Never mind that it is forbidden for Humans to leave Cerul."

"That is for you to solve, *Mate.* And gods save me, but I promise not to try to escape. Cerul is Brylie's home, and you are his Popa. But..." Nicole let him see the tears brewing in her eyes. "I would like to see my home one more time." Nicole stepped forward and lowered her voice as she took one of his hands, a move she knew punched through just about every defense he had. "Please."

P'alta gave a heavy sigh as he raked his hand through his hair, a gesture he'd picked up from Nicole. He wanted to consent to her request, but if things were as bad as they appeared, Cerul was the safest place for her and Brylie...maybe.

Unable to look her in the eye, he pulled his hand free and stepped away. "You cannot, Nicolette. I want to say yes, but we might be traveling into...difficult circumstances."

Nicole scoffed as she moved back into his line of sight. If he had wanted a mate that would keep sweet, he had certainly picked the wrong human. "What? Somehow in the last two years, Earth figured out..." The look on her mate's face stilled Nicole's tongue momentarily as her brain replayed what she heard at the table. In English, "Wait, he said *Regents*." Nicole stressed the plural. "There's a new Regent?" P'alta remained silent as her impressive intellect continued down the path. "But that would mean a Human is the new Regent...and somehow...the High Council would never allow her to rule. Cou'Parth H'arprom barely even respects Rory. He treats her like crap! Oh my god..." Nicole closed her eyes as something wiggled at the back of her brain. "Wait, something is missing..."

P'alta grunted and finally pulled his uniform from the closet. "I need to finish getting dressed and prepare for departure." Nicole could feel it through the bond. A vibration that carried an emotion she had never felt from him before. She could feel it consuming him as he struggled to hide it. Still, it transmitted across the thread between them to fill her own body with something she hadn't felt since waking up on the *Rising Star.*

Fear. *No,* Nicolette thought as she finally opened her eyes. It was abject terror.

"P'alta-"

"I cannot, Nicole."

"P'alta, look at me." Slowly he turned, and now that she knew it, Nicole could see it plain as day on his face. "We do not ask."

P'alta furrowed his brow, "I do not understand."

Nicole retook his hand and pulled him down to sit on the bed. "Have not any of you ever wondered why we, the humans, do not ask why the Cerulean females are sick?" P'alta slowly blinked and tried to stand, but she pulled him back down. "Even the ones who have been here since the beginning. Do you think we have not been observing and listening all this time? We talk amongst ourselves, and most of us have come to an understanding, P'alta." This got his attention, and his head swiveled on his shoulders. "This malady that affects Cerulean females was not a..." Nicole paused as she searched for the right translation but couldn't find it. So she continued in English, "...act of god, was it?"

Nicole watched his throat pulse as he swallowed. "No," P'alta answered thickly, "No, it was not. And I will lose my rank, if not imprisoned, for admitting that to you, should anyone find out that I did."

Nicole nodded as she pressed her lips into a thin line, then asked, "Are we in danger? Here, on Cerul?"

P'alta was ostensibly the second-highest-ranking male in the Cerulean military. His subordinates obeyed and admired him, and at times, his very bearing could fill a ballroom. Nicole knew, without a doubt, he would snap the neck of anyone who tried to hurt her or Brylie. But as he took a deep breath and glanced out the window he looked like nothing more than a frightened little boy. "I do not know."

Chapter Two

"Roger!" Maggie's panic-filled voice poured ice water down Michelle's spine even as her brain registered the acceleration of the blue threads in Domaas' exosuit. Without a word, they both pivoted toward the house. Michelle was at the glass slider before she even knew she was moving. The door was open, and she was rounding the corner from the empty kitchen and into the living room without a thought to see if Domaas was following her.

She first saw her father sprawled face down on the floor with Private Smith standing over him and his rifle pointed down at her father's back.

"Dad!" All heads swiveled toward Michelle as she moved to check on her father, but a strong hand grabbed her arm and stopped her dead.

"There you are!"

Michelle snapped her head to the side to find it was Corporal Turney holding her arm with his unholstered sidearm in the other hand. Then she noticed her mom and sisters cowering on the couch, with a third Marine holding his rifle aimed in their direction. In his other hand was a fist full of Jamie's ponytail. Michelle focused her eyes on Jamie's as she asked in Cerulean, "Where is Arya?"

"I do not know," she answered in the same language. "I was trying to put her in the crib when she suddenly threw a fit. I put her down, and she ran off and hid. That was just before..." Jamie's eyes danced around the room, "This happened."

"Enough of that freak language! You and that freak kid are coming with us," Turney said. "Call her to come out, and you might be able to save your dad's life."

Everyone felt a sudden pulse of static energy and looked about the room questioningly. "What the fuck was that?"

Only Jamie noticed Michelle's left hand slowly curl into a fist. "You want the money." It wasn't a question. "You were supposed to protect us. You are Marines." Michelle watched her father's back rise and fall, indicating he was still breathing. A small wave of relief passed through her.

"Yeah, well, turns out ten billion dollars can purchase a lot of morals," Turney answered. "Now find that little brat of yours. Before I start putting bullets through the walls." Michelle felt the pulse of rage across the bond with Domaas. She had felt him enter the living room behind her and move past deeper into the room. The cloak on the suit was perfect enough that she now had no idea where he was. Just that he was here and as angry as she was.

If Arya's abilities were what they seemed, then it made sense the child would find a place to hide. Michelle put out a probing thought. *Sweetheart, are you okay?* And got back images of someplace dark and cool. Fear was attached to the images, but so was reassurance that she was okay. Scared, but okay. *Talk to your grandfather,* Michelle thought as forcibly as possible. *Keep him company, and don't let him fade away.*

There was a grunt from the floor as Roger shifted.

Turney gestured to the Marine holding Jamie, "Put her on the couch with the others. They aren't going to do anything while he's still alive. Go find the brat and be quick about it. This is already taking too long."

Jamie squeaked as Private Holden roughly used her ponytail to drive her down to the floor at the feet of Michelle's mother and sisters. She quickly put her back to the couch and made herself as small as possible. "The kid's name is Arya; call out to her." The Marine moved around the furniture and took the stairs two at a time. Michelle felt Domaas follow the Marine.

"You were awake when I showed my Dad the video?" She asked in an attempt to draw this out.

Corporal Turney chuckled before responding, "I saw both, actually." He adjusted his grip on her arm. "Your hand-to-hand skills are impressive. Who taught you?"

Michelle pointed a manicured nail to her father's still-breathing body. "He did, one of two."

"Huh, well, I was top in hand to hand during basic, so don't be stupid. This is a target-rich environment. Why don't you call your kid and make this faster?"

There was another pulse of static energy, this time powerful enough that Corporal Turney released Michelle's arm as he stepped back. Michelle felt hot and then a flash of coolness as her anger came to a boil. Cold fury poured into her veins as her racing pulse suddenly slowed. This man had brought violence into her family home, a place of peace and safety. There would be time for regret and sadness later; now, it was blind anger. "What the hell is that?" She turned toward him, and his gun snapped up to point directly at her chest. "Freak, get on your knees. This bullet will be through you before it even knows it was fired."

Domaas returned down the stairs, a sense of grim satisfaction and purpose traveling across the bond. Arya was silent, but Roger was still breathing. Michelle could feel the energy collecting in her tightly coiled fist. She had not had an opportunity to explore her powers, and it was becoming a struggle to keep it contained. Distantly she scolded herself for trying to ignore what was now an intrinsic part of her. She doubted she could control it for much longer but did not want to let it out with her family present. Not when she wasn't even sure how to aim it. Maybe she had been foolish to think she'd be able to leave behind everything that had happened.

"Hey, Mike! Check-in!" Turney called up the stairs. But there was no response. "Holden, respond!" He shifted his gun from Michelle's chest to her forehead. "Who else is in this house?"

Michelle fought the urge to step back as she looked down the barrel of his handgun. The rifling was clearly visible. Death was mere inches away, perhaps even closer for her father still prone on the floor. Heartache suddenly threatened to bank the raging inferno at the thought of her dad dying, and with a blink, she shoved that thought away. *Not today.* She felt a chill race down her spine and spread to her fingers and toes. Cold resolve settled on her face.

"Everyone in the house is in this room except for my daughter," she answered as she forced her focus on his eyes. It was technically the truth.

Corporal Turney's back was to the living room, so he couldn't see Private Smith suddenly lift from his feet, his rifle swinging on its strap as both hands came up to pull at whatever gripped his throat from behind. "Maybe I should just put a bullet in you and give the aliens your kid, huh? What makes you so special any-" The barrel of Smith's rifle knocked against the coffee table as he silently struggled, and Turney began to turn.

The split second his eyes shifted was all Michelle needed. Her open hand came up to catch his wrist and yanked him forward as she stepped out of the line of fire. Corporal Turney barked his surprise and fired his weapon, but Michelle was already clear as she spun him around so they had switched places. Holding his gun hand pointing into the kitchen Michelle opened her fist, pivoted her bare feet into a fighting stance, then slammed her open palm into his chest with every ounce of strength she had. She released her hold on the energy in her arm, and Corporal Turney was thrown back in a flash of bright purple light. His body impacted against the wall with a sickening thud and crumpled to the floor as tiny bolts of purple energy danced across his still form. The wall where he hit had a perfect indentation of his body in the drywall.

Michelle was stunned at her display of power for a fraction of a second before she quickly moved to secure Corporal Turney's dropped gun. After checking the action and confirming there was a bullet in the chamber, she turned to see Domaas had become visible and was still holding Smith by the throat in mid-air.

"Domaas, do not kill him!" She yelled in Cerulean. Domaas lowered the man to the floor but did not release him, only lessening his grip. Michelle cleared the living room, crossed the space, and pointed Corporal Turney's pistol directly between the Marine's eyes. "Were you the one who shot my father?"

He had to blink several times to focus as blood rushed back into his head, and after several gasping coughs, he managed to answer, "No, that was the guy who went upstairs, Holden." The Marine's eyes shifted toward the staircase as if he was hoping for a last-second rescue.

"Twitch and I will let my mate finish you," Michelle said as her eyes narrowed. Her face was dark as if storm clouds hovered directly over her eyes. The fury in her voice left no doubt it was not an idle threat.

"Heartbeat?" The Marine stiffened at the sound of Domaas' heavy timbre and deeply accented English. When Domaas continued in Cerulean, Michelle saw it click in the Marine's eyes exactly who and what was holding him from behind by the neck. "The exo-suits have nanobots that deploy to heal injuries. Your father is alive but getting weak. We can save his life."

Michelle gestured with the pistol and said to Private Smith, "All the way down on your belly." Domaas released him, and he quickly dropped to the floor, crossing his ankles and placing his hands behind his back. This had not gone as planned, and at this point, he knew he'd be lucky to get out alive.

Michelle safetied the gun as she lowered it and turned to the couch where four sets of large eyes stared back at her. They needed direction before the shock set in. "Mom? Jamie? Can you undress Dad?" Jamie burst into action as she understood Domaas, but Maggie didn't.

Her voice quivered as she blurted, "We need to call an ambulance-"

"Mom, the suit that makes Domaas invisible can save Dad's life. It's already been too long; please hurry." Domaas had already pulled off his shirt, exposing the black material with pulsing blue threads. "Ellie and Shan, can you go get Arya and keep her company? She's hiding in the foundation of your bed Ellie. Just...keep her busy."

The living room was in a flurry of activity as everyone suddenly had a purpose after such a traumatizing event. However, as the rest quickly set to the tasks she had asked of them, Michelle found herself idle. She watched her mother and Domaas work on her father just long enough for the crushing reality of what had just happened to begin to gather into a monster wave that would consume her if she didn't busy herself fast. She couldn't let herself be swept away by that wave of self-blame. Not yet.

Pivoting on her bare foot, Michelle snatched her translator from the mantle over the fireplace and started walking to the kitchen.

"Wait," Maggie called from the floor as she carefully pulled her injured husband's pants down. "Where are you going?"

Michelle didn't stop but growled over her shoulder, "To tear a general a new asshole."

She threw the slider open hard enough it slammed against the stop and popped off the track. The deck remained pristine as if extreme violence had not just occurred mere feet away. The sun still shone warmly in a clear sky while birds chirped in the eucalyptus trees dotting the hillside. On the wooden planks of the deck were her pumps, which she didn't remember even kicking off, and in one was a pile of diamonds still sparkling in the sun. The translator beeped as she slipped it behind her ear, "Rachel!"

-*"Oh hey, Kiddo!"* Rachel's cheerful voice came back. *"How's your great reunion goi-"*

"The Marines General Hamlin sent to protect me just tried to kidnap Arya and me! Corporal Turney saw the wanted video, and my father was shot." There was silence on the other end for several long moments.

-*"Shit. Is...is your father..."*

The shakes were coming on from the adrenaline dump, and Michelle began pacing across the deck to bleed off the excess energy. "I don't know yet. Domaas is putting him in the exosuit to try to heal him."

-*"...Okay. Hold on a sec while I try to get a hold of the General."*

Michelle continued to pace and suddenly became aware she was still holding the pistol. She dropped it on the table while completing another circuit around the deck. *What if I fucking killed him?* She hadn't glanced at Corporal Turney's body when she walked out. *What if he had killed me? Or hurt Arya?* She felt her blood rush at that idea and was glad the doubting thoughts began to fade away. The man who had shot her father was dead if she felt Domaas correctly. And there was no remorse coming across the bond.

Michelle had done *exactly* what she'd promised Domaas she would do. If Turney were dead, if she had killed him, Michelle would not let herself feel remorse for that either. Not when it came to her family and the people she loved. -*"Michelle?"*

"Yes. Is he going to send someone to pick up the bodies?"

-*"Bodies? They're dead?"*

"One for sure, maybe another, but one for certain is still alive. Where's the General?"

General Hamlin's southern accent came through her translator. -*"I am here, Miss. Mizzi. Rachel has connected me through to you. What is this about my Marines?"*

"They tried to kidnap me and my daughter, General. And the name is Et'Kuraul. We need to speak in person; there's someone here you should meet."

-*"I will send a car to pick you-"*

"No, General Hamlin." Michelle took a deep shuddering breath before continuing. There was no going back after this. "I am the Regent of Cerul. *You* will come to me." She took off the translator before either the General or Rachel could respond and dropped it on the table. She picked up her pumps and poured the diamonds back into her hand as she entered the house.

Exiting the kitchen, she saw her father on his back and covered in Domaas' exo-suit. It was ill-fitting due to the size difference, but the ring was in place, and the blue threads were pulsing faster than normal. She stopped just shy of the carpet and finally felt the first sting of tears. "Is...is he going to be okay?"

Margaret looked up from where she knelt next to Roger, her eyes shimmering. "Domaas says the suit will heal him completely. The color is already back in his face."

Michelle nodded stiffly, "Good." She looked to where she had last seen Corporal Turney. He was sitting up and leaning against the wall where his body had left his imprint. He had a dazed look in his eyes, and what looked like burst capillaries covered his exposed skin in a vivid shade of lavender. Next to him sat Private Smith with his knees drawn up and head sunk between his shoulders. Jamie stood over them, holding Private Smith's rifle in a relaxed but alert position. "Jamie?"

"Not to worry, your Grace. As a Boy Scout, I received merit badges in shooting and gun safety. I also went hunting with my dad. I once took down a boar at two hundred yards." Michelle arched an eyebrow in appreciation of this new information. Those were skills she very much wanted watching over Arya.

She felt him approaching and turned just in time to embrace Domaas. Slipping her hands about his waist, she pulled him close and buried her face in his chest. His musk of clover and warm cinnamon enveloped her instantly, and Michelle finally felt the tension starting to bleed off. "A General is coming," she said into his chest. "It is the same one we were taken to when I made planetfall."

"General." The word was rough coming from Domaas. "I do not know what this is," he finished in Cerulean.

Michelle turned her head to be heard more easily but did not let go of him. "It is like the highest-ranking person in the military, sort of. I think he would be one rank below you if there were one in the...my fleet." She knew he looked down at her but wasn't ready to meet his questioning gaze. Michelle instead focused on her father's prone form. His breathing was looking more steady by the minute. "But since I named you my Regis, that makes you the highest-ranking person beneath me, right?"

Domaas' strong arms wrapped tighter around her body, and she settled even more into him. "Michelle-"

"This is going to be one of those things I am just not going to talk about, Domaas. I fought so hard to get here and return to something close to a normal life. I nearly lost my family because of what *I* wanted. I am not fighting against my fate anymore." She switched back to English, "Can we just leave it at that?"

Michelle felt the warm air from his sigh as his chest expanded and contracted. "Of course, your Grace."

This time her head snapped up, and she looked him in the eye. "No. Not from you, *not ever*. You are forbidden from calling me that."

He offered a gentle smile, "As you wish, Heartbeat." His arms tightened fractionally around her, and Michelle allowed herself to feel fragile - delicate, in his embrace. Grounded, if even for just a moment.

There was a groan behind them, and Michelle disengaged from Domaas and turned to see her father sitting up. Maggie struggled to contain her tears of happiness as Roger took visual stock of the exosuit he wore. Everyone but Jamie watched him go through a check of his legs and arms, slowly moving them as if to ensure everything was still working the way it should. Turning slowly, he looked to see Corporal Turney and Private Smith sitting with their backs against the wall and Jamie standing guard over them. Remaining slightly dazed, he nodded as if that answered his question and returned to Margarette with a faint smile. "Hey, you-" His wife couldn't contain herself and hugged him tightly as tears streamed down her face.

"Oof," he said. "Easy, honey, I feel like I was gut kicked by a mule." Maggie lessened her grip but did not let go as she cried into her husband's shoulder. He looked up as Michelle approached and sank to her knees, with Domaas standing behind her.

Michelle exhaled a breath she hadn't known she was holding and offered her father a grim smile, "I brought this to you guys."

Roger shook his head weakly and reached a hand for Michelle's. "Don't you dare." Michelle glanced down where he gripped her hand, the strength in his fingers, an expression of the life that had almost been lost. She hadn't given herself a chance to contemplate how much his loss would have hurt, but now she felt her chest painfully tightening as her vision blurred.

"If I hadn't come back, this wouldn't have happened. I put you all in danger, and you almost died because I had to be stubborn." The tears broke free and rolled down Michelle's cheeks in huge droplets.

Roger's grip tightened on her hand, and she looked up. "*No.* You do not have my permission to feel guilty for this. I am alive, and my family is whole. That is all that matters. Am I understood?"

Michelle flattened her lips into a thin line as she looked her father in the eyes and nodded, "Yes."

"Now," Roger said as he disengaged from Maggie. "Somebody help me stand up. I feel stiffer than wet sand."

Maggie protested, "Roger, you were shot..."

He waved away her protest as he held a hand up toward Domaas, who gripped it easily and began to lift. "Whatever is in this suit has me feeling fine, just sore." Roger allowed Domaas to gently pull him standing and looked up into the Cerulean's eyes. A simple nod was offered and returned, a vast amount of gratitude and appreciation transmitted through one simple gesture.

Releasing Domaas' hand, he turned again toward Jamie's hostages. "There were three of them?"

Domaas' accented timbre filled the room, "The one who wounded you will not hurt another."

Without looking back at Domaas, Roger nodded in understanding. He was taking in the appearance of Corporal Turney but elected to address that later. "There's another I need to thank." He glanced at Michelle, who was just getting to her own feet. "Where's my granddaughter?"

Chapter Three

The house was nearly empty. As soon as Roger felt well enough, Michelle practically ordered her family out of the house. The only one remaining, besides her Regis, was Jamie, who remained on guard duty over the two remaining Marines. Michelle had realized in the last hour that her daughter's nanny had been well chosen by the Elder Regent. Jamie generally kept a very placid face, but the fury in her eyes had not dissipated until Margarette's Suburban had been heard backing out of the driveway.

Domaas had brought down the dead Marine's corpse, which now lay at the feet of the other two, covered by a sheet. Private Smith sat leaning against the wall, his legs stretched out and crossed at the ankle while he kept his fingers interlaced behind his neck. This was the position Jamie had instructed him to assume. He wasn't exactly sure what he had seen happen to Corporal Turney, who sat next to him, nor was he eager to find out or experience the Specter's ire again.

Corporal Turney remained nearly catatonic. He was aware of his surroundings but seemed to be barely animated. He was taking long shallow breaths, and his bloodshot eyes blinked slowly as if he'd been heavily sedated. The jagged lines across his face and the backs of his hands had gone from lavender to deep purple - the same color as Michelle's energy blast. His lips had turned the same vivid color, and if one looked closely, the same pattern of blown, purple capillaries could be seen on the surface of his eyes.

"I should contact Colonel Cha'ol aboard the *Folded Fist*." Michelle felt a slight chill race down her spine as Domaas deep voice vibrated against her exposed neck.

Clearing her throat to remain focused, she asked, "Why?" From the corner of her eye, she watched him select another diamond and reach to match it against one of her spots. His touch was gentle but firm as he found the right spot and pressed it into place.

There was the now-familiar pulse of warmth as it fused to her skin. The diamonds were never to be removed. "Domaas?"

"As your Regis, I am responsible for ensuring your safety. To my eyes, my sovereign is now potentially on enemy soil. We should be doing this aboard one of your ships." It would take some getting used to the idea that she was now the head of an entire species, an Impire. Every ship grounded in the San Joaquin Valley ostensibly belonged to her, every ship in the Impirial fleet, for that matter. If she ordered Domaas to jump, he would actually do it.

The former Regent had explained in depth the full expanse of all that would be under Michelle's dominion. However, that had been after Michelle realized there was still a chance of escaping the *Rising Star*. By then, she had already stopped listening to most of the Regent's lectures. Now she was recognizing the enormity of what she had finally agreed to. Thankfully another bloom of warmth on her neck prevented the mental abyss she had just been about to dive into.

Michelle reached and clasped Domaas' hand. He stopped as his gaze shifted from her neck to her eyes. "I have you," she said softly.

Domaas' eyes crinkled as he smiled, showing his single dimple. "Always." His face turned serious as he returned to his task. "However, you know that we constantly studied Earth's culture, Heartbeat. Everything I have read and seen makes me firmly believe that once Humans *truly* understand who *and* what you are, it will not be safe to remain on Earth. If today's events result from greed, what could...pride? Yes, pride; what could that cause? I am learning that Humans can be a formidable species if given the chance."

Michelle blinked as she came to understand he was right to be cautious. Domaas hadn't used the right word, though. It didn't convey the right sentiment. She realized he most likely wasn't aware of the conditions and precautions she and Rachel had put in place. In exchange for the young women who had returned to Earth not being molested or experimented on, including the ones who had been pregnant at the time, Rachel had allowed them to download the vast amount of information she had brought with them. Over one hundred tablets with about sixty petabytes of Cerulean science, medical data, star charts, and the key to faster-than-light travel. Rachel was supposed to be in weekly contact with Makayla, Sean, Katie, and Chrissie to ensure they were being left alone.

"Rachel told me you cannot operate the ships?"

Domaas nodded as he pressed another diamond into its correct place, "Yes. Most systems remain inaccessible to us." Michelle noticed the faint growl in his voice. "However, the *Usurper* was kind enough to leave us in control of the defensive shields. It is how I got out. Allow me to contact my second and arrange for a proper guard."

He was right. She was now the sovereign of an Interstellar Empire; she'd be a fool to think she was completely safe now. "Do it. When Rachel arrives, I will see if she can arrange some transportation."

*****

Four Humvees rounded the corner onto Rancho De La Sur. Three stopped in the middle of the street and disgorged Marines who quickly set up a perimeter. It was a quiet suburban street that ended in a cul de sac but all errant traffic would now be strongly encouraged to get lost in a different direction. The fourth Humvee pulled into the empty driveway of the lone house in the arc of the street.

The General exited the front passenger side while Rachel emerged behind him. "This is the correct address? We're bound to garner attention," General Hamlin said as he turned to look at Rachel. She'd allowed her hair to grow into an approximation of a shaggy pixie cut and had moved from surplus BDUs to fitted women's jeans and polo shirts.

"Like I said on the way over, General. The wanted video offering that huge reward I showed you has broken my containment as of three hours ago. It's going viral."

The General harrumphed, "Maybe if you had been forthright with all of this, we could have provided better security."

"You have met her, General Hamlin. You tell me how well you think she would have embraced a platoon of Marines. Especially since three of them just tried to kill her father and kidnap her." Rachel gestured toward the portico over the front door. "Shall we?" The General turned and strode for the door with Rachel falling into step next to him and the two other Marines falling in behind them.

Rachel pushed the doorbell and listened to the three-note chime from inside the house. After several moments the door opened of its own accord to show Jamie standing in the foyer with both hands behind her back. "Please come in."

Rachel stepped through first, followed by the General and two Marines. "Jamie."

"Rachel."

"No hard feelings?"

The nanny smiled, "None."

"Good."

The door closed, again seemingly of its own accord, and the two Marines nervously shifted. Once she heard the click, Jamie relaxed her hands to her sides; in her right hand was Corporal Smith's sidearm. The two Marines were already in motion when General Hamlin spoke. "Stand down. It's a display of strength." He glanced down at the pistol and saw the safety was off. He looked back up to the young blonde's steady eyes. "It's not a threat."

"No disrespect intended, but my ward and my sovereign have both been threatened today. Your men may collect that," Jamie pointed to the sheet-covered corpse lying to the side. "And escort those two, but your men won't be allowed to remain inside of this house." She finished by waving her gun hand toward Smith and Turney.

He noticed how Smith flinched. "Sovereign, huh?"

"Yes," Jamie answered with a challenging lift of an eyebrow.

General Hamlin eyed Jamie's placid demeanor once more. The only thing giving away her state of mind was the tone she allowed into her voice. Whoever this young woman was, she had a face made for poker.

The General still had his doubts about the validity of what Michelle had announced over the radio. Rachel had given him a brief explanation of exactly what it meant but it all seemed ridiculously far-fetched. He turned to his escort and gestured to the sheet-covered corpse that had been left to the side, "Get him out of here. Wait outside, no one in or out."

"Sir?"

"You have your orders, Lieutenant."

"Sir!"

The two Marines stowed their weapons and grabbed the body first. Jamie looked down at Private Smith. "Now would be a good time to make yourself scarce; take that filth with you."

Without a word, Smith climbed to his feet and lifted the still-dazed Turney to standing. Rachel suppressed a smile at Jamie's behavior. *It's always the quiet ones,* she thought to herself. "Where's Michelle?"

"Her Grace is waiting." The door closed again, and only Jamie saw the deadbolt turn by itself. "This way," she said as she turned to walk through the house. General Hamlin and Rachel quietly followed her through the living room, where the General noted the blood-stained carpet and the wall with an imprint of a body, then through the kitchen to exit the glass slider still off its track. The General found himself standing on the rear deck with an impressive view before him.

He heard Rachel say in a breathy voice, "Oh, you were serious..." And turned to see Michelle standing in the sun. She was hard to look at as the left side of her neck was glittering with diamonds catching and refracting the sun. General Hamlin remembered that Michelle had her spots on the left side while all the other mothers had them on the right. Now, those spots had been replaced with diamonds cut to fit the shape of each one.

Michelle was calmly looking at him as he approached, but Jamie stopped a fair distance away and turned to face him. "I present Her Grace, Michelle Et'Kuraul, Regent of the Cerulean Star Impirium." Jamie, who had tucked her pistol into the back of her jeans, turned to face Michelle and offered a brief curtsy. "Your Grace, I present Major General Milton Hamlin of the United States Marine Corps to you." Jamie then stepped to the side so that she was standing between the two, most likely to act as a buffer.

General Hamiln stood at rest, clasping his hands behind his back. He glanced at Jamie and then back to Michelle. "She's a bit formal, isn't she?"

Michelle allowed the flicker of a smile. "It's what she was trained to do, but for my predecessor. She's also fiercely protective of my daughter." *That, and her comfort handling guns, will be an added plus,* Michelle thought to herself. General Hamlin glanced back at Jamie. "Still," his eyes snapped back to Michelle as she continued. "I'm pretty new to this, but shouldn't there be official introductions when the head of state of a foreign power presents themselves to a representative for the land they are in?"

The General sighed deeply through his nose. "You cannot expect me to believe they kidnapped you, turned you into a female with their DNA, *and* made you some..." Michelle moved for the first time. Her hand reached out to the side as if holding something back, but nothing was there.

She lowered her hand when she saw him looking and stepped forward. "The last thing that you will do in my family's home, the same home where my father almost died from being shot by Corporal Holden, is call me a liar."

She now had that same hard expression from just after they had landed. The same look that gave him the sense she had ice water in her veins. General Hamlin bowed his head. "Of course, you are right. My apologies."

"Thank you."

"However, you are seventeen? And somehow, you are now the queen of an entire alien species? Multiple, if I remember your debriefing correctly. The Specters, whom we still haven't seen, were so desperate for children that they made a human their leader? Do you see how that doesn't make any sense?"

Michelle barked out a laugh, surprising *everyone* present. "General, you have no idea how absurd this is for me. Imagine what it's like from my side of things. I'm Regent because I had a daughter. That's it, that's why. And I fought it so, so hard. I hoped I'd be able to live quietly and raise my daughter. All *I* wanted was to return home to my family - the family that refused to forget about me. The family that waved to a giant spaceship, doubting they'd ever see me again."

"And because of my single-mindedness, my father almost died on the living room floor of his own house. The previous Regent died trying to save the *Rising Star*. By now, word has gotten back to Cerul, and there is a flotilla on the way to Earth, who won't be happy when they get here."

"All because I refused to accept what fate had in store for me. So yes General, I am Regent. It is utterly ridiculous. And I'm learning as I go."

General Hamlin nodded at the humility in Michelle's words. "I'm sure you understand I'll have to bump this up to the President?"

"Actually, I expect you to. I'm sure she'll want to speak with me as I do her. My goal, General Hamlin, is to strike an accord of peace with Earth. This is my *home*."

The General nodded thoughtfully and pursed his lips before he said, "It is. Does that mean you'll be looking to add Earth to your...*Impirium*?" He knew as she rapidly blinked in surprise that the thought hadn't crossed her mind. "I do not mean to insult you, Michelle-"

"It is, *Your Grace*," Jamie interrupted. "She has used your title without fail, General. Please extend the same courtesy to my Regent."

General Hamlin was silent then grunted before responding, "I have earned my title, my rank, through decades of hard work and dedication." He spoke to Jamie but was looking Michelle in the eyes, "What has your *Regent* done to earn such loyalty, such respect? She just said so herself, it was nothing more than dumb luck."

Michelle lifted her chin at the challenge. It was a fair question. "Nothing," she said. "I've done nothing to earn it. I fought it, actually. Remember? As you said; dumb luck." Michelle gestured to Jamie. "But she believes in me. I don't deserve it, yet. Even still, I have every intention of earning it." Michelle paused and turned her head as if she was listening to something only she could hear. Rachel, who had been absolutely still and silent, noticed Michelle was wearing her translator again. And that someone was missing.

"Mich- Your Grace?" Rachel spoke in Cerulean. Michelle's eyes snapped to her. "Are you talking to Mr. Et'Kuraul?" The General was visibly annoyed at the foreign language, but he could be ignored for the moment.

"Yes, he is here. He has been chattering away in my ear this whole time. He dislikes the General and is a bit...salty about you being here. Destroying his ship and all."

Rachel's eyes shifted around the deck, looking for the tell-tale warping of light that gave away the near-perfect cloak of an exo-suit. She finally found it standing right next to Michelle. There was nothing but blue sky and distant hills behind her, so anyone who didn't know what to look for would not see it. "Do I have anything to worry about?" Rachel asked in English.

Michelle smiled, "No. You're my friend." She switched back to Cerulean. "Besides, technically, it was *my* ship." Her smile broadened. "And I forgive you."

The General pointedly cleared his throat, and Michelle shifted her gaze back to him. "If you would not mind...Your Grace, I would appreciate everyone speaking English."

"Of course, General Hamlin." The look on his face remained sour and Michelle realized he was waiting for her to tell him what they were discussing. With a sigh, she continued on.

"As I said, General. Earth is my home. You know we destroyed the *Rising Star* to prevent them from using a weapon that would have caused untold amounts of violence and suffering. As the Regent, I'm in a position to negotiate a peace treaty. Obviously, I have no experience on this level, so I will be leaning heavily on my mate, Domaas Et'Kuraul, Regis of Cerul."

There was a rippling of light next to Michelle as a transparent form appeared and then Domaas' tall figure faded into visibility. Impressively, the General managed to keep a passive expression as he took in Domaas' sudden appearance. When General Hamlin stepped forward, Jamie twitched but stayed her feet when she saw Michelle's shake of the head.

Looking up at the seven-foot-tall Cerulean, the General took in all the features. Brow ridges as described, pale skin, full mouth surrounded by a few days worth of sparse stubble, and in this particular alien's case, solid sapphire blue eyes. They had the same gemstone quality as Michelle's daughter. Dark hair cropped at the ear in a military cut, a strong, thick neck column leading to broad shoulders, and well-toned muscular arms. The exosuit the alien wore made it clear he worked to remain in excellent physical condition. All in all, he looked Human, albeit taller and better built than the average Human male. Domaas would have fit right in with any basketball team. He was exactly what Michelle and all the others had described, as for some strange reason, Rachel had not thought to bring any images with her when they left.

"Does he understand English?" General Hamlin asked without looking away.

"I understand your language," Domaas answered. Michelle was probably the only one present who caught the tone of annoyance in Domaas' deep timbre. To General Hamlin's ears, Domaas' accent sounded almost Russian. *That would have been interesting fifty or so years ago,* he thought to himself.

"You appear to be quite young. According to my understanding of your command structure, a Commander is equivalent to one of our Admirals."

"So I have come to understand," Domaas said with an arched eyebrow. "I am sure that does not diminish your hard-won rank, General. I have had my own experiences with those under my command going...out of bounds. We do not hold you responsible for what happened today." Michelle visibly turned her head to look at the back of Domaas' head. *Diplomacy?*

"I need to call my superiors. The President will want to speak with *you,* I am sure," he had been speaking to Domaas, and he shifted to Michelle.

"Both of you." He turned to walk inside but stopped; turning back, he said, "I will call before the day is out. I understand why you would object to this, but I will leave my Marines out front for your protection. Rachel will explain to you why."

He turned away again, but Michelle spoke. "I would think, General, that we've made it clear we can protect ourselves. I'd rather not have more guns around my family's home. My father was shot, after all."

General Hamlin glanced over his shoulder, "Yes, and I would very much like to know why he isn't lying dead on your living room floor. Either way, as you claim to be a foreign head of state, it is my responsibility to ensure your safety. Consider this house to be your Embassy until more secure, proper arrangements can be made. The President, the State Department, Congress...you've just set many wheels in motion, your Grace." He hoped she hadn't noticed he'd left the *Pentagon* out of his statement. "The men stay. If you have problems," the General glanced at the imposing Cerulean standing next to Michelle. "Let me know as soon as possible." He stepped through the slider and Jamie scurried to escort him to the front door.

Rachel watched them go then turned back to find both Michelle and Domaas looking at her. "That...was underwhelming..." Her voice dropped off as Domaas stalked toward her.

"You destroyed my ship," he growled in Cerulean. "You breathe because my Regent and mate wills it. Remember that, *Usurper.*" Rachel fought the shiver that ran down her spine. She had no doubts Domaas would have physically removed her head from her shoulders if it wasn't for Michelle. She knew he had the strength to do it. No preset transport beam was waiting to whisk her away to safety now. Still, she refused to look away from his penetrating stare.

"That ship was going to effectively destroy all technology on my planet. The same as Michelle's. You would have done the same if it was Cerul."

"Domaas? Stop trying to scare her. She needs to tell me why the General is insisting on leaving Marines out front," Michelle said as she stepped forward to slide her hand into Domaas', their fingers naturally twining together.

Rachel slipped her hand into the messenger bag slung over her shoulder and pulled out a tablet. After punching in her password, she held it out to Domaas. Looking at Michelle, she said, "The wanted video broke my containment and is going viral."

Michelle stood rooted to the spot as the color drained from her face.

Domaas took the tablet and scrolled through the display of social media postings. "I do not understand. Is this the video the soldiers spoke of? What is *viral*?"

"How..." Michelle had to swallow on a dry throat. "How bad is it?"

"If it's not on the news yet, it will be soon. It's already taken over the "big four" social media platforms."

General Hamlin waited until the Humvee had backed out of the driveway and maneuvered around the vehicle roadblock. After the vehicle rounded the corner, he spoke to the man seated in the rear. He had not arrived with them. "It was exactly as you said."

The Man In The Forgettable Suit nodded even though the General wasn't looking back at him. "And the Cerulean?"

"He was there. He was wearing one of those exo-suits. It made him invisible. The girls said they were tall, but you don't know until you see it, I guess. Their eyes are just...unnatural. No sense of emotion coming from them. It's not normal."

General Hamlin could hear scribbling on paper but didn't turn around. Many clandestine agencies had returned to writing on paper in code using cursive. It made it more difficult to steal secrets now that everything was digital and left a trace while paper could be incinerated. "Was she wearing the gemstones?"

General Hamlin nodded. "Yes, looked like diamonds. From her collarbone and up behind her ear." He gestured with his hand along his own neck as he spoke. Still not turning to look at the man sitting behind him.

"And the little girl, her daughter?"

The General shook his head, "The house was empty, or at least appeared so."

The rest of the ride back to Camp Pendleton was silent, except for the roar of the engine and road noise. The Marine driving studiously kept his hands on the wheel and eyes forward. When they pulled up in front of the command building, he simply shut off the engine, stepped out, and didn't stop walking until he had turned several corners.

In the Humvee, General Hamlin turned bodily in his seat to look at the man sitting in the back. "Is she really what she says she is?"

"Our source is insistent that she is. Evidently, Miss Mizzi caught the Cerulean Commander's eye early. She was suspected of being a subversive element, though, and my source was tasked with trying to befriend our young queen. However, she failed to gain trust before Miss Mizzi went into hiding aboard the ship. There was another, but she became loyal to her mark and stopped feeding information."

The General nodded as his eyes became slightly distant. "Jamie."

Forgettable Suit Man nodded, "That is the name I was given, yes."

"She was there as well."

"Interesting." There was more scribbling on paper. "Those markings on Corporal Turney were also quite interesting."

The General grunted in agreement, "I suppose he didn't return to the base?"

The Man In The Forgettable Suit offered a smile that didn't even reach his cheeks and opened his door. "Nor, Mr. Smith. I'll be in touch, General Hamlin." And then he was gone.

Chapter Four

It had been just over a month since Bailey had been transported out of her shower to a lifeboat. She had just enough time to register that she was dripping wet and naked when an unknown girl yanked her into an acceleration seat and told her to strap in. The restraint harness had clicked into place a fraction of a second before the lifeboat had ejected from its launch tube. The intense force of powerful rockets blasting them free of the Rising Star *was enough to steal her breath.*

They were seated in a circle of fifty seats around the craft's hull. As far as she could tell, there were three levels above them. Quick math said that would be two hundred passengers. On a pillar running through the center of the length of the craft were multiple screens. As the craft adjusted its heading, those screens flicked on, and they were all greeted with a smiling but serious face.

A Human face.

Mid to late twenties, if Bailey had to guess, with bright gray eyes and dark hair that looked like it was just coming back from a buzz cut. The interior of the lifeboat silenced as she spoke. "Greetings, my name is Rachel, and you've just been rescued from the Rising Star-"

"Hey!"

Bailey blinked, and she was suddenly back in the present. She sat up in her seat and glanced around the empty bus, then down the aisle to the driver, who had turned in their seat. "End of the line, sweetheart. You gotta get off here."

"Oh...sorry." Bailey stood, shrugged into her overstuffed backpack, and then slung her heavy messenger bag strap over her shoulder. The driver opened the rear doors, but Bailey went down the aisle instead. "I-I don't really know the area. I was trying to get to the train station?"

The driver grimaced, shaking his head, "Sorry hon, but Union Station is downtown. We're way out in Santa Monica. You should have taken the Eastbound."

Bailey looked out into the transit center as she bit her lip. *Fuck.*

"I was supposed to catch a train. You're going back the other way, right?"

The bus driver sucked his teeth. "Nah, this was the last bus of the night. I'm going off shift, so you must get off here."

Fuck, fuck, fuck. The door closed with a thunk behind her as she exited the bus. The driver had turned off the coach lights and pulled away from the curb before Bailey took her second step. The sky was darkening quickly as the sun made its final salute somewhere beyond the buildings to the west. Like most low-lying coastal areas, Santa Monica and Venice had been submerged with the arrival of the *Rising Star*. So even though the waters had been receding for over a month, Bailey could still smell the ocean on the evening breeze. Putting her back to the ocean and finding the rising crescent moon, she began walking east.

It started two weeks ago. The first time she had felt the tug. It was constant and unyielding like a tether had anchored around her heart and was under a constant pull. She tried to ignore it, tried to distract herself. It was fruitless. Her mistake was talking to her parents about what was happening and why she had to leave.

Their reaction was predictable on reflection. While Marquis had enjoyed a healthy, functional relationship with his parents, Bailey did not. Evidently, her parents had found warmth in the arms of an Evangelical preacher after she had been taken. She'd woken up to the reverend standing over her bed, and before she could even register why her father was holding her down, the reverend was attempting to "beat the impure thoughts from her soul".

"It was God's plan," Reverend Stakker had explained. "God has intended you and all the rest to become dutiful wives and child bearers for

goodly Christian men. Else, why would he have seen fit to return you whole and pure to us?"

The irony was not lost on Bailey as she felt blood trickling down the back of her throat. She had sent a scathing glare from the one eye that wasn't swelling shut and blooded to her mother, who stood in the corner.

Reverend Stakker railed for an hour afterward, starting with Genesis 2:18. "This is why the hands of God changed you. Too many young women have been soiled by modern society. But you, you and the others, you are pure. Born not of this world. This compulsion you feel to return to the Specters is just Satan testing the resolve of God's pure creation. He wants to corrupt your soul so you can't give birth to healthy, Christian babies. Do you not see?"

Bailey saw. And it filled her stomach with acid as she understood her parents had just allowed a lunatic to beat her. As she came to understand, Reverend Stakker had managed to convert her parents into people who would allow, help in the case of her father, to beat her until she was choking and coughing on her own blood.

Reverend Stakker prayed over her before leaving a Bible on the bedside table. Using his fingers, he gently wiped the blood from her left eye that had pooled from a split brow. "You are the first, my dear. In time and with faith, you will overcome this...compulsion that Satan's spawn has forced upon you and the others." The Reverend smiled in a way that sent ice forming over the churning bile in her gut. "I have a Godly young man in mind for you. My son. Take solace in knowing that others will soon join you, and together you will all give birth to God's Army."

Afterward, her mother used a warm washcloth to wipe away the blood, applied ointment to where her skin had split, and small bandages to where needed. Her father, meanwhile, had set to swapping out the door knob on her bedroom door for a deadbolt. As instructed by the Reverend.

Bailey laid perfectly still while her mother worked and prattled on about a religion she had not even spoken twice about a year ago. All the while, Bailey quietly had laid there, struggling to quell the sickening combination of horror and anger roiling through her.

She could hear her parent's bedroom door opening and her father fumbling with the new lock as Bailey tossed her two bags through the window she'd just shattered. By the time he had opened the door, Bailey had followed them. And for maybe the first time since that shaft of blue light had changed her life forever, Bailey was glad for the peak physical shape the Ceruleans had insisted they all maintained. She had vanished into the dark of the desert by the time her father made it outside with a flashlight.

It had taken three days to get out of Blythe. She considered herself fortunate that it was still mid-winter, as summers in the small desert city could be murderous. Although she had turned eighteen while aboard the Rising Star, a small city with a bored police force made getting out of town more difficult than it should have been. Bailey had seen flyers posted on telephone poles imploring her to return home. The number at the bottom was not her parent's but Reverend Stakker's number with the name of his ministry below; God's Love Ministries. When the significance of this struck, Bailey realized a target was on her back.

She finally escaped from town by slipping under the cover of a towed boat at a gas station just off the highway. Bailey's heartbeat roared in her ears as she lay under the stifling cover. She listened to the family noisily climb back into the SUV that pulled the boat trailer. She waited for the cry of alarm or the chirp of a police cruiser's growler as the boat was slowly pulled from the gas station. But none came, and Bailey didn't begin to take full breaths until she felt the acceleration and heard the road noise that signified they were at highway speeds.

Bailey had woken with a jolt as she heard vehicle doors slamming and the tired grumblings of children. Without waiting, she threw the boat cover back and climbed out with a "Thank You!" as she quickly shouldered her backpack and sprinted into the unfamiliar neighborhood. As she ran across their lawn, the look on the family's faces had been priceless.

Bailey smiled at the memory as she placed one foot before the other and walked into the night. Hopefully, she'd reach Union Station in time to catch the morning train to Bakersfield.

*****

She missed it by seconds. A last-minute dash down the tunnel and up the ramps had her huffing as she reached the platform. Her exhausted muscles and bones aching in protest as she turned just in time to see the rear of the Maglev train vanishing around the turn as it pulled out of the station. The magnets in the track were still humming with energy.

Bailey dropped her messenger bag, placed her hands atop her head, and swallowed lungfuls of air. She was much too worn out to verbally express her frustration and mentally berated herself for stopping to catch a few hours of sleep in that truck park. Turning into a pace to keep her shaking leg muscles from seizing up, she froze in surprise.

Her father, Reverend Stakker, and two men she didn't recognize had just come up the ramp to the platform opposite her, across the double set of Maglev tracks. Fortunately, she was standing in shadow, and neither had seen her yet. However, Bailey couldn't take the time to ruminate that they had *actually* come after her; she had to move. Now.

Rallying the dregs of her energy, Bailey forced her body into motion, scooped up her heavy messenger bag, and quickly walked toward the end of the platform where stairs led up to the old Metro line. Keeping her head down and willing herself to be invisible, she forced herself to take simple steps. Just another young woman trying to quickly make her way to the next leg in her morning commute.

Just like any other teenage girl trying to escape her suddenly physically abusive father and a preacher with questionable ideas on scripture-

"Bailey!" Her father's booming baritone dragged claws of ice down her spine. She had never feared that voice before. She fought off the shiver, and the urge to stop it caused but instead broke into a run, her legs screaming in protest.

"Bailey, you stop right now! The police are already on their way!"

"Great!" Bailey threw over her shoulder. "I'll tell them how you held me down and let him beat me!" The yelling cost her, though, and her lungs burned with needed oxygen. She gasped as she summited the stairs and dived into the crowd waiting for the MetroLine trains.

A glance to her left confirmed there was a staircase on the far side of the Maglev tracks, but Bailey didn't wait to see if her father and Reverend Stakker were giving chase. She'd be a fool to think they weren't at this point.

Of course, they had been waiting and searching for her here. The train to Bakersfield was the only option for mass transit into the San Joaquin Valley since the Arrival Cataclysm of the *Rising Star* had rendered the Grapevine Highway unpassable. It had taken nearly a week and most of her saved cash just to get to Los Angeles. It would have taken her father about four hours.

Bailey carefully slipped between the people so as not to leave a wake in the crowd. Just another commuter anxious to get to their destination. A train horn echoed down the track, and an overhead speaker announced the train's arrival and destination. There was a shuffling of bodies as some people shifted closer to the tracks, and some stepped back to wait for the next train. She knew she was now on borrowed time as she stepped back to keep a tall, overweight man on her left and slightly forward of her.

She was betting her father and the Reverend would expect her to attempt to catch the train as it pulled into the station. Presently she saw one of the men pass directly in front of her, but his focus was further down the platform. Bailey risked a glance from behind her human shield and saw Reverend Stakker and the other man lingering close to the platform's edge where the doors were marked to open. She looked back for the man who had passed by and saw that he had taken the same position at the far end of where the train would stop. Her father had vanished into the crowd.

Okay, Bailey thought. *Three are going to try to catch me on the train. Dad will probably wait behind me to ensure I don't give them the slip.* There was the sound of another approaching train, and Bailey looked to see a second train gliding to a stop at the farthest end of the platform. She glanced back just in time to see the doors open to the first train; as the crowd began to move, the three men quickly pushed their way onto the train and vanished inside. She knew her father would watch for her, but now it was just him. She could handle just one...maybe.

Her human shield turned and began walking toward the second train, and Bailey moved with him and broke cover as she increased her pace. She wanted her father to see her.

The first train was already pulling out of the station as the doors opened on the second one. "Bailey, you will stop right now! Enough of this! It's time to come home!" Bailey didn't turn. His voice told her how close he was; to do so would be acknowledging that he was speaking to her. She was nothing more than a morning commuter.

Bailey entered the first car and quickened her pace even more; now she was moving against the clock. Her muscles were burning. She'd have to find a warm, safe place to rest if she escaped this. She heard her father rudely pushing someone aside when he entered the front of the car as Bailey was already transiting to the second car. She passed the first doors and heard a warning chime from overhead that the doors were about to close.

Behind her, she heard the vestibule door to the car bang open and pounding footsteps. "You're coming with me, young lady!" Through the reflection in the window to her left, she could see her father's hand outstretched as if to grab her backpack. Calling up the very last of any strength she had left in her legs, Bailey broke into a sprint just as the doors hissed and began to close. She knew they'd automatically reopen for safety if she grazed the edge of one.

She leaped through the second set of doors and collapsed with a gasp of pain as they clattered shut behind her. Pounding could be heard, and Bailey rolled onto her hip to see her father angrily glaring back at her through the glass. With a smirk of satisfaction, she sent him a vulgar gesture as the train began accelerating out of the station.

Chapter Five

Michelle couldn't keep the sleepy smile off her face as she sat curled into Domaas' warmth on the couch, tucked into his side while he rested his arm atop the cushions. Rachel seemed vexed about the video breaking her containment and alternated between sitting in Roger's chair or pacing between the living room and the foyer. Jamie, her mother, and sisters were animatedly talking in the kitchen. Her father sat on the floor while Arya climbed over him like a jungle gym. The two had been inseparable since Roger had recovered, and Michelle was pleased about that. Secretly, she had harbored a slight fear her family would reject Arya for being part alien. Also, privately, she chastised herself for being so foolish. At this moment, everything was as perfect as it could be - even as she fought off the feeling that the events from only ten hours prior had been just the first rumble of thunder from over the horizon. General Hamlin had called and told her to sit and wait, that her proclamation had lit more than a few fires in the State Department, Congress, and the White House. "Someone from the State Department will be reaching out in the coming days," he had said. "I've been told to request that you keep as low a profile as possible. The wanted video has launched a nationwide manhunt for you and your child. By none of the type of people you would want to deal with."

Which was true. The family had agreed that leaving the television off for the evening was a good idea. Every channel had been full of *Breaking News'* and *'Special Reports'.* Nothing more than talking heads discussing absolutely nothing more than what the video told them. The video had not given her name or her expected location. So Michelle's security lay in her *unknowness*. She and Arya were now safely ensconced in digital black holes thanks to Rachel, who had quietly wormed her way into the military databases and erased all photos and information pertaining to the one returned captive with a baby girl and spots on her left shoulder and neck.

"Heartbeat?" Domaas voice rumbled through his chest and interrupted her thoughts.

Michelle lifted her head to see him looking down at her with unreadable eyes. She thought she might have missed a question. "Huh?"

"When did you last...cycle?" He asked in Cerulean.

Michelle made a face as she pulled back a bit, "Uh, why are you asking?"

He had the decency for his cheeks to color a bit at the rebuke. With a sheepish smile, he plowed ahead with his voice lowered to a near whisper, "Colonel Kea'rald told me where to meet Jamie in the mountains. I was focused on getting to you and did not ask him how he knew she would be waiting." His eyes began to sparkle with amusement. "It was Rachel who spoke with him, was it not?"

Michelle sat up and squinted her eyes warily, "Yes, it was."

"And you have cycled since you made planetfall, yes?"

"Yes." Domaas let his eyes shift to Rachel as she circled past the couch toward the foyer.

Michelle turned bodily on the sofa to look, and Domaas whispered, "Rachel is entering the *Quoy*. Do you remember how agitated you were after your first cycle? You will recall that I had you unlocked before meeting the first time? And I am sure you know the Regent had secretly unlocked Rachel."

Michelle watched Rachel stalk by in the other direction. She was angrily tapping at her tablet and unaware she was being watched. Oh yeah, Michelle remembered—all of it. "Oh my god," she whispered, looking at Domaas. "What do we do?"

"Remember that it goes both ways. If she is in the *Quoy,* so is Pitor; I am certain he will arrive shortly with the protective detail you requested. It was more controlled aboard the *Rising Star*... How was I to know my mate would become Regent? But I fear we are about to see even more damage done to your family home."

Michelle stood from the couch, stepped around it, and latched on to Rachel's arm as she began another circuit. "Rachel-"

"Let go of me!" Rachel snarled as she wrenched her arm free and then froze in shock of herself. "Oh my god, Michelle. I'm so sorry. I-I don't know why I'm so agitated..." Rachel stammered out as she ran a hand through her short hair. Roger and Arya had stopped playing and looked on in mild confusion. Arya's eyes were squinted as if she was struggling to understand something.

Michelle gestured with her head toward the stairs. "I think you should go to the bathroom."

Rachel shook her head in confusion, the tablet shaking in her right hand while the left slowly clenched into a fist. "Why are you telling me to go to the bathroom?"

Michelle ignored the hard edge in Rachel's voice. She understood all too well what the older woman was experiencing. Instead, she gingerly stepped close to whisper in Rachel's ear the very same words Michelle would never be able to forget, "Okay, so tough question. Are you wet?"

Rachel stepped back in mild shock at the question and then froze. Long seconds ticked by as her eyes went vacant, but then her skin suddenly drained of all color. "But...no...nooooooo..." She shook her head. "I haven't even been in a room with a Cerulean until today! And he's already mated to you!"

Domaas came to stand next to Michelle and slid his hands into the pockets of his trousers with a self-satisfied grin. "J'oons will be upset to find out he has lost to Colonel Kea'rald. The Phage can be entered through comms screens; it is just not as impactful," he said in Cerulean before switching to English. "I believe the term is *gotcha*?"

Michelle scoffed as she punched Domaas on the shoulder, "Don't be mean." Domaas absorbed the hit, but the smile didn't fade from his lips. He was not above enjoying the pebble in his boot, finally arriving at what she had managed to avoid for so long.

"He's coming, isn't he? With the others?" Rachel's hand was still tightly curled into a fist, and the tablet creaked under strain as she gripped it in the other. And yet her eyes were silvered with the threat of tears.

Michelle understood, probably more than anyone else could, what Rachel was experiencing. Especially after being unlocked, Rachel had become hypervigilant about not looking any Cerulean male in the eyes. "Michelle, this means they won, doesn't it?"

Michelle shrugged her bare shoulder. "Does it, Rachel? Have we really lost? I am Regent. You are my trusted advisor. We prevented that weapon from being used. Things will be changing when we get back to Cerul. I'd say you and I are breaking even, all things considered."

"Your Grace?" Michelle turned to see Jamie had stepped out of the kitchen. "I'm pretty sure a shuttle just transported some Ceruleans to the deck out back. Would you like me to greet them?"

"Yes, thank you, Jamie." The blonde turned away, and Michelle looked back at Rachel to see her friend's face had hardened. "My advice is to strike hard and fast. Make him bleed, but avoid the brow ridges. It took weeks for the swelling in my hand to go down. Also...wait as long as possible before attacking him. Let that rage build up a good head of steam."

"...now stand aside, or I will move you myself." Michelle wasn't sure she'd ever adjust to the hidden rod of iron that must have formed Jamie's spine. That was her first thought as she stepped out onto the deck. Jamie was boldly staring back up at the face of Colonel Kea'rald and the six equally tall Ceruleans standing behind him. He was the only one in uniform; the other six wore exosuits. Only their heads were visible above the active cloaks. Jamie's confiscated sidearm was out but calmly pointing down at the planks.

"This is her Grace's family home, and you *will not* enter it until she has given *her* permission. Attempt to enter and you will be shot," Jamie said in perfect Cerulean with all the authority of a pit bull protecting its children.

Pitor blinked, obviously unused to being spoken to in such a manner by a Human. *Get used to it,* Michelle thought as she stepped into the light. Well aware the diamonds across her shoulder and neck would catch fire.

As predicted, there was a gasp from the assembled males. Pitor looked up from glaring down at Jamie only to pale as he saw his Regent's crown. Instantly forgetting the biological compulsion that had brought him here, Colonel Kear'ald dropped to one knee, bowed his head, and brought his fist to his chest in salute. The six behind him followed suit.

"So it is done then?" He asked.

"It is," answered Domaas, who had stepped out behind Michelle.

"And confirmed?"

"I sang the Song of Ascension myself-"

"My first edict," Michelle interrupted in Cerulean. "Is that no one kneels to me unless I order it. I will lose my mind if I have to constantly speak to the tops of all your heads."

The Cerulean males stood as one. "Jamie?" Michelle asked in English. The blonde spun from where she stood before the Ceruleans, the gun in her hand quickly vanishing into the waistband of her jeans. "Please put Arya to bed. I will be up shortly to kiss her goodnight."

"Your Grace," Jamie said as she returned to the house.

Michelle smiled politely as she stepped forward and spoke in Cerulean to Colonel Kear'ald, "After this morning's events, she seems to have become quite serious about her job. I have decided to make her head of security for my daughter in addition to being her nanny. Domaas will work with your males to set security around the house."

The Colonel simply nodded, "As you wish, your Grace..." Michelle watched the Colonel's nostrils flair and his lip curl. A low growl rippled from his throat. The six males behind him nervously looked at each other and stepped back. Pitor's eyes narrowed into slits as Michelle heard the deck planks creak behind her.

She was just turning to look when Domaas took her arm and pulled her back, sliding his body in front of her. "I'm going to fucking tear strips from your hide," Rachel growled as she stepped into the light. The smell hit Michelle immediately, slamming into her nostrils with physical force. A pungent mixture of sweat, sexual arousal, and...*rage.* At least that's how the Cerulean DNA in her blood interpreted it. *Is that what I smelled like to him?* Michelle thought as she looked up at Domaas.

"Two of you go to the front of the house and ensure none of the Human soldiers come to investigate the noise. The rest of you, inside," Domaas ordered. The heads of two Ceruleans vanished in the cloak while the other males quickly made their way to the glass slider. Being certain to give their colonel and his soon-to-be mate a clear berth as they slipped past. Domaas then began backing up, guiding Michelle to follow the Ceruleans. "Give him hell, Rachel-"

Rachel roared and charged Pitor. He braced a foot back to absorb her hit, but she wrapped her arms around him and lifted him from his feet. Pitor's eyes flared in surprise as he was caught off guard by Rachel's *Quoy* amplified strength. His boots scrambled to find purchase as she drove him backward.

He winced as his back impacted against the railing and heard the threatening crack of wood. In a practiced move, he wormed an arm between their bodies and hooked his arm under one of Rachel's. Using his height, he managed to break her hold by wrenching up and pushing her back several feet. Rachel didn't pause and responded with a wild haymaker which Pitor blocked and forced Rachel back with another brutal shove to give himself a chance to get off the rail.

"Come, Heartbeat," Domaas said as he slid his hand into hers. "This is not for us to watch."

No, but he did have similar things on his mind. Michelle could feel it vibrating down the tether between them and her body tightening up in response. Once inside, Michelle scanned the visible parts of the bottom floor and saw that her family had vanished. Most likely upstairs if Jamie's presence at the foot of the stairs said anything. "Jamie? Has Arya already gone to sleep?"

Domaas slipped his hand from hers and went to speak to the four Ceruleans in hushed tones. Michelle watched their eyes flare and guessed that her mate was filling them in on the day's events. They furtively glanced in her direction but looked away when they saw her watching. Domaas gave his orders, and they each nodded before vanishing into the cloak. When he turned, the smolder in his sapphire gaze was almost enough to snatch Michelle's breath away.

Jamie's nostrils flared, and a slight blush crept up her neck. She would be as sensitive as the rest of them, but then the blush faded as quickly as it came as Jamie cleared her throat, "Arya decided she'd rather sleep with your parents. And," she paused as she swallowed. Jamie could see plain as day what was on the Regent's and Regis' minds. It was an odd juxtaposition against the sound of fighting coming from outside. "Your mother suggested you take the guest room downstairs to avoid disturbing Elsie or Shannon."

Michelle was almost embarrassed for herself or that her mother needed to say such a thing. Almost. Her birthday was in two weeks. She'd be eighteen then; after she had become a mother, was the equivalent of married and crowned the monarch of an alien race. She'd fuck her mate in her parent's house if she felt like it!

And after the day I've had, I sure as hell could use the release, Michelle thought.

Ignoring the continued gaze from Domaas as he returned to her side, she said, "Thank you, Jamie. Get some sleep. Take my bed. You'll be closer to Arya if someone is stupid enough to try again."

Jamie didn't fight the grin as she said, "My money will always be on you, your Grace. Every time." She turned and climbed the stairs.

Domaas' voice rumbled from deep in his chest as he turned to stand before Michelle. His hands were molten as they came to rest on her hips. "I can feel you across the bond, Heartbeat." Michelle felt her breasts firm and abdomen tighten at his touch, her pulse turning to a throb deep in her core. "You will show me where this guest room is." His voice softened to a husky rasp that sent shivers down Michelle's spine. "And soon, before I defile a male's daughter on her mother's kitchen floor."

*****

He'd been staring at it long enough to notice the swirling patterns on the surface of the steel table. Large swooping whorls in such perfect precision Corporal Smith was sure a computerized machine had finished the table. His father had begged him to go into engineering. There had even been money set aside for school. But no, his dumb ass ran into the ever-loving arms of the United States Mari-

The lock on the door suddenly buzzed and clicked open. The first sound he'd heard in minutes, hours, days? Long enough, the sound of his breathing had been his only company. Smith looked up slowly from the table to see the door swing open, and a man in a nondescript suit entered. He had dark hair, and dark eyes, with wire-rimmed glasses; the only items he carried were a notepad and pencil.

He set them on the table before taking the chair across from the corporal. "Are you Corporal Jainus Smith?"

Corporal Smith blinked and nodded.

"Young man, I will need you to use your words. Are you Corporal Jainus Smith?"

"Y-yes, Sir."

The Man in the Forgettable Suit smiled; it looked like it hurt him to do so. "I am no officer Corporal, but I may be able to save your ass. Would you like for me to make that happen?"

"Yes sir- I mean, yes, I would."

Picking up his pencil, The Man in the Forgettable Suit leaned forward and said, "Good. All you have to do is tell me everything that happened today. Beginning with whose idea it was to exactly what happened to Captain Turney. I need every detail, so expect me to demand clarification. I've ordered some food for you, which will be here soon. Understood?"

"Yes."

"Excellent, please begin."

*****

He'd been staring at it long enough to notice the swirling patterns on the surface of the steel table. Large swooping whorls in such perfect precision Corporal Smith was sure a computerized machine had finished the table. His father had begged him to go into engineering. There had even been money set aside for school. But no, his dumb ass ran into the ever-loving arms of the United States Mari-

The lock on the door suddenly buzzed and clicked open. The first sound he'd heard in minutes, hours, days? Long enough, the sound of his breathing had been his only company. Smith looked up slowly from the table to see the door swing open, and a man in a nondescript suit entered. He had dark hair, and dark eyes, with wire-rimmed glasses; the only items he carried were a notepad and pencil.

He set them on the table before taking the chair across from the corporal. "Are you Corporal Jainus Smith?"

Corporal Smith blinked and nodded.

"Young man, I will need you to use your words. Are you Corporal Jainus Smith?"

"Y-yes, Sir."

The Man in the Forgettable Suit smiled; it looked like it hurt him to do so. "I am no officer Corporal, but I may be able to save your ass. Would you like for me to make that happen?"

"Yes sir- I mean, yes, I would."

Picking up his pencil, The Man in the Forgettable Suit leaned forward and said, "Good. All you have to do is tell me everything that happened today. Beginning with whose idea it was to exactly what happened to Captain Turney. I need every detail, so expect me to demand clarification. I've ordered some food for you, which will be here soon. Understood?"

"Yes."

"Excellent, please begin."

Chapter Six

He knew as soon as her eyes opened. The switch to wakefulness came like a deep thrum across the bond between them.

Having her this close, the bond was at its strongest. The only time it was stronger was during their coupling. It was like a solid rod of the most sturdy alloy, unbendable and indestructible.

He continued to trace a familiar pattern across her spots. More gently now that her neck sparkled and shone in the morning sun that made its way past the blinds of the window directly over them. Michelle had once told him the pattern he traced was something the Humans called an *infinity loop.*

A thin smile broke his lips as the irony of that symbol struck him once again. Of course, the Ceruleans understood Infinity as a concept, they just had a different sign for it; and a different word. The humor was that every time he showed this bit of tactile affection, the word that continuously echoed in his mind was Har'edoi.

Forever.

Domaas hadn't shared this with Michelle and did not intend to. This was something he was going to keep for himself. For him only, forever.

He wasn't religious by any stretch of the imagination. Still, Domaas would be a fool not to thank whatever machinations had brought someone so strong-willed, so intelligent, so faithful into his life. He would eventually have taken a mate out of duty. It was expected of him as the commander of the *Rising Star.* And because of how the *Quoy* and *Phage* worked on a biological level, he knew he'd feel an equally strong bond with any he mated with. But Domaas doubted any would have fought so savagely in the Quoy. Would have made him feel like he'd won a rare prize. A prize that constantly made him strive to be always worthy of.

It is rare for a male to be so fortunate, Domaas thought as his smile broadened.

"I could order you to tell me what you are thinking, you know?" Michelle asked in a sleepy voice. "I can feel you getting all mushy across the bond."

Domaas chuckled softly, "If my Regent orders me into the vacuum of space, I will obey. If my Regent orders me to swallow poison, I will obey. However, I will never tell my Heartbeat what *mushy* thoughts I have of her when she wakes in my arms."

He knew she was smiling even though he couldn't see her face. "I could convince Arya to read your mind."

Domaas blinked and said, "So, it is exactly as it seems, then? Our daughter has...what is the term?"

Michelle spoke in English, "In English, we'd say she had ESP, or is a mind reader. It's not that crazy of an idea, I guess. Especially since I can throw lightning." She stretched languidly against him, tensing then relaxing her muscles in a slow ripple down her body. Domaas enjoyed the sensation. Switching back to Cerulean, she continued, "I will have to start practicing with that anyway. I do not like not having control over it."

"You seemed to have perfect control over it yesterday?"

Michelle shook her head against his chest, "Nah, I barely contained it. I think that is the reason why it came out like it did. On...on the ship, it felt like it was flowing out of me. Yesterday felt like a concentrated burst. Like a flash on a camera." Michelle fell silent for a bit, then added. "We will need to figure out a way to teach Arya, too. I do not think she is being invasive yet, but it is important to teach her early not to go rummaging around in people's heads. Unless I want her to find out what mushy thoughts her Popa has about me in the morning."

Domaas barked out a laugh as there was a knock on the door. "Your Grace?" It was Jamie. "I've prepared breakfast for you and the Regis. It is on the table when you are ready."

"Thank you, Jamie!" Michelle called through the door. "We'll be out in a moment."

"Yes, your Grace." Domaas allowed his mate to detangle from him as she sat up. The blanket fell away as she stood and turned to look back down at him. He knew she could see in his eyes that he quite enjoyed the view.

"You sure you will be happy with all this when it is old and wrinkled?" Michelle cocked a hip, taking a moment to enjoy her femininity.

Domaas smiled lecherously as he sat up and reached for her, "Come here, and I will show you how happy I intend to be."

But she swatted his hands away and stepped out of reach. "Nah uh, my boobs are full, and I need to feed Arya." Domaas laughed again and fell back to the floor where they had slept, as he was too tall to fit on the bed.

Arya yelled her approval at her mother's appearance and lifted her arms excitedly to be lifted from her high chair. Michelle sighed as she loosened the laces on her top and lifted the toddler into a cradle. "Arya, you're as big as a two-year-old but almost four months old. I'm gonna have to cut you off the nipple soon."

Arya's eyes were closed as she nursed, but her face scrunched up at her mother's words. Michelle tickled the girl's barefoot and then draped a thin blanket over her shoulder to give her daughter privacy. "You can put all the evil thoughts in my head you want, young lady. But you're ready to switch to solid foods completely."

Michelle finally looked to Jamie who stood across the kitchen. "You look like you slept well."

"Quite well, your Grace."

"Jamie..."

"Even when we are alone," Jamie smiled. "Besides, I like saying it. I feel like I'm actually part of something." She shrugged as she looked down at the floor. "I have a story, but let's just say getting Collected and becoming Arya's nanny is probably the best thing that could have happened to me." Jamie nodded to herself and looked back up to lock eyes with Michelle.

"So the way I see it, it's an honor to help however I can. And that includes always showing proper respect to my Regent...your Grace."

Michelle nodded and plucked a piece of toast from one of the plates Jamie had prepared. After chewing and swallowing, Michelle had come to a conclusion. "I need to start putting together my own council. I was serious about you being Head of Security for Arya." A smile slid across Michelle's lips. "Who knew my daughter's nanny had an iron rod for a spine? I want that around Arya at all times. But I also want someone who'll watch my back."

Jamie thought about the bright flash of energy that had propelled a man across a room hard enough to leave an imprint of his body in the wall, a wall everyone had studiously ignored since. She'd felt the growing pulses of static energy building in the room like everyone else. But she only knew what had happened because of the reflected angle of the dark wall screen. Something roiling and dangerous also flowed through Michelle's veins, and Jamie understood she never wanted to be standing in front of the Regent when she got angry.

Even still, this was a chance to do something. Anything was better than returning to her family. Although she *had* promised to return home tonight for some dinner guests, her mom and dad were hosting. Her family had been churchgoers, and things had been getting bad when she was Collected. Still, the religious preaching at the table had become unbearable after she had come out as an atheist. Worse than when the boy she had been had come out as gay before the Collecting.

Hopefully, tonight wouldn't suck. And it would give Jamie a chance to collect the important things since she planned never to return. "Your Grace has the Regis, guards, and an entire military with spaceships. What could I do?"

Michelle's smile broadened into a wolfish grin. "Be the one they don't see coming. The one they forget is even in the room. You are good at making that happen. Be the asp in the nursery." She stepped closer to Jamie as she lowered her voice. "You know how these Cerulean males can be. I know who put that video out for me, and I will deal with them when I can. But all they're going to see in you is just a *nanny*. Let them."

Jamie nodded as her eyes glinted, "I can absolutely do that, your Grace. Like an *asp in the nursery.*"

Michelle chuckled, "Liked that did you?" She switched breasts with Arya and then plucked a chunk of melon from her plate. "Also, you will be armed."

"Armed? Your Grace?"

Michelle went to answer, then paused as she finished chewing and looked around. "Where is everyone?"

"It's Monday, your Grace. Your parents have gone to work and your sisters to school. The Marines are still outside but have switched to vans not to draw too much attention. Two Cerulean guards went with your sisters under cloak, and the other four are on the back deck. Waiting for Rachel and the colonel to return." Her dad had just *gone to work.* As if he had not nearly died just the day before. Even if he had assured her multiple times that he felt perfectly fine...

Michelle forced a smile as she nodded, "I didn't order that to happen. With my sisters, I mean."

Jamie suddenly became a bit flustered. "They didn't know that. But I assumed you would have. All three of you are quite similar in appearance."

With a pointed finger, Michelle said, "That's why I want an asp in the nursery. Anyway, yes, you will be armed with a gun. Maybe a rifle *and* a side-arm."

Michelle noticed that Jamie didn't blanch but lowered her own voice. "Are you sure? Won't they..."

"No, they won't. I don't think they have them. Think about it, Jamie. You saw more of the ship than I did, and not once did I ever see an actual weapon. Or here's one better for you; how many shots were fired by the Ceruleans?"

Jamie's eyes squinted as she considered what the Regent was saying. No, all she had ever seen in use were non-lethal devices. Not even a "blaster" or laser pistol. "But...wait, they returned fire the first time the shuttles arrived."

Michelle nodded, "Exactly, the force fields absorbed the kinetic energy from our weapons and used that energy to return fire on us. Rachel showed me some of the old videos when I was with her, you can see it happening in slow motion. So really, the shuttles only fired in defense. If our military hadn't shot first, they wouldn't have been able to return fire."

The light dawned in Jamie's eyes. "Oh...I wondered why the sentries that arrived didn't have weapons even though they knew you'd just been attacked."

Michelle clicked her tongue with a wink, "The Ceruleans don't have offensive weapons. This means they probably wouldn't know what a safety switch looks like. So once I secure some money, you are to outfit yourself with what you think is best. I want you to practice, practice, practice. I want you to be able to clip a matchstick at fifty yards. And the only person who will know you are armed is me, so find a way to hide it if you can. Understood?"

"Absolutely, your Grace." Domaas chose that moment to enter the kitchen, but the conversation was done.

*****

Michelle had not been lying about their faces. Pitor was *handsome*. Rachel tried for a whole minute to convince herself it was just the oxytocin *and* Cerulean hormones still pumping through her system. However, that proved a fruitless effort as her mate *was* dangerously handsome. The idea that she finally felt some sort of attraction at all; after almost thirteen years on the ship - was one she'd have to process in pieces. It was too much to wrap her head around after the night she had just had.

Pitor was darker skinned than most Ceruleans. They tended to be pale from lack of natural sunlight aboard starships, but Pitor had the type of golden skin Hollywood starlets paid for. The kind that could make him racially ambiguous if it wasn't for his hair.

A strong jawline that appeared to be hewn from granite and a full mouth with lips that were indeed as soft as they looked. His closed eyelids had long, thick lashes that would have been feminine on a less masculine face, and his prominent brow ridges were deep enough to hold water.

Above all that was a head of thick dirty blonde hair sticking out in every direction from last night's activities and sleeping in the dirt under a bush.

Fuck. Damn. Shit...fuck.

Almost thirteen years, Rachel thought as she watched her mate sleep. *Almost thirteen years, and I got caught by a damned video call. I'm twenty-nine years old, for Christ's sake.* She remained kneeling in the dirt, her body aching, especially her nether regions. Michelle hadn't been wrong about that either. Rachel felt like she'd been sitting on a fire plug all night.

She could already feel it, though, that tether growing between them, strengthening even now as she watched her mate sleep. *Mate.* The word tumbled around and around in her brain like an echo that refused to fade; the hate and anger she'd felt last night had, though. Those emotions had faded to whispers for the time being and promised to fade away completely, she was sure.

At least, Michelle swore that's what it had been like with Domaas. But she had also had months of separation from him, which left plenty of time for the heart to grow fonder. Rachel would not have that luxury, would she?

Before she knew what she was doing, Rachel reached and gently ran a fingertip over Pitor's brow ridges. She was so lost in this simple act she was unaware his eyes had opened until his breathing suddenly changed. Glancing down, she saw his solid blue eyes looking back at her. The left was slightly swollen and bruised from one of Rachel's few lucky punches.

She backed away from him and rested on her heels as he sat up. Rachel didn't like how her body reacted when the muscles across his bare chest and abdomen rippled and flexed as he shifted to a seated position. "Good morning," he spoke in Cerulean.

Rachel didn't respond, instead becoming hyperaware of her own nudity. She covered her bare chest with an arm as she gazed about the small den they'd tumbled into. Her jeans were torn and shredded but wearable, while her top was nowhere to be seen.

Pitor's hand appeared in Rachel's vision as he gently grasped her chin and turned her head to look at him. "You are mine, and I am yours. Do you understand this now, Rachel Kear'ald?"

Rachel blinked several times as her brain tried to decide whether or not it liked him being so assertive. Her body certainly di- "Yes," She said, a bit too forcefully. "But do not expect me to like it so soon."

Pitor smiled as he released her chin. "This is fair. We shall have a lifetime together." Over a hundred years, if the Cerulean DNA in her blood had anything to do with it.

She frowned and proceeded to yank on her jeans, then quickly snatched up Pitor's uniform tunic and slipped it on. His scent of warm pine tar threatened to overwhelm her, but she managed to tune it out. "I am hungry, and you need ointment before the scratches on your back get infected."

Scratches she had clawed there because she had been the one on *her* back.

Rachel hid her face from Pitor as she searched for and found one, then the second of her shoes. It had been a farce, a weak imitation of Michelle's *Quoy*. Michelle had beat the crap out of Domaas until he knew he wouldn't win - she would have killed him if he had been Human! Only when he had known he'd lost had he then surrendered. Pitor hadn't submitted, not really.

She knew when the wooden railing had cracked and fallen away, and he had let her push him against it a second time. Rachel had become confident he was letting her win as he protected her body with his own as they rolled down the steep slope to the bottom of the canyon. She had repeatedly attacked him, but all of his moves had been purely defensive. Pitor had only submitted when Rachel had begun to tire.

Rachel wanted to spit.

Pitor watched his mate's face redden as she jammed her feet into her shoes. He busied himself by slipping back into his trousers and putting on his boots. "The hill is steep. Would you like me to carry you?" Her mouth twisted like she had just tasted the most bitter thing possible.

"Yes."

*****

Jamie had left to return her mother's truck. It was a decently long drive to Pasadena from Poway, and she hoped to complete it before the onset of afternoon traffic. Michelle had sent her a spare tablet so she could remain in touch and call for a ride when needed. Michelle would get Pitor to send a shuttle to get her if need be.

That left just Michelle, Domaas, and Arya sitting on the couch watching old recordings of children's programming (Arya seemed to really enjoy the talking red muppet) and four Cerulean guards sitting at the kitchen table. Jamie had nearly emptied the fridge for them and prepared a decent spread. The empty dishes and crumbs made it clear what they thought of Human food; or that they at least appreciated the taste of food that was grown instead of replicated.

All heads turned at the sound of the glass slider opening. Pitor entered first but quickly stepped to the side to make room for the storm cloud that entered behind him. Rachel looked haunted, tortured, angry...in love. Even as she stood motionless on the threshold, she was visibly fighting her eyes from drifting up to her new mate next to her.

Michelle left Arya on the couch and stood to slowly walk across the living room and into the kitchen, where the slider was. They were filthy, their clothing was torn, and Rachel wore the colonel's uniform tunic. "Congratulations."

Rachel's eyes snapped to Michelle's. "H-how long until the urges go away?"

Michelle offered an understanding smile and asked, "The urge to slit his throat or drag him back under a bush?"

She had to swallow first, but then Rachel answered deadpan, "Yes... I can feel his...his..." Rachel clenched her eyes shut and shook her fists. "It's cold and running down my thighs."

"Yeah, you get used to that. It took me about two weeks to stop staring at his neck while he slept." There was a grunt from the living room. "Showers helped." Michelle turned and pointed toward the staircase. "Top of the stairs, second door on the right. Take all the time you need. We'll talk more when you get out."

Rachel finally gave in and looked up at Pitor for a moment before turning and walking the way Michelle had pointed. "Colonel Kear'ald?"

Pitor watched his mate walk away and slowly blinked as he shifted to the source of his name. He could already feel the bond solidifying between himself and his new mate, as well. It was a sensation he had not expected. "Regent?"

"I am still new at this, but she is my friend. Domaas will probably try to talk me out of it, but if you ever hurt her, I will hurt you."

The tall Cerulean didn't even try to keep the stars out of his eyes as he said, "I would sooner leap from the Cliffs of Durbe'an."

She did not know of said cliffs but nodded, "Good. There should still be some food on the table. Eat something, and then Domaas can show you where the downstairs guest room is. You can shower in there."

"Yes, your Grace."

Domaas appeared at Pitor's side and clapped a hand on his shoulder. "Come, Pitor. I will help you understand what you are just discovering about Human mates. Perhaps the sentries have left some melon for us. It is quite delicious. There is something to be said for naturally grown food."

*****

"You."

He was the tallest of the four sentries. With dark hair and chocolate brown eyes so rich, they could have been liquid. According to Domaas, he was the highest ranking of the Cerulean cadre of guards that had arrived last night. It was almost comical when he glanced to his left and right, then over his shoulder. When he turned back to see Michelle still looking directly at him, his chair scraped as he leaped to his feet straight into attention.

"How may I be of service, your Grace?"

"What is your background?"

Confusion passed over his face as his brow furrowed. "My background? Your Grace?"

"Yes. What is your background? What does your Popa do?"

He continued to be confused. The previous Regent would never have spoken so frankly with someone of his rank or lower class upbringing. He and the others were supposed to be as intrusive as an empty chair against the wall. They followed orders, not engaged in conversations with their sovereign.

Michelle sighed in mild frustration and passed her gaze over the others. She had intentionally waited until Domaas went to put Arya down for a nap, while Pitor and Rachel were busy earning themselves another shower. "Listen, I know this is weird. I know it was not supposed to be a Collected Human who took the throne, and, for what it is worth, I am sorry the Regent died. I promise that was not supposed to happen. I kind of liked her in the end."

She was gratified to see the subtle nods around the table and the acceptance of her apology. "I did not want the Regency. I fought it. I skydived from space to escape it, and yet," Michelle gestured to the diamonds gracing her neck. "Here I am. I turn eighteen in a week, I have a daughter, and am the sovereign of a galactic impire, evidently. This *is* weird. Even so, I was raised that if you do something, you do it the best way you know how. That means I am going to do things my way."

Michelle finally looked back to the still-standing Cerulean sentry and was suddenly annoyed. "If I do not want you kneeling before me, do you think I would care for you to be still standing at attention?"

The Cerulean appeared to relax but remained stiff in the shoulders. *I guess that will have to do for now,* Michelle thought ruefully. "I am building a new council. Titles are irrelevant. As far as I am concerned, the members of the old one have abdicated their positions and lives. I want people I can trust around me and my family." Michelle allowed her gaze to harden. "Can I trust you?"

"Without reservation, your Grace. Every Cerulean in your military is sworn to the crown. Regardless of who wears them."

Michelle already knew this from her lessons with the Elder Regent. The intention was to prevent any attempts at a coup. It didn't matter *who* claimed to be in charge if the didn't wear the crown. And the crown was now a part of her very skin. Which made Cou'parth and his ilk attempt to control her an even more curious endeavor. Rachel had told her what had triggered their escape after making planetfall. However, she could only see their plan working if they were able to leave. Michelle wasn't sure yet if those old Ceruleans would ever leave Earth alive. "What is your name?"

"First Lieutenant Deron Ka'al, your Grace."

Michelle smiled, "See? Not so hard, right? Congratulations, Lieutenant Ka'al, you have just been promoted to the Regents Council. I name you head of my personal security. I advance your rank to Major and charge you with all rights and responsibilities herein." She had to stifle her giggle as his jaw dropped to his chest in shock.

Ka'al stumbled over his words, "B-but...your Grace... I cannot; there are many other males of higher rank, more experien-"

"Major." Michelle had known Domaas had returned and was standing to the left behind her, so she wasn't surprised by his deep voice. Major Ka'al stiffened back into rigid attention. "Will you deny an edict from your Regent?"

The young Cerulean's face colored as he snapped into a salute, "No, sir. I am honored by her Grace's trust in me. I will strive to serve her to the best of my ability and show that her faith has not been misplaced." What she had just done for his career and family's status was beyond measure, and he knew she had no ulterior motives for doing it.

Michelle looked at the other three, still sitting at the table, all wearing various expressions of shock. "You all and the two with my sisters are now my personal guard. Jamie is to be my daughter's personal guard. The only people who will know that are in this room right now. Understood?"

"Yes, your Grace," they said as one.

"Good," she looked back at the newly minted Major. "Looks like we both get to learn on the job." She winked. "I promise to make it interesting."

*****

Michelle knocked on her bedroom door and waited for the call to enter. It occurred to her that it was her bedroom, and she was sovereign; she didn't have to knock. She could have just walked in. The previous Regent had been doing that until Michelle snapped at her about it. The moment after, she had been suddenly afraid the Regent would follow through on her threat to replace Michelle's eyes with Cerulean ones, but nothing had ever come of it.

A soft "C'mon, Michelle," came back through the door.

Michelle opened the door and slipped inside, quietly closing it behind her. Rachel was sitting lotus-style in the middle of Michelle's bed. Freshly showered, again, and wrapped in a towel. Her shaggy hair was still wet and matted. Even though the window was wide open, the smell of sex still permeated the room. She made a mental note to swap out the sheets and have Domaas flip the mattress. "Hey, Rach-"

"I know I said it before, but I get it now. I really, *really,* do. Like when you were still pregnant, and you could tell when he was close? Yeah, I get it. This bond thing is going to be really weird."

Michelle gave a knowing half-smile and softly said, "Oh, you get used to it. I'll never admit it to anyone else, but I kinda like it." She clasped her hands in front of her and leaned back against the door. "And it has its uses. Like yesterday, knowing where Domaas was, even invisible, while everything was happening was remarkably useful."

Rachel pursed her lips as she picked at a thread on the edge of the towel in her lap. "It's funny how after all the planning and crazy stunts, we still ended up right where we would have if we just accepted their plans for us."

"Oh, I dunno about that," Michelle said as she pushed off the door and moved to sit on the edge of the bed. "I was trying to figure out how to escape from day one. Or rather, the first night. Domaas says that's what caught his attention, that he could tell I hadn't so easily surrendered. Arya and I being the Regent are just a roll of the dice, right? I could have just ended up being the mate of the Commander of the *Rising Star* and nothing more." Michelle gestured to Rachel. "And you? You are such a prize for Pitor. The great Micah! The one who hid aboard an alien ship for twelve years and was an unending source of frustration to the Ceruleans. The pebble in the boot that just refused to shake out." She winked. "I'll ensure your name is in bold when our story enters the history books. Both here and on Cerul."

Rachel smiled, but it quickly faded. Locking eyes with Michelle, she asked, "So you've decided to leave then?"

Michelle nodded as she sought out her friend's hand, "Yeah, I have to now, don't I? The General asked me if I intended to try to claim Earth as a colony, Rachel. How much do you wanna bet the military is not already trying to figure out how to force you to give over the defensive information you siloed? Or a way to nullify me, in case they decide I actually am a threat?"

"That's a suckers bet, Michelle."

"Exactly. Never mind the bounty on my head, but think of the possible global arms race once the rest of the world thinks we're just giving the United States alien technology. They probably already do, but they absolutely will once the world finds out about me. You think the United States government will share faster-than-light technology willingly?"

Rachel blinked, "Oh shit, I hadn't thought of that."

"Yeah." It was time to get to the real reason she was there. "I have a project for you."

"A project? For me?"

Michelle nodded with a smile. "What I really needed after mating Domaas was a project to keep my mind off the feeling of him inside of me for a while."

Rachel blushed. "Yeah...that. What's the job?"

"Jobs, actually. All the information we gave them? All the medical stuff, science, and engineering? I want you to find it all and secure it."

Michelle knew she was right about a distraction by the way Rachel's face lit up. "You want me to delete everything?"

Michelle shook her head, "No, but I want ensure we're the only ones with admin privileges. Wherever it is currently is where it stays, no copies or anything. Also, yes, I want you to be able to delete everything with the tap of an icon on your tablet or mine. Just us."

"Okay, it'll take me longer without my computer from the ship but I can use your rig boosted by the tablet. What else?"

"Find the money."

Rachel's eyebrows furrowed, "Money?....Ohhhhhhh."

"Yeah. Notice how all those grief counselors vanished when the fleet landed? I'm willing to bet the council is using the money in their hidden accounts as the reward for Arya and me. The way I see it, as Regent, that money is mine. I want it. I have ideas coming together, but I'm going to need money. So, if we create doubt the money even exists that might take the heat off Arya and me. This is my family's house. My parents haven't said anything to me, but there's only so long they can host a queen and her entourage."

Rachel nodded, "Okay, I'll have to code a crawler for that, but it shouldn't be too hard to find. Anything else?"

"Yes." Rachel caught the change in tone to Michelle's voice. "The ships up in the Valley have full archives, right?"

"Like historical?" Rachel asked as her eyes became unfocused. Michelle nodded, recognizing the calculating look on her friend's face. "I don't think they'd cover the entirety of Cerulean history, but it's a pretty long history. They've been space-faring for almost five thousand years."

Michelle blew a raspberry, "Okay, well, we're missing a big piece of the puzzle. I think it's kind of weird that the Elder-Regent didn't tell me about it, and I know it wasn't in my studies."

"What are you talking about, Michelle?"

Michelle blew a soft raspberry before answering, "Why don't the Ceruleans have weapons? You know how the shields work but think about it. You were on the ship for almost thirteen years. Did you see anything even resembling a pistol or *blaster?* I want to know why not."

Rachel gestured vaguely toward the ground floor of the house, "Why don't you just ask your mate? He has to tell you, you're in charge now."

Michelle canted her head to the side in thought, "Maybe. But I have a bigger question to ask him when I call my council meeting tonight. And I feel the no-weapons thing, and my question are connected-"

"Wait, council? What council?" Rachel looked confused.

Michelle grinned, "Ah yes, then there's that..." She stood and turned to formally stand before Rachel, who had yet to move. "Rachel..." Her mouth hung open in mild surprise as she realized something had been completely skipped over after all this time. "Shit, Rachel, what is your last name?"

Rachel burst into laughter so hard she rocked back, seemingly forgetting she wore nothing but a towel. Michelle dutifully looked away for modesty's sake. Rachel enjoyed a good ten seconds of laughter before wiping the tears from her eyes and righting herself on the bed again. "I'm sorry, we've done so much I can't believe I never told you. My last name is Wainwright or Kear'ald now, I guess. Do I *have* to take his last name?"

Michelle only smiled and said, "Rachel Wainwright, I name you to the Regent's Council. You are officially my Head of Information and personal advisor. I charge you with all the privileges and rights herein."

Rachel stilled, the humor completely sucked out of her. "The fuck..."

Michelle smiled again and winked, "Oh yeah, if I'm stuck doing this, I'm dragging your ass along with me. Think of it as being my personal liaison with Cerulean technology, *and* a well-paid trusted friend."

"Holy Hell, Michelle..."

"Oh and that; I know what this sounds like and I hate asking it of you, but could you please use the honorific whenever we aren't alone? It'll help with the Ceruleans, I think."

Rachel actually knew for a fact that Michelle hated the honorific, but as certain as the diamonds that twinkled on her neck she understood the required evil of using it. "Certainly, your Grace."

Michelle wrinkled her nose and turned to leave. "I'll check on you later. Council meeting tonight, after Jamie gets back. It's time to start things in motion." She paused in the open doorway and gave Rachel an appraising look. "Sooner than you expect you'll stop hating him, and then you'll start loving him and it'll hit you like a truck. I promise it will get better."

"It fucking better."

Chapter Seven

Jamie stood in the middle of her room and turned in a small circle with her fists on her hips. The room itself was abhorrent. Soon after returning, her mother had spent a proper fortune redecorating the room even though Jamie had asked her not to. Everything from Eric's old life was gone. Replaced by the most over-the-top feminine furnishings Jamie had ever seen. It was like being stuck in some nightmarish version of what a six-year-old girl was supposed to like. If it wasn't pink, it was cream-colored. Oftentimes, a sugary blending of the two; the walls, the curtains, the carpet, the matching furniture, stuffed animals. Even the dress of the doppelganger doll that now lay on its side against the pillows of the bed.

Jamie had tried explaining what it meant for her to have never been unlocked by the Ceruleans; that she existed in a weird grey area where it regarded her gender and absolutely had no interest in sex. She had thought this would have made them happy since coming out as gay and atheist months before she'd been Collected had been received so poorly. The next day her mom went shopping.

Jamie's only pair of jeans were the ones she was wearing when Rachel and Michelle started the mass exodus from the *Rising Star.* Along with the room redecoration came an entire hyper-feminine wardrobe; skirts, blouses, dresses, ballet flats, and heels with nothing more than three inches high. Of course, she could walk in them; the Elder Regent had insisted on it, but that didn't mean she had to, and she did not want to.

Currently, she was wearing a white sundress with scalloped cap sleeves. It was slim fitting and fell almost to her knees, while on her feet were a pair of simple white leather flats. Her hair was back in its usual ponytail, and she wore a thin, *thin,* coat of tinted lip gloss. Just enough so her mother wouldn't bitch about her *"...not looking presentable for their dinner guests".*

Jamie turned in a circle again, her eyes dancing over the room as she went down her mental checklist. She had decided this morning after Michelle had given her a title, that she would not be spending another night in this house. So, she wanted to make sure she grabbed everything she might want or need because she was *not* coming back.

The gym bag had been emptied of its pink sports bras and matching yoga pants and now sat half full, open, in the center of the bed. She'd emptied the underwear drawer because one should always have plenty of clean underwear. The toiletries were already stuffed into the side pockets. Her new driver's license and amended birth certificate were shoved into one of the inside pockets and zippered securely.

"What am I missing?" Jamie's eyes landed on the partially open closet door, and it hit her. She softly snorted as she took a few steps to the closet. She opened the door slowly to prevent noise and dropped to her knees to begin tossing shoes she'd never wear over her shoulder. "The money. I'm about to leave home for good, *again.* Then somehow get my butt back to Poway, and I was going to do it without my life savings?" She admonished herself as she cleared the space.

Once the shoes were out of the way, Jamie pinched the carpet near the wall and tugged. It took several mighty tries, but she finally got it to pull free from the carpet anchors and revealed a highly polished wooden floor underneath. This was the original flooring before her mother had insisted on a hardwood floor being *"much too masculine for such a pretty girl...".*

Her parents hadn't taken Eric being gay and atheist well, *at all,* but this new focus on Jamie was problematic, to say the least. It went beyond just being happy she had returned. Her father had grilled her when he got home from work to make sure she had not spent the night with some boy. Jamie had lied and said she had been visiting friends from before the Collection. It had gotten late, and she didn't want to drive late at night.

They really thought I was off with some boy? Jaime thought. Even after she had explained to them both, she had been intentionally left in some weird asexual limbo that she was perfectly comfortable with? It was so unnerving to have her father suddenly concerned with her purity. When just over a year prior, the man had damned Eric to Hell for being a *poof.*

The floorboard came up with practiced ease and Jamie lifted the shoe box from the space underneath. Flipping off the lid, she found exactly what she had left over a year ago. An old school adult women's magazine, a couple of USB drives that were full of gay male pornography, and after shoving that useless junk to the side; two stacks of hundred dollar bills. Eric had already started thinking about running when the shuttle arrived to transport him away. And now his life savings would serve its intended purpose.

"Jamie!" Her mother's voice called from down the hall. "Our guests will be arriving soon. Please come out to meet them!"

"Yeah, Mom! Be out in a sec!" Jamie snatched the cash and left everything splayed out across the floor but did close the closet door. *Let it be a surprise,* Jamie thought as she kicked the displaced shoes under her bed and dropped the cash into the bag. Right on top of the pistol she had taken and never returned to the Marine. She'd already decided she liked the way it felt in her hand. There was something primal to her about claiming the weapon of someone who would have done Arya harm.

After zipping the bag shut, Jamie carried it to the window she had opened hours ago and easily popped the screen free without letting it fall. It would not be the first time she had snuck out of the house. Holding the bag by the strap, she passed it through the window and carefully lowered it to the ground. The screen was back in place a moment later, and Jamie turned to survey the room again. Nothing but the doll lying on its side seemed amiss so she quickly set it upright against the pillows of the bed and opened her bedroom door.

Her mother was halfway down the hall when Jamie emerged. "There you are. Come now, you must give a good impression tonight. It is the beginning of the rest of your life!" She turned and began walking back toward the kitchen.

Jamie was too busy hiding her smirk at how true her mother's words were to grasp the importance of what she had just said. "So, who is this significant person coming to dinner?" She asked as she followed her mother. "I don't think I've ever seen the house this clean before, Mom." Carly was a stay-at-home wife who took pride in her vocation, and the house was at museum levels of cleanliness.

Carly glanced back with an odd gleam in her eye. "Well, things are changing now. For all of us. Now that God has returned to your father and I such a beautiful young woman, it is proof that the twisted perversion you were suffering from is irrelevant. One must treat all of God's blessings with the utmost respect. This includes keeping a clean and happy home. God doesn't like filth. Remember that, honey."

Jamie rolled her eyes and reminded herself just to breathe. This would be the last time she had to put up with her parents proselytizing. The last time she would have to pretend to be listening when her mom went on some Betty Crocker or Mrs. Manners nonsense. The Ceruleans were firm but flexible regarding a feminine aesthetic, and her mother was like a steel I-beam in comparison. The lip gloss was a concession Jamie had made at the end of a three-hour argument about makeup.

On the other hand, her father had become even more hands-off than after Eric had come out as gay. Instead, leaving most of the chastising and lecturing to Jamie's mother. Now, he was aloof and didn't engage in the girly stuff so long as Jaime did not show a masculine trait. *"I'd rather a daughter than a faggot for a son,"* he had said upon Jamie's arrival home. *"Sounds like those Cerulean demons even agree with God's plan for the correct roles women and men should have."*

And that had set the tone for the last month and a half.

He'd be apoplectic if he had seen me walking around with a gun all day, Jamie thought to herself.

All things considered, the last few days with Michelle and her family had actually been a pleasant respite from her parents.

"You didn't answer my question, Mom," Jamie said pointedly.

"You're right; I didn't. Remember to work on not asking too many questions, though, dear. Men don't like to be badgered too much, and as the head of the household, you should trust your husband to know what's right."

Jamie squinted, "I don't have a husband and have no plans to change that, Mom. We've been over this." She didn't know why she cared. Her parents' plans for her wouldn't matter in a few hours. "Who's coming to dinner?" she asked again.

Jamie's mom donned oven mitts and pulled open the oven door to lift a roasting pan from the oven. "Reverend Stakker, honey. He's the minister for the new church your father and I have joined. We've told him all about you, and he's very eager to meet you. He's also bringing along a handsome young man for you to meet."

She blinked once, twice. Suddenly, her mother's prattling about keeping a house and her husband happy made sense. Jamie was suddenly sick to her stomach. "Mom-"

Carly lifted the lid to the roaster and had a self-satisfied smile as she looked down at the prime rib roast. "That's just perfect! I'm so looking forward to teaching you my recipes. Your husband will never stray if you keep him satisfied." She looked to Jamie, who was still standing in the entryway to the kitchen. She mistook the barely veiled horror on Jamie's face for nervousness. "Oh, honey! It's okay to be a little scared. I was so nervous about my first date with your father, but I knew the Lord would only allow a godly man into my life and here we are twenty years later!

"Reverend Stakker was there for us when you were taken. Something was wrong about that grief counselor that came by the house. She just rubbed me the wrong way. But Reverend Stakker has really helped us anchor our faith in God and his plan for *all* of us. I'm so sorry that we failed you and allowed you to become an atheist and engage in that deviancy. I just knew God wouldn't let you go so easily. Our faith has been rewarded by having such a lovely daughter returned to us. I suspect I shall be blessed with the first of many grandchildren by the end of the year!"

The woman continued to chatter while Jamie glanced back over her shoulder toward the hallway. Her father was in his office, a space she was now not allowed to enter, with the door closed. Her path was clear. *I should do it now before this shit gets even crazier.*

Jamie began to turn away. "Mom, I forgot something in my room-"

The doorbell rang.

"Oh, that's them! I'm so excited!" Her mother slipped past Jamie to knock on the closed door to the office. "Honey? Reverend Stakker and his young man are here. If you let them in, I'll have Jamie bring refreshments to the living room."

He was taller than Jamie, who stood at 5'11", with light brown hair that had obviously been freshly cut and deep-set russet brown eyes. When he reached to shake her hand, Jamie kept both of hers stiffly at her sides. "Do not be rude, Jamie," came her father's gruff voice from behind her.

Shawn at least had the decency to look mildly uncomfortable as he said, "I don't mind, Mr. Shaffer. I'm quite nervous myself, but I imagine we'll have plenty of time to get comfortable together."

It had been less than five minutes. They had been in the house for under five minutes, and Jamie was ready to bolt. What was supposed to happen tonight had become quite obvious, even though none of them had said it out loud so far.

Maybe it was from being around Michelle so much, a person who spoke her mind. Clearly and loudly, her Grace would have already called bullshit and walked out. *So what are* you *going to do?* Jamie asked herself.

"No, I don't think we will." Jamie enjoyed a small bit of satisfaction watching the already weak smile on Shawn's mouth falter.

One could have heard a pin drop on the carpet as Reverend Stakker uncrossed his legs and stood from the couch behind Shawn. Jamie mimicked Michelle's 'already bored face' and relaxed every muscle in her face as she watched him stand and step forward to stand next to the young man. The Reverend was conventionally handsome with the same features as Shawn and Jamie suddenly realized they were most likely father and son. "First Timothy, Chapter Two Verse Twelve; Let a woman learn in silence with all submission. And I do not permit a woman to teach or to have authority over men, but to be in silen-"

"That's verses eleven *and* twelve, actually," Jaime said quietly, throwing down the gauntlet.

"Jamie..." Came her father's warning growl from behind her.

Reverend Stakker glanced at her father while holding up his hand, "It is fine, Adam. Do you see how the demons failed to teach them proper submission?" The Reverend looked back to Jamie, "Psalm 103:13; As a father shows compassion to his children, so the Lord-"

"Shows compassion to his children." Jamie crossed her arms and cocked a hip; she'd played this game before. It was amazing how many people thought atheists held no knowledge of the Bible. "Is there a point to you reciting scripture to me, Mr. Stakker?"

She hid it, but the saccharine smile that seemed to flow over the Reverend's lips sent a chill down her spine. "Your parents told me you claimed to be an atheist. It is good to know we will not have to teach you anew. Genesis 2:23; This is now bone of my bones and flesh; she shall be called Woman, for she was taken out of man... Finish that one for me, will you? What more evidence do you need that God's hand is at play here?"

Jamie couldn't resist the urge to step back as the full force of what was happening struck home. This wasn't her parents and their minister trying to play matchmaker. They intended for her to marry this boy who stood before her. "No. This isn't happening." Jamie turned to find her father blocking the living room entrance and her mother silently standing behind him, her face set in a resolute expression.

"Finish the passage, Jamie." Reverend Stakker quietly commanded.

Her spine hardened into that iron rod as Jamie exploded, "I am not marrying him! Y'all can enjoy this religious bullshit all you want! But like I said before I was *Collected;* I don't want any part of it. Especially," she gestured behind her without looking. "Any of this nonsense!"

"Oh Jamie..." Her mother whispered.

There were several quiet ticks in the room as the tension built, Jamie and her father locked in a staring contest. She refused to blink - to show any level of weakness. The ire was evident in his eyes. Reverend Stakker finally spoke after a full half-minute of silence.

"As I said, Adam," Stakker said into the taught silence. "They have all been resistant so far, but Proverbs 22:15?" *He couldn't be serious.*

Adam maintained eye contact with Jamie as he recited the verse, "Folly is bound up in the heart of a child, but the rod of discipline drives it far from him."

Jamie opened her mouth to rebuke the notion of someone beating her with a rod when white-hot fire sliced across both pits of her knees. She staggered and was just starting to turn when she heard a swish, and another slice of fire came from the lowest part of her thighs.

She was just starting to collapse in pain when a pair of strong hands caught her from falling. "No. It is time for you to learn proper submission." It was Reverend Stakker. "Come, Shawn, help me hold her to the wall so her father may teach your future wife some discipline. And so you may see how it is done. Your aim needs work."

Jamie got her feet back under her and surged forward to break free of the stronger man, but Shawn was surprisingly quick and took hold of one of her arms. It was in his other hand that Jamie spied the instrument they had used. A three-foot-long rod of bamboo. About as thick as a thumb. *Where in the hell was that hidden?*

"Jamie, don't fight them! It'll only make it worse!" Her mother cried.

They were suddenly moving her, keeping her upright and pushing her toward the only wall in the living room without furniture against it. "No! What in the hell do you think you're doing?" Jamie's flight or fight had ratcheted all the way past eleven. Adrenaline flooded her system, triggering her increased strength from the Cerulean DNA.

Wrenching her left arm as hard as she could, she managed to yank Shawn off balance toward her. Reversing that into a push caused Shawn's grip on her arm to slip, and he fell backward to crash through an end table. Not even giving the Reverend a second to compensate, Jamie brought her left arm around as if it were powered by rockets. The Reverend saw it coming and turned away, but Jamie wasn't aiming for his face. Instead, her fist pummeled his carotid artery in one savage blow. Just like the Cerulean fight sims had taught her when training to be Arya's nanny.

Reverend Stakker gagged from the hit, and his grip loosened as he staggered and then dropped like a stone, completely unconscious. Jamie spun, ready to fight her own parents to escape the house-

Only to be met by a full-force, backhanded slap from her father.

And then another, and another. Jamie quickly lost track of how many times he struck her. She was only aware of the impacts on her face as he held her standing with his left hand and repeatedly hit her with his right. Before long, she was barely registering the impacts and was suddenly moving with speed until something hard crashed into the side of her head. with incredible force. Her mouth filled with the coppery tang of blood. Soon after that she slipped away into nothing.

*****

Arya's scream struck like a hammer. Physically and mentally. One second the tyke was stacking the wooden blocks her grandmother had bought her, and the next, she was shrieking her lungs out. Michelle had never heard such a horrid sound from her daughter before and was on her knees on the carpet before anyone else could come out of their sound-induced paralysis.

Michelle's hands fluttered over the child, searching for an injury but found none. So she sat on her heels and gathered the child up into a tight embrace. "Baby, baby, baby tell me what's wrong. Are you sick, are you hurt?" Arya's small hands clutched at her mother's top as she buried her face in her chest, her scream fading into a more natural bawling. Michelle's mind exploded with pain, repeated impacts striking her head and the taste of copper filling her mouth even as it was dry with panic for Arya.

She hugged her daughter closer. She was sending this fear and pain into Michelle's mind, causing her to flinch from the feeling of something striking the side of her head. But it couldn't be Arya's own. It was too violent, and the house had been mostly quiet. "Who, baby? Who's hurting? Who is scared?"

A moment later, Michelle felt ice flood her veins. She heard Domaas curse in Cerulean as he knelt beside her and Arya. "Heartbeat, I felt this before, across our bond. Just before-" A static pulse of energy filled the room, causing everyone to go still even as they recovered from Arya's aural assault. "Michelle?"

Michelle gently kissed the top of Arya's head. "Okay, Baby. Mommy will go get her. Will you be okay if I leave you here with Grandpa?" The toddler nodded. Michelle climbed to her feet and turned to see her father had just arrived.

His jaw was set, and without a word, he took Arya and headed upstairs, with Maggie quickly in tow. "Colonel?"

Pitor materialized in the room, with Rachel soon standing behind him. "Your Grace?"

"Someone has *or* is attacking Jamie." Everyone cursed in their respective languages. "Colonel, get a shuttle here, and I want it here *now*. I do not care about stealth. Tell them to land in the street out front. Rachel?" Michelle held up her right arm to show the bangle she still wore; that they all wore. "All I know is she's somewhere in Pasadena. Track down her bracelet, *now*."

"Yes, your Grace," they said in unison.

She turned to the four guards inside the house, who had also come running when they'd felt the pulse. "Major, you're with me and Domaas. Pick one other. The rest of you will watch over my family until we return. Oh, and Colonel Kear'ald?" Pitor reappeared as if he had been just standing around the corner. "I don't care what ship he's on, but I want Healer Borlaas on that shuttle."

"Of course, your Grace."

She was conscious but didn't open her eyes. Keeping her body relaxed was a master exercise in meditative relaxation. Especially with how much her face hurt as her mother carefully cleaned her wounds and washed the blood away. "I really hope you're faking it right now, honey." Jamie didn't answer, but she heard a sniffle and a warble in her mother's voice. "I told him you wouldn't accept it. But he insisted you would see the light..."

The washcloth passed over a particularly tender spot just below her right eye, which she now realized was badly swollen, and she couldn't fight the wince and jerk of her head to get away. The movement sent raw fire up the backs of her thighs and across her backside. "Be still, sweetheart; I'm almost done." The washcloth reappeared, and her mother continued to whisper. "I am so, so, sorry. I just want you to be happy, but I see now that you really have turned from God-"

"What are you saying to her?" Her father's gruff voice came from some-where behind her mother, probably the doorway.

"A prayer," Carly smoothly lied. "So that the healing hands of God may see fit to heal her quickly and open her heart to his light."

"Finish soon; moving her before she wakes is better. It is obvious she was already planning on running away." Her father's voice faded down the hallway, "Probably to go whore herself to some boy..."

There was a minute of silence as she continued to work before her mother whispered again. "Reverend Stakker wishes to take you to the compound tonight after I'm done cleaning you up. They found your bag outside; it's on the floor by the dresser. I...What are you doing with a gun, Jamie? I pray you are not doing anything dangerous. You are still my child and will always be my womb's beloved fruit. So when you're ready, you're going to overpower me and take your bag. Everything is still in it. I moved the tennis shoes to the top; you won't be able to run in those flats. My sweet boy...I didn't know they would hurt you like that. I am so sorry... The keys to the Tahoe are inside one of them. Go out the window in my room, Reverend Stakker has men waiting outside yours, and it's on the opposite side of the house. Don't stay in the car too long, though - remember the truck has GPS. I love you. With all my heart. Be safe."

With one eye swollen shut and the other nearly so, it was difficult driv-ing at night. And she knew she was not okay. The warm wetness trickling down her neck had Jamie swiping at the side of her head to discover she was bleeding from her ear. *That explains the blurry vision, she* thought ruefully as a gas station appeared around a bend in the road.

She had meant to head toward Poway, but a rational thought told her not to. To do so would lead them in the direction of Michelle and Arya. So instead, she had headed west into the San Fernando Valley. It had been thirty minutes since she'd escaped, and she was certain she was already on borrowed time before they caught up to her. Every flash of headlights in the rearview mirror sent a shock of adrenaline through her system, and she was fairly confident she would have passed out if it weren't for that.

Jamie pulled into a hydro-fuel station but didn't pull to the pumps.

Instead, she pulled to the side of the convenience store and parked in the light well of the building. She just needed a few more minutes before getting out and trying to move. Just a few...

A knock on the window had Jamie jerking back to full consciousness and snatching the gun from beneath her leg in the same movement. The motion caused searing pain to flash from her backside and her head to throb. The barrel was pressed against the window's glass before she registered the deer in the headlights expression of a filthy girl now backing away with her hands up, her black bangle sliding down her wrist. "I-I'm sorry! Please don't shoot!"

Jamie lowered the window and sucked in the cooler night air. "Help...me...danger..."

Bailey stepped closer to the Tahoe; even in the dark, she could see the blonde's face was badly damaged. One eye was swollen completely shut, the other nearly useless. Her face was a heat map of nearly black bruises and a lip split in several places. Bailey could see blood flowing in a steady trickle from both of her ears.

"Oh my god, what happened to you?"

Jamie leaned her head against the pillar of the door and rolled it to look back at the girl, then squinted when she saw the black bangle on the girl's left wrist. It took serious effort to form the words, "Collected? Escape?"

Bailey followed the girl's gaze to her own wrist and nodded. "Yeah, I was on the *Rising Star*. What happened to you?"

"Have...tablet...get...get truck."

"You want me to get in the truck?" Jamie could only just barely nod.

The Marines hadn't much cared for the shuttle landing in the middle of the cul-de-sac in front of the Mizzi home and had been even more put out of sorts when several large Ceruleans materialized before them, seemingly out of thin air. The guns lowered themselves as the Marines took in their first glimpse of the Cerulean males. They'd heard the description that they were tall and *built*. However, seeing them was a different experience.

Michelle had ignored them completely as she strode with righteous purpose from the house's front door to the lowered shuttle ramp, clad in the same black suit the imposing Ceruleans wore. She ignored their calls and the people coming from their homes to investigate the alien ship that landed in their neighborhood. Many had already noted the increased military activity, which only added more questions.

Healer Borlaas stood in the center of the passenger compartment as they boarded, and his eyes flared when he glimpsed the exposed part of Michelle's neck, the diamonds gleaming in the compartment's lights. Rachel hustled past him to the cockpit to link her tablet to the navigation system. She had easily tracked down Jamie, who had been moving until a few moments before the shuttle arrived. The ramp came up, the doors closed, and the shuttle lifted from the ground, turning and quickly accelerating to the north.

"How long?" Michelle quietly asked when Rachel would return.

"Less than five minutes. I told the pilot his Regent was in a foul mood."

Michelle nodded and turned to Healear Borlaas. "Healer."

Borlaas smiled and gave a slight bow. "Your Grace. The crown fits you well. I am sure she would have been glad to see it." Michelle nodded but said nothing; she knew who he was referring to. "With such haste, your Grace. I assume my skills are in dire need. Is the princess well?"

She was vibrating, barely containing the energy that now coiled in her gut. It was a soothing balm when Domaas came to stand behind her and placed his hands on her shoulders. He applied gentle pressure, forcing her to anchor herself in the present. Five minutes from now was in the future. "Yes," she finally answered. "Arya's nanny has been assaulted." And despite her father's attempts, Arya had become increasingly agitated as they waited, blindly broadcasting a feeling of coldness and anguish filtered through bursts of pain.

Borlaas blinked and scratched at his beard. "It was my understanding that you guaranteed the safety of all those returned to Earth?"

"Yeah," Michelle growled through clenched teeth as she quickly wound her hair into a bun and secured it with her ubiquitous hair sticks.

"That was my understanding as well." Domaas could feel nothing but anger and violence vibrating down the tether between them.

Rachel came running back to the compartment and held up her tablet. An unfamiliar and frightened voice called out from the small speaker. "Hello?" It was dark, but the light from the screen illuminated the young woman's face, and the camera compensated for the rest. "Hello? Are you Miche... You're the one everyone is looking for!"

Michelle glanced over the screen to Rachel with exasperation. "I don't have time for this, Rachel."

"No, don't hang up! I'm with someone named Jamie. Someone's beaten her up really bad!" The girl turned the screen to show a blonde in a white dress stained with blood, her face nearly unrecognizable. Cold fire seized Michelle. "She showed me how to call you, then passed out. There's blood coming from her ears."

"Who are you?"

The image shifted again to show the girl's face. "My name is Bailey. I was on the *Rising Star*." The girl held up her wrist to show the black bangle. "I saw her pull into this gas station and was just hoping she'd buy me something to eat."

"Okay, Bailey," Michelle said to the screen. "I need you to keep my friend alive. I have the Head Cerulean doctor here with me, and he will give you instructions..."

Bailey's face and the cabin of the Tahoe were suddenly washed in light, and she glanced up. Michelle could hear doors opening and closing. Then there was a man's voice, "Well, doesn't the Lord work in wondrous ways?" Michelle watched the color drain from Bailey's face as her irises blew wide open. The eyes of a frightened and *trapped* animal. *Flight*.

The girl's lips trembled. "No..."

"It is truly a blessing to see you again, Bailey." The male voice approached as it spoke with a note of perverse satisfaction in its tone. Michelle watched Bailey's horror-stricken face as she tracked the man until he must have been standing at the driver's side window.

"Bailey, who is that?" Michelle asked. But Bailey didn't answer. Michelle felt like she was watching a horror movie. Right at the moment when the protagonist was faced with the monster for the very first time. There was a knock on glass from Bailey's right, and she flinched then leaned away from her door. Michelle looked up and saw Rachel holding her hands up with three fingers on one hand extended and the other forming an 'O'. *Thirty seconds.* "Bailey! Look at me!"

"-how lucky for us to be coming to take young Jamie to get some medical attention, and we find you here waiting for us. Has God finally spoken to your heart and sent you back to us? Who is that you're talking to? Another of God's precious gifts?"

"I'm not going anywhere with you!" The girl was shaking, and huge tears were flowing from her eyes. "You people are sick!"

"Bailey!" Michelle yelled again, putting every ounce of authority she had into her voice. The girl's fear-filled eyes looked down. "Fight! Make noise! We'll be there in less than twenty seconds!"

Michelle had to brace her feet as the shuttle suddenly slowed and swung around to land in the side lot of the gas station. The door was open, and the ramp extended before the craft settled on its landing struts. Major Ka'al beat her to the door, the shields of his exo-suit already activated and extended to form a moving wall. Domaas appeared on her left and the other sentry on her right. Their shields also activated and extended.

Screaming greeted Michelle's ears as they came down the ramp. Her eyes locked on two men carrying Jamie's limp form toward the open back door of a lifted white truck, then to a filthy redhead fighting for everything she was worth against two more men who were dragging her to another truck.

"Major," Domaas' voice was deep and commanding. "You and Sheel secure Jamie; get her aboard to Borlaas as soon as possible." Michelle pivoted as soon as the soles of her suit touched the pavement and began marching toward the redhead fighting for her life.

"Demons!" Everyone stopped moving at the booming voice.

A tall man in a three-piece suit stepped into the space between Michelle and her target. Perfectly coiffed hair, deep-set blue eyes, visibly soft hands, and what promised to be a massive bruise blooming on his throat. He screamed *used car salesman* from thirty feet away. "Be gone! We are about God's business!"

In the distance, Michelle could hear the whoomp-whoomp of a helicopter approaching at high speed, with the faint whine of police sirens not too far behind. She knew the shuttle would draw attention. "Who are you?"

"My name is Reverend John James Stakker. God Almighty has charged me to bring forth a race of pure, untainted Christians for His glory! These girls have been freed from the Demons to serve *His* purpose and none other!"

His head canted to the side as his eyes narrowed. "I recognize you. You are from the wanted video," He licked his lips as his eyes danced over Domaas and then across to Deron and Sheel. "It would appear Satan has swayed you to his darkness... But it is not too late for you. Come with me-"

"Enough." Michelle waved her hand as if dismissing the man and turned. "You," she said, pointing to the two men holding Jamie. "*Will* allow those males to take my friend, or you will not leave this parking lot alive." Michelle turned back and then closed the distance between she and Reverend Stakker, knowing Domaas matched her step for step. "Tell them to let Bailey go. Or the angry seven-foot-tall Cerulean behind me will break your fucking neck."

He tried. Oh, did he try to return her glare. She stood nose to nose with him, unblinking, with nothing but fury emanating from her faintly glowing green eyes. The helicopter flared overhead, and the entire parking lot was suddenly bathed in its spotlight. The diamonds on her neck flared to life, almost blinding him. From overhead came a voice from a loudspeaker, "This is the Los Angeles County Sheriff's Department. Do not attempt to flee. Remain where you are."

Michelle arched an eyebrow in a final challenge. Reverend Stakker sighed through his nose, then turned to the two holding Bailey. "Let her go!" He had to shout over the rotor downwash from the helicopter. There was no way the police would let them take the girls now. They were likely being recorded, and being seen taking two young women by force would not help his future plans. This evening was already a wash as it was.

Bailey sprinted toward the shuttle as soon as she was free. Michelle knew Rachel would get her settled. Sheriff and police cars poured into the parking lot with sirens blaring and were soon followed by a news van. Still holding her gaze on Reverend Stakker, Michelle said, "The likelihood that this is over is slim. But don't worry. I will come for you when I am ready. If you have kidnapped any other young women from the *Rising Star*, it would be in your best interest to let them go before I find you."

Police were rushing in now, with orders to freeze and to put their hands up. "Do not threaten me, little girl. I have God on my side," the Reverend said in a final attempt to have the last word.

Michelle didn't bother to respond, instead turning on her heel and walking toward the police. From behind her, in Domaas' thick English, she heard, "My Regent does not make threats. You would be wise to heed her words." The Major and Sheel were already heading up the ramp with Jamie's limp form, but Michelle didn't allow herself to feel that distress yet. Several police officers approached cautiously, their hands hovering near their weapons and their eyes on the hulking Cerulean behind her and the shuttle sitting quietly on its landing struts.

Michelle pointed to Reverend Stakker and his men. "Officers, that man was attempting to kidnap two women under my protection. One has been assaulted and savagely beaten by either him or one of his men."

The lead officer tore his gaze from Michelle's crown to finally look her in the eyes. "You're Human?"

"Yes."

He inclined his head toward Domaas. "And that...that's a..."

"He is Cerulean, yes. He is also my mate. He will defend me if I am attacked. There will be no violence from me."

Michelle finally saw what she was waiting for and began walking toward the crime scene tape that had already been stretched to cordon off the area. She turned her head as she walked and said to the three cops who had approached, "I'm about to answer some more questions if you officers would like to follow me."

"Oh shit, *oh shit*... Jim, call the control board. Tell Hank we're going live in ten seconds, and he will not want to miss this."

The cameraman activated his dual drones and guided them into a hover on either side of the reporter as he muttered into his headset. "...yes Boss, I realize it's the finals. Hank...it's the one from the video! Yes, *that* one!" There was a silent moment while he listened to the producer on the other end of the connection, then said, "Got it. Carol, we are live in five!"

The boilerplate blonde reporter had enough time to smooth her hair from the helicopter rotor downwash. She turned to the hovering camera on her left just as the little red light winked on. "Good evening from the San Fernando Valley. This is Carol Harbors breaking in with a special report. We're here at the Telco hydrogen fuel station on La Tuna Canyon Road, where it appears one of the smaller alien craft has landed. We don't have the full story yet. However, there appears to have been some sort of conflict between the Ceruleans and Humans." Carol could see Michelle patiently waiting from the corner of her eye and the hulking, handsome alien behind her. "In an unexpected turn of chance, we have here a human girl, one of the Collected that managed to return to Earth, with us. She appears to be the very same featured in the viral video that exploded across the internet only a day ago."

Carol turned to Michelle and forgot herself momentarily as her eyes drifted to the diamonds on her neck. "What is your name?"

Michelle felt Domaas' uncertainty vibrating across the bond. She wasn't sure either, but she was also tired of being reactive, of just waiting for things to happen. She was Regent, and it was time to be proactive. "My name is Michelle Et'Kuraul, Regent of the Cerulean Star Impirium." She turned and gestured to Domaas, "This is Domaas Et'Kuraul, Commander of the *Rising Star*, Regis, and my mate."

All chatter and activity within earshot stopped dead. Someone, just far enough away, muttered, "The fuck did she just say?"

Carol blinked rapidly as she tried to think of her next question. Michelle patiently waited. "I-I'm sorry. Did you say Regent? As in queen? But you're Human!"

Michelle smiled; this reporter was not being professional, but she'd also just thrown one hell of a corkscrew. "Yes. Yes, and yes." She looked directly into the lens of the camera to Carol's right. "I discovered tonight that there has been a man forcibly kidnapping returned captives, intending to force them into some sort of religious organization, if I were to guess. I feel I speak for all the Collected that we've had enough of being *kidnapped* and forced to do anything. Fortunately, we were able to save two of them tonight." *I hope,* she thought to herself.

"This is despite the fact that the United States government has assured me that all would be protected. From this moment forward, I will take on this task myself. If you were aboard the *Rising Star,* consider yourself under my protection. This means that I will personally see to it that any who would harm any girl wearing a black bracelet will have the same harm visited upon them."

Domaas leaned forward and whispered in Cerulean, "Heartbeat, the shuttle reports the military is approaching. They will be here shortly."

Michelle nodded, but Carol cut in. "I'm sorry, but what did he just say to you?"

She looked from the hovering camera to the reporter. "That I have garnered the attention of the military," Michelle answered. "I do need to see to my friends' injuries soon. Do you have any other questions?"

Carol snorted, "Many."

"Carol Harbors, correct? Channel eight?"

"Yes, that's right."

Michelle nodded and glanced back to the camera. "I am from Earth, and I am a United States citizen. This is my home. A general of the Marine Corps asked me if I intended to wage war on or attempt to make Earth part of the Impire I have recently inherited. The answer is *emphatically* no. I seek peace with my home. That includes the entire planet."

The sound of multiple approaching helicopters made itself known. Michelle looked up toward the sky and then back down to Carol. "I'll be in touch, Carol."

She turned away and began walking back across the lot toward the shuttle, Domaas again falling into step behind her. The gathered crowd of law enforcement personnel parted for her. The cameraman sent one of his drones after them. A glance at it told her it was still recording as it took a long tracking shot of her and Domaas from a respectful distance. Reverend Stakker and his cronies were handcuffed and sitting on the ground against the gas station convenience store. He shot daggers with his eyes, but Michelle paid him no attention.

"We still need a victim statement! And to see the injured girl!"

Michelle stopped walking. If she didn't comply and let them speak to Bailey, it would increase the chance that Stakker and his men would go free. There was no way she was letting them take Jamie, but it would be unseemly to flaunt the law. She also had no intention of leaving the terrified girl to the police or the approaching military. Michelle also wanted to know what had happened. "Domaas?" She said in Cerulean. "Go ahead and secure anything in the shuttle you would not want the Humans to see. Have Rachel clean Bailey up as well."

"Michelle, that is not wise. You will be alone."

"Do not worry. I have had my shield activated this entire time. It is just lying against me. I will be fine." Domaas reached and let his fingers graze her hip as he passed. Instead of touching her suit, his finger was repulsed by the faintly sparkling shield.

She turned to the cop who had called out to her. "She is under my protection, and I do not trust that I will be able to speak with her if I let her go with you. And you will not be allowed aboard my shuttle. Will a video recording suffice?"

"Uh, yeah, I suppose it would."

Michelle looked up at the hovering drone camera. It was still recording. "If you would like to know the cause of all this, please follow me." She started up the ramp into the shuttle cabin and was gratified to hear the drone buzzing behind her as she stepped inside.

The door closed, and the shuttle was airborne and moving before they reached the passenger compartment.

Jamie was hovering in the middle of the cleared space, suspended by some sort of stasis field and bathed in a yellowish light. Healer Borlaas loomed over her, using a medical instrument near her ear. "Healer?" Michelle greeted him in Cerulean.

"Another few minutes and she would be dead, your Grace. You Humans really do enjoy cutting it close, do you not?" He looked up and squinted at the drone hovering over Michelle's shoulder. "What is that?"

Michelle responded in English for the benefit of anyone who might still be watching; she didn't know the feed was now broadcasted nation-wide. "It is a camera drone. I am allowing them to see what was done to her."

Borlaas nodded as the translator behind his ear converted her words to him, then backed away and gestured to Jamie's prone body. Michelle nodded to the camera, and it moved in slowly. Panning up the young woman's bruised legs, the blood-stained white dress, and finally, her barely recognizable face. Michelle narrated in English, "Her name is Jamie. She is my daughter's nanny. She went home for a family dinner. If it wasn't for another girl seeking help to get something to eat, one of my closest friends might be dead." She gestured to the bearded old Cerulean, "This is Healer Borlaas."

The camera turned and raised to take him in. "He was the main doctor aboard the *Rising Star*. He personally saved my life and assisted in the birth of my daughter." Borlaas nodded. "Healer, could you please tell those watching what has happened to my friend?"

"She was beaten. Savagely," Michelle translated back to English as Borlaas spoke, gesturing around Jamie's head and face as he talked. "Here, you can see how her head was repeatedly forced into violent contact with a hard surface. Likely a wall or maybe a table. The blood from her ears are from ruptured eardrums, not brain damage, as far as I can detect. But I will be keeping her in stasis for a short while to be sure."

It took everything Michelle had not to scream in fury as she continued translating. Borlaas waved a hand, and Jamie's body rotated one hundred eighty degrees. "You see here she was struck repeatedly by some form of an instrument." Angry red lines cross-hatched the backs of Jamie's thighs. *They caned her!* "The marks go up to her buttocks, where the most damage was delivered." No one moved to lift the skirt of Jamie's dress for the camera, but blood had seeped through the white material.

Healer Borlaas continued speaking but stopped when he didn't hear Michelle translating. "Seriously?" She asked in Cerulean, her fists clenching until her knuckles turned white. Borlaas nodded.

In English, she said, "The healer says most of the damage you see was most likely done after she had been rendered unconscious. However, he can heal and bring her back to total health."

Michelle heard a door opening and saw Rachel leading Bailey out of a side compartment. The girl's face had been washed, and her hair brushed back into a greasy-looking ponytail. She wore a set of Cerulean casual clothing, a loose top and pants. Like scrubs but made of a silk-like material. They completely dwarfed her. Rachel nodded, and Michelle pivoted to follow them to a seating area toward the front of the shuttle. The drone whizzed along after her. The pilot/cameraman, who was probably a hundred miles away by now, fully intended to define his career with this opportunity.

Bailey drank deeply from the glass of water from the replicator and set down the glass. "When you're ready, Bailey," Michelle said. "Tell us everything you know about this Reverend Stakker." The drone settled into a hover just two feet away from Bailey's face, catching every word.

Chapter Eight

Jamie recognized the ceiling as soon as her eyes opened. Along with the bundle of warmth from the toddler curled into the crook of her arm. She took silent stock of her body and felt no aches or pain. Her vision was clear and there was no taste of blood in her mouth. There was no fire in her backside from being in contact with the bed. She was whole.

Slowly turning her head she saw Michelle sitting on the floor with her back to the door, head back and eyes closed. Jamie croaked, "You're going to get a crick in your neck like that."

A lazy smile slid over Michelle's lips as her eyes opened. They were bloodshot and now that she was looking directly at Jamie she could see her Grace's eyes were puffy from crying as well. "How close was it?"

"Healer Borlaas healed what he could right away, but you had brain damage. He set the nanites to keep you under for a while to give them time to heal you. But it was close, if they had managed to take you, you probably would have died. Disabled at the very least."

Jamie rolled her head back to neutral and blinked at the ceiling.

Michelle continued as she got her feet under her and stood. "I'm starting to think she loves you more than me." Arya shifted closer to Jamie as if she was listening. "She hasn't left this room for a day and a half. She was the one who alerted us that you were in trouble."

Jamie looked down at the sleeping child as tears stung her eyes. She'd be sneaking her ward all the ice cream she could get away with for the foreseeable future. Arya was a huge fan of cookies & cream and it was definitely not part of the fruits and veggies diet Michelle had started her on.

"If you ever want to talk about it, I'm here Jamie."

Jamie only nodded as the tears broke free and ran down the sides of her face. Michelle took that as her cue to give some privacy.

"I'll send one of the sentries up with food in a bit for you and Arya. Don't be in a rush to come down." Michelle turned and opened her bedroom door. She was through and closing it when Jamie called out.

"Michelle?" The shock of hearing that name out of Jamie's mouth reverberated as Michelle turned to see Jamie still looking at the ceiling.

"Yes, Jamie?"

"Thank you. Thank you so much for coming to get me."

Michelle went to close the door as she said, "You put your blind faith in me. It's the least I could have done."

Chapter Nine

Her eyes were closed. An image of serene calm as she sat perfectly still in the seating area of the shuttle. Her hair had been brushed until it shone like burnished copper and hung over her right shoulder in cascading curls. Her face bore only dark kohl over her eyes and a thin coating of something that made her lips glossy. Michelle wore a strapless lemon-yellow gown that nipped at the waist and fell to her knees. The shimmer of the shiny material against her dusky skin somehow increased the incandescence of the crown that graced her left shoulder and neck. *Satin,* she had called the material.

His mate was stunningly beautiful. Simply dressed and regal all at once. Much as her predecessor had been. Not for the first time, Domaas mused how fortunate he was to be the *Rising Star's* Commander. To have been in the perfect place and time to watch an unafraid girl reading her tablet in the dark of night-

"I can feel you getting mushy again, Domaas," Michelle said to him without opening her eyes. "Tell me what you are thinking?"

Domaas glanced at her father, Roger, sitting beside Michelle, was wearing a dark suit with a blue tie. Regis Et'Kuraul himself was wearing his dress uniform, with his exo-suit underneath. Just in case. "I am thinking, Heartbeat, how amazing it is to call you mine."

He watched a small smile play across her lips. Roger pretended to read his tablet, even though they were speaking Cerulean. "While you were watching over Jamie, Rachel told me about you staring down General Hamlin when you got back. And then the way you challenged this

Stakker human." Domaas grinned to himself. "I remember how you used to look at me in the same fashion."

He watched one of Michelle's eyebrows quirk upwards as her mouth twitched. She was amused. "And which way is that, Domaas?"

"As if you were *just* waiting for me to try something you would not like. Almost like you wanted me to cross a line just to teach me a lesson." Domaas paused as he thought back on those early days. "I never touched you, Michelle."

This caused her eyes to open and lock on to his. The question silently hung in the air. He continued, "The first time I touched you intimately was when we had dinner together the first time; I smoothed your hair behind your ear. I thought you were about to take my head off when I did. I could not stop myself; you so enthralled me. I was sure you noticed how much my hand was shaking. The second time was during our...date. The spacewalk. My heart was pounding so hard I was afraid it would burst." Domaas watched her brow furrow as she visibly thought about it. Then her head canted to the side as she realized the truth. "By then, I was craving to feel you, to hold you. I came up with the perfect excuse."

"Because of the way I look at you?"

Domaas shook his head and leaned forward to rest his arms on his knees. "No, Heartbeat, the way you *looked* at me. Some bluster, some roar and stomp to intimidate. But you, Michelle, when you are even slightly vexed, there is no fear in your eyes. Not violence either, just a...cold determination. *Cl'Thareu* herself could rise from the underworld, and you could make her back down with a stare. I am glad I am no longer on the receiving end of such a look. What is it that Rachel said?" Domaas had to switch to his thickly accented English. "Like ice flows through veins."

Michelle smiled as she shifted in her seat. "You say the sweetest things, Domaas." Turning to her father and needing to change the subject, she asked, "What are you reading, Dad?"

He quickly turned off the tablet and straightened up in his seat. "We're discussing in the family chat about what our next move should be."

Michelle nodded as she pursed her lips. None of them had said anything directly, but Michelle knew her family well enough to know they were all marginally upset with her. At a minimum. The stunt with the shuttle landing in the middle of the street and her subsequent introduction live on-air had made life difficult for her family. More than it already had become with a house full of Ceruleans.

She had intended to bring the spotlight directly on herself. Needing to rescue Jamie and Bailey had just moved her timeline forward. She had planned to be out of her parent's house before making a debut, but Stakker had taken that from her. She was forced to react instead of act. The harmful effect was a virtual media circus forming before the Mizzi home. Shannon and Elloise could not attend school once the connection had been made to whose home the shuttle had landed in front of. In two days, the problem had gotten bad enough that both schools had politely demanded that neither of her sisters return for the foreseeable future. Ellie missed an important soccer match because of it and was still understandably upset. And both of her parents had taken a leave of absence from work for almost the same reasons.

The good things that had happened in the last week were that the State Department of the United States had finally made its overtures to initiate contact, and she had an appointment to be officially recognized as a head of state in four days. Rachel had managed to secure all of the Cerulean data without tipping off the multiple agencies now controlling it and found the money. An unreal, enormous amount of money. $210 Billion and change. *Cash,* not stocks, bonds, or tied up in real estate. These were liquid funds. Michelle was now the richest single person ever to walk the Earth.

She still had trouble absorbing how much money that was. It was still difficult to comprehend, even after breaking it down into smaller units. Her father earned just over $145,000 per year. That meant it would take him earning that exact amount every year for nearly one million four hundred fifty thousand years to reach parity. It was *fucking* obscene, and this was before accounting for the vast wealth of the Cerulean Impire that was now titulary hers. Fortunately, she had plans to chip away at that ridiculous wealth.

In response to being forced out of their home, Michelle was finally returning to the Cerulean ships in the San Joaquin Valley with her family in tow. She was leaving for Cerul after securing a technology and peace treaty with Earth and ensuring the safety of any formerly Collected Hybrids who chose to stay. Or giving a chance for those who had mates to return with them. She hadn't shared her desire for her family to come with her, but she had certainly made it clear that they were welcome. If they chose not to, Michelle would install them in a comfortable home anywhere they chose, with enough independent wealth to be very comfortable. If they did stay, Michelle already had a good idea of how her father could remain busy.

They were headed for the *Folded Fist* specifically. The ship Domaas and Commander Kea'rald (recently promoted by Domaas) had been transported onto during the mass exodus from a dying ship. The Regis had made the official announcement there was a new Regent fleet-wide soon after Michelle's announcement. The response had been lukewarm at best.

It was known amongst many that the new Regent-apparent was a Hybrid. However, there seemed to be some questioning of the validity of Michelle's claim since the ceremony had not been performed according to tradition. According to Commander Kear'ald, there was a rising swell of discontent amongst the crews of the grounded ships, much of it being caused by the former Regent's Council. Specifically Cou'parth H'arprom. Sooner than later, she would have to deal with him and the others, but not today. Today was about pomp and circumstance.

"I really am sorry, Dad," Michelle said once her thoughts returned to the present.

Roger sighed as he nodded his head. "I know you are, Michelle. You were raised to be loyal. I would have been more upset if you hadn't gone to save your friend, and Arya probably would never have let you live it down either." Arya had always been a pleasant child in her months of existence, but she had become an absolute kitten with Jamie and her father.

"Well, whatever you decide to do, let me know before I meet the Secretary of State?"

Roger was about to ask why when Rachel appeared at Michelle's side. "Your Grace?" Michelle looked up in question. "The pilot says we'll be landing in about two minutes. The *Folded Fist* reports they are ready to receive their Regent."

"Thank you, Rachel." Michelle allowed her eyes to drift down Rachel's body as she smiled. "I thank you for not fighting me on the dress."

Rachel blushed as she self-consciously smoothed the flowing skirt of her tea-length black dress. She wore no make-up, but her shortish hair had been gelled into a somewhat feminine style. "Well, don't get used to it," Rachel said as she glanced toward her mate, who was quietly speaking with Michelle's personal troop of sentries. "Evidently, my mate knows what words to use. Are you sure this gets easier? The word *flower* isn't supposed to make my heart flutter, is it?"

Michelle glanced at her own mate, who was watching her with relaxed eyes and a half smile that showed the dimple she still hated to love. She laughed. "You get used to that, too."

Rachel needed to switch topics, "So anyway, we're still under escort from two military helicopters - our pilot keeps grousing about having to fly so slow, by the way. General Hamlin tells me they will remain in orbit until others come to take their place and so on."

Michelle didn't like having a military escort everywhere she went in a shuttle now either, which was always. However, she begrudgingly under-stood how the optics of it played to the public. Whatever she was doing, it *appeared* that the U.S. Government not only sanctioned it but was in control. She was in a shuttle that could leave Earth's atmosphere and enter orbit, with shields that would return what was fired at it but *they* had to pretend to be the ones in control. *Ugh...* "Thanks, Rachel."

The shuttle slowed even more and tilted as the pilot pivoted the craft so the door would open facing the *Folded Fist*. There was a ripple through everyone on board as Michelle stood and crossed to where Arya was playing with Jamie. "Hey, little one, are you ready?"

Rachel headed over to where Carol Harbors and her cameraman sat. Both were visibly nervous. "We're landing in about thirty seconds."

Rachel looked at the cameraman, Jim, and said, "Only one drone; get all the shots you want but keep the thing out of her Grace's face. Right?"

"Not a problem," he bobbed his head like a schoolboy. Seven-foot-tall aliens with the physique of Atlas had a way of instilling compliance. Especially when there was one that watched every move he made.

"Cool, so once we are aboard the ship, your live feed will cut, and I'll review the interview footage before you're allowed to leave-"

Carol stood, "Now wait, she said we'll have unlimited access."

"Within reason, of course. Can't have you sending that drone all over the ship, recording things it shouldn't."

"Fine by us," Jim said for both of them. He was on a very short list for several awards for his camera work on the night of the two girls' rescue. *And* he'd gotten a nice bump in salary, Carol as well.

There was a slight jolt as the shuttle settled on its landing struts, and Carol glanced out one of the few windows. "Oh wow....Jim? Jim, get that thing up right *now*."

The door opened, and the ramp extended then lowered. It rested on the very edge of a raised walkway covered by a blue carpet covered with weaving in gold filigree. The colors of the Cerulean Star Impirium. Her colors. Standing shoulder to shoulder on both sides of the walkway were Cerulean males. Each one wearing a freshly pressed dress uniform, standing at perfect attention, right fists to their chests in salute.

The *Folded Fist* sat hulking in the background, sleek like an elongated teardrop. Its dark hull gleamed in the bright sunlight under a crystal clear sky. Holographic banners and flags flickered to life to wave in a gentle simulated breeze.

And except for the two helicopters orbiting at a respectful distance, it was absolutely silent.

Michelle took a deep breath, held it, then slowly released it as she straightened her spine, elongated her neck, shoulders back - just like the Elder Regent had taught her. She looked down at her daughter, who was already looking up at her with smiling eyes. Her emerald gems caught and then refracted the bright sunlight, contrasting perfectly against her matching yellow dress. "Let's do this, kiddo," she whispered.

Behind her stood Domaas on her left and Major Ka'al to the right. Her Regis and Head of Security. Behind them would be Rachel and Commander Kear'ald, and behind them would be her family and Jamie. Carol Harbors and Jim would exit last and least, even as the drone camera quietly whizzed by. First, taking a long panning shot of the assembled Honor Guard and then settling into a hover with its lens facing Michelle.

Michelle took another deep breath and stepped out of the shuttle; Arya easily kept pace as she held her mother's hand. They stopped at the end of the ramp but did not step down. There were several beats of silence, then fifty yards down, a grizzled old Cerulean stepped out of line, turned crisply on a heel, and marched down the blue carpet toward Michelle.

She watched him approach at a perfect quarter-step march, hands no more than ten inches from his hips as they swung. His uniform was immaculate, and he even sported an impressive panel of awards and citations over his breast. He would have brought tears of pride to any drill instructor. *He probably is a drill instructor,* Michelle thought without so much a twitch of her eye.

He came to a stop directly before her and saluted. "What is the name of she who wears the Crown of Cerul? Who is this child that stands beside her?" His voice was high and clear in the surrounding quietness.

"I am Michelle Et'Kuraul," she responded in an equally high voice, speaking so it carried as far as possible. "This is my dopa, Arya Et'Kuraul. We are mate and child of Domaas Et'Kuraul, Regis, and Commander of the *Rising Star.*"

"Do you claim the title of Regent and accept all the rights and responsibilities therein?"

"I do."

The old Cerulean saluted once more as he lowered himself to one knee. twenty yards down the line, another member of the Honor Guard took one crisp step into the center of the walkway and snapped into a turn to face her. He held rigid attention for several silent beats, then his chest swelled, and he began singing the Cerulean anthem. The *Song of Ascension*. His voice was clear and strong as he sang the first stanza alone. Then Domaas, Major Ka'al, and the other Ceruleans behind her joined. The rest of the Honor Guard joined the chorus, their voices swelling and cascading, flowing through rounds and building to a second chorus that had every present Cerulean singing at the top of their voices. Strong and proud as they greeted their new Regent.

Michelle fought the sting of tears as its beauty sent a shiver down her spine. Protocol be damned, she scooped Arya up to rest on her hip so she could better hear the beautiful singing.

She had listened to the anthem multiple times but never like this. There were multiple tiers to the singing. A melody that rose and fell like a gentle breeze. A song that seized the imagination and turned every present mind into a master painter. Arya's mind pushed into Michelle's, into everyone nearby, and they saw verdant grasslands melt into deep alien forests full of mystery and life. Cities with towers so tall they threatened to shatter the bluest of skies melted into pastoral valleys filled with grazing beasts of burden. It ended with Arya's vision launching them into the sky until a field of stars surrounded them, hundreds shining brighter than the rest. As if those, too, were the locations of the species' planets in the Impire.

And then they fell back through every scene and image until Michelle stood again before the *Folded Fist*. Leaving the same soldier who had begun the song finishing the song alone, his voice gently falling silent until the only sound was a flock of birds chirping as they passed overhead. It was stunningly beautiful. Michelle did not bother to wipe away the tear that had escaped.

The old Cerulean rose to his feet and smiled. It was a gentle, grandfatherly thing. "Your Grace, your Impirium awaits. I would be honored to escort you and your cohort aboard the *Folded Fist*."

Michelle smiled as a rush of tingles spread throughout her body. She could feel Domaas' pride vibrating across the bond. "I would have your name?"

"Your Grace, I am Colonel Cha'ol, commander of the *Folded Fist*."

"Thank you, Colonel. To the Regent's Solar, please."

Colonel Cha'ol inclined his head. "If her Grace would follow me." The old Cerulean came to attention, snapped into an about-face, and began walking down the raised path.

*****

Cou'parth tasted acid in his mouth from the churning in his stomach. It was not supposed to happen this way. His spy reported that she was building her own council even. Without even having the courtesy to speak to him or the other council members watching the viewscreen. "She seems more formidable than we first gave her credit for."

"Yes," another hissed as if spitting venom. "It would seem our human ally could not move fast enough before *her Grace* began making her own moves."

Cou'parth turned to the frightened blonde standing beside her mate, Pouduit. "You will contact the human male again; tell him it is time we meet face to face."

"What about my son?" Pouduit pointedly asked. "He remains sick, and the healer aboard this ship has no experience with the Hybrid children."

Cou'parth glanced around to the other council members, who all gave dismissing gestures, then back to April, who cradled the sick child. "Please," she begged. "I did what you told me. Please let us go see Healer Borlaas."

"No. You are not leaving this ship. You said so yourself that *she* does not trust you. Letting you go would be tipping our hand. First, make contact with the human male, and then we will send a message requesting Healer Borlaas to transfer here."

April felt her heart ache as she turned to leave, her mate following. M'kylo had been running a fever for two days now and could barely keep anything down. She'd tried everything she knew, but nothing seemed to work. She was getting desperate.

Chapter Ten

Michelle sat quietly, sipping her braut as Carol Harbors spoke quietly with her producer on her mobile device. The interview wouldn't be live but he had evidently been expecting a direct stream to the news studio servers. He was upset they wouldn't get their hands on the raw video. They'd accept the rules Michelle and Rachel had laid down if they wanted anything at all. Carol was discovering how iron-willed Michelle could be.

"Yeah, yeah...okay got it, Hank. But you aren't here, she's not *just some girl*," Carol muttered as she glanced toward Michelle. She was pointedly looking out the floor-to-ceiling windows and barely suppressing a smile. "You should have seen how they greeted her, Hank. This is the real deal. I'll have Jim send the raw files as soon as we're given the clearance."

Carol ended the call without waiting for another rebuttal. She approached the table and slid into her seat. "Apologies for that, your Grace. But you understand that-"

"People find it hard to believe an eighteen-year-old Human has been made a queen of an alien race and galaxy-spanning empire?" Michelle asked as she slid into her own seat across from the reporter.

Carol had a small smile. She was indeed quickly learning that Michelle did not mince words. "Happy Birthday, by the way."

"Thank you, Ms. Harbors."

Carol blanched, "Please, Carol. Being called Ms. by a teenager makes me feel like a school teacher...your Grace."

Michelle nodded with a smile, "I'm still getting used to it myself. Shall we begin?"

Carol tapped the drone that sat on the table, a signal to Jim, who was out in the corridor with Major Ka'al. The drone burst into life and circled the room. Jim had not been allowed into the solar and needed to familiarize himself with the dimensions of the space. "Would you like something to drink? Eat?" Michelle asked as she picked up a tablet from her side of the table.

"Oh, I wouldn't want anyone to have to fetch something for me."

"Wine? Cola? A sandwich?"

Carol studied the glint in Michelle's eyes and decided to play along. The Regent was either flexing her control or about to show Carol something really cool. "A glass of water with lemon would be nice."

Michelle began tapping on the tablet. "Ice or no ice?"

Carol canted her head, "Ice, please."

"You might want to focus that camera on the circle in the center of the table," Michelle said as she made her final taps on the tablet and set it down. The drone zoomed down and hovered to the side as the pad glowed to life. Two tall glasses of water materialized on the pad, each filled with ice that clinked and settled with a wedge of lemon on the rim.

Carol did not blink. "Seriously?"

Michelle reached and lifted the glass closest to her and took a long sip. Carol reached out a shaking hand and lifted the second glass. "It's cold!" she exclaimed in surprise.

Her Grace laughed, "You did ask for ice." She watched Carol take a sip of her water.

The look of disbelief on the woman's face was palpable. "Wow. How does this work?"

Michelle shrugged, "I honestly don't know. But it's a technology I intend to share." The drone lifted up and panned to view Michelle from over Carol's shoulder.

Carol turned to the camera as she held up the glass, "For the record, this is the purest water I've ever tasted." Turning back to Michelle, "Can we start at the beginning?"

Michelle leaned back in her chair, water glass palmed in her lap, and looked directly into the camera lens of the drone. "My mate thinks I was unafraid the first time he saw me. It was after the orientation and lights-out on the first night. I had already decided that I was going to try to escape. They had given us tablets to read to...to familiarize ourselves with what was happening. Why they stole us, change our sexes *and* genders, really."

She paused long enough to sip her water, then continued, "I had stayed up late. I needed to know as much as I could, as fast as possible. I needed to know if it would even be possible for me to get back to Earth. One of the first things you should do in a hostage situation is to gain as much knowledge as possible of your captors." Michelle shifted her focus from the drone to Carol's eyes. "My mate thinks I was fearless because of what he saw that night. But Carol, I was actually scared shitless."

The professional journalist in her came to life as Carol set her glass of water down and leaned back in the chair to cross her legs. "I'd like to revisit your first days with the Ceruleans, but you just said something interesting. Could you elaborate more on the changing of gender? Did they really turn you all into females in both body and mind?"

Michelle's mouth twisted in contemplation as she glanced out the window to the cattle ranch outside. She quietly noted she hadn't smelled anything to remind her of that fact when they had arrived. *Interesting.* Turning back, she said, "Yes. But it wasn't that bad - hasn't been, not really." Carol raised an eyebrow in disbelief, causing Michelle to chuckle.

"I mean, yes, of course, it's bad. I'm one of twenty thousand, right? And it was done by force, against our will. But," Michelle's eyes became unfocused as she recalled the early days. "They at least made it as easy as possible to accept. Domaas started courting me early, and I peppered him with questions. There are mental blocks embedded into our psyche. The first time I saw myself naked in a mirror, it was a surprisingly clinical experience. Almost like just taking inventory that all the new bits were where my brain said they were."

She refocused on Carol's eyes. "And when you think about it, that's kind of the better of the options, right? They could have done this to us and done nothing to help us adjust, and even I can say I might have contemplated ending it then and there. Or, they could make it so that even though we didn't like it initially, we had time to come to terms with it. It helped that, in the beginning, I felt...genderless. All the things considered feminine; the feelings, thoughts, emotions, and...sexuality. All of that had been locked away from us. I could adjust to being in this body without going into an existential crisis."

Michelle squinted her eyes in thought; Rachel had described living like that for years. Long enough to develop a type of gender dysphoria. Dysphoria bad enough to even seriously consider suicide.

"Could you explain that a bit more?" Carol asked to prompt Michelle to continue after she had been silent for a moment.

"Sorry, I was thinking of a friend who had a different experience than most of us."

"Care to share that?"

"It wouldn't be right to share someone else's story. It would be better to say that not everyone had as easy a time as I did with the change." Michelle adjusted herself and took another sip of water before continuing. She was about to explain the *Phage* and *Quoy*. No videos would be shown, but that wasn't needed for Carol or the camera to understand the process. "It wasn't until I was unlocked before seeing my mate for the second time. They used the transporter pad to send me directly to his quarters and unlocked me in the process. This put me in something called the *Phage*..."

*****

Rachel grinned as she looked through the small portal window into the manufacturing chamber. The *Folded Fist* was a cruiser class ship, like all the others currently Earth-bound, a class that was the primary ship of the Imperial Fleet. As such, it boasted of similar facilities as the much, much, larger *Rising Star* had. Including a manufacturing plant that was capable of making just about anything if correctly programmed into the computers.

"Oh, that's coming along nicely." Rachel said to no one as she moved down to the next chamber and glanced in. "Perfect."

Pitor looked into the portal Rachel had just left. "What is it?"

"A sword," she said in English, knowing there was no word for it in Cerulean. Rachel didn't look at him as she answered. She was now in the stage where she could barely stand looking in his direction. The sexual rush had finally worn off, but Pitor could tell she was warming to him nonetheless.

"A...sword?" The word came out as *svard* in Pitor's heavily accented English. He had only started learning it in the last week and a half. "It appears to be very simple. What does it do?" He asked in his native tongue.

"It is a...tool." Rachel felt her mate approaching, then the palm of his hand sliding across her lower back. She stepped away before he had a chance to get too close. "It can be used for defense and protection, but most importantly, it projects a very particular image and idea."

"What would that be, Flower?" Rachel grimaced and fought the tingles in her chest. The actual word was *vio'stial*. Flower. Evidently, Cerulean males were fond of giving their mates pet names; and *vio'stial* came off her mate's tongue like warmed honey. Michelle had ungracefully cackled for a good thirty seconds the first time she had heard it. Rachel fully intended to go to the grave without ever again admitting how it made her feel when he said it, despite knowing he could probably feel it across the bond between them.

"Knighthood. I'll be sure to download information for the Regent's Guard to read up on it. It also says that anyone who gets close enough to our Regent with intent to harm her will be met with a very swift and personal death." Rachel wondered if Pitor would catch on to that last part. She'd done her research as Michelle had asked, and there was no reason in the archives why the Ceruleans didn't have weapons.

Pitor didn't seem to connect the dots as he asked, "Her Grace ordered this made? For the Regis?"

Rachel looked up at the ceiling and cursed. "No, but he should definitely have one." She brought up her tablet and began scrolling through her sword designs again. After picking the blade and hilt, she quickly took an image of the Cerulean Impirium crest, made some slight changes, and set that into the pommel. Finally turning to Pitor, she held up the screen and asked, "Yes?"

Pitor studied the image and found himself appreciating the object he saw. A double-edged blade roughly a meter long, with a bar across the top of the gold wire-wrapped handle. The solid circle at the end had the planet and stars crest in gold stamped into it. Something stirred in his chest. He would be proud to carry such an item. "That is beautifully designed, Flower."

Rachel allowed herself a small smile as she turned away from him. She quickly adjusted the original order to include one for Pitor, since she could tell he was about to ask. Then added the sword she'd just designed for the Regis to the order. The time to completion self-adjusted to just over four hours to being finished.

"How many of those will you be making?"

Rachel looked down into the third chamber and nodded before she spoke. "One sword, scabbard, and belt for Major Ka'al, and each of his cadres. The one I just designed for the Regis...and one for you."

She felt warmth blossom down the bond and into her chest. "Thank you, Rachel."

"Just ensure you learn how to use it. Otherwise, it is worthless. I sent Major Ka'al information on a training regimen for his cadre. Talk to him about training."

Rachel turned completely away from the row of manufacturing chambers and began walking across the compartment to another row of smaller manufacturing chambers. Pitor noticed the hand she braced against her stomach as she moved. "Are you well, Rachel?" He asked as he followed her to the only chamber operating on this side. She didn't answer as she looked down at the process underway in front of her.

The small chambers were used for replicating fine machine parts and the like. So these were shaped more like glass boxes. Inside, small robotic arms swiveled and turned through several axes as they assembled the much smaller item Rachel had designed and ordered. Pitor was quickly learning that his mate's intelligence had not been overstated. She was always working on something on her tablet. Designing, researching, refining, and creating.

Pitor looked down from over her shoulder. "That appears to be a more robust version of the bracelets," he observed. It looked like the black bangles that all of the Collected wore at one time or another that, with Rachel's help, had all dematerialized from the wearer's wrists but one. An effort to help the Returned be less recognizable and thus make it easier for them to blend in. The only one left was the white one her Grace wore, which she had considered equal to what Humans called a *wedding band*. A physical symbol that she was mated - as Pitor understood it.

"It is," Rachel responded after a moment. This bracelet was about an inch wide and marginally thicker than the regular bangles. "See the lip on one side?" Along the edge of one side was a depression that ran the circumference of the bracelet. "Her current band will lock into it. If it works as designed, all she has to do is put them together, and bam, her Grace has a temporary forcefield. Possibly longer if my guess is correct." A guess she didn't dare verbalize to anyone but Michelle.

Pitor moved to get a better look at the item being assembled before his eyes. Various waldos and armatures moved in a blur. They assembled the item molecule by molecule, building the microscopic internal electronics and band as they went. "How did you manage to shrink the field projection matrix? What about the power supply?"

Rachel chuckled softly, "It is amazing how far you guys have come technology-wise, but you do not do any refining once you figure out how to make something work. You have such powerful computers and barely use them to their full potential. Once they reverse engineer quantum computing, you will really see what Humans are capable of."

"Are they truly so formidable?"

Rachel turned to look up at her mate with an arched eyebrow. "Considering what one stowaway and a mother who wanted nothing more than to get back to her family managed to achieve?"

Pitor took the rebuke with a nod. "Fair enough, indeed."

Rachel took one last look at the small chamber and saw that in a short time, even more of the item had come into existence. "Hopefully, she will never need it, right? However, our Regent seems to have a propensity to walk toward danger, not away from it. She cannot always wear an exosuit, so this will be the next best thing. It is purely protective, though, and will only last about five minutes before it shuts off and needs to recharge."

"And how is that done if she is wearing it?"

"Kinetic Energy," Rachel lied. "As she moves, it will recharge, but that could take upwards of half an hour." Rachel hadn't asked about it, but she'd seen the purple marks that had covered Captain Turney's body. The same color as the lightning Michelle had thrown just before they were transported away from the *Rising Star*. She'd let her Grace know the device could be supercharged if her special ability was used again. If it worked as designed, even the strange pulse of static energy that filled a room when Michelle got angry would be enough to recharge the device. "Let us get something to eat," Rachel said as she turned to the door. "I am hungry, and I really want to get out of this dress."

Pitor watched her walk away for a few steps before following. Rachel obviously didn't know he could feel both lies across their strengthening bond. Rachel knew something about the Regent that he didn't, and she wasn't hungry; she felt sick to her stomach.

Chapter Eleven

The full moon hung fat and white in the dark sky. Its bluish light brightly lit the cattle ranch around the ship and muted what stars managed to shine through. That same light was brightly refracted into the Regent's Solar by the windows, filling the space with enough light that no artificial lighting sources were needed. Even though some light still spilled in from the dimmed lighting of the corridor through the open doors.

Michelle had changed into one of the silken tops and leggings. She sat curled, her feet tucked beneath her, on one of the couches she had asked to be brought in, with a mug of brut steaming on an end table next to her. A tablet cast its glow on her face as she quietly read, waiting for everyone to arrive from wherever they were on the ship.

There really wasn't much for her to do as Regent aboard a grounded ship. After grumbling about such to Domaas, after the journalist and her cameraman had left, he promised it would be different once they returned to Cerul. "It probably will be pretty intense for a while," he had said. "With both you and the council here, the only one left to run the Impire is Colonel Bil'tun and pure inertia. There are various ministers to tend the day-to-day, but Colonel Bil'tun would be the current leader in your stead."

The interview with Carol Harbors went very well. So well, Michelle had let them take the raw video file without having anything edited out. The Regent had been pretty forthcoming while leaving out very precise details and had even allowed Arya to spend some time demanding the older woman's attention. Carol had promised to send word of what time the interview would be broadcasted. Evidently, Michelle's lack of attention to the media had left her utterly unaware that the entire world was gasping for anything about the human boy-turned-Cerulean queen. Her blaise attitude toward notoriety had left the masses demanding every scrap of knowledge about her.

There had been several smaller interviews from others who had been returned. One of them Michelle remembered from the early days aboard the *Rising Star.* She had *definitely* overstated her importance to the escape and closeness to Michelle's inner circle aboard the ship.

Speaking of...

Michelle made a mental note to reach out to Katie, Chrissie, Sean, and Makayla. They'd all been tight-lipped as planned, but Katie and Chrissie should have had their babies by now or very soon. They'd probably want to be reunited with their mates as well.

"Forever studying something," her mother's voice broke into her idle thoughts.

Michelle looked up from the tablet she hadn't been reading - another long-winded article about her without the writer knowing anything - and uncurled from the couch to stand. Maggie waved her to stay in place. "Oh, please don't get up when I'm about to sit."

The daughter still made room on the couch and ordered a mug of herbal tea for the mother as she sat down. Maggie watched in fascination as the pad inset on the low coffee table before them glowed and a mug of fragrant dark brew rezzed into existence. "Wow," she said as she lifted the mug and cupped her hands around it to warm her palms.

"Everything we eat and drink comes from those things?"

Michelle nodded and smiled, "Pretty awesome, huh? Although nothing will ever come close to your chicken parm."

Maggie smiled; her eldest had always been a loud fan of her cooking. She sipped and sighed deeply, "This is probably the most perfect cup of chamomile tea I've ever tasted." The moonlight in the room flickered, and Michelle looked out the window in time to see one of the military helicopters completing another orbit with blinking running lights showing its path. "Your father and I talked, Michelle."

Maggie was looking at her when she looked back, "We won't be coming with you."

Michelle nodded her head. She had already figured. This was her mess to deal with; she was an adult now, a mother, a queen. *Regent*. Every child has to leave the nest eventually, even if the first time they do so isn't by choice. She understood. Her parents still had Shannon and Eloise to worry about.

In a different circumstance, she would probably be just as uncomfortable raising Arya on a completely alien planet. Only because she was Regent was she open to raising Arya on Cerul. Otherwise, she would have stuck to the original plan of living quietly with her family and somehow raising her half-alien child on a Human planet. It didn't have to make sense.

Michelle blinked as she realized that was exactly what she had been trying to avoid. Somewhere in the far recesses of her mind, Michelle knew that idea would eventually become a reality; it had to. It made her incredibly uncomfortable; having that thought would lead her to realize there was a high chance she'd never see any of her family again. The very same Michelle had skydived from orbit to get back to. Fear and sadness laid down that path of thought, and Michelle knew she wasn't ready to confront *that* reality yet. Not after everything she went through to get home.

"I understand, Mom. I kinda figured that anyway. And I really am sorry for uprooting you guys so much."

Maggie smiled warmly, "We know you didn't want any of this brought to us. We know you tried to avoid it, but sometimes you just can't escape what the Universe has planned."

Michelle huffed, "Don't I know it." Shadows cast into the Solar as several people arrived at the open door.

Time to finally have that meeting.

Michelle had originally intended to have it the night Jamie had been beaten, but obviously, that did not happen. Now it was time. She had questions that needed answering, directives to give, and balls to start rolling. "Come in, please." Even Domaas honored the ancient rule of not entering this chamber without the Regent's permission. Despite the fact Michelle had said if the door was open, it was to be taken as an invitation.

Colonels Kear'ald and Cha'ol entered after Domaas. Major Ka'al and Sheel followed them the former quickly moving to protectively stand behind the couch where Michelle sat. The others spread out across the room, with Domaas standing at Michelle's left side. Rachel and Jamie entered soon after, one of them chuckling over a joke the other had just told. Michelle made a note of the voluminous skirt of Jamie's dress and gave the nanny a questioning look. A simple nod was all that was returned. The girl was carrying at least one of her weapons. The last to arrive was Michelle's father, accompanied by a confused-looking Bailey.

That was everyone. "Doors closed and sealed," Michelle called to the sentries remaining outside. The door silently slid shut, and a blue light turned on near the control pad. They were now sealed inside. The only light was coming from the full moon shining into the room. Michelle looked around the assembled faces and had a moment of brevity. This was her first council meeting as Regent. "Shall we begin?"

There were small nods all around, but no one spoke. This was her Grace's show now, and the reception she received upon her arrival had truly ground home that fact. The mantle she had taken on had settled on her shoulders with a weight that could not be ignored. Looking around the assembled faces in the dim light, she saw support, hope, deep respect, and adoring love. Nothing but unadulterated pride and affection vibrated from Domaas down the bond. *But do I deserve it?*

"Arya?"

"Sleeping like an angel under the guard of one of Major Ka'als cadre," Jamie answered. She held up her tablet. "I had the doors sealed, and I have her crib on camera. I'll know instantly if there's a problem."

Michelle nodded and took a sip of her cooling brut. A grimace; getting used to the stuff had been one thing, but it went into the gutter when it was cold. *Enough stalling,* she chastised herself. "Bailey?" The redhead looked like she wanted to curtsy but, thankfully, only looked at Michelle expectantly. "Were you able to reconnect with your mate?"

The girl beamed brightly in the moonlight. "Yes, your Grace."

"And you spoke with him about our discussion yesterday?"

Bailey bobbed her head, "Yes. He will stay if I want to."

Domaas grunted as he sensed the sandbag about to drop on the young woman's head. He had noticed how his Regent liked dropping titles and positions on people. Traditionally, those on the Regents council came from noble houses or long, distinctive careers in the government and military. Michelle hadn't known Major Ka'al from a broken lightbulb, but by placing her trust in him, she was also asking for his loyalty. So far, the young Major had truly risen to the challenge. There would be no jockeying for positions in this Regent's Council. Ulterior motives would be hard to achieve while she remained so unpredictable.

"Excellent," Michelle said as a smile crept into her voice. "Bailey Et'Kanon, I name you Regent's Liaison for the Collected. You will be in charge of seeing to the safety, security, and comfort of all who returned from the *Rising Star* or those who may return from Cerul."

Bailey's already pale face turned ghostly in the dim light. "W-what?"

Rachel snickered, "Jesus, your Grace. You gotta start warning people before you do that." There was a soft tittering from the others Michelle had recently sandbagged.

Michelle could hear light humor as she said, "I can think of no one else who will understand how important it is to ensure the Hybrids who remain don't feel abandoned. But do not worry..."

Domaas' head snapped down to look at his mate as he felt a sudden...*tenseness* across the bond. "Dad?" Roger sat forward in his chair. "I would like to give you a job." Regent or not, she couldn't bring herself to make decrees or edicts involving her family. They were not her subjects and would never be considered such.

"A job?" He asked suspiciously, glancing at Bailey, who still had a look of utter confusion on her face.

"Well, it's safe to say you and Mom lost your jobs because of me; Ellie and Shan can't attend school either. You need money, and I have an obscene amount of it." Michelle had said nothing to anyone about how much money Rachel had found. She had, however, asked Rachel to look into finding what islands might be for sale in the South Pacific. For the job she had planned for him, Cerul would need a toe-hold on Earth. Just a tiny one that wouldn't be seen as a threat to the rest of the world. "I'd like you to take on the position of Cerulean Ambassador to the United Nations."

Roger blinked. He hadn't seen that one coming, either. Michelle noticed eyes shifting around the room as others began to wonder who else was about to get the shock of their lives next.

"Ambassador?" Roger asked as if the word didn't quite fit in his mouth. "To the United Nations?" His brow furrowed. "Why not the United States?"

"Because I don't want a treaty with just the United States, I want a treaty with the whole planet. How eager do you think the US government will be to share replicator technology that can solve world hunger over-night? Or faster than light technology? Quantum Computing? Shield technology and anti-gravity? Just the act alone of an entire alien impire aligning with one country would cause problems I don't want to be the cause of."

Regis Et'Kuraul and Colonel Kear'ald looked at each other and blinked in unison as if they finally realized something very important at the same moment. Unfortunately, none of the Humans were paying attention to them to see it.

"No," Michelle continued with a soft shake of her head. "I won't help start an arms race that could only end horribly. Will you do it? I promise you'll be paid well, Ellie and Shan's college funds will be covered and you can do whatever you want, Mom."

Roger shifted his gaze to Margaret, who remained on the couch next to Michelle. Husband and wife, father and mother, shared a long look together. A silent conversation; something Michelle was just starting to have with Domaas. Finally, after a full ten seconds of silence, her father looked back to Michelle and said, "We'll do it."

"Awesome, we'll talk more in-depth tomorrow about getting you vetted. Bailey?" The redhead blinked herself back to attention. She hadn't even known why she'd been invited to this meeting and now she had been given the full blind faith of this new Regent. If she hadn't personally witnessed the way the Ceruleans greeted Michelle earlier she would have had doubts this was all really happening. "I'd very much appreciate meeting your mate, I have a job for him as well."

"Yes, your Grace," she said with a touch more confidence in her voice.

Michelle took a pause and glanced down at her tablet to switch gears. "Rachel?"

"Your Grace?"

"What do you need to unlock control of the ships?"

"Your handprint and ah...um..." Rachel's face darkened a bit and as she visibly fought a giggle, "You singing Arya's lullaby."

Michelle's face went blank as color bloomed into her cheeks. "No." A statement of disbelief.

Rachel stopped trying to hide her amusement and chuckled out loud. "Sorry, I needed it to be two-factor authentication. They probably had your handprint and a voice recording, but you only sing to Arya when you're completely alone!"

"But how do you know about that?" Michelle pointed to the other blonde in the room, who was also fighting laughter. "Jamie doesn't even know about that!"

"Your translator, your Grace. Once I could talk to you again, I could listen in whenever I wanted." Rachel's eyes twinkled. *Whenever.* Michelle looked up at Domaas, who had canted his head to the side and showed his dimples with a smile. About the most amusement he was willing to show in front of subordinates.

"Colonel Cha'ol?"

The grizzled Cerulean stepped into Michelle's line of sight. Even he had a small grin on his lips. "Your Grace?"

"Since I utterly refuse to sing for the pleasure of present company. I will do it when we are done here. We don't need you for anything else; would you please signal the other ships to prepare for launch? I want the fleet ready to relocate before sunrise."

"At once, your Grace."

Colonel Cha'ol crisply turned and moved to the doors, which opened for him and then closed and sealed right after. "Heartbeat?" Michelle looked up at Domaas. "Are you sure this is wise? Given what I have seen and learned, the fleet taking flight will likely make the human military quite nervous."

Michelle pursed her lips and nodded, "You are right." She turned back to where her dad sat. "Dad, since you'll be the diplomat, can you message General Hamlin? Tell him the ships are just relocating. Rachel will set you up with his contact info."

"What do I tell him when he asks where the ships are moving to? Because he will ask."

Michelle shrugged in thought, "Domaas, these ships float, right?"

"Float?"

She looked back at him to see the question on his face as well. "Yes. Float? You know, if they land in water will they sink?"

Domaas cleared his throat as he began wondering just what his mate was thinking. "Yes, they *float,* your Grace. They will also submerge to three-thousand human meters before they develop problems."

Michelle turned back. "Tell him international waters, Dad. And that they're more than welcome to send escorts since I can't seem to go any-where without them making it seem like they're in control."

"But that's exactly the opposite of what we'll be showing them, isn't it?" Rachel asked. "You're telling the American government and the world that you...*we*, I guess, are independent of the American government."

"I believe that is exactly her goal," Domaas rumbled above her. "By doing so, she is showing the rest of Earth she has no intention of allying purely with one country, yes? It is one thing to say it, but it must be seen by the entire world so there is no question."

"Yes. Does anyone in this room have a problem with that?" Michelle asked the members of her council. "Seriously, if anyone has an issue with it, speak now. I have no intention of not listening if someone has a better or different idea." Silence. "Great. Domaas, you have overall command of the fleet, right?"

"Correct, your Grace."

"Great. See to it that all the other ship commanders understand exactly what I want. There is an area called Point Nemo in the Pacific Ocean. That is our destination."

"Understood, Heartbeat." Michelle stifled a smile. She could feel his pride and approval of her asserting her authority. In a moment, she'd see how deep that actually went.

"Okay, does anyone need a bathroom break? I have two more items on my list. The last one I feel might take awhile." No one spoke or shifted. *Okay,* Michelle thought to herself. *Here we go.* She looked at Rachel, who was watching her expectantly.

"Rachel? Are they ready?"

"The last one was finished just two hours ago. Scabbards and belts for everyone," Rachel chirped with a light note of pride.

"Major Ka'al?"

Michelle's head of security stepped forward. "Please summon the rest of your cadre to the Solar, except for the one at my quarters."

The Major reached up and tapped the communication device behind his ear. Something everyone in the room, but Roger and Margaret, now wore. "This is Ka'al, everyone but Kato to the Regent's Solar. Now." A few moments later, there was a low chime from the door.

"Enter!" Michelle called out. The doors opened, and the other three members of Michelle's security team entered the Solar. "Major, could you call your males to attention?"

Without a pause, the Major pivoted on his heel and barked the order. The males, having heard Michelle, were already in motion and formed up into formation in blisteringly quick order. Major Ka'al stepped to them and then about-faced once he stood before the cadre, snapping into perfect attention as he did so.

"Your Regent's Guard, your Grace."

Ignoring the querying looks from everyone else, she gave a nod to Rachel as she stood from the couch, and a blue light illuminated the room. A rack of swords appeared along the wall, complete with scabbards and belts. Six of them appeared black, and on closer examination, faint pulses of blue could be seen traveling along fine threads. The last, and seventh was a traditional brown leather sheath with a matching belt. Its hilt and pommel were more ornate than the others. Michelle glanced at Rachel to receive a pleased smile at the surprise.

"I didn't even think of that," Michelle said in wonder as she stepped to the seventh sword and lifted it from the rack.

"That is why you appointed me to your council, right?" The self-satisfaction was thick in Rachel's voice.

Michelle answered with a full smile as she grasped the hilt, and pulled the sword partially out. Pearlescent metal glimmered in the blue moon-light. "Lights," Michelle called out, and the overhead lighting came up until the Solar was well lit. The whorls and swirls in the alloy showed even brighter and the finely honed edge appeared sharp enough to slice stone. "Tell us about them, Rachel."

"They are made of the same alloy as the ship's hulls. Except, I was able to harden them even more by a factor of six. That's what causes them to have that rainbow-pearlescent swirl in the alloy. The edge is laser etched down to point zero-zero microns and will never, ever dull." The pride in Rachel's voice was palpable. "The other scabbards are designed to seam-lessly connect with the exosuits your security wears at all times, so if they are cloaked nothing will be visible. The material is even embedded into the blades, hilts, and pommels."

"Well done, Rachel," Michelle whispered as she resheathed the Regis' sword. Turning back to the room of curious faces, she sought out her mate's eyes, his curiosity vibrating hard down the bond. "Regis, please step forward."

Domaas arched an eyebrow in surprise. That would have been the first time Michelle had directly called him by his new title. "What have you two concocted for us?" He asked with a smile as he approached.

Michelle cradled the item in her arms as she turned bodily toward him. "Originally, these were supposed to just be for Major Ka'al and his cadre. But in Rachel's correct wisdom, she also made one for my Regis. I hope you like it." She held it out for him to take.

"How could I not appreciate anything my Regent has to give me? What is it?"

Michelle held it out as her eyes suddenly focused and bored into his. "A sword." There was no word for it in Cerulean; she had checked.

"This word is unfamiliar to me..." Domaas reached for the long object. The brown casing was made of fine leather, supple to the eye, the handle at one end made of fine metal with golden wire wrapping around the grip. A solid puck balanced the weight at the end where the planet and star constellation of the Cerulean crest was engraved, then relieved with Cerulean blue and gold. It was a work of art.

"A tool," Pitor offered. "Rachel explained to me they are tools of defense for the protection of our Regent."

Michelle wasn't looking, so she didn't see the way Rachel crossley glared at Colonel Kear'ald. Michelle did, however, hear the importance Pitor had placed on calling it a tool. "It is a tool, yes," she said while maintaining eye contact with her own mate. "It is also a *weapon*."

Domaas' hands froze in midair, inches from touching the sword. Michelle watched his vision narrow as a calm sort of panic traveled across the bond. "Clear this room." His voice was barely above a whisper but could have been a thundercrack for the burst of activity it caused.

"Who is the Regent in this room?" Michelle barked, freezing all motion. She let her eyes harden as she bore her gaze up at Domaas'. "Who is Regent, Domaas? Am I or not?"

Domaas swallowed. "You are, Heartbeat."

"Great. Just checking." She thrust the sword forward even as Domaas' hands drifted to his sides. "Take it, I want my Regis and security detail to carry swords at all times."

Domaas face crumpled - something Michelle could never recall witnessing before. "I cannot, we cannot, Heartbeat. It is forbidden." His eyes pleaded with her to leave it there, but he knew she was about to push.

Michelle returned to the rack, replaced the Regis' sword, and turned again to face the room. Every Cerulean face was pale enough to look sickly. Cold sweats had broken out across foreheads. The Humans held looks of confusion. It was incredibly rare for Ceruleans to show so much emotion at once, and they *never* showed fear. "Everyone take a seat, I don't care if you have to sit on the floor." There was quick compliance.

"Your Grace, it would be best if we discussed this private-"

Michelle cut him off, slightly irked Domaas had used her title, "The number one thing that frustrated me since that first night aboard the *Rising Star* was the Cerulean tendency to compartmentalize information," she turned to find Domaas still standing, and she angrily pointed to her abandoned spot on the couch. Like a chastised little boy, he obeyed and took his seat. Maggie made room for the larger male while barely suppressing her smile at seeing her daughter put the male in his place. "At first, it made sense," Michelle continued. "Of course, you all would want to keep us from knowing too much. Just enough to accept what our new lives held in store. Honestly, you guys were damned near artists at it."

Michelle paused. She could feel herself becoming properly angry, and so far her ire had been purely for looks. She walked around the room and, after taking several deep breaths, continued again, "It took forever for me to notice it. I even had to go back and look at videos from the arrival of the first Collection shuttles to verify it."

She turned back to the room. "I want to know why the Ceruleans don't have any lethal weapons, and *I want to know* what connection that has to the honest reason why Cerulean females are dying off."

Silence greeted her in response, with every Cerulean's eyes shifting to the Regis sitting behind her. Michelle spun, catching the look of extreme distress on her mate's face. "It's funny. We used to think you males never showed emotion, but now your faces are as easy to read as a book. There is a connection, isn't there?" Michelle came to stand before her mate and stopped moving. "Domaas, it would appear you've been elected as a storyteller."

Michelle watched her mate lose all composure. She watched the *Commander* evaporate like mist in the wind, leaving behind a scared little boy. A frightened child who wanted to be anywhere else but sitting under her intense glare. "It is forbidden to speak openly about it. Only the Regent's Council and high-ranking military are told the truth...it is part of the oath one gives once the rank of Colonel is achieved. You would have been briefed on it once we returned to Cerul. That is the law. I need you to give me a direct order, your Grace. So that all present may hear it."

Michelle cocked her head. The feelings she was getting across the bond were something she had never felt from him. *Fear, apprehension, dread.* "Okay. Domaas, I order you to tell us the truth. All of it. Start at the beginning."

Chapter Twelve

Almost three thousand cycles ago, there was a civil war. A war so devastating that it changed the very fabric of Cerulean society permanently. At the time, Cerul was much like nineteenth-century Earth... but worse, much worse. They thought themselves enlightened. They went from combustion engines to interstellar travel in roughly eighty cycles. It was a time of unprecedented advancement. But unfortunately, Cerulean society was not ready, ill-prepared to even attempt to keep pace with advancing technology and what it allowed.

Cerulean females had been not much more than chattel up to the age of Great Advancement. Often traded for property or used in arranged couplings to secure business deals and diplomatic goals. At the time, they were considered an inferior subset of the Cerulean race, and it was not even considered to give them rights. Cerulean females were good for breeding and giving pleasure, not much else. It was not uncommon for those who were known to produce superior sons to be highly coveted. As a result, there was a healthy breeding industry exclusively for Cerulean females. Sons were kept, and daughters were forcibly aborted or sold back to the Breeder.

The wealthiest of males would be known to keep several in his home. The more he had, especially if they were considered beautiful, the more status he could achieve in his community. Kept and displayed in his home like ornamental pieces of furniture. And just like a piece of furniture, a female could be sold off to pay debts or even simply tossed out once her owner grew tired of her. This was the worst thing that could happen. For if she was left with no master to claim her, then by law, she did not exist.

This all ended with a female named K'Iesta.

K'Iesta killed her owner. She had become pregnant with a female child, and her master had promised to allow her to bear and raise the child. Until he lost money on a bad investment.

She had never fooled herself into thinking him a kind male, but to allow her to become attached to a baby and then to take that from her was too much. First-born daughters were not permitted by custom and law; she had been a fool to think he would not find any reason to terminate her pregnancy.

It was not just that K'Iesta had killed her owner, though. She was defiant and showed righteous indignation even as they led her to her execution. It was unheard of. She spat in the faces of her executioners and cursed them. She denounced the authority of any Cerulean god who would allow her kind to be treated in such a manner. This shocked the world. Never in living memory had a female Cerulean spoken and behaved so contemptuously of societal norms.

They cut her in five places. The first four were nicked arteries so she would slowly bleed out, and the fifth was her womb cut open for her daughter to be thrown to the King's hunting varths. It was the last thing she witnessed before the darkness took her. Her body hung from the walls of the King's palace for a month before being removed and buried in an unmarked location.

Once out of sight, it was out of the male's minds; a female had thought herself above the law, and she had been dealt with. An example had been made to any others who might think to do the same. Secure in their own superiority and hubris, they did not see they had actually created a martyr.

The uprising started with a plea for freedom, equal rights, and fair treatment. All females who spoke up or spoke out were savagely put down. It was not four cycles past K'Iesta's slaughtering that Cerulean females were in open rebellion. Masters were no longer safe in their own homes. Cerulean males found themselves waking up with kitchen knives slicing through their throats or choking on a poisoned supper. The condemned taken to the butcher's block were often rescued and whisked into the uninhabited wilds of Cerul. The female rebels were hunted, but the hunters often never returned.

No one was sure which side introduced proper weapons into the fighting. However, it was not long until the Cerulean advanced technology brought offensive weapons into the mix. What had started with kitchen knives quickly turned into weapons of death. And, as with many things, there was no going back once the weapons were in play. The rebellion morphed into an all-out civil war. With the escalation of the conflict came more and more devious weapons. Weapons that killed all living matter, weapons that burned, weapons that caused madness, weapons that incinerated so thoroughly that nothing but carbon remained. Male against female, there were traitors on both sides. The war raged for nearly one hundred and fifty cycles. The planet was torn apart.

Until one day, the female faction leader stepped forward with an offer of peace. She had taken on the mantle of K'Iesta, as every rebel leader before her. Her demands were for the King to abdicate his throne and allow a female Regent to be installed. Only the mother of a firstborn daughter would be acceptable. As it had been long known there was only one firstborn daughter every generation. Both sides would destroy every offensive weapon and save one ship each. The females who wished to leave would take their ship and vanish into the depths of space, never to return. The females who had not fought for their freedom and continued serving their masters would stay and attempt to heal their fractured society. Even as the K'Iesta felt they deserved death for being traitors, she wanted the Regent to guarantee the females' safety and equal treatment under the law.

Exactly what happened during that time period is lost to time and echoes. All that is known is the King died soon after the rebel female-led faction had evacuated the planet. The first Regent was installed shortly after. Regent K'Iesta, who was pregnant with spots on her left shoulder. A girl child, a rarity in its own right. Also, one that had never before been allowed to come to term as custom required all firstborn children to be male to guarantee a master's lineage.

It wasn't until after the birth of her child that the first Regent's abilities manifested. She could throw and manipulate fire. Many tried to explain this new manifestation. Those who still had enough social clout to do so mused it was directly connected to having a first-born daughter. Although, *no one could say for sure as first-born daughters had never been allowed to be born as long as any could remember. Never mind their once-in-a-generation rarity.*

Time passed. Society healed and developed into something better. The Ceruleans traveled further than ever throughout the stars and discovered multiple other inhabited planets. Never conquering, but instead incentivizing other species to join for mutual benefit. Those planets which declined the invitation to join the Impirium *were left to their own devices but still allowed to trade freely. Most who witnessed the Cerulean's advanced technology were quick to sign the charter. If nothing else then to advance their own civilizations, often by hundreds of years.*

Peace reigned with a secured transition of the Regency every second generation. A mother, then a daughter would each serve as Regent. And only the next female to have a first-born daughter would be accepted to take on the next mantle of Regent.

For five hundred cycles, the Cerulean Impirium prospered and grew in near-perfect peace. Even the poorest of Ceruleans wanted for nothing. A class system remained, but its rigidness faded over time. It was during this time the biological phenomenon of mating *evolved. Children grew fat and happy.*

Until they stopped growing. And soon, they stopped being born. And then the Cerulean females began getting sick and dying.

And just as the Ceruleans understood how grave the situation was, the descendants of K'Iesta's tribe returned. A genetic weapon had been released at the end of the Great Schism, as the civil war had come to be known. A ticking time bomb designed to strike at the descendants of those who had chosen the wrong *side.*

The Kesta, as they now called themselves, in honor of their matriarch. They had settled and colonized a planet in an uncharted region of space and had thrived on their own as a matriarchal society. They had returned to ensure the Regent remained head of the Cerulean Impirium and offered a final truce.

Surrender the Regency to the Kesta and allow Cerul to become a vassal state to K'Iesta, they cared not for the Impirium, and the antidote would be delivered planet-wide. Refuse, and the Kesta would leave Cerul in peace forever, or at least until they were near extinction. Regent Hont'ia refused them and demanded the antidote.

But the Kesta only gave one warning, that they would be watching. If any attempt was made for the Ceruleans to weaponize their ships and come after the Kesta in a foolish act of vengeance, Cerul would not survive their response. If they caught wind the Cerulean Impirium made any attempt to expand the Impirium further, Cerul would not survive their response. They would return in another two thousand cycles to make their offer once more when the Ceruleans would be genuinely desperate.

The Kesta then returned to their ship and left. The Regent sent a small fleet of ships to track them, but those ships never returned. Soon after, Regent Hont'ia made a proclamation that all offensive weapons were to be destroyed, and only defensive, non-lethal devices were to be used or developed. This was for both personal and shipboard use. She also ordered that every possible effort be made to find a cure for the Blight.

It had been just over 1500 cycles since then, and once every two hundred cycles or so, a ship of unfamiliar design would make its way through Cerulean space. Never stopping, never answering hails, but ensuring it was seen and noted. And when it passed near Cerul, it always sent a short message. The date of K'Iesta killing her master. This happened twice before the Ceruleans abandoned the old communication network buoys in favor of subspace communications. The development of this technology came at great expense, but it was worth it to know that the Kesta could no longer monitor their communications.

The planet was discovered on long-range passive scans five hundred years ago in Earth's timeline.

Showing promise; a series of small, stealthy ships had been dispatched to take samples and run experiments on the dominant species on the planet. It was quickly discovered the young male of the species could be changed and adapted to suit the Cerulean's need for healthy, child-bearing mothers. With the added benefit that their Human DNA made them and all potential offspring immune to the genetic bioweapon that would eventually kill off all genetically-pure Cerulean females.

*****

"So you see, Heartbeat, that is why I cannot take this weapon; why none of us can," Domaas finished.

The Solar was as quiet as a tomb for a full minute. Michelle had returned to the window as Domaas had talked, and the moon had moved far enough that soon it would no longer shine through the window. "So what happens if the Kesta discovers what you guys have been doing to save the Cerulean species?" She asked without turning around.

Domaas got to his feet and moved to join her, but Michelle held up her hand, stopping him. He sighed, "We do not know for certain, although great reprisal was promised. The *Rising Star* went into construction just after a Kesta ship passed through but was not launched until after another Kesta ship passed by. But a ship of that mass cannot travel at high lightspeed for long periods of time without leaving a trail. It took five Earth years for it to transit to Earth. This was to make sure the Kesta weren't tracking the *Rising Star*. It could have done it in a few months if pushed. These ships can make the transit in two or three weeks-"

Michelle suddenly spun on her heel and lifted Domaas' sword from the rack. "I am issuing an edict," she said to the room. "You *will* carry the swords that have been made for you. Including you, Domaas. You will carry them and train with them. They will become an extension of your body." She locked eyes with every member of her security cadre, then Pitor, and finally back to Domaas. "You will use them only in defense of me, yourselves, your mates, or anyone worthy of being protected. You are never to draw your sword in anger, and you are never to draw your sword except to clean it, train with it, or defend a life with it. Does that work for you?"

Coming to stand before Domaas, she looked up into her mate's eyes, and both saw and felt the conflicting emotions within him. He didn't like it. He felt it was skirting a little close to the edge, but Michelle had been precise in her wording for that reason. She held the sword in its scabbard and belt out to him once more. "Yes, your Grace. I, we, shall bear them with honor and pride."

Chapter Thirteen

"Why have you left your ship, Cou'parth? We are in transit."

The Cerulean lord attempted to look down his nose at Colonel Cha'ol, which was challenging to do as they were the same height. "Know your place, Colonel-"

"My *place*, Lord, is the commander of this ship. And seeing as how the Regent is currently aboard my ship, that brings any unexpected arrivals directly under my concern."

Cou'Parth sighed explosively through his nose and turned to glance at his compatriots. Colonel Cha'ol was well within his rights and rank to question their sudden and uninvited arrival. Turning back to the Colonel, he said, "Yes, you are quite right, Colonel. We are here to greet our new Regent and invite her to hold a meeting with us. It is quite unusual that she has not requested our presence when we have made it clear we are eager to meet with her. There is much to discuss."

Colonel Cha'ol smiled faintly. He was not intimidated by these old lords. Males who had grown fat and lazy with their scheming for power. Males that had treated him as a second-class citizen because his birth wasn't high enough. The new Regent looked at him respectfully when she spoke and listened when he did the same. His loyalty had already aligned itself.

The Colonel had been deemed too old to take a human mate, but through their machinations, the five old council members each had a human mate back on Cerul. By all accounts, although not outright abusive, kindness was not a word that would be used where it was concerned with how their mates were treated.

It was with a small amount of pleasure that Colonel Cha'ol said, "Her Grace has already convened her council. None of us are simple-minded enough to think she forgot to invite you lot."

Cour'Parth waved the words away in annoyance and stepped down from the transporter dias. "Yes, yes, she named her mate Regis. What is that more than a ceremonial title?" Colonel Cha'ol did not move to clear the way for him.

"Regis Et'Kuraul is still my commanding officer, Counselor. And his authority supersedes yours as far as anyone aboard this ship is concerned. I will send word that you seek an audience with her Grace." The Colonel snapped his fingers, and the two sentries he'd brought stepped to block the corridor. "You will remain here until the word is sent for you or you are told to leave."

*****

The ship shields blocked nearly the entire wind effect that one would have felt in such a location. The fleet held elevation at one-thousand feet in perfect formation with the *Folded Fist* at point, the current flagship, and the rest following two abreast at one-mile intervals. They were heading for Point Nemo in the deep South Pacific. A point in the middle of the ocean that was as far as physically possible to be from any particular land mass.

Nothing but an uninterrupted blue sea spread out beneath them, and the sky was full of big fluffy clouds and a lone C-8 Paladin. A giant aluminum cloud of a military cargo plane. Roger had given General Hamlin a solid thirty-minute notice that the fleet would soon be airborne. The General had demanded an explanation, demanded to speak to Michelle, and had received neither.

The orbiting helicopters had quickly been replaced by the same fighter aircraft that had intercepted the *Arya Express.* And as each ship came to life and lifted off from the ground, more fighters arrived. Michelle had ordered that the ships were to remain at a low altitude, not to transit over any city centers, and to keep their speed at precisely three-hundred knots once they crossed over the ocean. It could not be said she hadn't considered the military's jumpiness. They had turned left near Hawaii six hours ago, and so far, that C-8 flying in formation a mile to port had been the only American aircraft able to keep up and not have to turn back for any type of refueling. Michelle had ordered the plane monitored for distress, just in case.

"You do know there is a very well-equipped exercise center aboard every ship, yes?"

Michelle smiled and blocked his strike only to counter with a half-speed blow to his temple with the back of her padded hand. It certainly would have at least stunned a lesser opponent. "Is there anything these ships do not have?" She asked between huffs. Domaas ducked low and charged her, going for a grapple. Michelle absorbed the tackle and fell backward, planting her foot in his midsection and using his own momentum to flip him completely over her.

Domaas grunted with the impact and slowly got back to his feet. Michelle was waiting for him, bouncing from foot to foot on the black hull of the ship. Sweat had soaked through her sports bra and tank top. Even though her hair was tied up with her hair sticks, strands had come loose and plastered themselves to the sides of her face in sweat. Domaas couldn't help the arousal from building as blood transferred from one part of his body to another. The last time they'd sparred together they had been aboard the *Rising Star*. The Elder Regent had no way of knowing how often she had sent a seething Michelle back to their quarters. And only Domaas knew Michelle's...temper could be quelled one of two ways. Both of them were highly physical.

"Ew, seeing me a stinky, sweaty mess gets you going, huh?" She feinted to knee him in the groin, and Domaas bent to protect himself by reflex - only to be met by what would have been a savage uppercut in an actual fight. "Besides, how many people can say they sparred with their mate on top of a spaceship while it flew over the Pacific Ocean? This is kinda fun!"

Domaas held up a hand and stepped back, asking for a reprieve. "You are giving poor Major Ka'al a heart attack, Heartbeat," he said, gesturing to where the Major and one other guard stood just out of earshot. "What if you slip and fall from the ship?"

Michelle grinned as she caught her breath and held up her arm to show the new bracelet that had joined the bangle on her wrist. "I will be fine. And I did promise him I would not make his job boring, Domaas." Her smile deepened to nearly predatory. "But I will tell you what," her voice dropped into a very husky note. One that she knew spoke to her mate's primal instincts. "You land a single strike on me in the next two minutes, and I'll let you put me on *my* back, right here on top of the ship below this wide-open sky and all the gods of this world." She sent the feeling of her heated, molten core to punctuate this down the Bond, to punctuate this. Domaas growled from deep in his chest and lowered into a fighting stance-

"Your Grace, I apologize for the interruption." Domaas whirled on Colonel Cha'ol, who had just appeared from the hatch on the top of the ship. The Colonel took two steps and froze when the breeze carried an unmistakable scent to his twitching nostrils. His face colored slightly when he realized exactly what he had interrupted. "Deepest apologies, Regis."

The Colonel stood perfectly still, waiting for his Commander and Regis to settle. A Cerulean male in a heightened state could be a danger-ous thing. He noticed how Ka'al and his subordinate stood at a much more discreet distance. "What do you need, Colonel?" The Regis' voice sounded as if he had just gargled gravel.

Cha'ol kept his eyes on the Regis but spoke to the Regent. "Your Grace, Cou'Parth Har'prom and the other council Lords have trans-ported aboard. They are demanding to speak with you." Since he wasn't looking directly at her, he didn't see Michelle's eyes turn to slits as her brows lowered and face darkened.

"They demand, do they? Have they not gotten the hint that I do not need them?" Domaas felt the lust turn into searing hatred down the Bond and turned back to view his mate. "Were they informed that I have already created my council?"

The first pulse of static electricity drifted outwards, causing the hair to stand on the arms of every male present. "Yes, your Grace. However, I am unsure how they would know this, as I did not tell them." Domaas could hear in the Colonel's voice that he was slightly unsettled by the waves of seething anger rolling off the Regent.

"Ka'al?" She called over her shoulder.

The Major stepped closer and inclined his head. "Your Grace?"

"Please go with the Colonel and escort the *former* council Lords to the Solar. Do not let them leave. I will be there at my leisure."

"At once, your Grace." Ka'al had been in the first group to arrive at the Mizzi residence after the Regents family had been attacked. Although her Grace had not fully explained everything, Ka'al had heard enough to know she firmly placed the guilt of that attack at Cou'Parth Har'Prom's feet.

Domaas did not succeed in her challenge. To be fair to him, he didn't have a chance once her cackles had been raised. Domaas was now on his way to Healer Borlaas to have his bruises tended to. She was strolling down the corridor toward the Solar, one of Major Ka'al's cadre following dutifully behind her. "Have you had a chance to practice with your sword yet, Captain..."

Michelle used her hand to brush the loose tendrils of hair from her face as she turned to look at him. She still wore her workout outfit of a sports bra under a loose gray and yellow-striped tank top with matching leggings. Positively scandalous, judging by the way the all-male crew struggled not to ogle their Regent as she passed by. "Kato, your Grace. James Kato. And I will be beginning training after shift rotation. The others are doing so now."

Michelle stopped dead and turned bodily to face the tall Cerulean. Hair the color of dirt, fair skin like most, and solid eyes the color of honey. He wore his hair long in a more shaggy cut that conveniently fell over his right brow, hiding his ridges. Which he quickly brushed to the side to show they were not nearly as prominent as she was used to seeing. They were shallow, much like Arya's.

Captain Kato knew the question before she could ask. "My Mopa was in the first group to be Collected. She was mated to my Popa and pregnant by the time they returned to Cerul."

That would make him around twenty years old. Michelle arched an appraising eyebrow, "I feel like I should not be as surprised as I am."

"That is not for me to judge, your Grace. But if I may say something?" Michelle nodded. "You may."

"If she does not know about you already; my Mopa will laugh in my Popa's face until she cannot breathe when we return to Cerul. She has a cackle that he loves and hates all at once." There was a gleam of amusement in his eyes, and a smile flirted on his lips.

"Is your mother happy, Captain?" Michelle watched the humor slip a little from his face.

"Not at first, I do not think, your Grace. But she is a wonderful Mopa to me and my sisters. I had a delightful childhood." Michelle nodded as she absorbed this new information and turned to keep walking. There had been such a focus on *having babies* that Michelle had not thought that some of those first children were now adults in their own right, many older than her. She was long used to hearing the assertion that the Humans on Cerul were not treated badly. And now that she knew the history, it made perfect sense why the Ceruleans had been so adamant about that. Still, it was more reassuring to have it confirmed by a product of the whole reason Ceruleans had come to Earth in the first place.

"Thank you for that, Captain Kato," she said over her shoulder as they continued down the corridor.

Sheel, Ka'al had officially named him his Second, was waiting with two others near the sealed doors of the Solar as Michelle and her escort came around the bend in the corridor. "Lieutenant?"

"Would you like us to wait outside, your Grace?"

Michelle shook her head once, firmly, "Absolutely not. Until I decide what to do with them, you will never leave me alone in their presence. Unseal the doors, please."

The doors unlocked and slid open with a faint woosh. Bright sunlight through the large windows filled the space with a warm glow. If not for the ship's life support, the Solar would quickly overheat. *There's an idea,*

Michelle thought ruefully as she stepped in to face the males who had sent violence into her home and almost caused the death of her father.

The four of them stood with their backs to the window, all attempting to appear placid and serene, but failing horribly. Like every other Cerulean, their faces were easy to read once you learned what to look for.

"What do you want?" Michelle asked sharply as Lieutenant Sheel and Captain Kato stepped into positions just slightly forward and to the sides of her. She watched their eyes flick across her two security guards and the slight twitching of frowns.

Cou'Parth stepped forward with a wave of his hand. "You have no need for those males here. We have much to discuss, your Grace." He gestured to Sheel and Kato, "You are dismissed." They did not move.

Michelle crossed her arms and cocked a hip. A move calculated for the four old males to find distasteful. It was considered a vulgar Human posture and something the former Regent, and the Cerulean etiquette holo-instructor before her, hated.

She was rewarded with a slight sneer from Cou'Parth for her efforts. "Last I checked, Lord, I was Regent. Is that still correct, Lieutenant Sheel?"

Michelle could hear the smile in his voice as he answered, "Yes it is, *Your Grace.*"

She smiled; a cold thing that bared her teeth in a wolfish fashion. "My daughter will be waking from her nap soon. What do you want?"

Cou'Parth's eyes darkened for a moment before he clasped his hands and said, "We have come to understand you have already created an advisory council without consulting us?"

"That is correct." How they knew didn't matter. It had been less than twenty-four hours, but males like this were bound to have spies. She knew it wouldn't be anyone on her new council. So whatever they were told would most likely be secondary or worse. Aside from the fact that by her actions, she was rendering them irrelevant anyway.

"Why would you build an all-new council of amateurs? Did her Grace, the elder Regent, not explain to you how important it is to have more experienced counselors to run the Impiruim?"

"Funny you should ask that," Michelle said in English. Something else she knew would frustrate them. "Her Grace once told me I'd have to play nice with you lot. She said you'd make my rule difficult if I didn't let you manipulate me or get in the way of your scheming."

Cou'Parth didn't bother trying to hide his self-satisfied smile. "The Regent understoo-"

"So I figure," Michelle intentionally interrupted, "Why even bother with you at all?" She let her power slip just a fraction. The anger she had forced deep down into the well where that beast lay curled flexed its muscles. A powerful pulse of static electricity filled the room. The council members stepped back from the physical push of the pulse; while the two sentries instinctively placed their hands on the hilts of their swords.

"So let me be clear," Michelle growled out with clenched teeth in Cerulean - all pretense of politeness gone. "I know it was you four who put that bounty out for my daughter and me. Your actions almost killed my father and brought danger to my family. If I were you, I would return to your ship and hope and *pray* that the new Regent of the Cerulean Star Impirium is *much* too busy to remember what you did. I *would not make a single sound, do a single thing...*" Michelle paused for a quick steadying breath; she'd needed to get out soon. "-that would catch her attention."

"Are you threatening us?"

"I do not threaten, Cou'Parth. It is in your best interest we never speak again."

Cou'Parth stepped forward with anger on his face but froze when Sheel pulled his sword halfway from its scabbard. "Do not approach the Regent unless you are invited to do so." The object in the Lieutenant's hand was unfamiliar to Cou'Parth, but he recognized hostile intent when he saw it. He did not move closer.

"Sheel? Will you and the Captain please escort the *former* council members back to the transporter? I want their DNA locked out of this ship," Michelle said as she turned to leave.

"Of course, your Grace."

"I will be in my quarters-"

"We will not be...*dismissed* by one of your kind."

Michelle froze in mid-step, then slowly pivoted on the ball of her foot. Her teeth were exposed in a sneer as a second, stronger, pulse ricocheted through the room, and her fists clenched. "One of my kind?" She asked quietly. "A lowly Human who *your* kind kidnapped and forcibly changed my gender and sex?" Control of her building, roiling, anger slipped, and Michelle's voice raised into a yell. "*Your* kind seems to forget about that when you are *fucking us* and when we are bearing *your* children!" She could feel the energy zipping around her body, struggling to find a point of escape as tears of fury stung her eyes. "You, and your ilk, Cou'Parth, nearly caused the death of *my* father by posting that wanted video! Do you deny it?" None of them answered, and her voice dropped nearly into a whisper. "*Do. You. Deny. It?*" A pulse of energy punctuated each word.

The former council members stood in mute shock. Tiny bolts of purple energy arced and danced up and down her arms, which remained stiffly at her sides, shaking as if she barely contained the full depth of her fury. Her eyes were glowing in the same color, pulsing in tune with the energy that danced across her. When no one answered again, she stomped until she stood toe-to-toe with Cou'Parth and looked up at him. However, instead of screaming like he expected her to do, Michelle's voice stayed down at a near whisper. Still laced with the rage she was barely containing; teeth fully bared as if she intended to tear his throat open like some beast, she asked again, "Do. You. Deny. It?"

Lieutenant Sheel slowly sheathed his sword to have both hands free. The Regent seemed prepared to remove the Lord's head with her bare hands and he would be the one to pull her off of him if he did not get shocked by the purple energy crackling up and down her arms.

"No," Cou'Parth finally answered. His voice shook slightly. Everyone in the room heard it and the other Lords traded nervous glances. Cou'Parth was the head of their council and had promised all sorts of things about how easy it would be to control or eliminate Michelle. Control would have been nice, but elimination would have made the Council guardians of the Regent's daughter. That would have cemented their slow, patient, takeover of the Impirium. They had not expected her to be so...*hard*. They had gotten too used to the Hybrids being relatively docile creatures.

"At least you are male enough to admit it," Michelle sneered. "*Your* Regis has counseled that it would be better to put you on public trial once we return to Cerul. It is his wisdom that ensures you still draw breath at this moment. It is only because I want you as far away as possible from me and my daughter that you are leaving this ship. If you are as smart as you think you are, you *will* be so quiet that I forget about you."

Michelle held up her tightly clenched fist, bolts of energy still danced and crackled across her knuckles. "Do not give me the *pleasure...*" She took a single deep, steadying breath and turned away from him, daring him to try something stupid. "Sheel?" She said looking at the lead sentry.

"Your Grace?"

"See that they are returned to their ship. Escort them there and speak directly with that ship's Colonel. They are to be locked out of all systems," Michelle glanced over her shoulder at the Lords. "I *do not* even want them to be able to use the food replicators."

"It will be done, your Grace."

Michelle exited the Solar and turned left into the corridor. She needed to find a place to release the energy pulsing through her body, fast. Every throb grew in strength, going from its usual dull pulse to a constant push like a capacitor taking charge.

The beast was awake now, raging like a drake discovering its horde stolen, and she needed to release it. She felt like an overcharged battery on the verge of self-immolation, her grip on keeping the power contained slipping every second. This was more than what she felt on the *Rising Star* and easily a hundred times more than what she felt at her parent's house. This was pure destructive power.

She needed to get outside of the ship.

Breaking into a sprint, Michelle left her escorts. She could hear their footfalls behind her as they struggled to keep up. However, it was as if the energy surging in her body amplified the strength of her muscles. Crackling, scorched deck plates remained where her foot landed, and overhead lights shattered in a shower of sparks as she passed. A bubble of static energy formed around her. It grew in strength and density enough to cause the walls of the corridor to buckle like a tin can. Distantly, over the sounds of destruction around her as she ran, Michelle heard Captain Kato order an emergency transport. Michelle thought he was ordering the ship evacuated until she was suddenly surrounded by blue light.

Cool, crisp air filled her lungs as the transporter deposited Michelle on the top of the ship. She had been transported in motion and so she didn't even break stride as she felt the hull buckling under her power. The alloy shredding and crumpling beneath her shoes as if some massive predator was clawing it apart.

Her focus zeroed in on the horizon of the hull, the edge where the top steeply sloped down into the side of the ship. She didn't have time to second guess the decision she had already made. Her family was aboard this ship, Arya, Domaas, Rachel, Jamie, and about a thousand Ceruleans who might die if she didn't.

One thousand feet up...she reached for her wrist and clicked the two bracelets together. *For what it's worth,* she thought as the edge loomed. Michelle felt the last of her control slip as she planted her foot and gave a mighty leap from the *Folded Fist.*

There was a fleeting moment of weightlessness-

Then the unforgiving pull of gravity as an iridescent bubble of purple energy replaced the static bubble. Bolts of lightning crackled from her entire body, and the sound of a shorting transformer about to blow filled her ears as she fell. The bubble grew, and Michelle still felt the surge filling her. The energy was now gushing from her body like a dam seconds away from total failure. Faintly, there was a tug on the Bond to her mate. Horror and anguish were all she felt from him. He was watching her fall - watching her turn into a glowing mass of raw energy. And he could do nothing to stop it.

Michelle barely felt the impact of hitting the surface of the ocean. The water hissed and flashed to steam as she slowly sank into the depths. The only light was her brilliant incandescence.

The dam failed.

Michelle didn't know when her clothing had incinerated but became aware of it as cracks of purple light spread across her naked body, spider webbing like shattered glass. They grew and ate away at her flesh until her entire body was a mass of pure energy. She could no longer tell where she ended and the universe began. Indescribable pain lanced through her very core, white-hot and infinite - she opened her mouth in a silent scream as she finally detonated.

Chapter Fourteen

He didn't bother hiding his smirk as the door opened, and two burly Secret Service agents entered. Dark sunglasses hid their eyes, but he watched their heads swivel as they scanned the room for threats. Without breaking a step, they both moved around the perimeter of the room until they came to stand behind him. Neither of their jackets was buttoned, and the tell-tale bulges of their side arms could easily be seen under the dark material.

Two more agents entered and took up posts on either side of the door. They also wore sunglasses and clasped their hands in front of their unbuttoned jackets. The Man in the Forgettable Suit stood from his and *buttoned* his suit jacket from his chair. He worked directly for the owner of the approaching clicking heels, but that didn't mean they trusted him. Not by a long shot. He had no name. He had no history outside of his government career. It was as if he had burst into existence the day he entered the personal employ of the Executive Branch of the United States. He was akin to the President's personal sniper rifle.

The clicking heels stopped, and a fifth agent entered the room. The Man in the Forgettable Suit smiled as he outstretched his arms from his body. "Morning, John," The Man said as the agent gave him a thorough pat down. "Good to see you, too," he chuckled.

John grunted as he turned away, "Clear!"

President Anne Willow strode into the room. Easily gliding on heels that would turn any man's ankle and wearing a fitted red pencil dress. Her chestnut brown hair was unashamedly streaked with gray, and it matched the story told by the wrinkles around her dark eyes and the corners of her set mouth. "Madam President," Forgettable Suit Man said with a nod.

"Christopher." A name only the President called him and only because she had insisted he had one. "The Joint Chiefs are all in a tizzy about the explosion in the South Pacific. I am busy."

"Have I ever been one to waste your time, Madame President?" 'Christopher' gestured to the briefcase, which sat open on the table next to the chair. "The explosion that damaged one of their ships? I am confident it was *her*."

The President narrowed her eyes, then reached into the open briefcase to lift the secure tablet that lay inside. She used her thumbprint to turn it on and watched the grainy video that began to play. It was an enhanced shot from the satellite that had been tasked to track the flotilla of alien ships. And she had just been viewing it down in the Situation Room in the basement of the White House. Sighing, she went to hand the tablet back to him. "I have already seen this. A glowing ball of purple light forms on top of the ship, then rolls off the side and falls into the water. The resulting explosion was equal to the bomb dropped on Nagasaki."

'Christopher' smiled as he held up a finger, "Yes, and if you look closely, you can see a running figure inside of that bubble, and I believe that is *her*."

"And you know this from your contact with these...Lords?" She asked with a vague gesture of her free hand. "The plane sent to surveil them had to ditch in the ocean, and we have yet to even send in search and rescue."

"No, as a matter of fact, Madam President, they've gone silent. I have not been able to reach them for four days now. "

"What about the girl, April?" The President asked as she attempted to return the tablet, but he didn't take it.

"She doesn't know a lot. Michelle never allowed the girl into her circle, so finding anything out is hard for her. She does say the Regent is alive, though. As for the crew of the C-8, she says the Ceruleans fished them out of the sea. They'll be returned as soon as they've recovered." He pointed to the tablet. "If you kindly select the next file, you will find the interview I performed with the only still functioning member of the Marine detachment that attacked Michelle's family. It is pertinent, I promise."

With an arched eyebrow, the President did as asked, and a shaky male voice came from the tablet speaker. "...I'm still not sure what I saw. T-the Specter had just lifted me by the throat from behind and was squeez...squeezing p-pretty hard. Turney must have heard me struggling, b-because as soo-soon as he turned to look, s-she attacked him. I swear I've never seen no one m-move that fast, sir. H-he never h-had a chance... And there was a bright ball of purple light from her hand where she hit him. And he j-just f-lew back and h-hit the wall."

Christopher's voice was heard, "And then what happened?"

"I-it was like hitting a switch, sir. She yelled something in the Specter's language and he put me down but she had collected Turney's weapon and was standing before me before I could b-blink. She had the barrel of the gun pointed right between my eyes. I could s-see the rifling."

"Did she threaten to kill you?"

"Yes."

"Did you believe her?"

"Yessir. Her eyes were g-glowing; the same color as the light she used against Turney."

The clip ended. Then a photo of Captain Turney lying in a hospital bed came onto the screen. He appeared alive but catatonic and mottled with deep, black, and yellow bruises, with purple striations across his exposed skin. "According to the doctors, he was hit with enough energy to kill an elephant. He probably won't live much longer," Forgettable Suit Man supplied.

"Why am I just seeing this now?" The President asked with deep concern in her voice. "Are they all like this?"

"I wanted to confirm it before bringing it to your attention. However, no, April insisted that Michelle was supposed to have some sort of special power. She just didn't know what it was. Supposedly, every Regent has a special ability, but the rank and file are just as normal as you and I. The girl insisted that the former Regent could manipulate their technology with her mind."

The President slowly blinked as the pieces he'd laid out began dropping into place. "Allow me to get you there faster, Madam President. It is an absolute certainty Russia, China, or anyone with a satellite was watching those ships. Which means they saw the same thing we did. A nuclear-like detonation without any sign of radiation or an EMP. We know the ship she leaped from was heavily damaged and scuttled." He held up a finger as the President opened her mouth. "I am aware, Madam President, that the Navy is already trying to figure out how to gain access to it or recover it. However, the Ceruleans towed it just above the Horizon Deep in the Tonga Trench. From satellite, it appeared that several large bays and ports were opened to flood the ship And most likely buried it once it hit bottom, according to the Navy's SOSUS net across the Pacific Ocean. That ship might as well be on Venus."

Christopher continued, "She has publicly stated that she intends to share much of their technology with the world, even though she has yet to give any data to any other country as far as we can tell. But if that was her, how badly do you think our adversaries would like to get their hands on her DNA? Or *her* even? My contacts with the NSA, CIA, and DOD have all reported a surge of clandestine activity. Especially with attempts at penetrating our government servers searching for what she already has given us."

"Is that information secured?"

"It would take someone physically breaching the server farms, and even then, they wouldn't understand what they were looking for. Sort of like failing to see a forest because of the sheer amount of trees in the way. But yes, every building has been air-gapped. Authorized access is a very short list, and no digital devices are allowed in the same rooms as the terminals. It would take a semi-trailer to carry enough storage media to copy the data. Those tablets of theirs hold an immense amount of information."

The President suddenly paled as she finally realized the original point, "Human bombs? Completely undetectable? Survivable?"

The Man in the Forgettable Suit nodded as he finally reclaimed his own tablet, "Yes, Madam President, at worst. Or imagine an entire infantry division equipped with those nifty suits the Ceruleans have, who can throw lightning with their hands. I think it's time to consider not accepting her petition for recognition as a Sovereign Head of State."

"What do you mean?" The President asked as she crossed her arms over her chest.

"She was born a citizen of the United States. By accepting the returned captives as maintaining their citizenry, does that not include Ms. Mizzi as well?" He gave a smile that barely reached the corners of his mouth. "That would make her accountable to the laws and regulations of the United States, would it not? It would be much easier to vanish a private citizen under some long-forgotten law, like the Patriot Act, than the acknowledged sovereign of an alien species."

"Kidnap her? Would they not see that as an act of war?"

'Christopher' wagged his finger in the air again, "According to the debrief, when she arrived, she was very confident they won't attack if they didn't know where she was. Also, although they haven't said it out loud, I have the feeling the Cerulean Lords really don't want her in charge. That wanted video wasn't for Michelle's return. They want her daughter, the princess."

The President nodded in understanding. "Okay, what do you need from me?"

"I am not sure yet, but I have a few ideas. We need to act soon, though."

"Why?"

"Because they're still waiting for the rescue fleet to arrive."

*****

"Status?"

"Sir, we dropped out of FTL just behind their fifth planet. Jupiter, confirmed as a gas giant. They will not have detected our arrival," came the reply from his science officer.

P'alta nodded as his eyes scanned the new cascade of information that scrolled down the holo-screen at his right hand. "Excellent, begin scans for debris. Comms, begin broadcasting on carrier wave only. And transmit only for one hour a day at random intervals. If our people are listening, they should pick it up."

"Yes, sir," both bridge crew officers responded at once.

P'alta's eyes drifted to the projected view screen on the far wall. A giant ball of reds, browns, and yellows dominated the view. Three months of puddle-jumping across the galaxy had truly worn on the crew. Three months of near-high alert as every male onboard knew why the *Regent's Mercy* had been pulled from the space dock.

The ship had been built before the *Rising Star*. They were, in fact, sisterships. Their base frames had been laid simultaniously and built side by side in the same specially constructed shipyards. Only the *Regent's Mercy* had been completed first. Bristling with ion cannons, plasma lances, and negative space torpedo launchers, it was a Galactic Class Warship - the first and only of its kind. The *Regent's Mercy* was the culmination of two hundred cycles of the most secret of weapons and technology research. And still, it was hoped it was enough.

Or not enough, depending on perspective. It was a warship, yes. But it was the only one in the Cerulean fleet—the only ship with offensive weapons. The *Rising Star* had only defensive capability aside from its integrated technology-destroying weapon. However, one must have been incredibly lucky to discover it, as *that* particular weapon had been built into the ship's power distribution network. Much as it was on the *Regent's Mercy*. The perspective mattered, though. Because it was hoped that if discovered, the Kesta would be more interested in hunting down the *Regent's Mercy* and destroying it, instead of investigating why the shipyard was big enough to build two ships of equal, immense size - or where the second one was.

But the distress buoy had broadcast through the old comms networks. If the Kesta hadn't completed a sweep of the Impirium yet, they would soon. And it would not take long for them to realize the signal came from a lonely backwater of a solar system. The nearest inhabited system was three weeks at FTL away, and its inhabitants had just begun to walk upright. As far as neighborhoods go, this would qualify as a rundown shack in the middle of the Zidmas Desert. If he were the Kiesta, he'd be awfully curious about what had dragged the Ceruleans so far out.

"Scans do not show a debris field, sir. However, there are residual traces of a singularity implosion and signs of debris in subspace. Most likely from the *Risings Star's* power core," the science officer reported. "If they lost magnetic containment, that could do it."

P'alta nodded silently. It was already known the *Rising Star* had been destroyed. "What of the transport fleet? Or the Regent's transport?"

"No sign of the *Regent's Grace*, sir. But it would appear the transport fleet made planetfall. No sign of their condition. They should hear the carrier wave, If they are still in control of their ships."

"Very well, set the ship condition to *shadow*. Minimize all energy output, passive scanning, thrusters only for station keeping - you all know the drill by now." After every FTL jump, they had to park the *Regent's Mercy* and switch to shadow running. If the ship was being followed this was the only way to prevent their discovery. P'alta stood from his chair and turned for the lift. "I'll be in my quarters; you have the bridge Major Milkas."

"Yes, sir."

Chapter Fifteen

Domaas' eyes flicked up as Michelle whimpered softly and shifted. He studied her calm face for a moment, then glanced up at the holographic display above her—steady heart rate, deep, slow breathing, and brain activity showing that she was dreaming. By every sign and Healer Borlaas, she was in perfect health. Nothing like the bruised and broken thing that had been found floating on the surface of the water; the bubble of her personal shield keeping her afloat. However, it had been thirteen days, and she still hadn't woken up.

The Regis settled back into his chair and continued reviewing the fleet's notes and dispatches. The *Folded Fist* had been scuttled into the deepest part of the ocean they could find. This was done by opening every airlock and internal hatch, excluding the seals around the power core, and, allowing the vessel to flood and sink. The magnetic locks of the contained singularity remained in place so the ship would remain fully powered close to eternity. However, between the security protocols and its physical location, it was ostensibly out of reach of any serious Human ability to reach.

Michelle's flag had first been transferred to the *The'rid Tal*, or *Gifted Oasis* in English, and then to the island once Rachel had taken possession of it. Now the remaining ships floated in formation, forming a ring around the island. The flags from multiple military vessels from as many countries now remained stationed just over twelve miles out from the island the Ceruleans now inhabited. Domaas had come to understand this was the agreed-upon distance one could approach without violating sovereign territory.

Through some mad stroke of luck, no one was hurt by the damage caused by the concussive force of Michelle's detonation. Colonel Cha'ol had been blessedly fast ordering the shields of the *Folded Fist* brought on-line, and those had taken the brunt of the impact. The worst damage had been to the ship's keel, and in essence, its back had been broken -- any attempt to jump to FTL would have torn the ship into atoms. The other nearby ships had managed to move away just far enough not to take the brunt of the blast as well. The Colonel's of the two behind, the *Depth's Silence* and *Binary's Light,* also reacted surprisingly fast to order course changes. They'd taken only minor damage.

Rachel had successfully purchased a small island just outside the Cook Islands, which the United States Government had protested after the fact. However, money had already been transferred, and Roger Mizzi had signed the documents personally. He was currently in a city called New York, working on his accreditation to become the Cerulean Ambassador to the United Nations, a global governing body geared toward world unity and peace. Bailey's mate, Lieutenant Kalko, had gone with him as a co-representative to provide security. The newsfeed had been buzzing for days around their arrival.

Fortunately, the island had already been developed by some super wealthy person, and Domaas suspected Rachel had thrown an obscene amount of money at the previous owner to get them to vacate so quickly. There was still food in the pantry when they had arrived, and the linens of the bed Michelle now slept on had been freshly laundered. On Domaas' orders Colonel Ch'aol, who had been given command of the island, had crews from various ships hard at work building and expanding the island's infrastructure. Tomorrow, the new fusion reactor will be coming online. Which was sorely needed to power the defensive shields, replicator systems, and other support for the troops staying behind.

Domaas eyes stung with the threat of tears once again, but he willed them away. His Cerulean masculinity would not allow for such displays of emotion. She had lost control of her power; one she was still working on understanding. Instead of panicking, she had made every effort to prevent harm to others, to the point of potentially sacrificing herself. She had done it without pause and leaped blindly from the ship. She had freely given her life to protect the thousand aboard the *Folded Fist.* And she had succeeded.

What grumblings of dissent there had been had gone nearly silent. The discontent the former Councilmembers had been stoking had suddenly lost all of its momentum. *How do you hate someone who would die for you?* Domaas asked himself with a grunt.

There was a gentle knocking from the door. "Come," Domaas called over his shoulder.

There was the sound of the wooden door opening behind him, and then Major Ka'al's voice, "Sir, Miss Jamie, and your dopa are here."

Domaas glanced at the time on his tablet. It was morning again, and evidently, Major Ka'al had come back on duty. "Send them in, of course."

"Good Morning, Regis." Domaas would have known who it was by her voice alone, and it was confirmed when his daughter skittered past him to climb up onto her mother's bed. He watched her burrow under the covers and nestle while he stood and stretched his stiff muscles.

"Good morning, Jamie," he answered back in English.

The blonde nanny stepped to his side, and he glanced down at her. She was wearing another of her voluminous tea-length dresses and simple white sneakers that seemed to have become her uniform. Today, it was blue with white flowers printed all over it. The material of the bodice seemed to be built thicker than needed, just as the shoulder strap on the right side was wider than the left. Jamie watched his eyes flicker between her shoulders, and when he opened his mouth to ask why, she spoke first. "You look tired, Regis. Her Grace would be livid if she knew you were running yourself ragged. She would not want you holding a vigil like this."

Domaas felt his body sag in agreement as he realized he couldn't remember the last time he had slept. "Yes, you are right. I will be back in a few hours," he said, tucking his tablet under his arm and turning from the lounge chair he had been sitting in.

"No, sir," Jamie said firmly as she turned with him. "Rachel will be here after lunch and Mrs. Mizzi for the evening. Commander Kear'ald has instructed Major Ka'al not to allow you back into this room until you have a full night's rest. We fear her Grace's wrath more than yours, Regis."

Domaas sliced his eyes to the Major, who was standing in the open doorway, his hands clasped behind his back. "Apologies, Regis, but Miss Jamie is correct. You do need to rest. It will do us no good if both heads of the Impirium are out of commission." Commander Kear'ald (recently promoted) was one of two Ceruleans alive who could give a command involving the Regis and have it stick. The other was Healer Borlaas, only because the healer was part of Domaas' executive chain of command.

"If there is any change..."

Major Ka'al nodded, "At once, sir."

Domaas took one lingering glance at his mate and saw his daughter's emerald eyes peeking out from under the blanket, looking at him. They seemed to be telling him the same thing as he felt a gentle mental push for him to leave. He indeed needed to rest if his dopa was nudging him away; she would be the one who could see how mentally tired he truly was. "Very well," he grumbled as he walked for the door.

Major Ka'al stepped to the side to allow him to pass, "Sleep well, Regis."

*****

It was the warmth of the sun on her bare skin that her mind focused on first. Like a blanket fresh from the drier, its heat seeped into her flesh and gave energy to her bones. Next was a gentle breeze, neither warm nor cold, filling her nose with the scent of wildflowers basking in the sun. Daffodils, daisies, and sunflowers. The smell of Spring. Michelle knew she wasn't dead, and this was not the afterlife. She could not have explained how, but she was sure of it.

She opened her eyes to find a brilliant blue sky open above her, framed by the stalks of flowers towering above her. "Gods, was this what it was like when you woke up on the ship?" There was the rustle of flowers as someone approached, and the sun was suddenly blocked by a young woman leaning over her. Cascading copper curls, olive skin, and...eyes that shone like emeralds.

The young woman smiled at the confusion on her mother's face. "Arya?" Michelle asked.

Arya's smile broadened, "Hey, Mopa. It's time to get up."

Michelle went to push herself up, and the young woman who was Arya took a few steps back to give her room. Once Michelle stood, she slowly turned in a circle to take in her surroundings. Rolling hills covered in flowers of every color stretched out in every direction. "Where are we?" Michelle asked as she turned back to Arya. A grown woman, with a grown woman's body.

Arya's nose wrinkled in amusement, "GrandPopa was right; you automatically dismiss things you deem unworthy of figuring out. I wonder why that is? Do you really believe I am your daughter, or are you just choosing not to fight it?"

Michelle glanced around again, then back to Arya. "Well, I know I'm not dead. I'm certain of that. So you're either my brain filling the void or really who you say you are. Both Dad and Jamie said you talked to them when they were hurt. And there's no point wasting energy on something if I don't have the power to change it. Sometimes you just have to go through it..." Michelle took in the young woman before her. Took in the hair, the brow ridges, the eyes, and the same familiar mouth. Her father's mouth, with the matching dimple on the left side. "They didn't mention you appeared to them like this, though. You look like your Popa."

Arya smiled and bounced on her toes. "That's 'cause I asked them not to. You would have demanded I show you, and you weren't ready yet."

Michelle squinted and asked, "You've been in my head?"

Arya's smile faltered a bit. "Mopa, you have to understand I've been in your head since my brain formed in your belly. I didn't even know what I was at first. Just that there was this...presence. That talked to me, and was protective of me. Singing to me when Rachel wasn't around. My first memory is of you discovering Rachel had been secretly talking to Popa. Remember? She was scared you might have turned native if you knew you were the next Regent?"

Michelle blinked, dumbfounded. Arya giggled and covered her mouth as delight filled her eyes. "You should see your face right now!"

"You should be glad I don't believe in corporal punishment, young lady."

Arya's giggling turned into a bark of laughter. "Mopa, I'm older than you here! This is what I will probably look like at twenty-five years old! Which one of us is young?"

Michelle pursed her lips and turned into a slow walk, wading through the flowers. Arya fell into step beside her. "So what is this place then?" she asked.

Arya spread her arms out wide. "I don't have a name for it. This is where I come when I'm asleep, though. It's peaceful. Sometimes, I just sleep under the sun or the rain. I really want to know what it's like to lay out in a thunderstorm. Rachel thinks it's awesome and she misses it." There was a rushing sound. Like wind through pine boughs and the wide-open expanse of wildflowers morphed into a beach with crashing waves. Michelle's nostrils filled with the scent of the ocean while a warm, stiff breeze was suddenly blowing her hair back from her shoulders. She stopped walking in amazement.

Arya continued, "I can make anything I want, though. Which is pretty neat, I think."

"But how do you know what these places look like? Smell like?" Michelle asked as she took in the view. It reminded her of the shore in Oceanside. There was a lifeguard tower about forty yards away that looked very familiar. "I've never taken you to the beach or seen a field of flowers like that."

"Oh, that's uh...I pulled them from the people around me. It's how I get to know people; if they're safe to be around or not. If they're nice. Nice people have pleasant memories like this. That old lord you met on the ship did not have nice memories; I did not like being near him." Michelle blinked several times. The only instance where Arya had been near him was when she was still an infant, just weeks old. "The flowers are from Jamie, actually; it's why I like her so much. She's always liked pretty flowers, and her Popa punished her for it." Arya gestured to the crashing waves before them. "This is where you had your first kiss, isn't it? When you were still Jason?" Michelle looked at Arya crossly, but her daughter studiously ignored the look. "Right over there," Arya pointed to the lifeguard tower. That was why it was so familiar.

Michelle didn't think too much about her former life as Jason. So much of who she was had carried through into her new life that, in many ways, the memories weren't exclusively *his* memories; something that had happened to someone else. They were her memories, and she did remember kissing Tilly Swire underneath the lifeguard tower that stood about a hundred feet away.

The scene changed again to show something else. Some type of control room aboard a Cerulean ship. She was standing behind a seated Cerulean, and hovering in the space before them was a holographic screen showing a darkened room. Michelle could see herself sitting on a bunk, face lit up by the glow of a tablet screen. It took her several moments before the scene finally clicked.

"Yes," Arya said with a wistful sigh. "That's the first night on the *Rising Star,* right?"

"How did..."

"This is Popa's favorite memory of you. The first time he laid eyes on you. He thinks of it a lot. Like, a lot, a lot."

Michelle felt her heartbeat accelerate and slow all at once. She could feel what Domaas had been feeling at that very moment. This was when she captured his heart. This memory is what made him send all those mushy feelings across the Bond between them. She knew at that moment that this was what he thought of when tracing the Cerulean symbol for Infinity over her crown. *The one thing he had wanted to keep to himself.* "Arya, I shouldn't be seeing this. Your father did not want to share this."

The scene instantly morphed back to the field of wildflowers, and Michelle turned to face her daughter. "You need to stay out of people's minds, Arya. It's a violation of privacy."

"Yeah, I know. I heard you thinking about it." Arya had the decency to look chastised from Michelle's pointed look. "Okay, okay, I'll stop. I just wanted to show you what I can do."

Michelle was careful to keep a soft tone, "Baby, I understand. It is cool what you can do. Jamie would probably be dead if it weren't for you. But I just learned that more than ever, we must master our abilities and not let them get away from us."

Arya pouted as she reached down and plucked a flower. She stood and spun the stem between her palms. As she did so, the flower's petals elongated into brightly colored feathers as it took flight, spinning up into the air, where it morphed into a brightly colored bird and flapped away. "Okay, Mopa. I get it. I wouldn't like it if someone was rummaging around in my head. But what about the bad people? Can I mess with them?"

"I'll let you know. But first, we both need to practice not to hurt anyone unless we mean to."

Arya nodded as they stood silently, watching the blue jay wheel turn on the gentle breeze. "So, how bad is it?" Michelle asked thickly.

"Everyone survived; nobody was hurt." Michelle arched her eyebrows but remained silent. Her gamble had at least paid off. "The ship was badly damaged, so they sank it. Rachel found an island like you asked; that's where we are now. Your people are doing the jobs you hired them for, and Commander Kear'ald ordered Popa to get some sleep. He wouldn't leave you alone for two days. Oh, and Rachel is pregnant. She's trying to keep it a secret."

Michelle would only involve herself with that if absolutely necessary. "What about me?"

Arya turned and beamed, "Oh, you're fine, Mopa. You were going to wake up soon, but I wanted to talk to you first." She hooked elbows with her mother and pulled her closer. "You aren't allowed to do something like that again, Mopa. I forbid it." An ache so profound it had Michelle gasping bloomed in her chest - a feeling of her heart shattering from anguish and loss. "That's what he felt when he watched you leap from the top of the ship. Popa is probably going to chew your ear off when he wakes up. You aren't allowed to sacrifice yourself ever again. You have to let people do their jobs, Mopa. You can't control everything. You can't always win."

"You wouldn't understand-"

"But I do. I'm in your head, remember?"

Tears burned in Michelle's eyes as the pain faded from her chest. "Then you do understand why I had to sacrifice myself. I could have killed everyone, including you."

Arya tugged her mother closer so that Michelle looked at her and said, "Did you not just say that we had to learn how to control our gifts?"

Michelle didn't answer. So instead, Arya leaned close and pecked her mother on the cheek. "It's time to go, Mopa." Arya unlinked their arms and stepped away. "I have a date."

Michelle's head came around like an owl's in time to see Arya shrinking and morphing into a child version of herself. Appearing to be maybe six years old. "What do you mean, a date?"

Arya shrugged a now narrow shoulder. "A little boy I met in my travels while dreaming, he's fun, and I think I might claim him as my mate. He's a year older than me but he makes me laugh," she said with a giggle. "Oh, and you know his Mopa! So there's that, too! They'll be here soon, make sure you ask for Brylie when they make contact."

Michelle was gobsmacked momentarily, then reached down to catch her daughter's arm. "Now wait just a second!" But Arya danced out of reach, giggled again, and winked. The field of flowers vanished into a white nothingness as Michelle felt herself being dragged up into consciousness.

"Oh, you little tart," Michelle said before realizing her eyes had opened again. Above her was a cream-colored ceiling with fan blades shaped like palm fronds slowly turning the air. She became aware of a tiny body scrambling off the bed with a mirthful giggle. "Come back here, you!"

Michelle was just starting to sit up when a hand pressed at her shoulder, and Jamie appeared at her bedside. "Welcome back, your Grace. Let me call Healer Borlaas before you start trying to move around. You've been out for almost two weeks."

Chapter Sixteen

"Thank you, Healer," Michelle said with a smile after he'd given his final assessment.

He turned to start slipping his instruments back into his shoulder bag and said, "Even though you appear to be in perfect health, your Grace would do well to take it easy for the next few days. Just in case something pops up that I missed."

"You? Miss something? Is it possible?"

"We are all fallible creatures," he said lightly. "It is important that we remember this." His message was well received.

Michelle looked to where Arya lay sleeping in the cot Jamie had brought onto the veranda. *Date indeed,* Michelle thought ruefully. *Just wait until I tell your father.*

Healer Borlaas had finished packing his things and turned to offer a slight bow. "With your leave, your Grace. I have a young patient to see."

Michelle looked back up in concern, "Young?"

"Yes, the infant son of Proctor Pouduit and April. He had become quite ill but is on the mend now."

The name registered, and Michelle made a mental note to have Rachel find out how April had returned to her mate. Especially since the last she heard, Katie and Chrissie were keeping her contained.

Michelle smiled once more, "Thank you, Healer. For everything."

The old Cerulean nodded. "Always a pleasure, your Grace." And he meant it too. Michelle could not recall ever having a negative experience with the bearded doctor. His bedside manner should have been taught in medical schools. With a shallow bow of his head, the healer turned and reentered the mansion, leaving Michelle alone in her chaise lounge with Arya sleeping nearby. Lieutenant Sheel was on duty, standing at a respectful distance next to the doorway.

Before her was a breathtaking view of a thick jungle sloping down a hill to end at a wide strip of blindingly white sand. Waves of crystal-clear ocean crashed against the beach. About half a mile beyond that, monster waves rose and broke early due to the coral reef that could barely be seen through the clear water. Even at this distance and elevation, the roar of those crashing waves was carried by the warm breeze. Big fluffy clouds drifted high above in a perfect sky. Michelle could almost believe she was back in Arya's dreamscape.

Michelle had just let her eyes drift closed, zoning out in the distant roar of the surf when she felt the pulse across the Bond. The memory Arya had shown her flashed in Michelle's mind, and she smiled despite herself. She opened her eyes to see her mate looking down at her with a blank face. "Heartbeat," he breathed.

"Domaas."

"You are well?"

Michelle nodded. "Yes, Healer Borlaas has given me a clean bill of health." She could feel his emotions broadcasting clear as a bell. He was so happy to see her awake and well but also harbored an echo of his fear and pain. Underneath that was a well-hidden current of anger that she had so carelessly tried to throw her own life away. "People would have died, Domaas. Cou'parth angered me, and I lost control of it. You, Arya, my family...it won't happen again."

He swallowed, and when he spoke, his voice was thick. "Swear it on our Bond."

Michelle swung her legs over to stand and pulled her mate into an embrace; wrapping her arms around his middle and burying her face in his chest. "I swear it." She listened to the steady rhythm thudding through his breast. His *Heartbeat.* She was the reason why it did so and yet had felt the pain of that same heart shattering like a pebble beneath a hammer. "I'll never make your heart feel like that again."

Domaas gently pushed her away but didn't let go. With his right hand, he tucked Michelle's loose hair back over her shoulder, exposing her crown. She was looking up at him with watery eyes. "You are brave and faithful, Heartbeat. Not in a thousand lifetimes could a male be so lucky."

Michelle gave a small smile and stood up on her toes to kiss him squarely on the mouth. "I love you too, Domaas. Now, first; I am starving, and second; you will fill me in on everything I have missed."

"What of Arya?"

Michelle glanced over her shoulder to see their daughter was still passed out and sleeping as if all was perfect in her world. A sly half smile slid across Michelle's lips. "She is on a date with some boy. Says he is supposed to be her mate." The Bond vibrated like a struck steel pipe as Domaas' muscles tensed beneath the palms of her hands.

"Boy? Mate?"

"Sheel?" Michelle called to the guard standing nearby.

The guard turned his head, showing the first animation she'd seen from him in at least an hour. "Your Grace?"

"Could you please send for Rachel and my family? I would like to have dinner with them."

"At once, your-" There was the sound of running boots on a wooden floor inside the mansion. Sheel spun and drew his sword in the same motion, bringing the blade up into the second position. "Name and rank!" He barked toward the unseen person who had stumbled to a stop.

"Lieutenant T'Rail Bilson!" Came the frightened voice.

"Stand down, Lieutenant," Domaas ordered. He separated from Michelle as he said to her and Sheel, "The Lieutenant has just started as my personal assistant."

Sheel stepped back and sheathed his sword in a practiced move. Michelle watched the way he moved and was pleased to see that her guards had been training hard at the martial art of swordplay. She made a mental note to watch them train when she had spare time.

T'Rail cautiously stepped out onto the veranda and turned to face Domaas. His eyes flared, and he suddenly dropped to a knee hard enough to make Michelle wince and the planks creak, "Your Grace! It is an honor to meet you finally!"

Domaas spoke before she could, "Lieutenant, the Regent does not like to be knelt to. Speak plainly, and she will do the same."

"Apologies, sir-Regent." T'Rail stood up, and Michelle took in the young-looking Cerulean. He was...average. Almost Human in his normalcy. Brown gem-like eyes indicated he was a 'test tube baby' like Domaas, thick brown hair in a military cut and short in stature. Tall for a Human male but short for a Cerulean (but still taller than Chief J'oons). His face was flushed, and his chest was heaving. He'd run here and probably did not even realize how close he had come to losing his life. Michelle watched his eyes nervously switch between herself and Domaas. Something had him excited, but he was waiting for permission to speak.

"Why is your name familiar to me?" T'Rail's eyes flicked to her and then looked down at the wooden deck of the veranda. He opened his mouth to speak, but Michelle cut him off. "Please look at me when you talk to me. I am not better than you."

T'Rail nodded and looked up, "I was the one Regis Et'kuraul assigned to find you aboard the *Rising Star*."

Michelle scrunched her face, thinking, "You were the one writing all the programs?"

He bobbed his head. "Yes, your Grace."

The Regent clapped her hands and laughed, "Oh, Rachel used to curse you in her sleep; you angered her so much. She did not know your name then, but I want to be there when she figures out who you are."

"They have already met, Heartbeat," Domaas murmured. "A week ago. Rachel was indeed quite...colorful with her language when she realized who he is. Lieutenant Bilson has been helping Rachel build out the communications and computer systems. He figured out how Rachel used the transporter system without a pad, thus allowing you to be transported outside..." Domaas cleared his throat. "Outside the ship and save almost one thousand lives."

Michelle let her gaze bore into T'Rail's brown eyes. "Thank you, Lieutenant."

He flushed and bobbed his head, unsure of what to say. He had not been aboard the *Folded Fist.* However, like every other Earthbound Cerulean; he was well aware of Michelle's attempted sacrifice.

"What is so important for you to be running from your station?" Domaas asked to bring things back into focus.

"Oh!" T'Rail was suddenly overly animated. "We have just completed setting up the communications array for the comms buoys! Sir, your Grace...there is a carrier wave. It is the lowest possible frequency, but judging by the signal decay rate, our people are in the solar system."

Captain Sheel's head snapped around, and Michelle felt a blended pulse of excitement and trepidation across the Bond. She looked up at her mate standing beside her in wonder at the odd mixture of emotions. "Lieutenant, pretend I do not know what that means," Michelle commanded.

T'Rail swallowed to slow himself down, "Your Grace, it means the long-awaited rescue fleet is here."

The roar of the surf suddenly grew louder in Michelle's ears, drowning out all other sounds. She'd hoped to have more time, and she had known every minute had been borrowed up to this point. She had wasted the last two weeks sleeping off whatever had happened to her. She wanted more time before leaving. She wasn't ready yet, and she hadn't secured a peace and trade treaty. She hadn't had a chance even to have this island recognized as a sovereign territory. She hadn't secured the safety of the other returned girls or even figured out how to help the others return from Cerul if they wanted to. She still hadn't...

Domaas' hand on her shoulder and a gentle tug on the Bond had her blinking as her eyes snapped back into focus, and she looked up at him. "You are Regent, Michelle. We leave when you are ready and not a moment sooner."

Michelle took a deep shuddering breath and offered him a smile as she placed her hand atop his. "Thank you, Domaas."

He spoke to T'Rail, "Have any of the other ships received the carrier wave?"

T'Rail emphatically shook his head, "No, sir. The signal is too low-powered and, as you know, our ships can't receive comms in Earth's atmosphere. It was never figured out why. The system Rachel and I constructed uses Earthen technology. She called it 'piggybacking' on some of the Human satellites. Our systems are too advanced to use their analog systems directly."

"This information is classified until the Regent decides to make contact with whoever is out there, understood?"

T'Rail bobbed his head like a schoolboy, "Yes, sir."

"I need to call a meeting," the Regent said quietly.

Domaas looked down at Michelle, looking out at the ocean and the many ships on the horizon. "I would have liked to have spent a few quiet days with you as well, Heartbeat. Perhaps a meal with my mate and daughter will have to suffice."

"How's it going, Dad? Bailey?"

Her father and Bailey's faces looked back from the holographic projection at the end of the long dining table. The room was large enough that it was obvious the previous owner of the island entertained large groups of people. Even with every other member of her council and Regent's Guard present, there was still room for at at least ten more people to sit. The French doors that took up the whole of one wall opened up to a northern view of the island and allowed in the warm breeze and natural light; making the space seem even more signifacant than it already was.

"Quite well, as a matter of fact. China, India, England, and Switzerland are supporting your petition to have the island designated as a sovereign territory. While Russia wants exclusive access to Cerulean technology before lending support. The Russian ambassador hasn't said that outright, but she's not exactly subtle." Roger reached up and tapped the translator behind his ear. "This little gadget is pretty handy; they think it's just a hearing aid. The main question I keep getting, though, is what exact purpose does the island serve? The second is why only the U.S. has been given access to Cerulean technology?"

Michelle furrowed her brow. "What do you mean, Dad? I thought I was pretty clear about that."

Roger nodded, "And that's what I told them, honey. But remember the part about how you aren't paying nearly enough attention to what's going on in the rest of the world? And you've been out of commission for two weeks now. The interview wasn't enough, sweetheart. We need you out here, meeting other heads of state. Right now, all the world knows is a teenager is in control of a vastly superior alien race. That makes old people a little nervous." The last part, he said with a smile that spoke volumes.

He had just strongly chastised Michelle in front of everyone who mattered, but only she knew his parenting style. The smile was to make everyone else think he was just giving a gentle reminder. For Michelle, it was on par with getting a full dressing down by a drill instructor. And it had stung. This was usually the point where she'd be sent off to run drills with her Uncle until her body gave out.

Michelle swallowed and nodded, "Understood, Dad. That's *actually* why I called this meeting so soon after waking up. I need to figure out my next moves." Michelle shifted her eyes to the redhead sitting next to her father. "Bailey, how are you settling into your role?"

The girl suddenly perked up and flushed when she saw she had the room's unfettered attention. "Um, not good, your Grace."

"What is the issue?"

"Well, I have yet to locate and contact everyone who came back, obviously, but..." Bailey glanced at Roger, and he gave a reassuring nod. "It's not good, your Grace."

"Yes, you've already said that, Bailey. I'm going to need you to be more specific."

"Prostitution, your Grace, and, um...d-dancing, like for money."

Michelle felt a chill settle on her skin as she asked, "There are Hybrids doing prostitution? Stripping? By choice or by force?"

Bailey's confusion by the last question was evident on her face. "I do not understand, your Grace." To Bailey's mind, there wasn't much difference.

"Are they choosing to do these things because they want to, is it for survival, or are they being forced into it?"

"I've found six so far, here in New York. I don't think anyone is forcing them into it, I suppose. Their parents didn't accept them back and…Well, we can't get pregnant from Human men, so…I guess survival."

Michelle held up a hand as she fought the bile trying to force its way up her throat. Even Rachel, who had been quiet so far, was pale in the face and green at the gills. There were several silent moments as Michelle looked at the different faces around the dining room.

Sex work in itself was not the issue. Not even remotely. It came down to choice. If one was doing it to put food on the table and keep a roof with no other options, was it really a choice? Not as long as Michelle was in a position to prevent the returned Hybrids from having to decide.

This was precisely why Bailey had a job, to avoid stuff like this. "Rachel, how much money is left?"

"More than enough," Rachel said without hesitation. "I invested more than half of it, and we're already seeing returns on the principal."

Michelle looked back to Bailey on the holographic screen. "Bailey, I know this is a bit overwhelming, but I have faith in you. Rachel will set up a fund you'll have direct access to. Every Hybrid you find in need gets a place to live, money for school, and whatever they need. Even a trip to the island for safe harbor if they want it. If you find any who are content with their chosen line of work, see to it they have easy access to healthcare. I'm going to send you your own security team just to keep you safe okay?"

Bailey smiled and nodded, "Thank you, your Grace. Otherwise, most of the girls I've been able to find in this part of the country seem to be happy for the time being. One other thing, though…"

"Yes?"

"I have had several requests if it would be possible to undo some of the changes the Ceruleans did to us?" Michelle opened her mouth for clarification but Bailey pressed ahead. "I know the physical stuff is permanent but for the ones who don't want to take a Cerulean mate. They'd like to be able to take a human one. I mean, we're all pretty, and I guess some would at least like to enjoy that fact…but with a Human partner."

Michelle looked at Rachel, who shrugged and had a sour face as if she was fighting nausea, then glanced to her right at Domaas and saw the contemplative look on his face. "I do not know, Heartbeat. I do not think it was something ever seriously considered."

Back to Bailey, "I'll have Healer Borlaas look into it and get back to you as soon as possible. Until then, keep up the good work." Bailey beamed but remained silent.

Michelle was about to go into her next topic when a thought struck out of the blue, and her eyes slewed back to Rachel. "April is evidently in the fleet somewhere, and isn't supposed to be. What are Katie, Chrissie, Sean, and Makayla doing? I haven't thought about them in weeks."

Rachel blinked slowly and then snatched up the tablet that had been on the table in front of her. She tapped it furiously through the navigation menus then slid her finger as if scrolling through a long list. She stopped, squinted and nodded, then scrolled more. "Chrissie and Katie's last message was a week ago. They're both still on that Marine Corps base in Louisiana. Both are due any day now and will be sent home. Last I talked to them, both were asking to be reunited with their mates. Chrissie sent a message stating April had left the base weeks ago. The Marines acted as if she never existed." Rachel's brow furrowed as she continued, "How did I miss this? But Sean and Makayla..." Rachel's voice drifted off again as she scrolled some more, then she dropped the tablet in her lap and looked up. "They've gone silent. Sean messaged about a month ago, says her dad was acting weird and seemed to have found some new religion."

Even with the wide open doors, the air seemed to get sucked out of the room. "She says he has been watching videos from *Reverend Stakker*." Jamie, who sat at the far end of the table, went rigid. Bailey gasped and covered her mouth, her eyes wide in horror.

Domaas leaned forward, "Would this be the same-"

"Without a doubt, Domaas," Michelle said through clenched teeth. "Rachel, how did we let them slip away like that?"

Rachel looked lost. Jamie and Bailey had talked at length about their experiences and what they understood of how vile Reverend Stakker's plans were. "I...don't know," she said. "Sean's last message came the day after your family was attacked. It must have gotten lost in the shuffle. Michelle, I-"

Michelle shook her head. Rachel and Commander Kear'ald had also sealed their Bond the same night her family had been attacked. Rachel had a bonafide reason for missing the messages.

"No," Michelle said. "The fault is as much mine. I should have remembered, and we've barely had a break since then... And I stupidly had you remove all the *bracelets*!" Michelle slammed her hand on the table in frustration. Everyone sat in silence. She turned back to the screen. "Bailey, I will need you to redouble your efforts to find everyone. See if those Hybrids you found on the streets would like to help others. I'll pay them well. Rachel, find where Reverend Stakker is hiding; we leave as soon as you find him. Meeting adjourned."

Without waiting for Domaas or the present members of her Regent's Guard, Michelle stood hard enough to force the chair to scrape against the teak floor and turned to leave the room. "Heartbeat."

The tone in Domaas' voice stopped Michelle dead in her tracks. The kind of tone that told her she wasn't going to like what he said next. Slowly, she turned toward him on the ball of her bare foot. "There is more to be discussed," he said without looking at her. "Please sit."

Her mate hadn't come so close to telling her what to do since just after they had completed the *Quoy*. A glance around the table and to the large video display showed her everyone present, even the Regent's Guard, was averting their eyes nervously. Except for her father, who was looking directly at her as if he'd climb through the screen if she misbehaved.

"What is going on, Domaas?" She asked in Cerulean. She did not like the change of energy in the room. She was about to hear something she would not like.

"Sit down, Michelle." This came from the only person who could ever explicitly give her orders. A lifetime of obeying her father's commanding voice had her gently resting on the edge of the chair, the balls of her feet braced against the floor so she could sprint away if she needed to.

"We don't have time for this. Sean and Makayla are in trouble. He could have had them for almost a month now." Why was she pleading?

Domaas cleared his throat and leaned forward in his seat to capture her eyes. They had all agreed upon this. However, he *was* second in command of the Cerulean Impirium and, more importantly, her mate. He had to be the one to speak. "We have discussed it-"

"*Discussed* what?" The knife-like edge in her voice was undeniable.

Domaas pressed on, "The Regent's Council, the people you have placed your trust in, have made a decision regarding your safety." Michelle shot daggers around the room, but the only one looking back at her was still her father from the other side of the world. "You are our leader now, of an entire race and multiple other civilizations. We can no longer allow you to place yourself in danger."

Michelle closed her eyes and didn't see the others brace for the expected static energy pulse. The tell-tale sign the Regent was getting angry. Instead, she whispered, "I promised you I would not lose control again, Domaas." She opened her eyes and looked around the room once more; this time, they had the decency to be looking at her. She saw concern and worry. It angered her. "So I am grounded, then? You're going to try to put me in some tower to rot away on a throne? I was very clear that's not the kind of Regent I would be," Michelle ground out through clenched teeth as her hands fisted in her lap.

"It is not about controlling you, Michelle," Domaas countered, keeping his voice calm and even. "It is about keeping our Regent safe. She has shown a tendency to rush into danger. We could not have a better Regent than one who would risk her own life to save others. It is time to let those who have sworn to defend and fight for you do the work. You have earned that right."

"I cannot order others to die for me or my friends, Domaas. I do not have that in me."

"Do not look at it that way, Heartbeat. Of course, you would not do such a thing. Instead, look at it as giving someone a job to do. They will do whatever they can to ensure their survival. This is part of the deal, your Grace, and it is non-negotiable."

Michelle's mouth twisted at her mate's use of the honorific. He knew she hated him using it, and she also knew he was making a solid point.

As Regent, she really should not be running off into danger. Rescuing Jamie and Bailey had been one thing, but evidently, leaping from the top of the ship had rattled them pretty hard. *They weren't the ones who felt the sickening pull of gravity,* Michelle thought to herself. *Or know what it feels like to explode...* She should have never been in a position to let the Lords rile her up so much. "You all voted on this?"

"Yes-" Domaas began to answer, but Michelle silenced him with a raised hand as she looked around the dining room.

"Yes," Rachel said, leaning forward. "We all voted on it, your Grace. It was unanimous. You are too important now." Every head that mattered nodded in agreement.

"Fine, figure it the fuck out and get back to me when you find them, I guess." Michelle stood and walked out of the room, leaving a trail of chilly air as Captain Kato silently followed with feather-light footsteps.

"That went a lot better than I expected," Roger quipped from the safe distance of a New York office.

"Did anyone feel it?" Major Ka'al asked.

"What?"

"There was no pulse," Domaas answered. "She contained her anger."

"That's not normal?" Bailey asked with a small voice.

"No," Rachel and Domass said in unison.

Chapter Seventeen

The sound of the sword blades clashing was different than one might have expected. The special alloy rang like a heavy bell every time it struck another of its kind. The guards moved faster than expected as well. Domaas kept himself in superb physical condition, but for some reason, Michelle had thought him more the exception than the rule.

She couldn't have been more wrong. Male Ceruleans filled the just recently built gymnasium. The length and width of a football field featured everything from a sand pit for an unknown form of calisthenics to a moving, adaptive climbing wall. There was also a large area for weight training using bars that manipulated gravity fields. From the ceiling, high overhead, thick ropes descended to sunken pits filled with foam blocks. Finally, a running track jutted out from the wall about 30 feet up from the floor and ran around the entirety of the building. The last two main areas were the bamboo floored sparring area her guard used for sword practice and the space Michelle occupied alone.

Her corner had a concrete floor and nothing else. The walls were open to the outside but protected by force fields. The fields were set to Michelle's DNA and would drop if she attempted to pass through them. All she had to do was leap onto a transport pad linked to another pad on a floating steel box moored two miles offshore. Rachel only needed to explain what to do, not why.

The gymnasium had been open for two days, and already there was a waiting list for the Ceruleans on the ships to come to the island to use it. Nearly all crewmen had been confined aboard the ships since leaving Cerul almost half a year ago, so a desire to disembark for a short time was understandable. Michelle also suspected they wanted to get a view of the Regent as she practiced with her unique ability.

"I've made some decisions," Michelle said quietly in English to the tall Cerulean as he approached. She didn't turn to him but remained focused on the ball of purple energy suspended between her hands. She had been focusing on growing and shrinking it at will, wanting to ensure she had solid control of her ability before attempting to play with it.

"Oh?" Domaas asked as he stepped into view. Michelle had been...cold to everyone for the last couple of days. However, Domaas had experienced an especially icy shoulder. She had even gone as far as sleeping in the Regent's Solar that had been built on the island. He had only approached from his sword practice because he had felt her tug on the Bond. It was probably as close as she ever got to *summoning* him. He had tried several times to speak with her, and each time she had turned and walked away before he had the chance. She was bitter, even if it was for the wrong reasons. If Michelle had wanted people afraid to speak their minds and act decisively, she would have picked different people for her council.

"Yes," she said as she turned so he wasn't in her view again. "Have T'Rail ping the carrier wave or whatever. I want to talk with whoever is out there before they approach the planet."

The Bond between them had long gone quiet. What was usually a luminous strand of adamant that hummed with energy was currently nothing more than a gray cable that periodically transmitted her heartbeat. Domaas opened his mouth to speak, but she continued, "I also need an assistant, like what you have with T'Rail. Not another person for the council. I need someone who won't vote against me, who *can't*. Someone who can run messages and carry out my orders to the Council so I don't have to see your traitorous faces-"

Domaas' voice boomed, echoing off the high concrete walls. "Give us the space!" There was a beat of silence before a quiet stampede poured through the exits.

Domaas silently stepped directly before Michelle as he unbuckled his sword belt. "Ka'al?"

The Regent's Guard changed course and jogged over to where his

Regent and Regis stood facing each other, the pulsing ball of blue energy now crackling between the former's hands. Major Ka'al took the sword and belt that his Regis held out, then snapped into a turn to follow out the last of the stragglers. "No one enters," Domaas commanded to the Major's back as he stared down into Michelle's hard green eyes.

The last door thudded closed with finality. "What the fuck do you think you're doing-" For only the second time ever, he caught her off guard. A slap. Hard enough to make her stumble to the side and her ball of energy fizzled out as her arms waved for balance.

Then Michelle planted her leading foot, pivoted through a complete turn, and lifted off. Her fist struck his cheek, but Domaas absorbed the hit and completed his own spin to come back around to drive his elbow down into her back. Michelle hit the concrete with a thud and leaped back to her feet with the grace of a cat. "You learned some new moves," Michelle said as she rotated her shoulders and craned her neck side to side to loosen her tense muscles. She slowly circled him as Domaas settled into a defensive stance, turning to keep her in front of him.

"I hope you aren't expecting to get laid after this," Michelle said as she feinted left; Domaas showed her what she wanted to see by shifting his right foot. When she swung with her right fist, Domaas stepped into her swing, blocked with his elbow, hooked her arm, and swept her legs from underneath her. Michelle rolled away and sprang back to her feet again. "Oh, you've *really* been practicing," she snarled.

No, he hadn't. Not hand-to-hand combat, anyway. Perhaps his building skill with the sword was making him faster but that wasn't why he had just been able to floor her twice in a row. Michelle's fighting style had always been hard and fast. It was disarming to anyone who had picked the fight and constantly kept her opponent on the back foot in defense. Domaas had only begun to realize it the last few times they had sparred. However, Michelle had minimal experience being on the defense herself. It was time she learned how much of a liability that was.

Her loved ones had made the collective decision to protect her, and that made her defensive. Angry. The last few days proved she wasn't prepared to deal with it. Michelle didn't feel like she was the one who needed protection. Domaas guessed that she might even be thinking herself unassailable. All while giving paltry notice of the literal flotilla of Earthen military vessels floating just over the horizon.

The fleets of four different nations were holding stations in battle formations. Rachel reported at least three satellites had been moved into geostationary orbit over the island. Roger's negotiations were suddenly stalling out. Michelle had told the world the Ceruleans weren't a threat, but Domaas had a steady din of alarm bells going off in his head. The world didn't believe her. When they struck, she would not see it coming.

The Regent wouldn't see it coming because she allowed her pride to blind her.

Michelle tried to strike first again, and Domaas easily caught her arm and spun with enough force that she flew a short distance when he let go. His mate landed in a heap on the rubber matting that covered the rest of the gymnasium floor. She was still momentarily before she cursed and slowly returned to her feet. "Okay, asshole. Is this what our arguments are going to look like then? Fine, it's you Borlaas is going to be healing." Michelle shifted fighting stances.

Domaas calmly walked toward her and stopped once he was back inside her circle. "Why don't you just say it so I don't have to beat it out of you?" Domaas settled back into his fighting stance but wasn't still for long as Michelle unleashed a barrage of punches and kicks. A fury that would have left lesser opponents bleeding and bruised on the floor. He blocked every single one. Elbows that should have connected with temples sailed through empty air. Feet that should have weakened knees were blocked by shins with higher bone density than hers. Fists that should have been gut punches were deflected away.

Through it all, Domaas kept a perfectly calm demeanor. Even though his heart was pounding with exertion, he appeared outwardly to be taking a stroll in the park. It served its purpose when he switched to offense again and forced Michelle to concede space. The frustration showed itself quickly. Step after backward step, her face reddened in anger, and he felt the first pulse of energy.

Perhaps the swordplay training really had improved his skill set.

Her defensive blocks became more and more sloppy, his strikes getting closer and closer to finding their marks. He'd walked her backward all the way into the sand pit and saw her face crumple as she realized just how much distance she'd given up. Michelle went on the offensive again, trying to force her way through his suddenly impenetrable defenses, but he was now countering her every move. What were once simple blocks now became counterstrikes.

She had never had this much difficulty fighting him before. She couldn't get in close enough to use any of her finishing moves, and whenever she tried to back away to regroup, he would close the distance, staying just inside of her bubble. If she tried to advance, Domaas would concede just enough to block, then counter and continue to press his attack.

Strike, block, and another part of her body exploding in pain. Another step backward in the sand-

No!

The energy was traveling down her arm as she feinted and swung her right fist as hard as she could, aiming for the dead center between his eyes. But this was what Domaas had been pushing her toward, and he saw the color shift in her eyes - the tiny bolts of energy traveling down her arm into her tightly clenched fist.

Both of his hands came up and caught her wrist. He then turned his back to her and dropped to a knee in one fluid move, transiting her captured fist from left to right over his head as he spun - just as a blast of purple energy released from her fist. With a twist and thrust of his shoulder, Domaas forced Michelle to flip over him to land on her back. By the explosive gasp, he knew the wind had been knocked out of her, and in a spray of sand, he was quickly straddling her, pinning her arms beneath his knees.

He hovered over her hips but kept his weight off her and waited until she caught her breath. When she finally looked up at him, he said, "My mate just tried to kill me because she was losing a fight."

Michelle blinked rapidly and shook her head as her eyes cleared. "No-"

"If my Regent orders me to take my life, I would do so without hesitation. If she wishes to *take* my life, I will give it without hesitation." Domaas leaned forward so that his hands rested in the sand on either side of Michelle's head. "However, until that time, I will defend my *mate* until the day I die. Even if that means I have to teach her that she is not invincible. Even when she becomes guilty of the very thing she once rightly accused me of."

Tears were pooling in her eyes and sliding down the side of her face, but she otherwise remained perfectly still. She was beaten. "And what is that?" Michelle asked in a tiny voice.

"Overconfidence, Michelle. You have enemies on your doorstep, and you are either too stupid to notice or think it does not matter. Let people do the jobs you have given them. Tell us what to do. We will not fail you."

"But *you*, we can no longer allow her *Grace* to place yourself in danger. You need to *delegate.* It is not about controlling you or taking advantage of you. You are the Regent of the Cerulean Star Impirium; almost ninety different species and a hundred civilizations in total. Your very word is law. It is time you start acting like it." Domaas leaned back and then slowly got up from his knees. He looked down at where she still lay, then turned and walked away.

Michelle lay still as she listened to his fading footsteps, then the opening and closing of a door. The flat gray concrete ceiling high above gazed right back down at her. Domaas was right. "Fuck."

Chapter Eighteen

Brylie was bouncing from foot to foot, bubbling with infectious excitement. His father fought the smile that tugged at the corners of his mouth as he scooped his son up into his arms. "What is this about, P'alta?" Nicole asked as she came in through the door behind Brylie. Her escort stopped at the door and nodded to the Colonel before turning his back to the closing doors.

He waited until the lock switched to blue, then spoke. "It would seem that your insistence in coming along has worked to our benefit."

Nicole crossed her arms and paced about the room. A relatively small space for a vessel of this size and empty except for the glowing blank holographic screen hovering near the far wall. "Are we finally moving closer to Earth?"

"Maybe," P'alta said as Brylie climbed up to his father's shoulders. "We shall be finding out momentarily."

"So why do you need me and Brylie?"

"I am not sure. But the coded message we received instructed Brylie to be present when we made video contact."

Nicole squinted her eyes as she came to a stop. "How would they even..." She looked up at Brylie perched on his Popa's shoulders. The boy was grinning ear to ear. He had never stopped talking about his 'friend' the Princess. Nicole had honestly started thinking it was just an imaginary friend. However, just two mornings ago, he had been tweeting about meeting his friend soon. "Brylie?"

"It is her, Mopa! I know it!"

"Something I should know?" P'alta asked with a flat voice.

Nicole shrugged, "Ask your son."

Brylie was happy to volunteer. "In my dreams, I have a friend. She came when we were still at home. She is a princess and says Mopa and her Mopa were friends when they were still like me and you, Popa."

P'alta's face turned contemplative as he locked eyes with Nicole. "He is serious?"

"Very." Nicole looked up at Brylie. "Tell Popa what you told me about your friend's Popa."

"He was in charge of a big ship like this one! But it was for turning Popas into Mopas!"

"Commander Et'Kuraul?"

Brylie shrugged his little shoulders as he rested his chin on his father's head. "I do not know. The princess never told me his name. She just said her Mopa likes to beat up her Popa, and then they make weird noises."

Nicole held a small smile as P'alta's face showed discomfort with his son talking about such things, innocent as it was. A speaker clicked on overhead, and Major Milkas' voice came through. "Colonel Bil'tun, we are receiving a signal from one of the human satellites. It has the royal authentication codes. However, it is audio only. Shall I have it put through?"

"Yes, of course."

There was a series of faint beeps, and a male's voice came through the overhead speakers. *"This is Lieutenant T'Rail Bilson speaking on behalf of her Grace, Regent Et'Kuraul. We have received your signal. Due to Earth's atmosphere, we are not able to communicate directly. Therefore the Commander of the fleet is ordered to come to Earth in a shuttle. If a child named Brylie is in your fleet, the Regent also requests this child be aboard the shuttle. Approach speed is to be no more than six krikams. We are secure, and there are no hostilities with the Humans. If you are approached by Human craft, do not engage or adjust posture in any way. Embedded in this message are the coordinates for landing."*

"Come, meet your new Regent."

*****

"How long will it take them to get here?" Michelle asked as she touched T'Rail on the shoulder to express her thanks for sending the message. She had wanted it to be a video call, but the hodge podge comms system Rachel and T'Rail had put together was evidently weak against solar flares.

He stiffened and then relaxed as he looked back and up at his Regent. He was still adjusting to her relaxed way of doing things. He had never met the elder Regent. Been in her presence, yes, but those few times she had not even acknowledged his *presence*. Regent Et'Kuraul spoke to him directly; knew his name even. That was a difference he was growing to appreciate. "If they obey your orders, your Grace, it will take them roughly four days."

"Pretty sure the military will pick them up as soon as they pass Saturn," Rachel interjected in Cerulean for T'Rail's sake. "I shou- No, *you* should call General Hamlin and let him know the fleet is here. I think it would be more official that way. He has been wanting to talk to you anyway."

Michelle arched an eyebrow as she glanced at Rachel, "Why?"

Rachel shrugged, "I do not know, your Grace. That is why I have not bothered forwarding his requests. He refuses to talk to me and demands to speak to you."

"He demands? After the Secretary of State has canceled with me?" Michelle figured it had been in reaction to naming her father an Ambassador to the UN, not the United States. It did not matter to her goals, though. Her history teacher, Mrs. Tiffle, had thoroughly covered the Cold War and the subsequent arms race. Michelle would have no part in causing that to happen again.

"He demands."

Michelle harrumphed and gestured toward the communications console. T'Rail set to work contacting the Marine Corps installation in San Diego as Michelle asked in English, "Rachel, have you ever noticed how alike the males of both species are?"

Rachel snorted as her hand rested on her stomach, which wasn't as flat as it used to be. "I really thought it was just me adjusting to being...complete. But yeah-” She laughed out loud, “I thought about reaching out to my mom. She still lives in the same house, but she’s the kind of woman who would just love to pick my brain apart about what I think of males now.”

“And?”

“And I will keep my opinions to myself, your Grace.” Rachel’s eyes found a fascinating spot on the wall. ”I will say I don’t want to kill him anymore if that’s what you’re asking.”

Michelle glanced over T’Rail’s shoulder to see that he had made contact but was waiting for them to answer. This was supposed to be a direct line to General Hamlin’s desk. “When are you planning on telling him?”

“Tell him what?” It would be impossible to miss the note of apprehension in Rachel’s voice. She had come a long way from the cocksure and bravado-filled Micah whom Michelle had met over a year ago. Still confident, still capable, but certainly different. It was interesting watching the evolution of Rachel as she settled into the very existence she had mocked Michelle for once upon a time.

Including motherhood.

“That you’re pregnant with his son,” Michelle said as she turned to look at Rachel again. The older woman studiously refused to return the favor as her face paled, and a hand drifted up to her bare neck. Her hair was long enough now to reach her nape but not nearly long enough to hide the spots that were currently covered by a thick coat of makeup.

“Would you believe me if I tried to say I don’t know what you’re talking about?” She asked in a hopeful tone.

“Would you *really* try to lie to me about it?” Michelle answered deadpan.

Rachel’s hand hovered over her neck, and then with a firm wipe of her thumb, she rubbed away enough makeup to expose spots just beneath her ear. “I thought I was hiding it pretty well.”

“Two things; first, you forget I know what morning sickness with a Cerulean baby looks like. Second, how long did you think you were going to hide being pregnant? Were you just going to go into labor and be all, *Oh yeah, Pitor, by the way...?*”

Rachel nodded and sighed dejectedly, "Yeah, I'm not exactly sure what my plan was. I just didn't want *Them* to think they won, Michelle. I feel like this is the final nail in the coffin for Micah."

"*They* who, Rachel? Pitor calls you '*Flower*'. He adores you. For Christ's sake, he has stars in his eyes every time he looks at you. I'll say no more about it, but you're starting to show. You've hidden the sickness better than I did, but it's only a matter of time. And I guarantee he knows you're hiding something. He'll feel it across the Bond every time you lie."

Rachel continued to stare at the spot on the wall but bit her lip and nodded in understanding.

"Your Grace," T'Rail spoke. In the last few minutes, his Regent and her friend had spoken in their native tongue. He knew enough that his Regent had just gently chastised her friend, and if he turned to look, he would have known why. But T'Rail wasn't so bold to think the Regent was that casual. They would have spoken in the language he knew. If they had wanted him to know. "The General is holding for you."

"Put him up on the screen."

The holographic viewscreen rezzed into existence above the console. General Hamlin's face appeared, bracketed by the United States and Marine Corps flag against the wall behind him—several plaques and glass-framed certificates could be seen over his head. In one of them, there was a reflection of someone else in the room standing opposite the General.

Michelle smiled, "General, I see your people were able to install the equipment we sent you."

"The instructions provided by Rachel were concise enough." The General's soft southern accent was as clear as the image hovering before her. "I have come to understand you also have offered this technology to other...entities."

Michelle tilted her head as she pursed her lips, "I have." She wouldn't bother asking how he knew. Michelle had made the offer to China, Russia, England, and Germany after the dressing down by her father. Both the hologram *and* radio technology had been freely given. "Is that a problem? Is this why you've been demanding to speak with me?" Not that it would matter too much to the Regent. The United States government dragging its feet had given Michelle time to think more clearly about her goals.

General Hamlin leaned back in his seat, away from the display on his end. "Please look at it from our point of view, your Grace. You refuse to share the Cerulean defensive technology, you've restricted our access to the information you have already given us, and now you are sharing technology with two countries that have an interest in weakening the United States."

Her original purpose for calling set aside, Michelle narrowed her eyes and asked, "At what point did I ever say I would only be sharing Cerulean technology with the US? I have always been clear that I wish to share with the entire planet. Isn't that so, Rachel?"

"*Very*, your Grace," Rachel responded, curious how this would go. She wasn't sure if Michelle knew it, but she had adopted the Elder Regent's ability to *code-switch* her personality. Just moments ago, the Regent had been a kind and caring friend and, in the span of two sentences, had emphatically stated her position in a stunning display of diplomatic directness in the span of two sentences. And the Regent was still warming up to deliver one of her infamous verbal takedowns. Rachel had learned to see those coming miles away.

"I recognize that you still see me as too young to have the wisdom a head of a galaxy-spanning impire should have..." *Here it comes,* Rachel thought. "But it would seem to me that when the Human race has a chance to advance its technology by orders of magnitude, it would be prescient not to start a global arms race. Wouldn't it? If I remember correctly from my US History class, it was an arms race that brought the world to the brink of nuclear war. Several times... I mean, it was only high school history, so maybe I'm wrong. Either way, I think it would be *quite* obvious that it is in the entire planet's best interest that I do what I can to prevent that. Don't you?" The saccharine sweetness Michelle added to her voice at the end was sickening in its effect.

The General nodded his head softly, as if he had forgotten who he was talking to, then smiled. "I have told them repeatedly that you aren't some stupid eighteen-year-old girl. Please understand, I have my orders to speak to you about these things. Between you and I, I wish they would allow someone else to be your liaison. To what pleasure do I owe this...phone call?"

"The rescue fleet has arrived."

The resolution of the holographic display was so sharp Michelle could see the color drawing from the General's face. "How many ships?" He asked around a thick tongue. Just over a hundred currently floated around the island, Michelle had claimed. *How many more ships could they have?* He silently wondered.

"We don't know. They're currently parked out past Jupiter somewhere. They didn't want to come in too close since they don't know what happened to the *Rising Star.* I have ordered them to remain there and for one shuttle to approach Earth slowly. It should be here in four days."

General Hamlin's eyes appeared to be running fast calculations before he asked, "And what of the fleet moored around your island?"

"What about them? They don't move without my say so, General. My plans remain unchanged since your Marines attacked my family. I seek a peace and trade agreement with Earth. This island will be a toehold presence as a non-voting UN member state. One ship will remain in defense of my sovereign territory. Then the rest of us leave."

The General's eyes flicked off the screen for a fraction of a second and Michelle watched the reflection shift. "Us?"

"Yes, General, I will be leaving as well. I *do* have an impire to learn about and run, after all."

General Hamlin pressed his lips together into a thin line as he processed the information Michelle had just given him. "I would like to think we understand each other, General. Please speak plainly."

He sighed heavily through his nose before speaking, "The President has directly ordered me to request that you decrypt the defense data you have restricted from us. Also, we are still waiting for an explanation for the massive explosion that took out one of the Cerulean ships and our plane."

"No on both counts, General. Didn't I just explain why I won't be releasing that technology to you or anyone for that matter? And tell the

President she can ask me herself next time; there is an open invitation for her to visit anytime she likes. Also, it isn't polite to have someone eavesdropping on the line. They should at least have the decency to let themselves be seen."

The General's eyes flicked to Rachel on the Regent's right, then off-screen again. Michelle rested her hand on T'Rail's shoulder again and gently squeezed. He understood the silent message; the tone of her voice was evident even if he didn't understand the language, and he killed the connection.

Michelle turned to Rachel. "Find April and have her delivered to the island. That's the second time they've had information they shouldn't have had. I want her before that shuttle passes Mars."

"I have a pretty good idea of what ship she is hiding on," Rachel responded as she got to work on her tablet. "That was a good catch on the reflection, by the way."

Michelle grunted, "If there's one thing the Ceruleans have taught me, it's to pay attention to things they don't want us to notice."

******

General Hamlin looked across his new desk through the derezzing holographic screen. "She doesn't miss much, does she?"

The Man In The Forgettable Suit pushed his glasses up the bridge of his nose as he answered, "I *was* curious if she would notice. The more I learn about her, the more I want her in a box with glass walls. Our young Queen is a special breed indeed. It's time to start moving the chess pieces."

Chapter Nineteen

"You know April," the blonde began to turn as Michelle paced around her but stopped when she saw the subtle shake of Captain Kato's head. "I knew someone like you at my high school. His name was Mark..." Michelle eyed the young woman as she passed to see if life could be that ironic but saw a lack of recognition. "I figure every school has that one kid."

"I... don't understand, your Grace," There was a nervous warble to April's voice. *Good,* Michelle thought to herself.

"Oh, you know, the kind who just can't be trusted, ever, with anything? The school snitch. The one who everyone knew never to do anything they didn't want to get in trouble for in front of?" Michelle came to a stop in front of the shorter tanned blonde. April's blue eyes nervously darted away to where Pouduit stood holding their son. "Don't look to your mate for help, April." They were a long way from that empty corridor on the *Rising Star.* "Now, you know I, at the very least, suspect you of something. So I tell you what; you tell me what you are guilty of, and I won't punish you or your mate. I'll even send you two to the country of your choosing; with plenty of money. Rachel will create some documents for you three, and I'll have Healer Borlaas perform some cosmetic surgery so Poudiut and your sopa have a better chance of fitting in. Either way, you're done being under my protection."

April swallowed and, as expected, didn't hesitate to start talking. "It's the council members, the old ones. I was on a base with Chrissie and Katie, and they kept me from talking to anyone because I kept asking to be reunited with my mate. My son had just been born. I don't know how he knew about me, but some guy showed up and wanted to know about you."

"So you spoke with General Hamlin?"

April shook her head. "No, I don't know who that is. It was someone else...I can't even remember what he really looked like. He was just...plain." Michelle's doubt must have been obvious as April quickly added, "I swear, he never even told me his name. He just said he worked for the government, and if I told him everything I knew about you, he'd get me back to Poudiut."

Michelle turned to April's mate, who looked much more comfortable holding an infant than Domaas ever did, "Lieutenant? Is your mate telling me the truth?"

Poudiut cleared his throat and nodded as he said, "As she told me your Grace, and I am not sensing anything. When she first appeared with our sopa aboard the *Gifted Silence* I only trusted it wasn't a trick because of the Bond."

Michelle returned to pacing, this time in a large circuit around the Solarium. She glanced at Domaas to see suspicion but not doubt on his face. Her Regis wasn't doubting Poudiut's words, but the male had lost any trust he might have held in the Regent's military. "So you told this forgettable man everything you knew about me?" She asked April.

"Yes, your Grace, but I honestly did not know much. I just told him you were mated to the Comman-Regis and had become Regent. Oh, and how I originally supposed to be the princess' nanny, but they knew you would never trust me. But..."

Michelle glanced over her shoulder from the window. "But?"

"I think he knew who you were before then. He wanted to know who and why they wanted you so badly to offer that much money. He never really asked me *who you* were, and I think he already knew where you were."

Michelle returned her gaze out the window as she stepped away, nodding in thought. She glanced over to Domaas and Rachel against the far wall, both had been quiet this entire time. Domaas' face had turned grim, and Rachel was looking contemplative. "How does Cou'Parth and his ilk fit into this?"

"They were on the same ship with Poudiut and Chief J'oons. The Chief interrogated me when I showed up outside the ship's force field. I guess he told the Lords because I didn't even get a chance to see Poudiut before they threatened my son's life if I didn't help them contact the government guy again. He had given me a business card with just a phone number, so I did what they said. When M'kylo got sick, they refused to call for Healer Borlaas until I swore to keep helping them. They did not want to lower themselves to use a translator to speak to him, so they made me do it."

"Made?" Michelle had been calm so far, eerily, but she did not attempt to keep the ice out of her voice. It was enough for Captain Kato and Domaas to alter their breathing.

"Y-yes, your Grace." April fought the urge to curtsey randomly; she had caught the vocal shift as well. Suddenly feeling like a tiny mouse staring down the open maw of a cat, she continued, "They threatened Poudiut's family on Cerul and m-my sopa. By then, I knew I had gone too far, but I did not know what to do."

Michelle whirled and let her beast slip a fraction, just enough that April felt the static charge raise the fine hair on her arms. Just enough that M'Kylo shifted uncomfortably in his father's arms. Just enough that Poudiut was looking to the sentry and his Regis to know if there was any real danger. Judging by the tension on their faces and shifting of stances, there was. "So instead, you helped the males who almost caused the death of my father and the kidnapping of my *own daughter*? You could have asked for help, you *dumb bitch*."

April visibly shrunk away. Michelle's eyes were faintly glowing purple. All words of defense or excuse lodged in her throat. Silence filled the Regent's Solarium until Domaas cleared his throat and spoke. "Who has been giving you information from the Regent's Council?"

"It is Proctor Co'in," Pouduit offered. He could feel the abject fear of his mate across the Bond and sought to pull the Regent's focus on himself.

Captain Kato hissed a curse as Domaas growled. "He is one of your Regent's Guard, Heartbeat," Domaas rumbled, his voice brimming with anger.

Michelle looked at him, brow furrowed. "The quiet one? The one who gets stars in his eyes around Jamie?"

"Yes," Poudiut answered. "The Lord Hrar'prom promised Jamie as his mate if he spied for them. He was her Proctor on the ship when she was in training for service to you. He was very upset that she was re-programmed to never go into the *Phage,* your Grace. Cou'parth and the others knew your dopa would still need a caretaker after you were..."

"Finish it," Michelle demanded as she glared at her own mate, using him to ground herself before she let her anger slip. She had much better control of it now, but that was the problem; she *wanted* to detonate.

"I believe their words were '*Disposed of*'...your Grace." Pouduit sounded like he would have rather eaten a shard of glass than utter those words out loud.

The Solarium was so silent the whisper of the air conditioning could be heard through the vents high overhead. Michelle closed her eyes and took several deep breaths before opening them again and turning back to April. The girl's entire body was visibly tense with fear. "When was the last time you relayed information to this secret agent?" The calmness of the Regent's voice was the most frightening thing April had ever heard.

"The night we left California," April said as her bladder suddenly threatened to empty itself. "The Colonel on the *Gifted Silence* won't let any communication leave the ship unless it goes through his console." This Michelle knew.

Domaas had been quite thorough with the communications blackout she had ordered. But there was no such restriction in place for communications anywhere else in the fleet or on the island. No restriction of movement either. The old Council Lords couldn't leave the *Gifted Silence,* but a guard in his private time could move about unbothered just fine.

Michelle spoke to Domaas even though she still held eye contact with April. "Have Healer Borlaas prepare for surgery." She glanced over at Poudiut holding the infant M'Kylo. "For two, they both need to look as Human as possible." Back to April, "Rachel will set up a *well-funded* bank account for you to live on. Your sense of self-preservation will serve you well. If you're smart, you'll do nothing to get my attention ever again and allow me to forget about you."

"This is a kindness I do not feel, April. You could have kept my secret. It would have cost you nothing if you needed help. It would have cost you nothing to ask. Instead, your words and actions put me and my child in danger. You and your mate are walking away because I will not rob a child of their parents, as you would have done to Arya."

Michelle began walking for the exit, "Domaas, I don't care how, but I want them off this island and anywhere else in the world by this time to-morrow. Do what you will with Proctor Co'in." The doors opened and then closed as Michelle stepped out into the bright sunshine of the South Pacific. She didn't hear the collective release of breath that had been held for the last five minutes.

******

He would love to know how he had never been able to find her aboard the *Rising Star. Perhaps the Bond had not truly settled yet,* Domaas mused as he sat on the fallen remains of a palm tree to remove his boots and socks. *I feel as though I could find her across the galaxy's vastness now.* Domaas stood and regarded his mate standing at the water's edge, bare-foot herself; he watched the dregs of a wave surround her ankles before being sucked back out to sea. The breeze was strongest here at the shore, a constant warm pushing of air that seemed to ebb and flow with the tide.

Michelle's hair was loose and danced on the breeze like strands of curled copper filament in the afternoon sun. The skirt of her knee-length dress, a *sundress* Domaas remembered her calling the style, danced in time with her hair. And other than that, she appeared to be perfectly still.

She was a statue of the finest tawny stone, an homage to the ocean placed for some long-forgotten goddess of this world.

Her head turned slightly in his direction, and he could barely see the upturned corner of her mouth. Then, he felt a gentle tug on the Bond.

Domaas nodded to the grim-faced Major Ka'al standing in the shadows as he stepped out onto the sun-warmed sand and approached to stand on her right side.

He doubted she had noted his way of signifying what role he was tending to depending on which side he stood of her. To the left and one pace behind, she was his Regent, and he, her Regis. For that was the side on which she wore the crown. Anyone looking upon her Grace would know she was his sovereign, and he fully supported her. However, to the right, he was her mate, his equal. And he, hers. Even if she was unaware he did this on purpose, his *Heartbeat* tended to follow the pattern.

He turned bodily to look at her, "Tell me how you feel, Michelle." This was not a demand but a male seeking to provide support to the mother of his child. She was silent for a long moment, her gaze fixed on the horizon and the large ships that floated in formation there.

"I wanted to incinerate her." She turned her head to look at him, then back to the waves. "I could have done it, too. The energy was there and I could have turned her into a pile of ash as easily as snapping my fingers. And for what? Because she wanted to get back to her mate and the father of her son? I helped to destroy an entire ship and it could be said it is my fault the Regent is dead, just so I could get back to my family."

Michelle looked down and dug the toes of one foot into the wet sand as the last of a wave swirled around their ankles. "God, I have been a selfish bitch, have I not?"

"It is as I said before, Heartbeat. Now that I have had met your family, I completely understand why you wanted to return to them so badly. It is not selfish to wish to be with one's own family. I know that feeling well."

Michelle shrugged a shoulder, not entirely convinced but catching his meaning. "And what about now? What about what I am trying to do here on Earth? We could have left right after my coronation..."

Domaas snorted as he turned to take in the view for himself. "As I understand it, Heartbeat, everything you have done since returning has had the goal of fostering peace and safety for everyone. You only become...dangerous when those you love suffer violence. I often think back on that night when Jamie was assaulted."

"Oh?"

"Yes, but not for the reason you think."

Michelle reached and took his hand, interlacing her fingers with his own. Domaas looked down at their hands and allowed himself a smile. Michelle could be very tactile at times, a thing he very much enjoyed. "Oh?" Michelle prompted again.

"It was the first time I had witnessed you *commanding*. Surely you had given orders and made proclamations by then, but it was the first time you had spoken with absolute authority. When you ordered the shuttle, the way you commanded Bailey to fight with everything she had, the way you spoke to that Stakker male. When you stood alone and spoke to that reporter and properly claimed your title... That was the moment you had truly become Regent Et'kuraul. You spoke, leaving no room for someone to misunderstand or misconstrue exactly what you meant. You *commanded* the very space you were in."

He continued, "Heartbeat, you are providing for the returned Hybrids to have a comfortable life here. You are attempting to provide your first peoples with knowledge and technology that will solve much of this world's ills. Which, by the way, is what would have happened anyway with Earth if...things had been different. So no, you are not being selfish at all, you are being Regent."

Michelle was silent for a long time. Long enough to allow Domaas the pleasure of simply standing on a beach with his mate with nothing but the breeze and surf to keep them company. But eventually, she asked him, "Even when I am still struggling to delegate? When I am still working on controlling my temper?"

Domaas chuckled softly as he squeezed her hand, "Your temper is fine, Michelle. You do not get angry over little things. And remember the Elder Regent wore the crown for nearly one hundred Human years before she transitioned. You have more than enough time to reach perfection."

Michelle was silent for a long time once again. Minutes rolled by as massive waves crested and broke on the barrier reef a half-mile offshore. This close it was like thunder she could feel vibrating through the sand beneath her feet. Her shoulders were well-warmed by the sun, and her spirit was buoyed by her mate's support. Michelle could have stood there for another hour. Just basking in the sounds of a living ocean, while holding Domaas' hand. However, with a sigh, she released his hand and walked back toward Major Ka'al.

"What are you going to do about Proctor Co'in?"

"I instructed Pitor to deal with him. I am too close, too..."

Michelle picked up that Domaas couldn't think of the right word in English, so she said it for him in Cerulean. "*Feltsuad.* Emotional, and I understand. I also understand this will not be the last time it happens. I do not know if I could ever actually order the death of someone though, Domaas. That feels like something I could never come back from."

"There may come a time when you do not have the choice, Heartbeat," he said quietly.

"I know," she said just as they reached the shaded spot where Domaas had left his boots.

Chapter Twenty

"I'm sure he'll be a handsome boy," Michelle said quietly. Fiddling with the new bracelet Rachel had recently given her. Her 'wedding band' had survived her detonation, but the shield-generating bracelet had failed permanently shortly after Michelle had been pulled from the water. This new one was fractionally thicker in width and had a bit more weight to it. It evidently had a few more functions, but Rachel hadn't taken the time to explain them yet.

Rachel looked back at her Regent. Pitor had walked in on Rachel covering her spots with make-up and the argument that ensued had been heard halfway across the island. It had been the first time Michelle had ever seen an angry Cerulean male and honestly...it had been impressive. Domaas had told her about his rage when he learned of what Chief J'oons had pulled in the atrium aboard the *Rising Star*. However, witnessing a Cerulean male with his blood up had been something else.

"He better be. If I'm gonna have a kid, he better not be ugly. Now focus, your Grace. They're on final approach," Rachel said as she looked back out to the horizon and pointed to the approaching dark spot in the sky.

"You informed General Hamlin my guests were arriving?"

Rachel shrugged her shoulders, "I sent an email. Her Grace does not need anyone's permission to have friends over, right?"

Michelle felt the small tug of a smile at the corner of her mouth. "Correct." Turning to her left, "Domaas, are we sure they are not going to be like the Lords and cause more problems?"

"There will always be some who do not agree with you on the throne,

Heartbeat. Fortunately, their opinions are irrelevant when you have already sealed your claim."

"Right."

In the distance, Michelle watched two unidentified fighter jets peel out of formation as the shuttle crossed the invisible line denoting the threshold of the island's territory. The shuttle then passed through the forcefield that was always kept on now that so many naval ships were holding station just over the horizon. Every nation that could float a navy had a fleet keeping station around the island. Eventually, she'd need to do something about that.

A landing pad had been hastily constructed on a stump of reclaimed land, large enough that four other shuttles sat silently on their struts off to the side. There was still room for at least three more to park comfortably and plenty of open space for the approaching shuttle to land.

No phalanx of Ceruleans lined up to receive whoever was on the shuttle. Just Michelle, Domaas, Rachel, and the Regent's Guard minus one. All of whom wore their swords secured at the hip. Jamie and Arya stood even further off to the side with Captain Kato.

There had undoubtedly been a change to the posture of the males as each had grown comfortable with the tool they now carried at all times. During Michelle's tantrum, Rachel had taken it upon herself to introduce her Guard and Domaas to the idea of Knights. Chivalry, honor...the whole bit. A pity the concept came too late for Proctor Co'in. Their acceptance of the idea had certainly made their chests puff out just a bit more, their strides had a bit more swagger, countenance a bit more profound-

Michelle blinked, and the shuttle was already settling into a hover as its landing struts deployed. The soft, throbbing hum from the shuttle's propulsion ceased, and the hatch opened for a ramp to extend out and down to the concrete that had taken three days to pour and cure.

"Although," Rachel continued, unaware Michelle had spaced out. "I have to admit we're all curious as to how you knew they would have brought a child with them. It was my understanding that children weren't allowed to leave Cerul until they became adults." Michelle glanced over to where Arya stood with Jamie. The blonde tightly gripped the toddler's hand even though Arya was looking to break into a run any second.

She was just turning to give Rachel a vague answer when she heard, "Brylie! Wait!"

A young boy appearing to be about six years old came racing down the ramp at full tilt. He had solid eyes the color of sky and nearly platinum blonde hair. He stumbled to a stop and looked around until there was an excited yelp. Michelle glanced to see that Arya had finally broken free and was running as fast as her little legs could move. Brylie's face lit up like the sun as he opened his arms to receive Arya in a hug and was rewarded with a tackle to the ground. Pure childish laughter erupted from both of them as they continued to roll around on the concrete.

Michelle couldn't help but notice Arya was the more aggressive one of the two children. The feeling of '*Like her mother…*' came across the Bond from Domaas, and Michelle snorted as two more figures appeared in the hatch. The first, a woman with the same coloring as the boy, rushed down the ramp with admonishment on her tongue. "Brylie Bi'ltun! You get off that little girl right now! You promised to behave!" Her Cerulean was flawless, whereas Michelle knew she still spoke with an accent.

Michelle canted her head to the side and didn't fight the smile as she watched the scene play out. Even with Arya in the middle of it, she had watched from the corner of her eye as Jamie drifted closer, her right-hand drifting into the folds of her dress' skirt. Michelle had never really watched Arya at play, and her mirthful giggles as she rolled about in the rubber duck dress warmed a special place in her heart.

"Bi'ltun?" Domaas murmured. "Colonel Bi'ltun?" He was tall like all the other Ceruleans. However, instead of being fair-skinned, as Michelle was used to seeing, he was swarthy like her father. With dark hair worn rakishly long and solid light eyes like the flesh of an almond. Michelle had never seen this combination of features on a Cerulean before and made a mental note to ask about it.

"Do you know him?" Michelle asked as she noticed Jamie giving her a questioning look. She shook her head - *Let them play.* Besides, if that was the same Brylie Arya had spoken about, Michelle was okay with it being innocent for as long as possible.

"He should not be here..." Domaas answered as he stepped forward to greet the new arrivals. Michelle looked at Rachel, who shrugged a shoulder, then fell into step with Domaas.

P'alta stood at the end of the ramp and snapped into attention, then saluted. "Commander Et'Kuraul, I greatly apologize for my sopa's behavior..." His eyes drifted to the Human standing next to him, and Michelle was treated to watching the realization slowly arrive as his eyes caught on Michelle's crown burning in the sun. His eyes flared, and then his head snapped to where the children were now lying on their backs and laughing at nothing but the sky, the blonde mother quietly admonishing her son as he paid her no heed. Colonel Bi'ltun's face suddenly seemed to lose color as he made the connection. "Y-your Grace! You have my *deepest* apologies for my sopa's behavior."

P'alta was halfway down to one knee when Michelle jumped forward and caught his arm. "You do not kneel to me, Colonel. And your sopa is forgiven, as I am pretty sure those two have been waiting for a long while to meet."

Colonel Bi'ltun appeared dumbstruck as he allowed himself to be pulled standing and looked down at Michelle, then Domaas, and back again. "She looks us in the eyes?" He asked Domaas in confusion.

The Regis chuckled softly. "She also hates being knelt too. Has a temper you do not want to challenge, could potentially give Master Gulon a run for his title, is fiercely loyal, and has already sacrificed herself for the entire crew of the *Folded Fist*. My Mate, Michelle Et'Kuraul, Regent of the Cerulean Star Impirum, Mopa to Princess Arya."

Colonel Bi'lton saluted once more, even more stiffly this time. "It is an honor, your Grace-"

"Shannon?" It wasn't so much the voice, but the *lilt* of the voice. "Shannon Mizzi?" Michelle slowly turned her head to the tall Nordic blonde who was approaching slowly.

"Nicolette, do not be disrespectful," P'alta quietly admonished.

Michelle turned bodily and stepped to meet her. "Who- No, *how* do you know my sister's name?" Domaas was the only one in earshot who knew enough to hear the edge sharpening in Michelle's voice.

Confusion washed over the blonde's face, her eyes turned to slits, and her brow furrowed. Then her eyes nearly bugged out of her head. "No! Oh my god, really? Jason?" A thousand-watt smile lit the blonde's face as she leaned her head back and roared in unabashed laughter. She managed to catch her breath long enough to take in the Regent's Guard, the shuttles, the island, and finally settled back on Michelle with her crown of cold fire across her bare left shoulder; she took a deep breath and then erupted into laughter again.

Colonel Bi'lton appeared at his mate's side and gently took her elbow. "Nicolette, you made promises..." Nicole managed a few more deep guffaws before she was fanning away the tears of mirth and collected herself.

She turned to P'alta. "This is Jason Mizzi, my best friend since we were children. There surely is a God, and his sense of humor is perfect." She pointed to Domaas, all decorum forgotten. "Oh, I would give anything to have seen what he looked like after the Quoy! I managed only to give you a scar, P'alta. Do you remember when I told you I trained with my best friend, but he was better?" Nicole looked at Domaas with naked humor on her face. "If he could get out of bed the next day, I would have been surprised!"

Domaas cleared his throat but said nothing. After their fight in the gym, he had been sore for days. Whether or not Michelle had technically lost, a Human male probably would not have walked away.

"*Louis!*" Michelle blurted, both in realization and shock at what this woman had just said. "*You're* Louis Royce?"

"Well, Nicolette Bi'lton now, but yeah. You seemed to have done well for yourself." Nicole reached to touch Michelle's crown, but the Regent turned her shoulder away. The action was enough that Michelle heard several swords be loosened in their scabbards.

Nicole heard it too, and her smile faltered a bit. "They don't like it when someone they don't know tries to touch me. It's kind of their job. And last I remember, Louis didn't look like he'd just stepped out of Hitler's wet dreams," Michelle said cooly.

Nicole looked down at the backs of her hands as darkness clouded her pretty face; all happiness sucked out of her. "Yeah, well, I won't be trying to see my parents while I'm here. How do you convince two proud African American parents their only son is now a Swedish supermodel?"

"I'm sorry...what?" The Royce's were incredibly proud of their heritage and where they came from, even the dark beginnings of how their ancestors had arrived in North America. Mr. Delroy Royce had, however, spent twenty-eight years in the Navy before medically retiring. Ten of those years as a Navy Seal and the rest in Special Forces. In contrast, Dr. Jani Royce was still a practicing NICU thoracic surgeon. Together, both of them were *Black Excellence* at its finest.

"It is me, Jason. They," Nicole jabbed an accusatory finger to where both Domaas and P'alta stood watching, "Played with our genetics in the last group. They didn't discover the Black part of me carried a latent gene for Sickle Cell until the transformation process. I wasn't the only one, either. There was a Japanese kid who came out with blue 'round eyes." She huffed. "Far as I can guess, some slaver who raped my ancestor hundreds of years ago, and now I have to wear sunscreen. I turn into a frikken lobster if I forget. Which I do, a lot," Nicole finished as she glanced up at the bright sun warming the landing pad.

Michelle narrowed her eyes as she asked, "Who was I dating when you left?"

"Tilly Swire," Nicole answered without hesitation. "I'm still mad about how she treated you in tenth grade." She glanced at the approaching Regis as her smile returned, "But you always did have a thing for dark hair and blue eyes."

Michelle hadn't talked with anyone outside of her family about Tilly Swire. The girl who had broken up with Jason as soon as she saw the black bangle on his wrist. The likelihood of any Cerulean knowing about her was fractionally slim. Hell, she couldn't even remember ever uttering that name to Domaas or the elder Regent. "Well...shit."

"Forgive me, Heartbeat," Domaas' deep voice rumbled. "There is much to be discussed, and the children have wandered off without us." Michelle spun around to see Arya and Brylie holding hands as they made their way up the shady path leading to the mansion, with Jamie quietly walking behind them.

"Are they going to be okay?" Nicole asked - a concerned mother.

"Jamie is the only person, other than my family, I trust to be alone with Arya. She is frighteningly calm when the pressure is up and can probably handle a gun as well as your dad."

"My dad was a Navy Seal..."

"I remember," Michelle said with a faint smile.

Nicole took a long hard look at the blonde walking away with her son. Ponytail swinging as she walked, arms relaxed at her sides, calm stride, and dressed like she just stepped out of the 1950s. "Where is she hiding it?"

Michelle's smile broadened as she linked elbows with her best friend and began walking across the landing pad for the same path. The day had taken quite a delightful turn. One of the guards took the lead while everyone else fell in behind them by order of rank. "Where would she hide anything in that dress?" Nicole asked.

"Why would you assume she's hiding anything?" The lilt of Michelle's voice confirmed Nicole's suspicions.

"It may have been almost two and a half years, but don't think I've forgotten how that mind works." Michelle only smiled as they continued down the path. "Gods, it is so nice to speak in English. I want to know everything; I need to know everything..."

As they made their way up to the mansion, the de facto nerve center of the unnamed island that represented the Cerulean Impirium on Earth, Cerulean males cleared the way as they approached - primarily offering polite greetings to the Regent and nods of acknowledgment to the Regis. She did not respond to every male they passed, but Colonel Bi'ltun certainly noticed she at least made eye contact with them. Even as she quietly spoke to the pregnant woman with short dark hair on her left, she turned to point out something interesting about the island to Nicollete. "She treats them as her equal," P'alta said softly to his Regis.

"Quite so. I fear she will bring great change to our social structure," Domaas said in an equally soft tone. "She has no care for titles or the caste of one's family."

P'alta gave a doubtful look, so Domaas continued. "Major Ka'al," Domaas pointed out the Cerulean guard walking ahead of the group, "He was a Lieutenant when we made planetfall. Her Grace formed her own personal Regent's Guard and advanced him to Major in maybe three sentences. His father is a farmer from the southern continent. She did this without knowing who he was or his background." Domaas' hand rested on the weapon's pommel hung at his side. "That is just one example."

P'alta snorted, noted the object hanging from Domaas' belt, then said, "I am willing to bet the Council fought her on that."

Domaas caught the Colonel's elbow and turned to face him. "The Councilors have forfeited their lives as far as she and I are concerned. The Regent's father was nearly slain in his own home through their actions."

P'alta felt his blood warm at the thought. A male's home was sacrosanct. One did not bring violence to a place of peace and safety. It was anathema to civil society. He cursed at the very idea of it.

"Quite so," Domaas agreed. "They live because I convinced her to put them on trial once we return to Cerul. As of now, they are somewhere in the fleet, the *Gifted Silence,* I believe. They are not even able to access the food replicators."

P'alta glanced up the path in time to see the three females disappear into the mansion. Glancing around, he saw they were completely alone. "What is it?" Domaas asked, picking up on his friend's sudden discomfort.

"Sir, we were unsure what had happened to the *Rising Star.*"

Domaas nodded and turned to continue walking, "That is understandable. Especially with the return fleet present at the same time. How much of the home fleet did you bring?" But P'alta stopped him this time.

"One, Sir." Domaas froze mid-step and turned bodily to face P'alta full-on. "The *Regent's Mercy,* sir."

Domaas felt his blood slow in his veins as he asked in a near whisper. "Why would you launch *that* ship?"

P'alta met his Regis' eyes as he said, "The *Rising Star*'s emergency beacon transmitted through the old comms network. If the Kesta heard it, they are certainly trying to find out where it came fro-"

"HOW!!!" Domaas bellowed so loud the jungle around them went silent. He spun on a heel and began briskly walking up to the mansion, tapping his translator as he did so. "Lieutenant Bilson, get everyone to the council room as soon as possible...I am aware of that, but this requires her Grace's attention, *and Rachel.* Do this right now." Domaas did not even bother to see if P'alta was keeping up.

Domaas nearly tore the doors off their hinges as he threw them open and stormed into the dining room turned council chambers. He sent a powerful pulse down the Bond, strong enough that Michelle winced as she looked from her blonde friend to him. "Domaas, what is-"

"The Regent, Rachel, Colonel Bil'tun..." He glanced around the room and saw T'Rail quietly standing at the far end of the room. "Lieutenant Bilson, transport Commander Kear'ald to this room right now, then leave."

Michelle noted the authority in her mate's voice, a timber he rarely used unless he was vexed. "Domaas, what is going on?"

Domaas made eye contact with his Regent to let her know he had heard her but did not answer. Instead, he pointedly looked at Nicole. "She is neither on the Regent's Council nor a high enough ranking member of your military to remain."

"Domaas-"

"It is okay, your Grace," Nicole said with a smile. "I am very used to being asked to leave when my P'alta needs the room. Where can I find the children and that nanny of yours?"

Michelle flicked her eyes up to the ceiling, "Two floors up. T'Rail can show you the way." Nicole smiled again and left the council room, gently touching P'alta's arm before stepping out and T'Rail closing the doors behind her. The Regent looked back to her own mate as a blue light pulsed in the corner of the room, to deposit a confused-looking Commander Kear'ald.

"What is this about, Domaas?"

Still not answering her, Domaas looked to his first officer. "You are here out of respect, Pitor."

The sandy-haired Cerulean arched an eyebrow as he moved toward his pregnant mate, "Sir?"

Domaas finally faced his Regent to answer her. "You and Rachel have put us all, and possibly Earth, in grave danger."

Michelle blinked rapidly, "Excuse me?"

Domaas pointed a finger toward Colonel Bil'tun without breaking eye contact with Michelle. "Please tell the Regent what you have just told me."

P'alta cleared his throat. "The emergency beacon from the *Rising Star* transmitted through the old communications buoy system."

Rachel snorted and began to respond when Pitor was suddenly clutching her arm. "Do *not* speak, *Flower*." Rachel looked up at him in shock. It wasn't the tone of his voice; she had learned how loud his volume could go. No, the Bond between them had gone taught as if she had a leash tugged to heal. She remained quiet.

Michelle's voice carried the question as she slowly asked, "Why does this qualify as an urgent matter? Why is there danger?"

"The only way this would have happened is if someone reprogrammed the protocols on the beacon. It would have had to have been brute forced," Domaas answered as his eyes slewed back to Rachel. That annoying pebble in his boot back to irk him again. "The only one I can think of capable of or even wanting to do such a thing is Rachel."

Rachel yanked her arm free from her Mate and stepped away from him as she stiffened her spine. "Well yeah, big whoop. It is slower than your subspace network, and I needed to guarantee her Grace and I had a chance to make our plan work. A plan that got completely blown out of the water, by the way. What is the issue?"

"The issue," Domaas snarled. "It was discovered that the Kesta had thoroughly penetrated our communications. We created the subspace network to secure our official communications and it is uncrackable. We send harmless traffic through the old system to prevent the Kesta from learning too much. So, through your stupidity has essentially put a locator beacon on us and your homeworld." Pitor gently retook Rachel's arm and pulled her back next to him. His Regis had taken a menacing step toward her as his voice dropped into a threatening growl. Domaas Et'Kuraul *was* his superior officer and Regis, but that did not negate that Rachel was Pitor's pregnant mate, and he would protect her if need be.

Michelle saw it, too, and called his name to shift his attention. "Domaas?" He turned back to his Regent and caught himself before another snarl slipped from his throat. "We did not know about the Kesta then. Remember that whole thing about you guys keeping secrets?" There was a beat as the Regent glanced around the room to the highest-ranking members of her military. "If they come-"

"When," Domaas interrupted.

Michelle clenched her teeth in annoyance but continued, "Fine, *when* the Kesta come, how likely are they to attack Earth?"

"I believe, your Grace," P'alta ventured. "It would depend on whether or not the Cerulean fleet is still here. My ship, the *Regent's Mercy,* is hiding inside the gas planet you call Jupiter-"

"Really?" Rachel asked in disbelief as she stepped forward. "I thought those were alternate plans for the *Rising Star.* I guess not." Looking at Michelle, "It is a battleship, your Grace." She then switched to English, "Think about all those navy ships, out over the horizon and how itchy the planet will get when a ship as big as the last one and bristling with actual *weapons pulls into orbit.*"

Michelle stepped away from Domaas to her place at the head of the table, asserting her position. "I was given the explicit impression that Ceruleans did not have weapons of any kind on their ships."

"The former members of the council pushed for its construction when plans were being made for the *Rising Star,*" Domaas volunteered. Michelle's penetrating green eyes told him to continue. "Their thinking was that we had gone too long being unable to defend the Impire. Also, if the Kesta made contact again, and saw that a solution had been found for their bioweapon, they might attack Cerul outright. This is the main reason why the Hybrids are not allowed to leave Cerul once they arrive." Domaas' eyes flicked over to Colonel Bil'tun. "We know the Kesta have spies on other planets and could not risk them knowing about you and the others before the program was complete."

Michelle was silent for a long time, then clicked her tongue and looked over at Rachel as she rested her arms on the back of her chair. "Rachel, I want everything you can find about the Kesta in the Cerulean archives. I don't care if you have to crack the servers, or whatever they are, open and physically pull the info bit by bit. I'm tired of only getting half the information I need. Also, Colonel Bil'tun will be needing a sword as well. Get on that now, please."

Without a word, Rachel turned on her heel and exited through the French doors onto the veranda. "Stay, Pitor." The sandy-haired male stopped at the threshold of the doors and simply closed them before turning back around. "If I am understanding things correctly, you three are essentially my Joint Chiefs of Staff. Do you know what that means?"

"No, your Grace," Pitor answered.

"It means you are the highest-ranking members of my military. I see my Regis, a commander, and a colonel. A high-ranking Colonel, if he has enough power to bring a ship that is not supposed to exist, yes?"

P'alta bobbed his head like a schoolboy. "That is correct, your Grace, with Regis Et'Kuraul and the former Regent away, I was left in command of the Imperial fleet. With my departure, the role went to Colonel Ge'arche; he commands the Home Fleet. The Council Lord's proxies keep the government running until you return."

Michelle clapped her hands together, then stepped back to pull her chair out before sitting, "Great! Take a seat then, Gentlemen. I name you three my Defense Council. Welcome to the club." She watched their faces as they all came to the table and pulled out chairs for themselves. Colonel Bil'tun was the only one who had a look of shock on his face.

Domaas explained, "Her Grace has a way of...what is it your mate called it, Pitor?"

"Sandbagging."

"Yes, dropping something heavy on someone in surprise. You will adjust, I am sure. It shows she is placing her trust in you. It would be wise not to abuse that trust." Try as he might, Domaas couldn't keep the edge out of his own voice as they had dealt with *that* problem just days before. Glancing across the table, he could see the darkness in Pitor's eyes as well.

The Commander had not volunteered what had happened to the young Proctor and no one had asked.

"So what now?" Michelle asked, bringing the focus back on herself. "What are the chances they are on their way here right now?"

Domaas remained silent, so P'alta answered, "It is a certainty, your Grace." Colonel Bil'tun had just watched the new Regent assert her dominance over a room full of Cerulean males without hesitation in her voice. If he understood exactly what had just happened, she had formed a new sub-council, named it, and assigned him to it in *one* sentence. Without so much as a consulting look to her mate. Nicolette could be a force unto herself, but still understood her place as most of the Hybrids had come to. Her Grace was different. P'alta made a mental note to extract everything he could about this young Regent from Nicole.

"And what makes you so certain of that?" Michelle asked as a follow-up. "Why would they care about a distress signal from a downed ship of their enemy?"

Domaas cleared his throat and leaned forward to rest his arms on the dark teak of the table. "Remember that they are waiting for us to grow so weak as to not be able to defend ourselves. Earth is quite far outside of the Impirium's borders. Do we know for an absolute certainty they are coming? No, we would have no proof of that unless Colonel Bil'tun has more to share?"

The colonel shook his head once. "Then," Domaas continued. "It would be best to assume they are at the very least sending a scout ship. It is what we would do if in their position. For nothing more than curiosity's sake. The issue is they will absolutely want to know why an entire Cerulean fleet is at anchor on the surface of an unknown planet. We will have a problem when they discover the answer to that question. And they will, your Grace.

Everything we know about them is second-hand at best. Over the ages, they have consistently visited every planet the Impire has made contact with and invited under our banner. They always arrive after to ensure that we are not *conquering* other species. A simple scan of Earth's media and global networks will tell them all they need to know about why Cerul is here." He looked at her as he said the final part, well aware of his mate's unwavering thoughts on the subject.

Michelle was quiet as she thought. These were things Domaas had said before in one fashion or another. However, it hadn't been a real concern until now. Rachel's thoroughness had set into motion something that could severely hamper, if not make entirely impossible, what Michelle was trying to achieve. "What should be our course of action?" She knew what they'd say, but she needed to ask anyway.

"Immediate evacuation of the planet of all Ceruleans and make the best possible speed out of this quadrant of the galaxy."

Michelle slowly turned her head to fix her gaze on Colonel Bil'tun. Perhaps it was cruel to have set the trap, but she needed this new member of her new council to understand some very important things about her. There was a gentle caress across the Bond from Domaas - *Be nice*. To his own credit, the Colonel's face held a look of slight apprehension as if he had realized he'd said something wrong. "Colonel, that is not going to happen. I understand it has been less than an hour since you arrived, and you do not know me. So let me be clear about several very important points."

"I did not want to be Regent, I fought very hard against it. It was I and Pitor's mate, Rachel, that brought down the *Rising Star*. However, Regent, I am, and I do nothing half effort. I was not raised that way. I have set my mind on establishing a peace and trade agreement with Earth and I will not be leaving until this is done. Earth is my home as much as Cerul soon will be.

"If my actions brought the Kesta here, I will not leave Earth to defend herself. When the Rising Star arrived, the most well-equipped military was brushed aside twenty years ago. What do you think will happen if the Kesta, whom I have come to understand is even more advanced than Cerul, arrives, and we are gone?"

"It would be a slaughter, your Grace," P'alta answered.

"I think so too. What kind of Regent would I be to leave my home planet helpless to an alien species that just might attack out of spite?"

"She wants honesty, always," Domaas cut in before P'alta could answer.

Colonel Bil'tun nodded in understanding. "Not a very good one, your Grace."

"Exactly. So what I need from you three is an action plan for if or when they show up. Yes?"

"There is already a plan for scenarios similar to this. However, we will work to tailor something specific," Domaas answered for the group.

P'alta watched as the Regent reached and rested her hand atop her mate's without looking at him. "Domaas understands what I want." She stood and waved them back into their seats before they could jump to their feet. "We will dine together tonight, Colonel Bil'tun. We have much else to discuss, like my daughter's intention to mate your young Brylie."

Colonel Bil'tun stared as if he didn't trust what he had just heard. Michelle winked and turned to leave. Only Domaas saw the self-satisfied smile as she walked out. *I knew it,* he thought as the door closed behind her.

Chapter Twenty-One

Her heels struck out their staccato rhythm as she walked across the lobby floor toward the elevator bank. She moved with her head held high, shoulders back, and curled ponytail swaying with every swivel of her hips. From her soft pink silk blouse and gray wool pencil skirt to her black-patent opera pumps; from her full face of carefully applied make-up to the delicate and dainty, lingerie she wore beneath her outfit. Bailey had come to love being a young woman.

In the brief time she'd been in New York with her mate and Mr. Mizzi, Bailey had blossomed into a self-confident and highly feminine creature. She was unsure she could ever pinpoint exactly what had started the change. It had just become who she was once she'd felt a sense of safety and purpose. She wasn't the only one of the returned Hybrids who had gone *high femme*, but many had. Many had also seemed to settle into a tomboy-like aesthetic, butch, goth, girl-next-door - an amalgamation of all and in some cases, none at all.

Having her Grace's support at her back also went a long way, both financially and as a way to gain trust from those she was continuing to find, help, and settle. Many had been skeptical of who she said she was and what she was trying to do. Most of the captives aboard the *Rising Star* had been completely unaware that one of their own had even mated with the Commander, let alone ascended the throne. However, as in all things in the United States, money had a great way of smoothing over many wrinkles.

Bailey wasn't giving them money directly, per her Grace's instructions. Every Hybrid that accepted help got an apartment and a small stipend for life's monthly expenses. This was contingent that they did something, anything, productive.

Mrs. Mizzi, having quickly grown bored with financial independence, would soon be taking over control of the liaison duties in New York and the Eastern Seaboard. Today would be Bailey's last day in New York before branching out into other cities. Chicago and the Midwest were next. A replacement had been sent for her Mate's position in Mr. Mizzi's security detail and another two to form her own protection detail that would be arriving by stealth shuttle this morning. Bailey would then begin canvassing the country for other Hybrids needing help. A call had been sent out across the 'Net for any returned captive in need of help, and nearly thirteen hundred had answered so far.

The security detail was because she was becoming known, and her Grace was nothing if not cautious for the safety of others in her sphere. Bailey had yet to experience any real threats. However, a strip club owner hadn't taken well to his top three money earners quitting within minutes of Bailey's arrival. The man mysteriously lifting from his feet and being thrown across the stage had stopped any ideas the bouncers might have had.

Speaking of which...

She felt a phantom hand slide across her lower back as they waited for the elevator. Co'ta was a syrupy romantic who never missed a chance to express his affection. Bailey smiled and fractionally leaned into him as her eyes became hooded. Anyone who might have been watching would only have seen a well-dressed redhead quietly enjoying a fond memory as she waited for the elevator, and to Bailey, that made Co'ta's clandestine show of affection all the sweeter.

He'd never de-cloaked in public and had only once, in the strip club, he had to make his presence known. His very presence had given Bailey the fortitude to go into the seedier parts of the city to find girls in need. "You are resplendent in this outfit," he whispered in Cerulean. His hand drifted slightly lower to rest at the top of her rear end, his favorite part of her body. Bailey suppressed a smile as she arched her back, forcing his hand lower; all of her skirts were fitted for exactly this reason.

"I still think it is rude they made those suits so difficult to get in and out of," she said as the elevator dinged and the doors slid open. She stepped in and felt the sudden coolness as his hand left her. It was only from feeling the elevator shift under his weight that she knew he had followed.

The elevator swiftly lifted them to the sixteenth floor, and the doors opened again with a ding. Bailey went to step off but was greeted by Co'ta's arm suddenly blocking her. "Something is not right," he said out loud.

The elevator doors opened at the end of a long hallway, at the end of which were the double doors of the leased office space she used to conduct interviews and business. There were several other doors along the way, but they all led to unoccupied workspaces. "I do not see anything. Go, you have to meet them on the roof, do you not?" There was a long pause as the doors attempted to close and then reopened. "I will be fine. No one else is on this floor." Bailey raised her hand and felt the smoothness of the bubble surrounding her mate's head. Blue glowed faintly under her fingertips, making his eyes just barely visible. He may have been invisible, but she'd be able to find the center of her universe at night in a rainforest. *I will be fine,* she sent to him across the Bond. Co'ta lowered his arm, and Bailey entered the hallway as the doors closed behind her.

Bailey's heels continued their staccato rhythm as she transited the corridor and then muted as she unlocked the glass doors and stepped into the carpeted anteroom. An empty desk sat against the far wall. A receptionist would soon occupy it once Mrs. Mizzi took over the New York operation. The older woman had plans to branch out into charity for LGB and particularly T youths who also needed a hand up from the gutter their families had put them in. The last twenty years had been especially difficult for trans youths - an unfortunate side effect of *The Collecting.* There was a small closet to the left and another hallway to the right, which Bailey headed down. At the end of which was the office she used.

The various other doors led off into a room with a set of bunk beds for emergency overnight stays, a clothing closet full of quality clothing, and cold weather gear. They had arrived in February, and even Bailey, who had grown up in the desert, had been completely caught off guard by the frigid New York winter. There was a full bathroom with a shower stocked with lots of towels and surplus toiletries from hotels across the city. And opposite her office door, the hallway opened into a modest kitchen with a fully stocked fridge and overstocked pantry. All in all, Bailey thought she had done quite well getting this project up and running. She had already helped many and looked forward to helping even more. Much more. Not too bad for a nineteen-year-old who was learning to love the life she had been given.

The phone was already ringing before she managed to sit behind the desk. Bailey snatched up the handset and slid her tote bag off her other shoulder to set it on the desktop blotter. "Office of the Returned Collected Liaison, with whom am I speaking?"

There was no answer as Bailey cradled the phone with her shoulder and pulled out one of her tablets. "Hello?" Still nothing, so she dropped the handset back into its cradle and set the first tablet flat on the desk as she sat down. The holographic display exploded into view above, and she started going through the emails that had come in overnight. Being one of only two publicly known people to be connected to the Cerulean Regent, she received many of them. Most were deleted outright, and many were forwarded to Mr. Mizzi, the rest were passed on to Rachel.

The phone rang again. This time Bailey let it ring several times before she punched the speaker phone. *Maybe they had a bad connection,* she thought. "Hello?"

"Why, good morning, Bailey. It is good that the Lord has seen fit to keep you in good health."

Bailey's vision blurred then focused on the desktop phone all at once. "H-how did you get this number?"

Reverend Stakker laughed softly, "You have made a name for yourself, helping the rest of God's returned vessels. You have indeed been doing the Lord's work, but it is time for you to come and serve your true purpose. And now, with the work you have done, it will be much easier to bring others into the flock and to serve as our Lord has intend-"

Bailey stabbed the disconnect button and stood from her desk...just as she heard the distant ding of the elevator. Her heart was pounding in her chest as she left the office and walked down the hallway, eager to feel the closeness of her mate. Reverend Stakker had just rattled her cage pretty damned hard. She was sure that if he threatened to try to grab her again, he already would know where she was...

All thought evaporated, and her body froze mid-step as she entered the anteroom to see her father, Kyle, and three large men just steps from the doors. "Do not make this difficult, Bailey. Just come peacefully," he said, stepping through.

His eyes scanned her from head to toe, and he sneered, "A good man would not want a wife to be so obscenely dressed."

Co'ta gasped as a pulse of...*terror*, sheer terror, slammed into him from across the Bond. His mate was in trouble. Then he felt the *yank*, as if she was pulling on the Bond like a lifeline. Bailey was calling for him, for his help, to be saved. The shuttle was not due for another few minutes, so he turned and charged for the roof access door without a thought.

She got to her bag, still sitting on her office desk, slipped a hand in, and spun on her toes. In one smooth motion, she grabbed the folding knife she kept for defense, flicked it open with her thumb, and swept her arm in a sweeping arc. Her father cursed as the razor-sharp blade sliced through the sleeve of his shirt and just barely cut his skin. He jumped back, looked at the superficial wound, then back at Bailey as she swiftly put the desk between her and her would-be captors.

"You would dare to injure your *own* father?" He boomed as he stalked toward her.

Bailey lunged forward and swung again, forcing the larger man to back up again. "You are no father of mine, asshole! You and that crazy reverend can go to hell! I have my mate now, and he is a better male than you could ever be!" Bailey caught motion from the corner of her eye and was just turning when a massive fist crashed into the side of her head.

Stunned, the knife fell from her fingers, but she still managed to remain standing in her heels.

Her father wasted no time sliding in and grabbing both of her arms, then quickly turning her to apply zip cuffs to her wrists. "It is a shame you allowed yourself to be defiled by one of those Demons. With the Lord's mercy, perhaps the Reverend can absolve you of such a foul sin." He started force-walking the dazed Bailey toward the office door, saying to the other men in the room, "Make sure you grab that tablet. She'll have names and locations of others on there."

There was a mighty, animalistic roar - like a firedrake had just discovered its hoard was stolen. Bailey's lungs filled with air before she even knew what she was doing. "Co'ta! It's my fath-"

Bailey's father clamped a hand over her mouth, but Bailey had come back alive and fought him. Even with her hands cuffed behind her back and her ankles threatening to snap in her heels; she struggled against him. Her father cursed as she fought and stopped moving her to prepare to lift her into a fireman's carry. However, Bailey took advantage and stomped the stiletto of her opera pump right into the toe of her father's left shoe. He roared in her ear and released her arm, the other hand falling away from her mouth. Bailey didn't even let a heartbeat pass before she was moving down the hallway. Barefoot now that she had kicked one off and the other pump had stuck in her father's shoe. "Co'ta, help me!" She grabbed the Bond again and *yanked;* reeling her mate in like it was a lifeline.

There was a loud crash of breaking glass as the front office door was ripped from its hinges and shattered against the empty desk of the anteroom. Co'ta appeared at the end of the hallway. He was completely visible. Clad in the black of the exosuit, its blue threads pulsing faster than Bailey had ever seen. There was fury on Co'ta's face as he took in the fear in Bailey's eyes as she ran toward him, her hands behind her back. His mate's irises were blown wide open, the tang of her terror clawed up his nose, the thin trickle of blood on the side of her head. She sobbed as she focused on him and cleared the distance between them.

Ca'to curled an arm around his mate and propelled her over the broken glass toward the portal where the glass office door had once been. "To the roof, Ke'elsa." *Delight.*

Bailey did not stop moving; she did not even look back. She knew Ca'to could handle himself. The corridor seemed to lengthen as she ran its length, made even more difficult by her restrained wrists locked behind her back. She slammed into the wall next to the elevator with her shoulder and pivoted to push a call button by feel. A glance up at the display over the doors let her know the elevator had returned to the ground floor and was now moving upwards. Behind her, the sounds of fighting could be heard. Mostly the sounds of bodies hitting solid objects followed by Human male voices grunting in pain.

"C'mon, c'mon, c'mon..."

The elevator dinged behind her. "Ca'to! The elevator is here; hurry!" Bailey heard the doors open behind her and turned - just in time for her eyes to register Reverend Stakker's slimy smile and something hard slamming into the same temple that had been struck before. She was out before she hit the floor.

Ca'to dodged a wild punch by the largest of them and was the only one still putting up a fight. As a fist sailed past his face, he hooked the human male's arm with his right elbow and slammed his left fist into the male's right shoulder. Ca'to had eight inches with nearly sixty pounds of solid muscle on the Human, and his fist, with the knuckles reinforced by the same alloy as a cruiser's hull, struck like a sledgehammer, shattering the joint into splintered bone and pulverized sinew.

Bailey's father screamed in agony as his arm fell limply at his side. Ca'to caught the man's shirt and prepared to finish him when he felt the sudden spike of fear, and then the Bond went silent. Not severed, but as if his mate had been rendered unconscious. Ca'to dropped the Human male and turned for the anteroom.

He rounded the corner and arrived at the open portal just in time to see the elevator doors starting to close. Bailey's limp form was over the shoulder of yet another Human male, and there was Reverend Stakker. Bailey had been certain to make sure Ca'to knew the face that gave his

Ke'elsa nightmares. The doors were closed before he was even halfway down the corridor.

*****

"So basically, she's his mistress and I have to play nice to her because...because it's expected. All the high-profile males have taken one of us and a Cerulean female. Pretty sure the Regis would have been pressured into it as well if you hadn't won the lottery of all lotteries," Nicole finished as she took a very unladylike bite out of her second apple. The food replicators could produce Human fruit, but it wasn't the same as the fresh produce Michelle had flown in.

Michelle pursed her lips in displeasure. She'd feed Domaas his entrails if he even considered taking a *mistress*. It was a good thing she had already made her position clear about the subject. "And this...Zouma?" Nicole nodded as she chewed. "How is she with your son?"

Nicole had to finish chewing and swallowed, "She treats him like a favored nephew. She's actually sort of afraid of me, I think. On that count, anyway. But Zouma is respectful. She knows I don't want her there and tries very hard not to make her presence more complicated than it needs to be. She's lucky to have a safe place to live since she's technically in hospice care." Nicole took a final bite of her apple and tossed the core in the small trash can under the tea table between them that was a smartly hidden matter recycler. The island was carbon neutral and produced zero pollution. A point of pride for Michelle. "At this rate, she won't be around much longer any-"

Rachel exploded onto the veranda. Her arrival was so sudden Ka'al, always at a respectful distance, had loosened and began to draw his sword before his brain registered who it was. Michelle looked up at her friend in surprise. The pregnant woman was flushed and panting as if she'd just run from wherever she had been.

"Rachel? What's wrong?" Michelle had come to understand people only came running to her with pressing news.

Rachel had to bend over to brace her hands on her knees as she staggered and struggled to catch her breath. Ka'al was at her side, gently steadying her by the arm in two long strides. She *was* pregnant. She held up her tablet. "Bailey...." A swallow of air. "Stakker has Bailey! Attacked at the office...Ca'to gave chase...but was visible and lost them in traffic due to crowds! Family..." Another swallow of air followed by several deep breaths. "Your family is safe in their apartment and under guard."

A chill rippled over Nicolette's skin as a frosted voice spoke next to her. "Ka'al, I want a ship ready to launch in ten minutes. Notify the Regis." Nicole turned to look at the source of the spine-shivering words and was greeted by green irises crackling with tiny bolts of purple energy.

Domaas and P'alta caught up to Michelle and her Regent's Guard at a jog as they crossed the landing pad. The Regent was wearing her exosuit. A shuttle sat with its door open, and ramp extended as they approached. "Michelle!"

Michelle didn't even turn around, "No, Domaas, I am going! It is time for him to be dealt with. Rachel is tracking Bailey's tablet. We can take him out and rescue everyone."

Domaas was only one of two people on the island who could touch the Regent and not face the pointy end of a sword. Jamie and Nicolette, with Brylie, were watching over the other. P'alta stopped dead mid-step as the Regis caught his mate's arm, and she whirled angrily at him. She opened her mouth and then snapped it shut when she saw that he was already in his exosuit, his sword swapped into its matching scabbard hung at his hip. "This is not a debate, Heartbeat. This is fact; I cannot allow my Regent to go into a known hostile situation."

Michelle's lip curled as she wrenched her arm away and stepped into his space, "You would have me send others to-"

"Yes. We are trained military personnel. You are not. We are expendable members of the Cerulean Star Impirium Military. *You,* your Grace, are not." Domaas watched as his mate clenched her teeth, a muscle feathered on her jaw. Her eyes were faintly glowing, and her face set in a fierce mein. She was serious. So was he. Domaas met and held her glare with his calm gaze.

"I am getting on that ship, Domaas."

Domaas gritted his own teeth. Now was not the time, or place, for this argument. Although he was sure, she would want to finish it later. "Very well. But aboard the ship you remain, or my Regent remains on her island."

"Fine," Michelle said with a clenched jaw.

"I will have your promise, *your Grace.*"

Michelle bared her teeth. He would know if she tried to lie to him - she would *not* lie to him. A sigh exploded through her nostrils as she spun on the ball of her foot to continue to the shuttle, her cadre falling right back into step along with her. "Fine."

Chapter Twenty-Two

She had woken on the private plane Stakker owned. Bailey had been allowed to use the facilities before receiving a jab in her thigh and being sent back under. Wherever they were now, it was warm and smelled of pine trees. The single window was barred and set high in the wall, so Bailey could not even verify if they were in the mountains.

It did not matter.

The first thing Bailey did when her eyes opened was reach for the Bond and give a gentle tug. It took long moments but eventually, elation, love, and then blood-chilling fury came back to her. And then what she wanted to know most. Ca'to was coming; her Regent was coming. The thought of the level of violence about to come down around Reverend Stakker and his friends was enough to make Bailey smile, just enough.

The Regent had never displayed open violence in her presence. However, Bailey knew the look of a hardening gaze. The way Michelle shifted her body, or the change in her voice, indicated a raging internal beast was kept on a very short and tight leash.

She was sitting on the thin cot when she heard keys in the lock and the door swung open on silent hinges. What remained of her father stepped through. His face was swollen, with an obviously broken nose, two black eyes, and his right arm in a sling. What she could see of his shoulder was so purple it was nearly black. Ca'to had done that to him. Her mate had defended her, savagely. Bailey wisely chose to suppress the smile that almost bubbled free. "Hello, Kyle."

He ignored the barb, threw a pile of clothing at her feet with his good arm, then reached into the hallway and produced a simple pair of white tennis shoes. "You will change out of that slutty clothing and dress more appropriately. Including your underwear," he said with a sneer as he looked at her own shoulder. She followed his gaze and saw that her blouse had torn at some point and the thin lacey strap of her red bralette was showing.

Bailey looked down at the clothing and saw a simple white cotton sports bra and what could only be called granny panties. *Shame.* That's what Bailey saw in the pile of material. She was supposed to feel ashamed of her body and womanhood. "And if I refuse?"

Her father's answering stare was cold. He was angry he'd had his ass handed to him. "Then, as your father, I will be within my biblical rights to discipline you."

"Where's mom? Does she know you kidnapped me with the Reverend?"

Her father sneered, "Your mother has learned to obey her husband in all things. As you soon will."

Bailey shifted so that even though she was still sitting, she was looking down her nose at him, "I have a mate who is quite protective of me-" Her father took the two steps needed to cross the small room and backhanded Bailey with his one good arm.

He struck with enough force that she was knocked to the side and slammed her head into the wall. The same temple that had been struck twice before. Bailey blinked rapidly as stars danced in her vision and a headache roared to life. "God does not recognize such a foul thing. Get dressed, properly. *Obey.*" He turned and stepped out into the hallway, pulling the door closed behind him.

******

They were in a geosynchronous orbit. The Human ships lit off their targeting radars as soon as the *Quaalf-Sasnuar,* Star's Blessing, lifted off from its watery birth. Fighters from the aircraft carriers of five different nations scrambled off their respective decks. General Hamlin had called only to be told the Regent was not available. On the Regis' advice, the ship's colonel ordered a vertical ascent into space. None of the human aircraft could follow.

One hundred and sixty miles below them was a small city called Sho-Low, Arizona. Ten miles outside Sho-Low was a twenty-acre compound with various recently built-rough buildings. They had indeed been able to track Bailey's tablet. They had to wait until the location hadn't changed for a few hours before being sure that it would not change.

However, in that time, word had come from her father. The UN General Secretary, Mr. Jon Basatuti, had invited Michelle to speak before the General Assembly in five days. This was what her father had been working toward this for the last two months. This one thing went a long way to mollify Michelle's ire with Domaas tugging on the leash to prevent her from freefalling into danger.

"It is easy," Michelle said as her Regent's Guard stood at attention. "As we speak, Rachel is sending an update for the rings of your suits. Just let the auto-pilot guide you in."

"Your Grace?" Major Ka'al asked. Michelle turned her head to him, signaling that he had her full attention. "What are your rules of engagement?"

"Defend yourselves, defend any of the Hybrids, avoid killing if possible, no one gets left behind, and…" Her voice took on an icy chill. "I want Reverend Stakker."

"Alive? Your Grace?"

Michelle nodded, then spoke to make it official, "Yes. Although I will not be mad if he limps when he arrives." Her eyes shifted to the end of the line where Ca'to stood, the very image of a male who was using every ounce of willpower to remain calm and steady. A muscle feathering in his jaw and a fist clenching until the whites of his knuckles showed were the only indication that Bailey's mate had heard and registered what his Regent was saying. Ca'to had refused healing, instead claiming the battle scars he had earned.

"Understood, your Grace. We will not fail you." The conviction in Ka'al's voice was palpable. His Regent had sworn the returned Hybrids would be protected. That made it his oath as well.

"I know. Now go. You have a green light as soon as you are ready to depart."

Ka'al called his cadre to attention, and with a crisp salute, the four turned as one and exited the Solarium with Ka'al trailing. He had selected another five members from the ship's crew to fill out their numbers. Michelle had wanted to replace the lost guard, but on Domaas' council, she was leaving that to the Major. He was being incredibly thorough with the vetting. *Good.*

Michelle had already changed from her exosuit and was wearing black leggings with a cable knit sweater that exposed her crown shoulder. She was barefoot, which was just one more thing he enjoyed about his mate. Her being barefoot was her claiming the space she was in. Almost as if she needed to keep herself grounded. Just one more thing that Domaas wondered if she was even aware of. Surely those who interacted with the Regent noticed. When Michelle was being the *most* Regent-like, she appeared the most casual, at ease.

"You were right, Domaas."

Domaas was well aware his eyebrows were trying to climb into his hairline. She turned to face him. He had stood to her left but several feet behind her. The symbolism was as important as Michelle (and others) was coming to understand that she stood alone regarding her position. He supported her as his Regent and Mate; she knew this. But under-standing the symbolism of such things had taken a bit longer for her to grasp. She understood it now, though. The mission she'd just sent Major Ka'al on was as much a declaration as a rescue mission. "That is twice now," he answered.

"I am still amped up from earlier, gloat anymore, and I will kick your ass."

Domaas did not fight the slight smile. "A male could get used to being right. A third time and I shall be claiming my prize."

"Keep it up." Michelle closed the distance between them and took his hands in hers, interlacing their fingers. "I just sent males on a mission. I am sending you on a mission."

"Yes," Domaas said as he looked down and held her gaze.

"They might get hurt; you might die."

"Yes."

"I feel sick to my stomach. I should be going with-"

"*You* gave them a job, yes?"

"I did."

"Yes, *you* did. Our Regent has given us a mission, and she has given us the tools to complete that mission. This concept Rachel taught us; *Knighthood.*" The word was unfriendly to Domaas' English tongue. "Chivalry? Yes? To defend the weak, to defend our sovereign, to correct what is wrong. This is the mission you are sending us on. You said these *swords,*" He gripped the pommel of the one at his side. "Are tools for protecting those who cannot protect themselves. Be concerned for our safety, but do not rob us of the honor you have given with your trust, Heartbeat. We go because we know you would be right in front if we let you."

Michelle harrumphed and buried her face in his chest. "You are making a habit of this," she mumbled into the black fabric of his suit. Domaas merely cleared his throat. "Distract me. What should I say at the Assembly?"

Domaas was quiet long enough that Michelle stepped back to see if he planned to answer. He was smiling. "I have an idea."

"Oh?" Michelle was intrigued.

"Oh yes, I think my mate is finally rubbing off on me."

"This should be good. I do like to put on a show."

"Exactly. Walk me to the transport pad, and I will tell you."

*****

Pitor was smiling in the background. Rachel's face was blank. Michelle had a big dopey smile like she'd just fallen in love. It was a genius idea and just the thing she needed to not think about what her mate was currently doing. "Are you serious?" Rachel asked in disbelief.

Michelle nodded. "Frankly, I'm sort of surprised I didn't think of it sooner. It turns out he has a brain, after all. It was even his idea to have you run the logistics." Rachel understood Cerulean technology to a frightening degree. Much to the chagrin of some of the engineers in the fleet who were still learning Humans weren't as simple-minded as they had thought. T'rail would spend weeks trying to figure out how to do it. "Can it be done?"

"Well yeah, of course, it can. I will have to use every ship's manufacturing plant, but they can handle it. The other part is child's play." Michelle could already see the calculations running behind her friend's eyes.

"How long?"

"If you order the colonels and commanders to give me remote access, the manufacturing should be completed just in time for your address. The other is just setting up an IP address with an open directory. The servers here on the island have most of the Cerulean archives. I'm guessing nothing that could be used to jump-start an arms race?"

"Correct, no shield technology and no weapons."

Rachel nodded in thought as she tapped a finger to her lip. "What about the server farm where the US government keeps the stuff we gave them?"

Michelle shrugged as she asked, "Isn't it air-gapped?"

"Yeah, by Human technology standards." Rachel chuckled, "There's no such thing as a computer I can't reach with Cerulean tech, though." Pitor snorted behind Rachel in amusement. How many times had they thought they had managed to lock the *usurper* out of the *Rising Star's* computers?

*****

It was hot but not oppressively so. The clothing was a voluminous yellow ankle-length skirt and a simple white cotton blouse with half sleeves that stopped just above the elbow. Over that went a white ruffled pinafore. Bailey's father gave a cursory glance at her and grunted in approval before grasping her arm and pulling her out of the room into the hallway.

She was hauled past doors lining both walls, and Bailey was sure she heard quiet sniffling from one of them. "So I'm not the only one you've kidnapped recently?" Her father's grip on her arm suddenly tightened enough to hurt, and she winced.

"Be silent."

They entered a larger room that looked to be some sort of receiving space for when they brought new girls in. There were various bins and stacks of folded clothing in cubby boxes mounted to one wall and a simple kitchen on the other. There was a brunette elbow deep in the sink, cleaning dishes. She didn't look up when they entered. Her shoulders hunched slightly, and she seemed to shrink as if she desperately hoped her father wouldn't take note of the girl's presence. "Your death is a virtual guarantee," Bailey muttered in Cerulean. She was oddly okay with the prospect.

Her father whirled as his face colored with anger. "You will not speak the Devil's tongue in the Lord's presence!" He let go of her arm and wound up to strike her again but checked himself when she didn't flinch or cower.

"I will ensure your future husband knows not to spare the rod with you. You will learn humility and submissiveness." He pointed to a wicker basket overflowing with dirty clothing. "There is washing that needs to be done." He pointed out the open door toward a large yard covered in gravel. "There's a laundry area off to the right. The whole compound is fenced in and patrolled, so don't even think of trying to escape again."

While monotonous, the task was straightforward enough and quiet. Periodically young men would walk by, eyeing her like a side of beef but saying nothing. Multiple Hybrids were working on different tasks— everything from churning butter to tending chickens and menial cleaning. Once in a while, there would be a raised masculine voice, followed by a slap and exclamation of pain. Bailey couldn't help but grit her teeth every time she heard it. Her job had been to prevent herself and the others from ending up like this.

A clink of metal and crunching gravel intruded Bailey's thoughts. "You're the one they brought in last night? We heard them talking about you from the dormitory windows." A female voice, the first she had heard speak openly since waking up.

Bailey finished wringing out the pants and turned to hang them to dry along with the rest; she was about halfway through the basket. "Yeah. Bastards finally caught me," she answered quietly as she turned back to the tub and stopped.

She was vaguely familiar. Ebony skin as smooth as lacquer with a crown of curly hair, full lips, and dark almond-shaped eyes. She walked with a limp that wasn't from the chain connecting her ankles. Even with her dark skin, Bailey could see dark patches denoting serious physical abuse. "You've been fighting them," Bailey whispered.

Makayla grinned, then winced as if doing so caused her pain. She dropped her own basket of laundry on the gravel. "Stakker calls it 'corrective copulation'. Usually likes to cite some bible verse about why I should submit beforehand. I don't *let* them do anything willingly."

She caught the context of Makayla's meaning, and her stomach churned. "Why the chains?" Bailey pointed to Makayla's feet.

"Me and another kept trying to escape. They killed her, hoping to teach me a lesson, and because she tried to kill her *husband*. Stakker signed his death warrant with that one. Sean and I are both close with the Regent...what?"

Bailey's eyes had grown wide as she stared across the metal tub. "You are *Makayla*." A statement of fact uttered in Cerulean.

"Yeah..."

Bailey plunged a shirt into the tepid water so she was looking down, hoping her voice wouldn't carry as she continued in Cerulean, "I am the Returned Liaison. My job was to help prevent Hybrids from ending up in places like this. Michelle Et'Kuraul personally saved me when the Reverend almost caught me the second time and one other before, Jamie. They beat her pretty badly, too."

"Arya's nanny?" Makayla whispered hotly. "They tried to take Arya's nanny?"

"Shhhh..." Bailey cautioned. "Her Grace has been looking for you, Sean, everyone here, but evidently, Stakker was good at hiding this place.

Wait," Bailey looked up. "Sean is dead?" There was a crunch of boots on gravel, and Bailey went quiet. However, the boots didn't walk past this time but stopped behind her.

"Bailey." She righted and turned away from the washtub. The young man lewdly scanned her from head to toe before he said, "You are to meet your father and Reverend Stakker in the main lodge in ten minutes. Finish what you are doing here, and don't be late."

Bailey bobbed her head but remained silent. The young man turned and walked away, continuing his patrol. Turning back to the tub, she plunged her arms into the dirty water and said, "Stakker has my tablet. I can feel my mate's fury across the Bond." She looked up and fixed her eyes on the perfectly still Makayla. "They can track the tablets. I will bet my life she is already on her way here. Tell the others to be ready. I would not want to be anywhere near here when her Grace finds out about Sean."

Bailey pulled out the half-clean shirt and wrung it out before hanging it on the dry line. She risked a glance back to see a savage smile on Makayla's ebony face and was given a slight nod. Bailey snapped back around and quickly made her way toward the large building in the compound's center.

Chapter Twenty-Three

Two young men that appeared to be Bailey's age but shorter than her stood watch on the front porch as she arrived. Both cradled long barreled shotguns, which was an odd juxtaposition against their boyish features. "Reverend Stakker wanted to see me?"

"Wait here," the taller of the two said and turned to rap on the wooden door twice then opened it and stepped in. He came back a moment later to take Bailey's arm and lead her inside.

"I'm not a dog-"

"Learn your place. A good wife only speaks when she is spoken to."

Bailey looked at the boy as they entered the front room. She opened her mouth to retort when her father was suddenly in front of her once again. He grabbed her jaw with his good hand and forced her to look at him. "Young Reginald is correct. First Timothy 2:12…"

"I do not permit a woman to teach or to exercise authority over a man; rather, she is to remain quiet. Apt, but not quite. I feel Colossians 3:18 is more fitting to the purpose of our movement."

Bailey's father released her jaw and stepped aside in deference to the slimy used car salesman that approached from behind him. "Thank you, Reginald. I will call for you when we are done here." The young man left, and the door closed behind him with a soft click. Bailey didn't shift her eyes as she gazed at Reverend Stakker. A man who had no idea there was a target painted on his forehead. Oh, how the Regent had raged and cursed when Bailey had finished telling her story so long ago in that shuttle.

He gazed back at her, a lazy, self-satisfied grin plastered on his thin lips. "You have provided quite the adventure, young lady. I would have thought someone who escaped us twice would have avoided making a name for herself." Bailey didn't respond. "So, of course, once I realized you were helping so many others, lifting so many from the depths of despair, the Demons have left you all in - well, I just had to help you achieve the Lord's purpose-"

"Do you truly believe this crap you say? Or are you just splattering the walls with shit to see what sticks to the smooth brains you keep around?" Bailey's father raised his hand to strike her but stopped when Stakker deliberately cleared his throat.

"Now Bailey, that language is quite unbecoming for a future vessel of a soldier of Christ."

"I have a mate, and we have sex, *a lot*," she stressed as she glanced at her father. "Even then I'm on birth control that will last a year. *And,* even then, we can't get pregnant by Human males. I'm sure you realized this by now, judging by how others avoid even looking at your men."

Reverend Stakker wagged a finger as he turned and stepped toward a large desk sitting diagonally in the corner - and sitting square in the blotter was one of her tablets. "Something about you returned ones; words so full of bravado. So obstinate and in denial of the natural order of ways of the Lord. Did they teach you all to refuse the commandments of men, which hold sway over the inferiority of women as thy Lord commands?"

Bailey stepped toward the desk unbidden as Stakker slid into the expensive-looking leather chair behind it. "Quite the opposite, as a matter of fact, but you knew that."

He leaned back and looked up at her, "Quite right." He was silent for nearly a full minute as she stood there, staring at each other. "*You* are different than when we first met, however. What changed?"

"Got into a fight with my mate, and then we fucked ourselves silly. Getting laid has a way of changing a girl, I guess." The back of Bailey's head exploded in pain as her father cuffed her, and she stumbled forward. Kyle's hand was suddenly on the back of her neck and pushing down hard. Bailey tried to brace her hands on the desktop but missed, and she found her cheek pressed firmly into the wood.

"I examined the clothing you were wearing when you arrived here.

Such a foul, sinful choice of undergarments you wore. Women who wear such filthy things often get more than they bargain for."

Bailey stilled.

"I see that I have your attention," Stakker said quietly. "I already have a decent young man selected for you, Bailey. My son, as a matter of fact. By the Lord's commandment, we do not need your consent for marriage, just your father's. And I can have him in here to consummate that marriage before you can think of something else witty to say."

Bailey felt bile rise into her throat as her stomach churned. He *really* was threatening her with rape. Baily was not ignorant enough to not know men like this existed in the world, but she never would have thought the man who raised her would go along with something so vile. She braced her hands on the desk and pushed against her father, but his large hand squeezed her neck. The pain was nearly unbearable, and she relented after a brief effort. "What do you want?" She asked with her face still pressed into the wood.

"Your job was to find and keep track of every other returned girl you could, yes?" Bailey didn't answer as her heart stuttered in her chest. She knew what Stakker wanted. In that tablet were the known locations of nearly one thousand, three hundred Hybrids. Many of them were in very vulnerable situations.

"Yes," she answered slowly.

"You will help me recruit them. And in exchange," he continued before Bailey could respond. "You will not be forced to consummate your marriage with my son; for a year, at least. As you said, there would be no point in trying until then and sex for pleasure is a sinful act before the Lord. I need you to input the unlock code to your tablet."

Bailey closed her eyes as she breathed deeply. Her muscles were starting to strain in her precarious position but she tuned out the dull aches. *Her Grace would tell him to fuck off with a smile,* she thought to herself. *Her Grace would die before letting others get hurt...* Bailey reached for the Bond anchored to her chest, her heart, and gently caressed it. She sent her love and hopes, her dreams, and the way she felt when her mate called her *Ke'elsa...*

The response came back a lot faster than she expected; almost instantly. It hammered into her chest hard enough she gasped. The Bond filled and rippled with glowing light. The emotion of nights lost between the sheets and the dream of ten thousand sunrises with her in his arms. Ca'to was close, very close, and he wasn't alone.

Bailey smiled and shifted her head just enough to see Stakker sitting behind the desk. "No."

She watched Stakker's eyes crinkle as his mouth fought a frown. "Your father warned me that you would be obstinate."

"We're all obstinate. You said so yourself." Her father's grip on her neck tightened fractionally. She had no doubt he would be doing more if he had use of both arms...

Another pulse came from Ca'to. An image of her father dropping to his knees and clutching his shoulder filtered into her mind. Ca'to wanted to finish him. Bailey was momentarily surprised at the lack of concern she felt at that. "Ca'to says he's looking forward to finishing the fight, Dad." His grip on her neck tightened even more. Which was fine so long as it distracted them from what they wanted from her. *Hurry,* she sent back to Ca'to.

"I fell," her father growled.

Bailey surprised herself again as she laughed out loud. For someone in her precarious position, she had lost all fear of her situation. "If you say so, Kyle."

His grip turned rigid as he leaned over her, his breath hot on her face. "You will respect me! I am your father!"

"Enough, Brother Kyle. Stand her up." Bailey's father yanked her standing hard enough that she rocked to find her balance. His hand slid down to grasp her arm. "How do you know your father didn't hurt his arm falling?"

Bailey lifted her chin, "If he did *fall,* it was because my mate assisted him." Stakker's eyes narrowed in doubt. "You're right; Ca'to destroyed the joint." She turned to look at her father with a smile. "He hooked your right arm and taught you a lesson. I'm no doctor, but you'll be lucky ever to use that arm again, won't you?" Was mocking him the smartest move right now? Probably not, but Bailey was enjoying herself. Kyle's face turned red with rage.

A clearing of the throat brought her attention back to the used car salesman behind the desk. "It would seem you will need a more proper education before marrying my son."

"I won't be marrying your son and I won't be unlocking that tablet. You can beat me all you want. Rape me if it'll get your rocks off, but I suggest you get to it quickly."

Reverend Stakker leaned forward and rested his arms on the blotter to frame the tablet. "And why would that be, young lady?"

"Because my mate has come for me, and the others." She looked back to her father, "And he's going to finish what *you* started."

*****

Domaas could feel the energy coming off of Proctor Caltsua. So intensely it was surprising not to see the young male vibrating. And Domaas understood. "There." The male's arm shot out, pointing to a redhead being roughly escorted from what appeared to be the compound's main building.

Ca'to took a halting step forward, but Major Ka'al caught his arm. "Hold," he said.

They were cloaked but standing on a rise that gave them an elevated look into the compound. Surrounding them was a copse of young trees with reddish bark and green needles instead of leaves. Their smell was quite pleasant. Ka'al had chosen this location wisely, as even though the cloak was near perfect, the shade provided by the trees did not leave the prism-like warping of light. They were shadows within shadows. The cadre could not see each other either, but with their bubbles activated, each male was nothing more than a bluish outline with a name floating above it.

The second sentry appeared as he trod a well-worn path inside the fence line. Domaas recognized the item he carried as the same weapon the Marines had held in the Mizzi home. The man slung it by a strap over his shoulder and allowed it to swing freely as he walked - head down and not even scanning as he should have been. Ka'al grunted softly next to Domaas, and the Regis agreed. That male would have been assigned to a month of cistern duty for such an utter lack of discipline in the Imperial Military.

Ca'to intently tracked where his mate was being taken and who led her by the arm like some beast of burden. They crossed the center of the gravel yard and disappeared behind another building.

The sentry stopped just before he was out of sight and pressed the earpiece he was wearing deeper into his ear. He looked up and around as he unslung his weapon, and tension began radiating from his body.

"Something has alerted them," Ka'al said quietly. "Look." As he pointed, more Human men appeared from the various buildings. Most of them carried similar weapons as the sentry, who had since moved on. Others were seizing the Hybrids doing various chores and dragging them all to the large building to the left of the one they'd seen Bailey get dragged from.

"It was Bailey," Ca'to offered. "She told them I was here."

Domaas turned to look at the silhouette that was Proctor Caltsua. "Why would she do that? It has ruined the element of surprise."

Ca'to was silent for a moment. *Probably asking her across the Bond,* Domaas thought to himself. Then, "The leader, Stakker, threatened to have her raped if she did not comply with his wishes."

The temperature dropped perceptibly as every Cerulean male present felt ice pour into their veins. Rape was a personal assault to the very core of every Cerulean male. The very smell of the violation could send a male into a violent rage, especially if the female were a personal relation. Which, at least one of the Hybrids below them was.

"Her Grace ordered that no life be taken," Ka'al whispered to his superior officer, knowing they were both feeling the same thing.

"Her Grace would have already charged down this hill with the fury of *Gueth'Chopius* if she heard what Ca'to just said," Domaas said icily as he gripped the pommel of his sword. "Ka'al, this is your mission. I will follow your lead, but I am overriding her Grace's command. Every male who carries the stench dies here. I will accept her wrath, but it is doubtful she will have any."

"As you say, Regis." Ka'al turned as his cadre circled him, and he began to lay out his plans.

*****

"Does Mom know you've caught me?"

Kyle looked back from his place next to the window. Periodically, he would pull the curtain back a fraction of an inch, look out into the darkness and then let it drift closed. It had been three hours since Bailey had made her proclamation, and the compound remained in total lockdown. As darkness fell, large spotlights flicked on. Many parts of the compound were now bathed in bright light, but this also created many light wells that were pitch black. In his waistband was a black pistol; against the wall next to him leaned a double barrel shotgun which he had made a show of loading it with slug shot. *"Let's see if those fancy suits really are bullet-proof,"* he had said with a smug smile.

"Your mother has left the church," Kyle muttered into the silence.

Bailey blinked, then laughed, "Why? She get tired of being treated like garbage?" That he had lied was utterly unsurprising at this point.

"You," her father said as he stretched his neck and tried to roll his destroyed shoulder, earning a stab of pain for the effort. "She left because you rejected the Reverend's Teachings. After Los Angeles, she snuck away in the night, just like you. After getting you back and then losing you again so quickly, your mother wasn't ready to accept God's purpose for her without you." He studied Bailey's face for a moment, then said, "Your...*Mate*..." Like the word tasted vile in his mouth. "How did he get you to accept being a girl?"

"That's the funny part, Dad. I had already accepted it, but Ca'to made me enjoy it. Love it, actually." Her father visibly didn't like that. So Bailey pressed on. Her mate had gone quiet, but she could still sense him preparing, like a compressed coil waiting to burst free and release its energy. "We have something you could never understand-"

"Yes, your *Bond*. We have learned about it. Some connection the Demons have forced upon you all."

Bailed chuckled, "So much more than just a *connection*. And no, not all, Kyle. Some of us never want it and hope to find a Human mate. I liked my Proctor. He was kind and treated me well. As far as I knew, we were never coming back, so I decided to make the best of things. Before someone else tried to put me with someone I didn't like."

"That was not God's plan for you. It won't matter when *she* comes, though. The Reverend has made arrangements..." His eyes narrowed as he realized he had said too much. "Why are you trying to distract me?"

Bailey smiled as a bell started ringing outside. Simultaneously, she grabbed a tight hold of the Bond and poured every ounce of energy into it, lighting herself up like a supernova to Ca'to. Her father had been talking about the Regent. Bailey was sure of it.

Stealth.

Even on gravel, the special soles of the exosuits prevented any sound from giving them away. The sentries at the perimeter fence had quickly been dispatched. Only one had lost his head for his crimes. The others were unconscious and wrapped in a mesh of wires that would not be easy to cut through. Ca'to came upon two human males lurking in the shadows between two buildings, both wearing odd contraptions over their eyes. *Night Vision Gear;* his suit ring provided against the heads-up display.

Then the stench hit him. One of these two males was guilty of raping one...no, two of the Hybrids. Ca'to made no sound as he approached the male head-on. The Human was probably just starting to see the faint light distortion through his headgear when Ca'to's large hands gripped his head and snapped to the side. The sickening crunch of bone shattering caused the second man to jump back in shock as he watched his partner's head nearly twist off his body from some unknown force.

"What the-" Something small and silver hit him in the stomach, and there was a pop of sparks as an unseen mesh surrounded him and forced him to the ground. He was out before he could utter a second sound.

Ca'to moved on, following the Bond to the pulsing beacon of his mate.

Savagery.

Ka'al and two others nearly gagged as they approached what they knew to be the main building, where most of the Hybrids were kept. Six men stood out front, and each one of them carried the stench of multiple violations. On Ka'al's signal, the three of them deactivated their cloaks.

The men started yelling and giving orders as they brought their weapons up to bear when the three Specters materialized from the darkness. The pulsing blue threads gave a bowel-watering otherworldliness to the figures. Their drawn swords held their own light in the darkness like glimmering shafts of pale light. "Defend the weak," Ka'al murmured as they rushed the group. The gun muzzles ignited with fire, and Ka'al could feel the impact against his body, but it hurt no more than getting hit by a pebble. They could not use their swords effectively with the shields activated.

James was the first to strike with a mighty upward swing of his sword. The Human's gun fell away, along with his arms. The man barely had time to notice this as James turned the swing's momentum into a spin and cleaved the man's head from his shoulders. The Proctor was already swinging for the next man before the first's body had dropped. This was his Mopa's kin he was rescuing.

Vengeance.

Ka'al kicked the door hard enough that it came off the hinges as it swung inward with a great crash. Before him was a long space with simple beds lining the walls down both sides. There was an aisle that ran down the center, and standing a dark-skinned Hybrid was brandishing what looked like a broken table leg. Behind her were about twenty-five others cowering in fear. "Duck!" She bellowed.

Ka'al was moving before he fully registered the word and felt the air split a fraction of an inch from where his head had been. Spinning away, he brought his sword into a guard position to see a human recovering from his failed attack. He brandished a one-handed short blade that looked better for chopping than cutting. The man swung wildly, and Ka'al parried easily as the *stench* once again clawed up his nose. The man lunged again, swinging wide and leaving his body open for attack. Ka'al turned his shoulder into it for the blade to harmlessly scrape against his suit. Using his free hand, Ka'al reached and grasped the man's neck to pull him forward while simultaneously thrusting his sword through the man's belly with enough force to lift him from his feet.

Blood erupted from the man's mouth as he gasped in agony, and his own blade fell to the floor with a clatter. But that was brief as Ka'al pulled his blade free and removed the man's head with a flourish before he collapsed to the floor. Silence fell on this corner of the compound as the other two Ceruleans cautiously stepped into the barracks.

Ka'al snapped his sword to the side to clear it of blood and quickly sheathed it. Turning to the Hybrids, "We are here to rescue," he said in broken English.

"Name and rank!" The dark-skinned Hybrid demanded of him in Cerulean. She had lovely dark eyes.

"Major Ka'al, commander of her Grace's Regent's Guard. Michelle Et'Kuraul has sent us to bring you to safety." A masculine scream of horror and then sudden silence from somewhere outside punctuated his announcement.

Makayla dropped her makeshift club as she said, "Fucking took her long enough! We have wounded."

Ka'al produced an orb the size of a fist from the pouch strapped to his thigh. "This is a device made by Rachel. One holds it and link hands with others. Everyone will be transported away at once." He approached slowly and dropped the orb into Makayla's hand. His breathing hitched as he looked into her dark eyes again, and he swallowed before asking, "Are there others? Elsewhere?"

Makayla shook her head, "Except for the new girl, Bailey, no. They put us all in one place for easier defense." She took in the dark stains over the pulsing blue threads and the red splatter on his face. "It seemed not to have mattered."

Ka'al allowed a faint smile as he activated his translator. "Prepare to transport, lock on to the orb." He watched as the Hybrids quickly took hands and reached for those unable to get out of bed. Far too many of them showed signs of abuse. "By the way," Makayla jerked her head to the corpse by the door. "I was his favorite. Watching him die like that was more therapeutic than any amount of counseling."

Ka'al nodded as he stepped back. "Transport." The familiar shaft of blue light appeared, encompassing all of the Hybrids. Just as she vanished, Makayla winked.

Mercy.

She was warning him now. Wanting him to come but letting him know her father was waiting. Having long since dropped the cloak, Ca'to stepped over another unconscious body tightly wrapped in wire mesh and slowly strode down the hall. The door was unlatched, and he gently pushed it open. It swung easily, and his six-foot-seven-inch frame filled the doorway.

"Ke'esla," he whispered.

"Hello, Ca'to. I believe you have met my father, Kyle." Bailey gestured to the man standing next to her, holding a gun to her head.

"Are you well?" He asked.

"They like hitting me in the head, so I have a headache that just will not quit, but so much better now that you-"

"Enough of that foul language! That is Satan's tongue!" Ca'to's eyes shifted to the Human male holding a weapon to his mate's head. In another world, Ca'to would have shown proper respect to his mate's father, much as his Regis had. However...

"Release her," he said in accented English. "You go and live."

"Every one of you shall revere his mother and his father, and you shall keep my Sabbaths; do you know what that means, demon?" Ca'to canted his head in question. Only Bailey understood what the increasing speed of the pulsing blue threads meant. Ca'to was getting ready to move. "Of course not, you evil bastards have shown you care no for parents' rights. Robbing me of my son wasn't good enough? You must turn my... *daughter* against me? *I* am her father! *I* know what is best!"

"I see no father here, just dead male."

Kyle's face twisted in anger and pain as he dropped the pistol and raised the shotgun from behind his leg with his bad arm. Bailey was moving before Ca'to, and caught the barrel of the shotgun before her father could lift it level. The man roared in pain from the strain on his ruined shoulder and backhanded Bailey with his good hand.

Ca'to was on him before he had a chance to recover. First, knocking the shotgun from the man's hand and then wrapping his own fingers around Kyle's throat. Ca'to looked back to see his mate wiping blood from the corner of her mouth. "Ke'elsa?"

"Take his other arm," she hissed. Without missing a beat, Ca'to pivoted and drove the man back against the wall and wound up a fist; the reinforced knuckles of the exosuit provided a satisfying crunch as Ca'to drove his fist into Kyle's other shoulder. The man erupted into a wail of agony which was promptly cut off as Ca'to followed up with a punch to the gut. Kyle's breath caught in his throat as his diaphragm seized and he crumpled to the floor as Ca'to released him.

Reaching a hand toward Bailey, he felt her fingers lace into his and he led her out of the room. Bailey did not look back.

Diplomacy.

Domaas gently pushed the door open with the tips of his fingers, ignoring the muffled grunts from the two young men now secured in a web of mesh. Inside the office, the only illumination was a desk light with a green glass lampshade; behind that desk sat Reverend Stakker.

"Demon," he said as Domaas stepped deeper into the room. Stakker watched the alien's unnatural blue eyes shift about the room and then settle on him. Stakker's eyes shifted to the open door leading outside and back. "Where is she?"

Domaas canted his head, "Where is who?"

"Don't play coy with me, *Demon*. You know who."

Domaas looked about the room again as his sword hand came to rest on the pommel of his sheathed weapon. "Her Grace could not be bothered with small matters."

Stakker was like most Humans and not very good at hiding his thoughts or emotions. It was evident on his face he had been expecting Michelle to come. May have even been planning on it. "Did you kill my men?"

"Males who commit such filthy violations are no males that live." Domaas was unsure how he felt that Stakker did not carry the stench on him. While it would be easier to remove Stakker's head and be done with it, his Regent had ordered the Human captured alive. Domaas had already gone against one of her orders; he didn't want to go against another. He took several unearthly quiet steps to stand just before the broad oak desk. Stakker's eyes shifted to the door again as his hands fidgeted in his lap. Domaas could see it was a small black box and that the Human was frantically pressing a single red button. "No help comes for you."

The Human's throat bobbed as he swallowed. He was beginning to realize that himself. "Then be gone from this place, Demon. This is consecrated land." The bluster fell flat before the words even crossed the desk.

Domaas narrowed his eyes as he said, "You expect my Regent to come. Why?"

Stakker tossed the box on the desk blotter and stood in a weak attempt to show strength. He was still looking up at the much taller Cerulean. An alien who appeared mostly Human except for his brow ridges and solid sapphire eyes - could have been a stone statue when standing still. He gave Stakker nothing to feed off, and it was unnerving for a man who was used to reading people's emotions to get what he wanted. He opened his mouth to answer when running steps were heard on gravel, then stomping on the wooden porch through the open door.

Inhumanly fast to the Reverends' eyes, Domaas had spun and lowered on the balls of his feet. His sword was half drawn from its scabbard. Bailey managed to come to a dead stop as she raised her hands in surprise. "Regis!" Ca'to arrived on silent feet a moment later.

"Clear?" Domaas asked in Cerulean.

"Clear, sir. We passed the others on the way here. The Hybrids have already been transported away."

Domaas nodded and relaxed, sliding his sword back into place. He then noticed Bailey's eyes shifting about the office, looking for someone who wasn't there. "The Regent is not here. She did not come." Bailey instantly relaxed. "Why were you expecting her?"

Bailey pointed to the Reverend, who stood behind the desk and appeared wishing he was anywhere else. She said in English, "He had something planned. I almost got my dad to spill the beans, but they wanted her Grace here for a reason. I think I was the bait."

Domaas slowly turned to fix his gaze on the human, then looked down at the little black box on the desk. "It would seem so." Looking back up, he said in English, "You are to be guest of her Grace, the Regent of Cerul."

Stakker vigorously shook his head. "No, absolutely not. I will go nowhere with you Demons or be a guest of your whore-" Domaas sword was unsheathed, and its tip pressed into the soft flesh of Reverend Stakker's neck in a flash. The Reverend's spine locked up in surprise as his eyes grew as big as saucers.

"She did not request. She would not be upset if you were bleeding when you arrived. Speak ill of my Regent again, and you will lose your tongue." Domaas spoke in Cerulean, but Stakker understood just the same as his teeth clicked shut.

The Man in the Forgettable Suit was, in fact, not wearing a suit. Instead, he wore the same black Nomex jumpsuit as the squad of Navy Seals. Twelve men and women surrounded him, using the darkness of night to camouflage themselves. "Sir, they're exiting the office building with Stakker. Target one is nowhere in sight. I have a bead on target two," came the hushed whisper next to him. The sniper kept his eye firmly pressed to the night vision-enabled scope atop his rifle. Through Christopher's own night vision goggles, he could see a group descend the front steps and head toward the central open area of the compound. Stakker was being led by one of the soldiers, with Target Two leading the way and Bailey and her mate following. The others of the squad had already gathered in a small cluster, boldly standing in the wash of one of the bright security lights. "I have the shot, sir."

"No joy," 'Christopher' said into his radio. "Abort mission. Taking down Target Two will only make it harder to grab Target One, and she's not here." He stood up and stepped out of the bush hide he'd been sharing with the sniper as a spotter. The Seal team materialized out of the darkness around him.

"Sorry to have wasted your Saturday night," he said as a shuttle hummed out of the darkness and used its transporter to collect the Ceruleans. He watched the shaft of blue light appear, and the entire group was gone. Christopher was unsure if he'd seen Target Two turning his head in their direction just before he vanished. The shuttle lifted away into the darkness. Dead silence settled on the compound. "Anyone else curious to see the carnage? Was it me, or did those swords appear to almost glow in the dark?"

Chapter Twenty-Four

Michelle was standing in one of the cargo holds hastily transformed into a barracks. Beds had been clustered on one side with a partition separating the hold; on the other was a triage area for any needing medical care. Those needing surgery would be quickly triaged and taken to the medical bay for treatment. Healer Borlaas and the ship's Healer stood quietly with their assistants.

"Your Grace?" She turned to Sheel, who had one hand on the translator behind his ear. "They're about to be transported up."

"Thank you." Michelle stepped closer to the large white disc set into the cargo bay floor as the familiar shaft of blue light appeared, and a large group of Hybrids appeared. She didn't bother looking for Domaas, doubting he would return with the first group. No, he and Ka'al would want to get the Hybrids to safety first and as soon as possible. The Healers and their assistants rushed in, straight for those who appeared lying on the floor. Hovering orbs were used to lift them in a bath of yellow light, and they were quickly taken out of the hold. Others visibly wounded or showing signs of physical abuse were escorted beyond the partition.

"No!" Michelle's eyes snapped to the location of that voice. "Where is she?"

"Please come with us, you are hurt-"

"You think I do not know that, you idiot?"

"Hey Makayla," Michelle said quietly, as she approached from behind. The healer's eyes flared for a second then he gave a slight bow as Michelle waved him away. "They're just trying to help..." The words died on her lips as Makayla spun, and the clink of metal drew Michelle's eyes down to her friend's still shackled ankles. Her dark skin was raw, bruised, scabbed, and bloody, with a thin clear fluid leaking from some of the wounds. There was a roaring in her ears as Michelle turned in a slow circle and looked at the bruised faces and bodies that she now stood in the middle of. "The fuck..." Sheel, who had followed her, even cursed under his breath. Turning back to Makayla, "Where is Sean?" Michelle asked thickly as she felt her anger starting to build. "I don't see her."

"You don't know?" Makayla asked. Emerald green eyes flickering with tiny bolts of energy focused on her. "Fuck, of course, you don't know. Michelle, this isn't even the worst of it. Sean's dead. Reverend Stakker had her throat slit for attempting to kill the guy he married her to. Used that as a threat to keep the rest of us in line."

"Sheel?" The guard stepped forward and felt the hairs on his arms rise as he got closer to his Regent.

"Regent?"

Michelle almost pointed but stopped at extending her finger, less the coiled beast she kept at bay slipped loose. "Find something to get those off her, *RIGHT NOW!*" The vehemence in the Regent's voice was enough to silence the hold for a solid five seconds as if her voice had been focused and amplified.

Makayla watched as her friend clenched her fists so hard her arms shook, and she took several *deep* breaths. When the Regent opened her eyes again, the faint purplish glow faded. "For what it's worth," she offered quietly. "I never doubted you'd come for us. Everyone here," Makayla gestured around the once again bustling hold. "I told them all about you, and as soon as you found out where we were, you'd come running. Lo and behold, you send sword-wielding Cerulean shadows to remove the heads of every man that hurt us. So thanks, for that, I guess," she finished with a shrug.

Sheel picked that moment to return and quickly knelt at Makayla's feet. "Please hold still," he said in Cerulean. A small cylinder in his hand sprayed a fine mist on one shackle and the other. The metal glowed green and then disintegrated into piles of rust-colored dust. Makayla went to step away, but Sheel said, "Wait." He produced a second canister and sprayed its mist onto her blistered and bloody ankles.

The skin took on a faint sheen as the patient sighed blissfully, "Oh, that is nice…"

"It is only temporary until the healers get to you. Try not to walk too much."

"Understood, Proctor," Makayla quipped.

Sheel stiffened as he rose and silently returned to his place behind Michelle. Makayla saw the deference he paid to Michelle and arched an eyebrow in question. "I have my own group of guards. *Lieutenant* Sheel is one of them. The others were the ones who rescued you."

"Why would you need guards? Aren't you in charge of everything now?"

Michelle nodded as a healer assistant approached slowly, the same Makayla had chased away before. "It seems we both have a lot to catch up on. Please let this healer see to your injuries. I need to tend to…other things." Speaking to the healer, "Please see to it that they all get fresh clothing and something hot to eat."

The healer touched his fist to his chest, unaware of how casual his Regent was about such things. "It will be done, your Grace."

Looking back to Makayla, "I'll have Sheel find you in the morning, okay?"

"Sure, I'm just looking forward to a comfortable bed and sleep without being woken in the middle of the night." Makayla allowed herself to be led away, walking stiffly to not stress the coating on her ankles.

Michelle watched her go and then let her eyes drift over the group of Hybrids she was surrounded by. Sean was dead for defending herself, *for killing her would-be master.* The haunted look in many of their eyes told a tale Michelle was struggling to comprehend. However, she could not ignore the way many showed fear of the male healer assistants that were trying to help them.

Makayla had said, *removing heads.* That wasn't a verbal slip. Makayla did not mince her words. "Sheel?"

"Your Grace?" His voice was strained, and she turned to look at him and saw it plain as day on his face. He heard the question before she could ask it. "We can smell it, your Grace. All Cerulean males can." Sheel's hand was gripping the hilt of his sword tightly. "The Regis is arriving with your guest as we speak. Perhaps it would be best to discuss this with him." *Not here,* he didn't say.

"Lead the way then."

Deep down, the beast rumbled.

Domaas felt her coming just as the doors opened and turned to face her as Ka'al tightened his grip on Stakker's shoulder. "*You* will kneel." The Human obediently lowered under the force being applied.

"Domaas..." She stopped some distance away as her eyes took in the crimson blood splattered across their faces and exosuits.

"We are whole, Heartbeat."

"Why are you covered in blood?" The cadre all kept silent as their faces remained grim.

Domaas straightened his spine as he looked his Regent in the eyes. "Counter to your orders, Regent, lives were taken."

"Why?" She had a very strong suspicion but wanted to hear him, *someone,* say it out loud.

"Because they were raping the Hybrids, your Grace," Bailey said as she stepped forward. Her hand remained tightly held in Ca'to's. "Corrective discipline, he called it," Bailey pointed to the kneeling Stakker. He looked around with wide, frightened eyes as they spoke in Cerulean, and Bailey had just pointed to him. "He threatened to have me raped if I did not unlock my tablet and give him the information of the Hybrids I was helping."

"Every Cerulean male can smell the violation, Regent." Michelle glanced back at Sheel. Domaas continued, "It is part of the...*curse.* There is no reason to have let those men draw breath after committing such heinous acts."

Michelle was silent as she recalled back to Domaas' initial courtship of her. She had been quite combative then and demanded to know if the Ceruleans raped the Hybrids to get them pregnant. Domaas' reaction to that accusation had been barely contained anger. He had been offended that she had even asked the question.

"If there is to be discipline, Heartbeat, it must fall on me. I countered your orders."

Michelle took in all of their faces. The simmering remains of fury she had never seen before and a grim satisfaction. They had taken lives for something that offended the males deep in their primal core. Depending on whom you asked, rape could be considered a more vile crime than murder on Earth. But serial rapes, rape as punishment, and a matter of course of the day...

No. Michelle would not be upset if Domaas had countered her orders. Rape *was* vile.

Defend the weak.

"There is something else," Domaas said. "I believe it was a trap. For you." He fished in the pouch strapped to his thigh and stepped to hand her the small black box with the button. "He was pushing this when I arrived. And when we were leaving, our suits detected a targeted beam of light. I believe you call them laser scopes."

Michelle's eyes slewed over to the kneeling Stakker, who began shifting as he understood he was now the focus of attention. He wasn't safe on terra firma anymore, with his acolytes around him to perform for. Or with the distant security of some type of law enforcement. Like Jonah, he was now in the belly of the beast. "Was it a trap?" It took a long second before he realized she had spoken to him in English.

"Was what a trap?" He dared to ask, playing dumb. His way with words had served him well, but first, he needed to understand the dynamics at play.

Michelle gestured, and he was suddenly hauled to his feet. "So what are you not going to do," she said as she slowly approached him. "Is play dumb with me, Reverend. You have been accused of using rape as a punishment. You have kidnapped those who were under my protection. You have beaten and shackled those who would not bend to your will. You have *killed* one of my friends." Stakker looked down when he felt the hair on his arms rise as she neared.

"Your demons slaughtered my Brothers in Christ," he said loudly. The iron he attempted to add to his voice did not appear, making him sound like a frightened child.

Michelle smiled as she stepped closer. It was wolfish, unnerving, and predatory. "Yes," she hissed. "Removed their heads clean from their shoulders if I understand correctly. For *rape*."

"They lie! They've even fooled you into thinking you're one of them!"

"You have no audience here, Reverend. Just me. Ka'al, if he lies again, hurt him." Stakker winced and groaned in pain as Ka'al tightened the grip on his shoulder. "I ask again, did you have a trap set for me?"

Michelle watched his eyes dance about the shuttle bay once more before he swallowed and said, "Yes."

"So you intentionally kidnapped Bailey to draw me out? Was I not clear that we shouldn't cross paths again?"

Stakker felt a faint pulse of static energy pass over him. He noticed all but the Specter holding him take several steps back from Michelle.

"They were supposed to sweep in before your Demons did too much damage. He said there was a way to hack into your tablets if Bailey didn't comply. So he'd give me the information needed if I helped them capture you."

A deep, dangerous growl emanated from Domaas' chest.

"Who," Michelle asked, eyes taking on their faint glow.

"I... don't-" Stakker winced as his knees buckled in pain. Ka'al's fingers were pressing deep into the soft tissue of his clavicle. "I swear! He never gave me a name! He said he worked for the government!"

Ka'al cursed under his breath, and Michelle's eyes shifted to him. "Apologies, your Grace. Did not April say the same thing about the one who returned her to the fleet? Perhaps it is the same male?" Michelle's eyes lost focus as she tried to recall that conversation with April before exiling her and her mate.

"Yes, she did. And I think I've seen him." Michelle looked back to the Reverend. "Brown hair and glasses?"

Stakker nodded quickly, "Yes! And he was wearing a plain suit! It was gray...I think!"

She nodded and turned to pace in a circle, obviously in deep thought. Stakker watched her nervously while the Specters could have been statues; they stood so still. They had made a point of letting him see the remains of his men. The movies had it wrong; there was nothing clean about having one's head removed. It was a bloody affair, and John Stakker was certain he'd never get the look of a silent scream of agony out of his nightmares. Even the men restrained in some steel-stranded mesh looked to be in their special place of hell. Many had lain helplessly in bloody puddles of the dead man next to them.

Michelle tightly clenched her fists at her sides and shook her arms. Stakker blinked to check his vision as he thought he'd seen tiny bolts of electricity fall from her knuckles. When she turned back to him with a grin that made him think of an apex predator, he felt his stomach drop.

Standing a few yards away now, she held up her right hand. Tiny bolts of purple lightning sparked and crackled between her spread fingers as she looked at him. When she spoke, her voice came from a frigid place and did not sound of this world. "My first impulse is to incinerate you where you stand and make the universe a better place. You are an abomination to religion and the antithesis of Christ's teachings. You have taken advantage of parents in their deepest moments of weakness. You have abused and twisted a belief meant to bring joy and happiness into people's lives for some perverted ends that I cannot even begin to fathom. Nor do I even want to try. I believe you have caused immeasurable suffering and pain, and you do not deserve to live."

Michelle continued as a single bolt of lightning flipped between her spread fingers, like a poker chip, "Fortunately for you, I am not now, nor ever will be, in the habit of executing anyone. So I have decided the next best thing. Eye for an eye, I think the Old Testament says." She watched his brow furrow, and then his eyes grew big in realization. "Yes, that would be a just punishment for someone like you, but that's exactly why it won't happen. Despite what you may think, there is nothing shameful *or weak* about being a woman." Michelle enjoyed the confusion that washed over his face. Of course, a man like him would think being turned into a female would be the worst thing possible. So now he had to be wondering; what could be worse?

Michelle looked at Domaas and spoke in Cerulean, "Domaas, I am guessing there is some sort of labor camp or prison in the Impire?"

Domaas grunted, then said, "Several, Heartbeat, if I may suggest the penal colony at *Hase'Fernte* -the Cerulean version of what Humans would call 'Hell'. It is an asteroid that orbits a star. No one ever leaves; prisoners and provisions are delivered via one-way pods."

"How bad is it?"

Domaas turned his gaze on Stakker and said deadpan in English, "Prisoners do not survive long on the surface. The thin atmosphere and its closeness to stars make the interior very hot. Food and water are used to ensure obedience."

"So, no escaping, then?" Michelle asked, holding eye contact with Stakker.

"Impossible."

"What are the chances for a Human male to survive in a place like that?"

"Not promising unless your Grace orders him kept alive, no matter what."

"Good. Send a message to Rachel. I want his very existence erased, including the birth certificate. No trace of this piece of shit ever living." Michelle let her wolfish grin show. "And yes, I want him kept alive. I want him to die of very old age in *Hell*."

"Y-you can't do that!" Stakker bleated. "I'm an American citizen! I have the right to a trial! I have done nothing you accused me of. I raped no one, I killed no one!"

"Turn you over to the police? I don't think so. Even if you were found guilty, you'd just spend the next twenty years in a comfy prison. That isn't justice for what was done at your behest. Besides, you did it to the citizens of *my Impire!*" Michelle angrily pointed at the floor for emphasis, and a bolt of purple energy slammed into the deck plating before crackling and reaching toward where Ka'al held Stakker.

Ka'al jerked him back several feet, and it was just enough to dodge the bolt as it fizzled out a few yards past them. It had been an accident, but Michelle took grim satisfaction as she saw wetness form in the crotch of the Reverend's trousers and run down his leg. The room was stone silent as she closed her eyes and took several deep, shuddering breaths.

"Domaas?" she asked without opening her eyes.

"Yes, Heartbeat?"

"This ship has stasis pods, yes?"

"No, but one can be built."

She opened her eyes to see Stakker still holding the look of absolute shock and fear at her display of power, standing in a puddle of his own making. "Please see to it that they start on it tonight. I want him in it before we return to the island. I want the next thing he sees to be the inside of that asteroid."

"At once, Regent."

"Enjoy the time you have until then, Reverend. This is the last bit of cool air you'll ever breathe. Know that once I walk out of this room, I will never think of you again."

*****

Jamie could not sleep. Even though she knew everyone was safe back on the ship, she felt too energized for her eyes to remain closed for long. Which was telling that there truly was something on her mind, a pressing sense of urgency that would not go away. Arya with Brylie was like trying to herd cats, and that was with Nicole trying to keep her son in order. Jamie should have been dead-tired, and yet...

With a toss back of her thin blanket, Jamie stood from her bed and began to dress, which always took longer than most people would have thought. The night's crescent moon had set hours before and it was near total darkness outside her window. The paths across the island were lit using motion-activated dimmers so as not to waste energy, but also provide illumination as needed. Jamie looked toward the gymnasium, two hundred-fifty yards away, and only saw the barely illuminated path leading up to it.

She knew there were sentries keeping night watch, but they would be cloaked in the jungle or out on the beaches. Jamie wasn't concerned with being seen walking to the gym with Arya, so long as no one saw what she was planning on doing.

She left her room and silently walked down the hall to Arya's, where a bog-standard Proctor stood at relaxed attention next to the door. "Miss Jamie? Is there an issue?"

Jamie couldn't place his name but he was familiar to her. Unlike Proctor Co'in who played spy; this one kept his eyes squarely on her face and never attempted to flirt. Arya trusted him, and coming from a toddler who could read minds and force project virtual reality that was high praise indeed. "No, just taking Arya down to the gym," Jamie answered as she pressed her hand to the black glass panel next to the door. Only hers, Michelle's and Domaas' palm prints could trigger the lock. That the Proctor didn't question the odd hour for calisthenics spoke well for his ability to keep his thoughts to himself. Jamie would know soon enough if he decided it was a good idea to gossip about her and Arya's comings and goings.

Once inside, she found her ward already sitting up in bed, still wearing her footie pajamas but having squeezed sandals onto her feet. The child's emerald eyes seemed to glitter in the dark room. Jamie sighed, "Your words, Arya. You could have just told me you wanted to practice tonight." There was a pause as Arya responded silently. She hopped down from her bed and took Jamie's hand. "I know, your Popa is worried about it too. But that's why we practice, yes?" Another pause, and then, "That's right. We practice now, so we get it right when it matters."

Chapter Twenty-Five

Makayla eyed the Nordic blonde sitting across the table from her. Took in the blue eyes, narrow nose, and the signs of a healing sunburn. "Tough luck," she said.

Nicole shrugged as she finished chewing, "Eh, it could have been worse. My mate got to enjoy seeing me in a bikini." P'alta choked on the fruit he'd been about to swallow. Nicole grinned at that before saying, "Besides, I could have ended up being Regent." P'alta coughed again into his glass of water as he tried to rinse the fruit down.

"Careful, Nicole," Michelle murmured as she watched the Regis try to hide his smirk. "I may abdicate and nominate you to take over." Domaas was suddenly choking his way into a coughing fit.

"So," Makayla said, leaning with her elbows on the table and leveling her eyes at Nicole. "Any good stories to tell about our Regent? From the *before times*?"

Nicole opened her mouth to answer, but Michelle cut her off, "I will have P'alta assigned to an orbital ball-bearing factory if you utter one word. If the Ceruleans don't have one of those, I'll have them build one just for him."

Nicole chuckled and shrugged her shoulders, "Worry not your Grace," she said formally. "I have not forgotten our pact of mutually assured destruction."

Michelle took another bite of her toast and smiled as she chewed. Her friendship with Nicole went back to childhood. There were more stories of shame, defeat, success, and triumph than could be counted between the two of them. Their fathers had even trained them together. Nicole had been a solid fighter and a great marksman. So even though both of them were now mated mothers, one a sovereign, and with near certainty, they were to be in-laws; some stories were just better left in the past, fond memories or not.

A quiet morning enjoying breakfast with friends and family had become quite a rare thing. For this morning, she had even had Ka'al station one of his cadres at the end of the hallway so there would be no running surprise entrances. It was all pleasant enough, but this would also be a meeting. Not a full council or anything, but some things needed to be discussed. All gathered around the breakfast table was as good a time as any.

"Makayla?"

The returned and trademarked smirk dropped as she asked warily, "Yes?" It had only been a few days, but Rachel had already availed her of Michelle's penchant for sandbagging.

"You have a choice. Well, I'm offering you one."

"Heartbeat..."

Michelle didn't even glance at Domaas as she ignored him, "As you know, I'll be leaving for Cerul soon with most of the fleet. You can either come with us or stay here."

"I'll be staying here," she answered without any thought. "If it's all the same. My mothers did not know what Reverend Stakker was doing and want me home. He had convinced them it was a camp to help Hybrids *reintegrate* into society or some nonsense." Makayla thought that was the end of it until she saw the sly smile spread across Michelle's lips.

The Regent struck before anyone had a chance to stop her. "That's perfect. Makayla Tyler, I name you Liason for the Returned of the West Coast. You'll work with Bailey Caltsua and my mother to keep all the at-risk returned Hybrids out of dire straits. Do you accept?"

Makayla's eyes flashed with interest. "How's the pay?"

"*Very* nice," Bailey quipped from the other end of the table. "It is almost obscene. Our Regent is not stingy with her money."

"Well...I accept. With one caveat, though?"

Michelle arched an eyebrow in surprise as the others the Regent had sandbagged looked at each other. *You can do that?* They all seemed to ask each other. "Oh?"

"Yeah, so I know a lot has happened since the ship and all, but did you forget that we were all unlocked by the former Regent?"

Michelle blinked; she had forgotten. "But that was so long ago. I asked Healer Borlaas about it, and he said the *Phage* resets if the *Quoy* isn't completed."

"Yeah," Makayla said. "Why do you think Sean, of all people, was so violent? They tried to time her forced marriage to it; Stakker was hoping that would be the magic pill to make us compliant." There was a quiet beat of reflection then Makayla pushed on. "Either way, I felt it click on again the night you had us rescued."

"Who?" Domaas asked.

Makayla smiled and pointed to the brown-haired Cerulean with chocolate eyes. He was standing perfectly still. Looking resplendent in his uniform, with one hand braced on the pommel of his sword and the other tucked behind his back. Michelle turned in her seat, as Makayla was pointing behind her, to see Major Deron Ka'al with his eyes wide open in surprise. "Ka'al?"

"He was the first one through the door and dispatched my rapist in a way that could rival any love letter or bouquet of roses." Makayla's frankness about her experience would take some adjustment. However, no one in the room would tell her to dial it down. Everyone deals with trauma differently.

"Well..." Michelle turned back to look at her mate, who shrugged his shoulders and nodded; a silent conversation carried across the Bond. "Major?" Ka'al stepped until he was inside his Regent's line of sight. "What say you?"

The male's mouth opened and closed several times before he answered. "Your Grace..."

"You will not be abandoning me or your position, Major. You will hold your rank. Recent history has taught me that those I leave behind *must* be protected. Bailey and my family will have their own security detail; Makayla will have the same. Who better to lead that detail than her own mate? We have seen the benefit of that with Bailey and Ca'to." The redhead at the end of the table squeezed her mate's hand. She rarely let go of it.

Ka'al swallowed on a suddenly dry throat. Everyone in the dining room was looking at him. Especially Makayla with her dark, almond-shaped eyes. They were deep, soulful pools of calculating intelligence. Any male would be a fool not to notice.

He had been too full of adrenaline to notice the *click* at the time, but he had noticed something different. Now it made sense - but to leave the service of her Grace? After she had up jumped his rank and social status, thus ensuring security and comfort for his family on Cerul and any future children he may have. But first, he would need a mate to have those children with.

"Well?" The Regent prompted.

Ka'al straightened his back. "If you will have me, then I would be honored to complete the *Quoy* with you, Makayla." Silently, she stood and approached Major Ka'al. He held her gaze as she reached and gently tapped his cheek with the palm of her hand. Ka'al's eyes flashed in under-standing as he said with a smile, "I submit to you, Makayla Ka'al, do with me as you wish."

"Later." Makayla flashed a grin as she looked at Domaas, "See, that was so much easier than keeping it a secret and then him getting his ass kicked, was it not?"

Domaas made a show of straightening his tunic and looking displeased as the rest of the table snickered. Michelle's whooping of his ass on that night had reached legendary status. It helped that even to this day, Regis Et'Kuraul wore his bruises proudly, and it was not uncommon to see the Regent with a slight limp the morning after they were known to spar.

"Great," Michelle said, bringing the table back to focus. She rather enjoyed that when she spoke, everyone else went silent. To Makayla, "Get with Rachel, and she will get you guys all set up, okay? Oh, and Major?"

"Your Grace?"

"Please congratulate Sheel on his promotion to Major and help him find two replacements before we leave?"

"It will be done."

Rachel, for her part, was laid up in bed. A stack of pillows propped up her back while a wedge pillow supported her knees. Mate's orders. Rachel had stumbled on a set of steps the day prior and nearly fallen. A Cerulean Proctor heading the opposite way had just managed to catch her. Of course, he had reported it to Pitor, mostly because he'd had physical contact with Pitor's pregnant mate.

So, of course, Pitor had demanded an examination by the resident healer on the island, who had insisted on a day's bed rest. Rachel had been working herself ragged getting the food replicators built and prepared for delivery, along with coordinating all the shuttles and crew needed to deliver and set them up.

Pitor had been insistent, and Rachel had already discovered it was hard to tell him no. There was something nice about how protective he could be over her, although she'd swallow acid before ever admitting that out loud. But after being alone and in a constant defensive posture for so long, it was...pleasant. And that was about as far as she was willing to think about it.

So instead, she lay in bed, a tray of half-eaten food on the side table and multiple tablets stacked against her lifted legs. The baby promised to be large but wasn't so big yet to cause difficulties. Pitor reclined next to her. Pillows propped him up as he perused the *internet,* trying not to mother-hen her too much.

"I do not understand, Flower."

"Understand what?" Rachel asked without looking up from her current tablet.

"Your species has barely managed to stave off environmental collapse for another two centuries at best. So many of your native species have been erased, yet they do nothing to stop it? Humans are such an intelligent species, but yet so many ignore the advice of your scientists. Why?"

Rachel harrumphed to herself as she switched to a different tablet. Each replicator had to be programmed to draw its base materials from a local source. Aboard the *Rising Star* and other ships there were tanks of matter and recyclers, but in this case, she'd have to be quite selective. The wrong location could turn a forest into a desert or aquafers to run dry. As it was, most were either to be located near garbage dumps or, even better, be given access to sewage treatment plants. The Cerulean servers had been easy enough to bring online and the purchase of multiple gateways to prevent any potential overloading from the guaranteed load soon to be placed on them. A large payment to one of the global backbone ISPs, and all that was needed was for Michelle to say when.

"Money," she answered. "Money is the driving force for everything on Earth. Those that have much of it want more of it. Often to the detriment of other Humans and definitely to the detriment of the planet. We had a decades-long *cold war* because of two different ideologies concerning wealth and its means of production."

"Oh...yes." Pitor thought for a moment then said, "Cerul uses currency for the exchange of goods but not to the detriment of our environment. Certainly not enough to go to war over it."

Rachel shrugged, and the collar of her oversized t-shirt dropped over her shoulder. "Well, on Earth, it is often thought what good is a forest if you cannot make money from it? You also have matter replicators that can create anything needed. That makes a huge difference." She turned to look at him, "There are no poor or hungry Ceruleans, correct?"

"Not in the entire Impirium. How could some be allowed to go without when we have so much?"

Rachel smiled and tapped the side of his head. "That right there is what we Humans have yet to figure out. It'll be interesting to see how these replicators affect that. Between those and the ability to build more, that promises to disrupt the pursuit of money and people needing it just to survive. Factor in medical technology and that fancy energy source you guys use- Hell, nanobots alone... Things are about to go through a seismic shift on this planet."

"Do you think her Grace is aware of that?"

Rachel chuckled, "Oh yes. That brain of hers always seems to be crunching numbers. She knows quite well what she's doing. If she just let the United States keep all that data, the likelihood of them sharing before taking full advantage is next to zero. *That* will start wars. This way, the entire planet is on the same start line. Some countries may have difficulty taking advantage of the new technology, but…" An icon on the tablet near her hip started flashing. A message had just been received via one of the comms stations her Grace had gifted.

Curious, Rachel tapped it, and the message popped up in holographic view. Pitor looked to see what had drawn her attention and leaned into his mate to read it as well. Pitor did not need the Bond as he felt his mate suddenly tense next to him. His English wasn't excellent yet, but he had been making a point to learn when he could. So far, he had found that reading English went a long way to helping him understand the weird syntax the language used-

Pitor was the one who cursed out loud as he got to the last line of the short message. "Am I understanding what this message says, *Flower?*" It *was* in English, but written in a very clipped and precise language, leaving no room for doubt. Pitor could not recall reading something so…terse when it came to his mate's first language.

"Yes," Rachel hissed. "I need to tell her."

Michelle heard him enter and glanced up to see Lieutenant Bilson quickly make his way around to where Domaas sat at her left. He bent to Domaas' far ear and whispered something that made the Regis' hand go still. He looked at the Regent and then said to T'Rail, "Get the Regent's father online as soon as possible and have Rachel and Pitor conference in." To the room, "I must ask that everyone, but the Regent's Council and Colonel Bil'tun take their leave."

Makayla looked around in surprise as Bailey's mate, Ca'to, and Nicole promptly stood and turned to leave without protest. "What's going on?" She asked as she stood, but Domaas gestured her back down.

"You have just been appointed as a member of her Grace's Council, you are to stay." Makayla plopped back down and looked at Michelle. Her Grace had her head back and was looking at the ceiling with the most annoyed expression on her face.

She must have felt Makayla's gaze because the Regent said in English,

"God, I fucking hate this part. It was such a pleasant morning." Bringing her eyes back to neutral, she watched a squad of stewards quietly enter and clear the table of its platters and left behind dishes. "What is it, now?" She asked the room. The mood had shifted in a matter of seconds and left Makayla leaning back in her chair to absorb what was happening in silence.

"If I may, your Grace?" Lieutenant Bilson laid his tablet flat on the cleared table and activated the holographic view. He waited until stewards had left, then tapped the glowing icon. "This was sent directly to Rachel from General Hamlin." An image of a letter on beige paper appeared. T'Rail tapped the image twice and pushed it to one of the two large view screens that hung on the far wall. The same message appeared there for everyone else to read.

Roger Mizzi appeared in a split screen with Pitor and Rachel on the second screen. Without being prompted, T'Rail pushed the message to them as well. Roger's eyes scanned the text while the other two sat quietly, waiting for the Regent to read and absorb the message. Makayla wasn't sure if anyone else noticed, but she watched Michelle's hands grip the armrests of her chair until the wood creaked. Curious, she turned to read the message.

May Sixteenth, 2029
500 hrs PST
From The Office of The Secretary of State
Orville P. Sturgis

To: Michelle Mizzi-Et'Kuraul, Regent of The Cerulean Star Impirium

Members of your military have conducted an unauthorized action inside the sovereign territory of the United States of America. This un-sanctioned action resulted in the massacre of American citizens and the abduction of one Reverend James J. Stakker. The United States does not take kindly to this action and demands the immediate repatriation of the aforementioned person.

In addition, we assert the sovereignty of all land and airspace over the continental United States and its territories. Permission of transit by any and all craft of off-world origin is hereby revoked indefinitely, effective upon receipt of this message. Violation of this order will be considered an act of war.

The Regent is reminded that many of the returned victims retain their United States citizenship and are thus subject to the laws and regulations in their current country of residence. If suspected of clandestine activity, such persons will be arrested according to our laws.

Regards,
Orville P. Sturgis
Secretary of State, United States of America

Makayla had to drag her eyes away from the wall screen and took in the eerie stillness of the room. It was as if the air had been sucked out of the space, and everyone was afraid to exhale. Long seconds ticked by, and Makayla spoke first, not knowing she was breaking protocol, "Did they really just say *or else?*"

"Yes. They. Did." Michelle turned to look at Colonel Bil'tun, her head moving slowly as if the muscles in her neck were too tense to move. "Contact the *Regent's Mercy.* I want them parked just outside of Earth's gravity well yesterday."

*****

The President looked up from her tablet at Christopher, who stood a respectful distance away, with a Secret Service agent standing between them. "Do you know my reaction if I received a letter like this from China? Or Russia? Or any number of other countries?"

Christopher smiled, "The same I am hoping for from Miss. Mizzi. We used the wrong bait before. Of course, the Ceruleans would not let their queen go on a search and rescue mission. However, we just told her she couldn't go to New York and threatened those she considers under her protection. Now our bait is her own hubris."

"Do you really think she'll return this Stakker fellow?"

Christopher waved his hand in dismissal. "No, Madam President. She has done us a favor with that one."

The President looked down at her tablet again and sighed tensely, "If this goes wrong..."

"It won't."

Chapter Twenty-Six

The ship was floating two hundred miles outside of Pearl Harbor. After submerging in the dark of night, the *Blissful Wake* surfaced two days later at the coordinates that had been transmitted to General Hamlin thirty minutes prior.

Fortunately, Carol Harbors and her cameraman managed to catch a flight from California and make their rendezvous. A somewhat bewildered helicopter pilot who now had more money in his bank account than he'd earn in a lifetime already had his rotors turning as his passengers stowed their gear and buckled in. His only instructions were to fly to the same coordinates sent to General Hamlin. He had no way of knowing the time he'd been told to arrive meant he would have a half-hour lead.

He would never forget the sight of that massive dark hull breaking the ocean's surface. He knew what it was instantly; the whole planet knew what those ships looked like. Especially now that another moon-sized ship had appeared in the daytime sky.

Jim had his handheld camera out and was recording as the seawater sluiced down the ship's sides and the hull began to sparkle in the morning sun. "This is completely bonkers, Carol," he said. "Where's the military?"

"She's not giving them time to respond. There's no way we'd even get this close if they were here already." Carol looked to the pilot, who'd tossed a questioning glance over his shoulder. "Oh, yes," she said over the intercom. "They're expecting you to land on it." She gestured down, and the pilot shrugged. He'd be sure to tell his grandchildren this story and earn him more than a few drinks at just about any bar around Pearl Harbor.

A large white X appeared on the hull, slowly pulsing as he descended and circled to check the wind. As he approached, the X split in two as huge doors lowered and then opened to reveal some kind of landing pad. With a slow and steady breath, the pilot maneuvered his helicopter inside.

A woman with dark hair that grazed her shoulders and was visibly pregnant was waiting for them as the rotors slowed to a stop. Beside her was a tall and powerful-looking male Cerulean wearing a black form-fitting suit with glowing blue threads and the hilt of a sword poking over his right shoulder at an angle. Carol recognized both.

"Congratulations," she said after disembarking from the helicopter and reaching to shake hands. "Pregnancy suits you." Carol turned to Rachel's mate and smiled. "Colonel Kear'ald, a pleasure."

Pitor nodded in greeting, "Commander now, Ms. Harbors." He turned to several Ceruleans standing off to the side and gestured toward Jim, who was struggling to remove his crates of equipment. He said something in their language, and they burst into action, quickly relieving Jim and opening the pilot's door for the pilot to step down. He said something to Rachel, who quickly nodded.

"What is your name, sir?" The pilot took a step away from the much taller Cerulean near him before answering. "Uh, Stephan, Stephan Morritz... I have a family..."

Rachel grimaced at his obvious trepidation but easily understood the reasoning. "You have nothing to fear here, Stephan. These males can understand you even though they can't answer. They've been instructed to make you comfortable and meet your needs."

"What assurances do I have?"

Now she smiled, "You are a guest of the Regent, Stephan. They won't harm the hair on your head." Turning back to Carol and Jim. "We do have a timeline to keep, shall we?"

"Whenever you're ready, Carol." Carol observed Michelle sitting across from her, idly turning a metallic-looking cuff around her wrist and looking resplendent in a silver tea-length dress with undertones of pearlescence, legs crossed at the knee, and barefoot. Copper on the cusp of melting draped over her right shoulder in liquid waves that nearly reached her lap, and her crown sparkled under the studio lights Jim had just finished setting up. They were in this ship's Solarium. Carol had learned that every ship had one just for the Regent, but it was below the ship's waterline, and nothing but dark water lay beyond the windows.

"How do you do it?" Carol asked as Jim checked his light meter and adjusted the mic stand that would sit just out of camera view. He'd wanted Michelle to wear a mic but had already learned one does not approach, let alone touch, the Regent without receiving some dangerous glares from the sword-wielding Ceruleans in the room.

"Do what?" The Regent asked with a cant of her head.

"Look so comfortable? As if you're completely unbothered that the American Navy is scrambling to surround this ship."

Michelle smiled, "It helps to know they can't hurt us."

Jim cleared his throat. "We have a signal, Carol. The anchors are vamping, and the studio is waiting for us to begin transmitting." He looked at Michelle, "The signal will go live as you requested, broadcast and internet live-stream. Anyone on the planet with a screen will be able to see this. We'll start with Carol's introduction and then switch cameras to you. I won't turn them off until your signal."

Michelle nodded, "Let's do it." She made a gesture, and one of the two Ceruleans stepped away to get out of the camera shot. The other, Domaas, remained where he was. Standing one pace behind her left shoulder in the same dress uniform Carol had first met him in. However, now a rather ornate-looking sword hung from his waist. His left hand rested gently on the pommel while his right hand was tucked behind his back. He was standing so still that if Carol had not known better, he could have been a statue.

"Let them know we're ready, Jim."

Jim mumbled into his headset and said aloud, "In five, four, three..." He finished the countdown silently as he stepped back and pointed to Carol.

The lights brightened a fraction to signal the feed was live, and Carol smiled brightly into the camera. "Hello world. I am Carol Harbors from

KCVX News out of Los Angeles, California. I come to you now aboard the *Gist'tine Dua,*" Carol mentally praised herself for not butchering the pronunciation, "Two hundred miles west of Hawaii. You will remember our first introduction to Michelle Et'Kuraul, crowned Regent of the Cerulean Star Impirium. You will further remember the in-depth interview we had together after her coronation, just before boarding a ship much like the one I am on now. In that interview, she told us about her experience aboard the *Rising Star,* where we learned the true purpose of why the Ceruleans came to our planet just over twenty years ago. We met the male she married and even spent time with her beautiful daughter."

"Today, upon the invitation of her Grace, we are to learn what her intentions are for the planet she calls her home..." Carol saw Michelle grimace out of the corner of her eye. "But perhaps we should let her tell you. This will not be an interview but an address to the people of Earth." Carol smiled once more for her camera and gestured toward Michelle. "Your Grace? You have the world's attention."

The red light over the camera facing Michelle blinked on, and she silently counted to five before speaking, "The ship that has recently appeared in the sky is called the *Regent's Mercy.* It is a battleship capable of immense levels of destruction. I tell you this not to threaten you or give cause for alarm. This is the ship that was dispatched to rescue the Ceruleans when my friends and I destroyed the *Rising Star* after escaping. For the last month, it has been hiding inside Jupiter, where I told them to stay so as *not* to frighten you all. It is here now because a threat has been made against the returned captives, or Hybrids as we've come to call ourselves."

"This threat was made due to my having some of them rescued from a cult that was using *corrective rape* to bend them to the will of the cult's leader. He is now a permanent guest of mine and will not be returned. There is no established death penalty in the Cerulean Impirium, bar one. Rape."

"Cerulean males can *smell* when a female has been assaulted in such a fashion. In Cerulean society, summary execution is the only answer to such a thing. It is an offense that strikes at a Cerulean male's core sense of being. I ask look to your mothers, sisters, and daughters before making any judgment upon those who rescued the victims. Personally, I think the world has been made better with those men removed from it.

"The response of the United States was to bar any Cerulean vessel from entering their airspace, which is perfectly fine and acceptable. I have no issue respecting the wishes of any sovereign nation...so long as they hold to agreements made regarding the safety of those who also hold Cerulean citizenship, which the Hybrids do.

"Today, I intended to speak before the United Nations General Council, something I have sought since accepting the crown." Michelle gestured to her left shoulder as if no one had noticed how it glittered. "However, since that is no longer possible, I am speaking to the world directly. I believe they intended to prevent me from speaking at all."

Rachel blew a thin stream of air between her lips. Michelle had just thrown the United States' threat back in their face. Twice in five minutes, while looking as if she was about to have a high-end Sunday brunch.

"Now, the last time I spoke with Ms. Harbors. I told you all that what I want is peace with Earth. This is and forever will be my *home*. The place I was born and the place my family will be long after I leave. I wish Cerul to join *your* global community, which is the purpose of Regent's Island in the South Pacific Ocean. I do not seek to add Earth to the 'Impirium'," Michelle made quotation marks with her fingers, "As a vassal state."

"I simply wish to help and, when Earth is ready, help you all join the galactic community. I am just starting to learn about all the civilizations out there."

She paused and took a sip from the glass of water on the tea table next to her seat as she glanced at Rachel. The signal received, Rachel lifted her tablet and executed a series of commands, then nodded grimly back to Michelle. Back to the camera, "When I arrived, I brought information, over sixteen terra quads, if I remember correctly. This data is just about everything this world could want or need. Technology for medicine, faster-than-light travel, clean energy production, quantum computing, communications, and astrophysics. This is information that will change this world by immeasurable factors. Stupidly, I gave all of that to the

United States government when I returned. I wanted to help my people advance technologically because I still had anger in my heart. I naively believed this was the right thing to do and now realize I was mistaken. My eyes have been opened, and I know this data belongs to the entire world. For it will take the whole planet working together to join us amongst the stars."

"The information I gave to the United States has just been deleted. They will not get to decide who benefits from cancer-curing medicine or clean energy, and money won't get to decide either." Michelle gave a sly smile pointed directly at the President of the United States. "Right now, an IP address should be on the bottom of your screens. This IP address leads to a vast database, a library that will take the whole world working together to understand and take advantage of the gifts being given. There are no ulterior motives in giving this information but for my *home* to be made better. To see my fellow Humans walk on a distant planet like Cerul."

"I am now speaking directly to all heads of state. I have shuttles that are currently waiting outside each of your country's internationally recognized territories. With your permission, these shuttles will deliver a food replicator to a preselected location, along with detailed instructions on how to develop the technology and build more. If you are willing to accept this gift, free of any strings, please have your military broadcast the encoded message currently being sent to each head of state. My shuttles will fly to the location, and a small group of Cerulean males will deliver the kiosks, set them up, and *leave*."

To the UN, all I ask is for you to grant a *non-voting* membership to the Cerulean Impirum. I also ask that a meeting place be set so I may introduce myself properly and further tend to any concerns you may have personally." Michelle smiled faintly, again subtly jabbing the President, "Perhaps somewhere in Europe? South America or Africa? Until then, have a good day, be well, and thank you for giving me your time."

Michelle smiled pleasantly at the camera until the red light winked out. "And we're clear," Jim said.

Carol started clapping. "Eighteen years old, huh?"

"Only my mother knows for sure," Michelle answered with a laugh. Turning to Rachel, "How are we looking?"

Rachel was watching her tablet. "Servers are spooling up to handle the load, but right now, we're looking at eighteen million individual connections to the library and climbing by tens of thousands every second. That will taper off once most people realize they lack the education to understand gravity drag coefficients caused by using a magnetically contained singularity. The chat boards are literally on fire and twenty-six governments have granted permission to the shuttles, so far." Rachel looked up with a smile. "Including the United States; and before you ask, they are *screaming*. I've already rejected calls from both the Secretary of State and the White House."

Michelle stood and stretched, "Good. Let them stew for a while. Or better yet, forward all calls to my dad. He *is* the ambassador. Domaas, please let the ship's colonel know he can resubmerge the ship. No point in being here when an angry Navy shows up." She looked at Carol and Jim. "Join my mate and I for an early lunch?"

*****

"Stephan, is it?" The pilot's eyes flicked open to find an olive skin-toned redhead smiling down at him. Her emerald green eyes were sparkling nearly as bright as the diamonds scattered across the left of her neck and shoulder... Stephan's brain stuttered to a stop, and then he was suddenly surging to his feet as he realized who it was.

"Uh, y-yes, your highne-"

"*Grace*." Stephan blinked in confusion as Michelle gently guided him back into his seat. "Call me your Grace, if you don't mind. Or Michelle if that makes you more comfortable. Is it okay if we join you?"

Stephan took in the reporter and cameraman he'd flown out, the sizeable Cerulean male hovering behind and to the left of her and the dark-haired pregnant woman. "Well, it *is* your ship." She stepped around the table, where another sword-carrying Cerulean quickly pulled out a seat for her.

"It *is*, and it isn't," she said as she sat down and pulled her chair in. "This ship belongs to the Impire." The Regent gestured to the male on her left, "Blue eyes over here will tell you the Impire belongs to me, but I refuse to see it that way." There was a quiet tittering as the rest of the Regent's party, except for the one who pulled her chair, took their seats around the table.

Stephan noticed the way the indicated Cerulean cut his eyes toward the Regent, but there was amusement there. "Is this your mate?"

Michelle beamed and kept her gaze on Stephan, "He is! Why? Is he looking at me with disapproval in his eyes?"

Stephan slowly flicked his eyes between the two, unsure if it was safe to laugh or not. "Yeah, uh, something like that."

Food began appearing from stewards, the Regent receiving her plate first. Stephan watched as she captured the steward's eyes and said a foreign word with a smile. The steward blanched for half a second, then nodded as a return smile flickered across his lips. "So, Stephan, did you watch?" Her piercing green eyes focused on him as she took the first bite of her steak salad.

He glanced at the others and noticed they weren't wholly focused on him. The only one was *Blue Eyes*, but he could easily understand why. "I did. Is what you said true? About not trying to conquer Earth?"

Michelle took another bite and swallowed before answering. "You know anything about history, Stephan?"

"As much as the next person, I suppose."

Michelle huffed in amusement. "Besides being a star receiver for my high school football team, History was, *is*, my favorite subject. The one constant with war is it's always over resources. The men who start them use fancy words or false reasons to justify their cause, but it's *always* resources. You have it, and I want it. That's really why the Ceruleans came when you boil it down. They needed a resource that Earth had, and now that the need has been met..." Michelle shrugged as she took another bite of her salad and chewed.

"So anyway," she continued after swallowing, "I just removed food as a resource worth fighting over. In the library is technology to desalinate water without the huge energy requirements. So now even the poorest of countries have easy access to food and clean water. There will also be a fund set up for any country needing financial assistance to take advantage of Cerulean technology that is a net positive for the populace."

Stephan's face went slack as Michelle watched his gears click in place. "You just caused a paradigm shift in the history of Humanity," he said as the enormity of her actions settled on him.

Michelle, with a mouthful of food, covered her mouth and said glibly, "Gods, do I hope so. Hey Rachel?"

The brunette looked up from her plate of fruit, "Your Grace?"

"How many more countries have signaled they want a replicator?"

Stephan watched the pregnant woman activate her tablet and tap a few commands in. "It looks like all of Africa has requested one. Central and South America are nearly all on board as well. It's almost exactly as predicted."

Michelle only smiled at Stephan and took another bite.

"They're going to hate what you've done," he whispered in awe. Did she genuinely understand exactly what she had done? Solving world hunger? Not talking about it, not spreading *awareness,* but actually solving it...then eating a steak salad!

"Certainly. Too bad it will amount to nothing more than the gnashing of teeth. There is a thriving galaxy out there, evidently. When we leave, I'm going to have to go on a tour of the entire Impire, according to my mate. That's nearly a hundred planets of differing civilizations. Be kinda cool if Earth could come out and say hello as well. But that's not going to happen with Russia, China, and the US controlling Humanity's advancement, is it?" Michelle tapped a finger on the table, one manicured nail clicking as she did so.

"Maybe there's a child in India," she continued. Michelle had not had a chance to verbalize her thoughts fully, and she was doing so now. "Who won't starve now from lack of money. Maybe that child will be the one to decipher the designs for anti-gravity generators this very ship uses to fly. Maybe her mother won't die from a cancer that could soon be cured in minutes. Or better yet, maybe her mother won't get cancer at all since pollution from power generation in her hometown will decrease. And just maybe that child's father won't die in a war over clean water." Michelle shook her head as she pushed her plate away. "Nah, let them be upset. Let them squeal and gnash their teeth. It's worth it if it means Humans survive into the twenty-second century."

Chapter Twenty-Seven

She was tall for a woman, even sitting, The Man in The Forgettable Suit could see that. Blonde hair swept back with a pearlescent comb on the right side. Blue eyes lined and darkly smoked with shadow under well-manicured eyebrows, and thin lips accentuated by dark red lipstick. She was the captain of the cheer squad that managed to turn her charisma and leadership skills into a high-earning income. And she wore the designer skirt suit to devastating effect. He helped himself to a seat.

The woman darkened the screen of her mobile device, placed it face down next to her coffee cup, and stared at him silently. Christopher lifted the lapel of his suit jacket and reached into the inner pocket to extract a sheet of paper. After unfolding it, he read the writing he had carefully transcribed earlier. "Felith quor'it keesh." He had used one of Michelle's gifted tablets to ensure his pronunciation was correct.

"Koesh quar'is lith'fe," she responded, finishing the passphrase. "You have five minutes, Mr..."

"Christopher is just fine," he said as he returned the slip of paper to his pocket. "I must admit, I am surprised you returned my email. For anyone paying attention, it was obvious you and your...compatriots had gone underground as the *Rising Star* was destroyed."

"It seemed prudent that we make ourselves scarce." Christopher was impressed. Her mouth moved but nothing else, a talking statue. Far from the caring and emotive persona she and her ilk portrayed on television. "Your...reaction, to the truth of why we were here, was expected to be much more hostile. Humans continue to be an interesting species."

He glanced around the busy coffee shop. No one was sitting close enough to hear them directly and with the low-fidelity music playing, they would need to be nearly yelling for them to be heard. He would have gone for a public location like a park bench but appreciated her picking this place all the same.

"I was in communication with your Council Lords, but they seem to have been cut off." Christopher had questions, lots of them. However, she had set a time limit and he had more pressing issues.

"This is correct, our understanding is that *she* had them isolated in strict confinement. It is possible to send a message to them either way. It will just take longer to get through and a response is not guaranteed."

Christopher arched an eyebrow. That had been essentially what he intended to ask for. "I have a rule that I do not work with someone willing to give something of that level so easily. Unless they are willing to tell me why and how much."

Ire flickered across her perfectly made-up face, "That little tart took our money and has made no effort to bring us back into the fold. It would have cost her nothing more than to call for us. By the time we thought to present ourselves to her, she had taken the ships and left the continent."

"Why have you not contacted her or the Cerulean Lords?"

A wave of the hand with a flicker of disgust on that pretty face. "These old males you are so eager to work with are only out to aid themselves. It is they who assigned us this duty so long ago. Our names are not in any records. Only they and the former Regent could verify our identity, and the Regent is dead." She met and held his gaze. "I am trapped in this body and was supposed to be returned to my natural state months ago. Do you understand what I am saying? Maintaining this facade is bad enough; we will not remain destitute if she plans to leave us out in the cold."

Oh, he understood. "How much?"

"One hundred million. There's twenty of us."

"And if I were to say that was too much?"

She lifted her mobile device, and the screen illuminated. She allowed him to catch a glance to see there was a messaging app open. "Then I let them know the American government isn't as desperate as you let on and that we'll need to find another source of income. Please understand,

Christopher, I have been here for fifteen years. There are others who have been here since the beginning. It will not be difficult to blend back into your society, and you'll never find us again. That is the plan either way, but we would prefer to do it with a bit of wealth if we are trapped on this shithole of a planet." Her thumbs hovered over the screen as she looked back up at him. "Please make your decision; our time is almost up."

Chapter Twenty-Eight

Truth be told, T'Rail Bilson missed the days of his quiet nights in the dorm monitoring center aboard the *Rising Star*. He had arrived just a year before the last cycle of Hybrids had been brought aboard. An escape for himself, really, as he had not been getting along very well with his father. In the end, both agreed it was a good idea for them to be as far apart as possible. The mission at Earth was about as far as a Cerulean could go. Even still, the long quiet nights of watching the Hybrids sleep were now nothing more than a pleasant memory. That and the brief bursts of excitement he'd get when the *Usurper* showed her face.

Now, his days were mostly occupied with pouring through the dispatches being sent to the Regis. Most of it he would respond to himself, as he had the full faith of Regis Et'Kuraul, much of it pertained to things that fell under Colonel Cha'ol's purview as the Colonel of Regent's Island or Colonels Kear'ald and Bil'tun if it was a military issue. The few remaining dispatches directed to the Regent he forwarded to Rachel, the *Usurper,* to filter through.

It wasn't staring at holo-screens all night, but it was sufficient for T'Rail to turn his brain off and let his thoughts drift away into...

Thoughts that suddenly sharpened into focus as his eyes caught a line of text as he scrolled through the messages. Sliding his finger down the screen of his tablet, he read each subject line until the one that had caught his eye came back into view. Tapping it, the message exploded into holographic view.

It was from the Colonel of the *Gifted Silence* reporting that an airlock had been tampered with and allowed to flood with seawater. Damage teams were able to reseal the hatch and purge the water with no permanent damage. Except that ship surveillance had been tampered with, and a complete census of the ship was underway to check if anyone was missing and, if so, who.

So it was just a report, nothing special about it. A true emergency would not have been a simple dispatch in the middle of the night. But, *Gifted Silence.... Why is the name of that ship ringing bells?* T'Rail asked himself. *Who would want to leave through the submerged part of the ship in secret?* There were plenty of other ways to get off a ship. *Where would they even go?*

T'Rail forwarded the message to Commander Kear'ald - the fleet was under his command. The Commander would decide if it was worth following up on.

*****

Michelle knew before she opened her eyes. The sun's warmth on her face and the smell of wildflowers told her everything she needed to know. Keeping her eyes closed, she said, "You know, sweetheart, you can just talk to me with your voice when I'm awake?" A shadow passed over her face, and Michelle opened her eyes to see young adult Arya leaning over her, smiling, and blocking out the sun.

"Hey, Mopa."

"Sorry I haven't been around much kiddo-"

"I know, you've been busy. Changing the world has a way of keeping people occupied." Arya took her mother's hand and pulled her standing.

"How do you know about that?"

Arya smiled and tapped her temple. "It's amazing what I can hear when everyone around me thinks out loud." Michelle made a sour face. "I'm not reading minds, I promise! It's like there are thoughts, and then there's the stuff people are saying out loud but just in their heads. Popa has a dirty mind when he watches you walk, by the way. I had to start tuning him out." Michelle smirked, then sobered when she remembered how old Arya actually was. "I can hear you when you look at Popa shirtless, too." Arya said before Michelle could chastise her. "All that mushy romantic stuff you two send back and forth over the Bond, blech!" Arya made a show of shivering.

Changing the subject as she took in the infinite field of flowers, "So, I'm guessing you want to talk to me about something?"

Arya slipped her hand into Michelle's and began to walk. The field of flowers sifted like colored sand, and they were soon walking down a trail in an old-growth forest. "The Redwood Forest," Michelle whispered in wonder. "Your grandfather brought me up here with Brylie's Mopa when I turned twelve. We were up here for a month so he could teach us survival skills." Birds chirped overhead, and a cool ocean breeze sighed through the pine boughs. It was as if they were walking through a memory. A nearly forgotten one at that.

"You're doing a good job, Mopa." Michelle turned her head to look at her daughter as they walked. Highly developed mind or not, Arya wasn't even a year old yet. "I hope I'm as good as you when it's my turn."

"But..."

"After the meeting tomorrow, we should leave." Arya continued looking straight ahead, refusing to meet her Mopa's questioning look.

"Why, Arya?"

Arya didn't answer right away; instead, she bit her lip, and her face took on a pensive look as the environment changed again. Instead of flowing like paint on a canvas, this transition was hard and jolting. The air was suddenly cold as they stood in what looked like an operating theater. And on the table was Michelle. Her hair hung free, touching the floor, the color of rust instead of her normal coppery shine. Her arms were spread out wide from her body to form a T and were securely strapped down with a series of wide leather straps. Over her hands were metal balls that fitted tightly to the wrists with thick cables attached, leading to a large bank of electrical panels against the wall. Multiple IV drip lines were tapped into the veins of both arms, and her body was covered by a single white sheet with dried blood patches over her lower abdomen. Bruises of yellow, purple, and black mottled the entirety of her legs and arms - as if she had been in the fight to end all fights.

The body on the operating table, the equipment, and even the lights were hazy, as if just out of focus. It was an image right out of a torture porn horror film, and Michelle felt a trickle of ice race down her spine to settle in her gut. The image, the scene, was incredibly violent. "Arya..." Michelle's voice had thickened in her throat. "Arya, what are you showing me? What in the hell is this?"

Arya spoke quietly as if she was afraid her voice would catch someone's attention. "I found Brylie because he was broadcasting his dreams. Lots of people do it. There's someone on Galavix Prime I wish to meet; their dreams are beautiful. But this isn't a dream, Mopa." Arya finally turned to look at her mother, "This is like an echo from someone who knows how to shield or hide their true thoughts but doesn't realize how loud they really are. This...this was a fantasy. Whoever this is, they are actively thinking about what they want to do to you."

"Why isn't anything moving?" Michelle went to step toward the table, but Arya tightened the grip on her hand and pulled Michelle back.

"Don't." Michelle snapped her head back to Arya. That had been fear in her daughter's voice. "This is just a picture after they were done with you for the day. I don't know if they'll become aware of us if we interact with their memory."

"But you called it an echo, a picture."

"I said I don't know, Mopa. Please..."

"Am I dead?" What an odd thing to ask, but Michelle knew she'd die before letting herself into this situation.

"No. They're experimenting on you. Whoever was thinking about this was loud, so, so loud, Mopa. I tried to ignore it and just couldn't." Michelle idly remembered Jamie reporting a few days past that Arya had been having a very rough week.

"Who is it?"

"I don't know." The scene returned to the infinite field of flowers. "But he wants to hurt you and make you suffer. You embarrassed him to someone significant, and he intends to make you pay for it." Arya turned fully to look her mother in the eyes. "So we have to leave. Very soon."

Mother and daughter stood silently for a long moment, staring into each other's eyes. "Why don't you talk, Arya?"

Arya shrugged her shoulders. "The people that I care about most hear me just fine. I talk to Jamie directly, and sometimes Popa will send a thought to let me know he's thinking about me. His jokes are awful, but he thinks he's funny... And Brylie is a chatterbox, but I adore him, so it's okay. Oh, and I even said hi to Rachel's babies. Well, sort of, I don't think they even know they're alive yet. One of them is hiding from the scanners, he's shy."

Michelle somehow missed the use of plurals as she felt the pull of her body in the real world beginning to wake up. "Is there anything else before I go?" She asked.

Arya shook her head, "No. Just be smart, please?"

"I promise, Kiddo."

Michelle's eyes slowly opened to find her mate lying on his side and gazing at her. "How is our daughter?"

"She says your jokes are not very funny." Michelle stretched and rolled over to get out of bed, but the gentle tug on their Bond stilled her movements. Rolling back over she saw the concern etched across his brow. "She showed you first, huh?"

"Even looking as she does in her world, she is still a child, Michelle. She was frightened and wanted to know if she should be worried or even show you."

Michelle settled back on her pillow. "And should she be? Worried, that is?"

Domaas sighed heavily as he said, "Quietly, I had Pitor order the fleet to make ready for the transit back to Cerul two days ago. We are leaving the day after your summit is complete."

"And if I was to order that we stay longer?"

Domaas sighed as he rolled onto his back, prepared for her to be angry with him. "Then I will call for a council meeting and request a vote. The safety of the Regent of the Cerulean Impirium overrides even the Regent's own command."

Her head turned slowly to look down at him. Her voice was flat as she said, "And my predecessor? She died trying to save the *Rising Star*. Did you take the time to vote then? What stopped you from dragging her onto a shuttle before it was too late?"

"You forget her Grace could manipulate our technology. When the mass transports started, she prevented the beam from taking her. Her last words to me were to ensure your safety. She never truly believed you had accepted your fate. Also," he turned his head toward her, eyes dark and hooded, "You are my mate and the Mopa of my child. I would burn every Earth city to cinder if something like that were to happen to you. So please, Michelle, do not make us override you."

Michelle stewed in silence, and Domaas let her. As far as he was concerned, it had been a statement of facts, and no amount of arguing would change that.

Chapter Twenty-Nine

Rachel was sure the President had thrown some muscle about to make this happen. A site had been selected in the Serengeti of Tanzania and nearly all the heads of state had agreed to the location. Michelle had even offered to fully cover the costs of hosting such a large summit in the middle of the African continent, far from civilization. Instead, enough of them had suddenly shifted and requested to hold the summit on Regent's Island instead.

If Rachel did not like the idea of so many Humans and their entourages on the Island, Pitor and Colonel Cha'ol were damned near apoplectic. Bungalows were quickly erected to house most of the *lesser* world leaders and their various attendants. Colonel Cha'ol established and assigned dedicated security teams to patrol while cloaked and deploying hardened force fields around the various sensitive locations around the island. Such as the structure housing the digital library her Grace had already given the world access to. Fortunately, the United States, England, Russia, China, and France elected to stay aboard their respective flagship Naval vessels. All of which had already been holding stations just outside of the island's recently deactivated forcefield.

From the veranda just outside the dining/council room, Rachel watched Colonel Cha'ol glide down a meandering path leading a group of men in dark suits. He walked with one hand tucked behind his back, while with the other he seemed to be randomly pointing at various things as they went. "Who are those males the Colonel is walking with?" Pitor asked as he came out onto the veranda.

"The Secret Service, Russian Federal Protective Service, UK Special

Forces and whatever the protection detail for the French President is called."

Pitor slid in tight next to his pregnant mate and kissed the side of her head, an affection he'd picked up from watching Human television. He noticed Rachel just barely leaning into it. "What do they do? Why is Cha'ol showing them the island like that?"

"Each one of those men is basically the same as Major Sheel with their own versions of the Regent's Guard beneath them."

Pitor squinted into the distance. "They do not carry swords."

"No, they carry *guns*. Much more lethal than swords. There will be an insane amount of guns on the island for the next few days."

"How many?" Pitor had read the after-action report of the compound raid Ka'al had submitted to the archives and after some research of his own, understood that guns could deliver devastating and, often fatal, damage to the body if one was not wearing an exosuit.

"Well," Rachel looked down at her tablet which rested on the railing and continued scrolling through the dispatches T'Rail had sent the night before. "The United States President will have at least fifty people on the island at all times. Even when she's on the carrier," Rachel vaguely gestured out to the harbor where the *USS Gryphon* sat. "So that's going to be fifty for them at a *minimum*, add in all the other security teams, and a firefight on this island will be the stuff of legends." She held up her hand, "And before you ask why, look up a person called Franz Ferdinand and how his death shaped the last hundred-twenty years. That will make you understand why heads of state take security so seriously on this planet."

Rachel snatched up her tablet and turned toward the French doors. "That reminds me, I should eat something before this circus starts."

He wore his sword in a surprising fashion. Vertical, over his left shoulder with the belt going diagonal across his chest. Purely in an ornamental fashion as it would be incredibly difficult for him to draw the three-foot-long blade. "I like it like that."

"Your Grace honors me with such a fine gift," Colonel Bil'tun said with a smile and a dip of his head.

"And you have no issues with its intended purpose?"

A shake of the head as he understood her true question. "None, your Grace. The Regis was quite clear. I look forward to the training regimen."

"Excellent!" Michelle glanced over to Nicolette who was smiling up at her mate with pride. The young woman looked resplendent in her own dress. A simple affair in blue and gold satin with her hair brushed over her left shoulder to show the dark spots on the right, counter to Michelle's own hairstyle. Every female in Michelle's retinue was wearing an identical dress and similar hairstyling, except for Rachel, in Cerulean colors that matched the dress uniforms of the Cerulean males. "Are you sure you're comfortable doing this?"

Nicole nodded her head, "Yes. I answer any questions about life on Cerul to anyone who asks. Are you sure you don't want me to edit? It's not all roses for every Hybrid there."

"Yes. That is why I want you to be honest. If you tried to convince me it was perfect I would call you a liar and then tell Auntie and Unk you were back on Earth."

Nicole laughed, "Do you know the ass-chewing I would get if my mom knew I had come thousands of light years and did not even call? Even if I have been turned into a Barbie doll. Truth it is, your Grace."

"You stay with her, Colonel, and keep your translator on in case anyone wants to speak with you."

P'alta bobbed his head. "Yes your Grace, however..."

Michelle waved her hand, "Use your discretion, but obviously don't say anything involving the military." He bobbed his head once more. "And neither of you take issue with Brylie getting some attention?" P'alta looked down at his mate in question. The discovery that Brylie could speak English had caused a small argument, but it was difficult to argue against a child being bilingual. The boy was a chatterbox and to fully expect him not to slip up when even the Regent regularly spoke his mother's tongue would have been unfair. "Arya will be there too of course, with Jamie and two Proctors in cloak."

"Yes, that is fine," Nicole answered. "That nanny of yours is hiding a spine made of iron, but you know that."

Michelle felt Domaas approaching and turned toward the door as he entered. He was looking magnificent in a uniform Michelle had never seen before. His tunic was deep Cerulean blue with a gold filigree brocade. High-collared, the left shoulder was black leather with a constellation of diamonds in the same pattern that matched Michelle's crown on her shoulder. Black pressed trousers and boots polished to a mirror finish along with his sword swapped into its leather belt and scabbard finished off the look.

Domaas smiled, showing his dimples, as he felt his mate's approval across the Bond. He sent the same back to her as he took in her strapless dress in the same Cerulean blue and gold brocade. "Jesus Christ, you two look good together."

"Thank you, Nicole," Michelle murmured as she rose up on her toes to peck Domaas on the mouth.

Roger had no uniform, however as the representative of Cerul on Earth, he did wear a gold-bordered blue sash over his bespoke Savile Row suit. A glittering of diamonds in the Cerul Imperial Constellation rested directly over his right breast. Not for the first time, Roger thought about how the job as ambassador for an alien species was proving to be more difficult than he expected. He'd of course known it would be no walk in the park, but international politics was a brutal thing to learn on the fly, and *then* add galactic politics to that.

He thought of his wife and daughters back in New York for a brief moment and then refocused his attention as the first shuttle turned and then settled for a butter-soft landing. This one would be the Norwegian Prime Minister. The first in a long line of heads of state Roger Mizzi would be officially greeting them as they arrived at the island. Michelle would be greeting the United States, Chinese, French, and British heads of state personally later in the day.

He smiled as the door to the shuttle opened and the ramp extended. To say he was proud would have been the same as calling concrete hard.

He had trained his eldest child everything he could about survival, but none of that had included becoming the sovereign of an alien species. What she had done so far, what she had done for Earth... Roger wasn't sure he could put a word to how proud he was of her now.

"Prime Minister," Roger said loudly as he stepped across the landing pad. "Welcome to Regent's Island..."

*****

"Madam President," Michelle stuck her hand out to shake. "Welcome to Regent's Island. It is a pleasure to finally meet you."

The President's face was a cool mask, giving and taking nothing. "The pleasure is mine, I assure you," her voice was nearly flat with a minimal amount of pleasantness added at the very end. As they shook hands, Michelle noted that the President's palm was smooth and soft in contrast to her calloused hand from fight training. The Regent saw the flicker in the older woman's eyes as it registered and they broke contact. The older woman had expectations that were already being broken.

President Willow shifted focus to the tall Cerulean standing directly to the left and behind Michelle. "And *you* must be the great Regis Et'Kuraul, former Commander of the *Rising Star*?"

Domaas sketched a slight bow in difference. "The same," he said. As with most humans, this one was easy enough to read. This female was not happy to be here, at all, and he got the feeling she'd wring Michelle by the neck if possible. He sent the thought across the Bond and received a pulse of acknowledgment.

The President pointed to the sword hilt at Domaas' side. "My father was a collector of ancient weapons, may I?"

Ancient, the Regis thought ruefully. It was doubtful that it had been anything else but an attempt at an underhanded insult. A very weak attempt at that.

Feeling the eyes of her Secret Service detail hardening on him, Domaas slowly pulled the sword free of its scabbard with his non-dominant hand and held it out, blade down and pommel first. Cloaked, the Regent's

Guard tensed as well. "Such a fine instrument," the President said, holding it up in the light of the sun. "What type of metal is this to glimmer like that?" She looked down the length of the blade. "And no hammer marks? How is that possible?"

"An alloy," Michelle answered. "The same that makes up the hull of the ships. I can have one of my people send one of yours the link to the metallurgical portion of the Library if you like. They were made in one of the shipboard manufacturing plants. Those can also be found in the Library, although, my understanding is you'll need a physicist, a highly skilled chemist, and a master engineer working together to understand the technology."

Michelle stood silently as President Willow admired the blade a little bit longer. "I am assuming this is one of the weapons used to liberate that camp in Arizona?"

The President looked to the Regent to find the young woman's eyes waiting for her. "The very same," Michelle answered. She had known the question was coming.

Domaas leaned toward Michell's ear and spoke in Cerulean. President Willow looked at Michelle expectantly as she handed the sword back to Domaas. "We do have a schedule to keep," Michelle gestured to her right and turned to fall into step with the President.

"Sir?"

Colonel Sut'ok grunted and took another sip of his braut. The doors hissed closed behind the Major as he fully entered his Colonel's ready room and approached the desk. "What is it?"

"The census, sir." Major Gult held out the tablet, but Sut'ok waved it away as he continued reading his own. The fleet would be departing in a few days and he wanted to be sure his ship was in top condition for the trip. Transiting the Galactic core in FTL would be a bad time to lose the stabilizing thrusters.

"Everyone accounted for?"

A very pregnant pause; long enough for the Colonel to look up. "No, sir. I missed them on the first count, ran the scan twice more, and then had a security team check their compartment."

The Colonel blinked slowly as the braut soured in his mouth.

"They are gone, sir. The Council Lords have escaped."

"Escaped to where? They would not dare go to the island; her Grace would not give them a second chance." The older Cerulean surged to his feet as his voice boomed. "Who helped them? I want to know who helped them and where they went!" Colonel Su'tok paused briefly, long enough to run a hand through his longish hair and contemplate the blue sky behind his window. His voice boomed again, "Comms!" Loud enough to penetrate the walls to the bridge beyond.

A youngish voice returned through the hidden speakers in the office, "Comms, sir."

"Flash a priority message to Colonels Cha'ol, Kear'ald, and the Regis. Council Lords have escaped, whereabouts unknown, accomplices also unknown. Will advise."

"At once, sir." The speakers clicked off.

Su'tok looked to his subordinate, "Find out who disabled the surveillance system, quietly."

Major Gult nodded his head grimly, "It will be done, however..."

A steeply arched eyebrow, "Yes?"

"One of the repair technicians had to access a nearby storage compartment to access a power coupling. He noticed water on the deck and reported it to the Cargo Master. A crate of exosuits is missing, along with their matching rings. Upon further investigation, Major Plis'Kursaul discovered the locking mechanism on the door had been bypassed. Most likely in the same fashion used to bypass the lockouts on the airlock, we think."

Major Gult stood stock still, waiting for his Colonel's wrath to wash over him. He was not at fault and knew it. He knew his Colonel knew it was well. Nevertheless, he was also the closest target.

Colonel Su'tok looked at the muted wall screen on the far wall. On it was a live feed of her Grace standing at a lectern and speaking to an audience of Earth's leaders. If he was honest with himself, the Colonel still wasn't sure a Hybrid was right to be the Regent of Cerul. To her credit, every male with whom she dealt reported her as being fair, kind, and respectful. She looked those beneath her in the eye and spoke directly. While she had yet to actually display her lethality, it was said the last place any male should want to be is the focus of her ire. Regis Et'Kuraul himself had needed to prevent her from going on the rescue mission to save the Hybrid prisoners, and she had heeded him. She had recognized wise council when it was given, whether she asked for it or not. The fact that she had intended to take part only added to what she had done for the *Folded Fist*.

Leaping into thin air and thus saving the thousands of lives aboard the *Folded Fist...*

The Colonel's eyes focused on the Regent's left shoulder, where the Crown of Cerul spread across her bare skin and disappeared up behind her ear. She wore it well, and Colonel Su'Tock would be damned if someone thought they would cause her harm. There were still rumblings amongst some members of his crew, and other ships, he was sure, but the Colonel also knew those same voices were finding it increasingly difficult to be heard.

Instead of the booming voice the Major expected, his Colonel spoke softly. "Find the ones responsible, Major. Someone would have needed to operate that airlock from inside or the ship would have flooded. Find them...*now.*"

The only response he got in acknowledgment was the sound of the doors hissing open, then closing as Major Gult hurried off to his task. Su'Tock stiffly slid back into his chair and quietly waited for a response to his message.

Chapter Thirty

"All teams check in." There was a series of clicks through his earpiece. "Acquire targets and prepare to execute. Do not move until I give you the go. " The same number of clicks acknowledged the order.

*****

"I'm sorry, this is all very interesting, but...you are *pregnant,* yes?" The translation came in real-time through the device behind her ear, but Rachel was sure it had been Farsi. She was giving her third tour of the second day through the recently built manufacturing plant. Around them sat twenty assembly chambers of varying sizes, all inert and silent. Rachel had been explaining how the machines used some of the base technology as the food replicators when the President of Iran had cut in.

With a smile that she hoped appeared pleasant, Rachel answered, "I am around five months." For all of them, Rachel would be the first pregnant Hybrid they had seen.

The man's mouth formed an O in surprise along with the others as the Swedish Prime Minister said what the rest of them were thinking. "That is not possible; you appear to be ready to give birth."

Rachel nodded as she subconsciously rubbed at her lower back. "And I feel like it, but no, still two months to go. I'm having twins, which I am told are rare." That it had taken Michelle demanding she get scanned again to find that out was another issue altogether. "Cerulean babies gestate for six months. Have you all seen Princess Arya? She is less than a year old. The Regis is only in his late twenties as Ceruleans age differently than Humans."

"And what about you?" The Prime Minister pressed, "I heard a rumor you were the one who hid on the *Rising Star* for twelve years."

Rachel canted her head in interest; that was not something publicly talked about - just that she had been instrumental in helping Michelle escape. "It is true. I'll actually be turning thirty soon...I think. I sort of lost track over the years."

There was a light tittering of laughter as Rachel turned back to lead the group to the next point on her tour - and she froze. *Too many, was* her first thought. There were only supposed to be two Cerulean Proctors providing security for her. Turning back to her group slowly, Rachel was careful to keep her eyes moving as she passively scanned. She saw two faint warpings of light standing between her and the group of world lead-ers. *Okay, so then who in the fuck are they?* Behind the group, standing far back, were two more warpings of light. Faint, but visible to someone who knew - and they were now moving. Watching without looking, Rachel saw them break apart and slowly start to circle the sides of the room toward her.

"Mrs. Kear'ald?" The Swedish Prime Minister asked, concern etching her face. "Are you well?"

Rachel realized she had been still for too long and nodded quickly, "Yes," she lied. Warning sirens were going off in her head, but she couldn't communicate with her security without tipping her hand. Why hadn't they seen the unknown two in the back? Exosuits could see each other when in cloak. The IFF - Identify Friend/Foe - system made sure of that.

There was no practical reason for her to suspect anything, right? Maybe they were just rank-and-file Ceruleans with too much spare time on their hands. And yet... "If you please follow me; I'll show you the cold fusion power plant." Rachel tried to remember how Michelle explained how she and Domaas communicated across the Bond as she stiffly turned back toward the exit and began walking toward the door.

The pulse almost startled her. Pitor must have picked up on her accelerating heart rate and change in demeanor. It felt like he was asking, *"Are you okay?"*

Rachel used that as a guide to collect her thoughts and emotions, gathered them into a ball, and sent her response blasting back across the tether. *"No! Something is wrong! Where are you? I want you here now!"*

Technically, Colonel Bil'tun had no reason to be present for the final part of the conference. However, Nicole and Brylie were having lunch with the Princess, and he wanted to be present for what could be a historical moment. It would not be such a bad thing to ensure his name made it into the archives when this day was committed to the historical memory of his people. A young Regent, barely carrying the mantle for less than a year, forging a pact of peace and prosperity for a doomed people? Yes, he would have his name attached to that-

P'alta's head snapped to the side when he heard the grunt from Commander Kear'ald. The Commander's hand flew to his chest as if to grip the base of the tether anchored there. "Sir?"

Pitor spoke quietly so as not to interrupt the Regent, who was actively engaged in treaty negotiations, the reason she had called this summit. "Rachel is distressed. She is calling for me...and still learning how to use the Bond-" Then he received an image. Pitor's brow furrowed as he slowly stood. Bowing to his Regent and Regis, Pitor silently left the overly large conference room.

Once outside, he tapped his translator and called Rachel directly. "Flower, what is the matter?"

"Something is wrong," came the hushed reply.

Pitor started walking down the nearest path, turning left at an intersection and following the tether to his mate. "Are you well..."

Pounding footsteps could be heard, and Pitor turned back in time to see T'Rail going through the intersection at a full sprint. "Lieutenant!"

T'Rail stumbled to a stop and spun, his eyes wild and panicked. Humans and Ceruleans nearby and alike looked on in interest. "Sir! A flash message from Colonel Su'Tock!" T'Rail jogged the distance between them and held out a tablet.

"It can wait, do not go running into that room with all this Human security about," Pitor said, taking the tablet and continuing toward Rachel.

T'Rail took a heaving swallow of air to calm his racing heart before saying, "No sir, it cannot wait. The message is for you, the Regis, and Colonel Bil'tun."

Pitor continued walking but began to read the message as he moved...then stopped dead in his tracks. "Rachel?"

"Where are you?" She hissed back at him.

"What, exactly, is the problem?" Pitor could feel his heartbeat accelerating as he finished the message.

"There are two more Proctors following my group. I *do not* think they're part of the security you assigned me. My Proctors don't seem to know they're there. Something is very wrong."

Pitor slowly turned back to see T'Rail was still there and looking at him with wide eyes, chest still heaving from the sprint. "*Flower*," Pitor stressed the word and sent a pulse of calmness toward her. "The Council Lords have escaped the *Gifted Silence*. It has been determined they had outside help, and twelve exosuits are missing."

"Shit," came her reply.

"Execute."

Arya froze and tilted her head, the slice of apple halfway to her mouth. Nicole had been talking about something that Jamie instantly forgot as her ward's head snapped in her direction. The image slammed into her mind a fraction of a second later. Arya was relaying from someone else. Multiple minds, Jamie realized as the view flickered between perspectives. Three of them were quickly approaching the second flight of stairs. Cold, calculating, malice, and cloaked in exosuits. These were minds on a mission, and Jamie didn't need to figure out what for. They were approaching the nursery with guns and ill intent.

"Get Brylie and stay behind me," she said as she surged from the table, not giving Nicole a chance to ask questions.

The change in demeanor was enough that Nicole burst into action herself, jumping from her place on the sofa and scooping Brylie into one arm then reaching for Arya. "No, she and I have trained for this." Nicole watched as Jamie grasped the shoulder straps of her dress and yanked. There was the snapping of threads as the seams came free and the bodice dropped away. From behind, Nicole was gobsmacked to see a semi-automatic pistol affixed, barrel up and lying flat against Jamie's spine. Below that and across her lower back were multiple clips in individual pockets.

Arya ran up behind her warden and yanked at the skirt of Jamie's dress, which fell away to reveal dark leggings that stopped at the knee. Nicole instantly recognized the blue pulsating threads as Arya quickly gathered the skirt and returned to her. Brylie's eyes were as wide as saucers taking in the sudden burst of action. "The skirt is bulletproof; wrap Brylie with it," Jamie said without looking. She was busy taking up the P90 submachine gun that hung from a clasp at her waist, already loaded, with another six clips affixed to an apron slung around the Nanny's hips. Strapped to her right thigh was another holstered pistol with four extra clips in sleeves circling her leg.

Nicole quickly dropped to her knees and wrapped the skirt of Jamie's dress around Brylie like a cocoon. "What the hell is going on?" She couldn't keep the shaking out of her voice.

"Danger," Jamie answered as Arya took a position behind her. Facing backward with one hand on the older woman's leg to detect movement. "Show her, Arya." Jamie took her stance, the iron sight of her P90 already beaded on the closed door.

There were several beats of silence, then Nicole leaped forward and pulled the pistol free from Jamie's back. After checking the slide and clip, she pulled two more magazines and stuffed them down into her bra cups. "Get behind me, Brylie," Nicole said as she thumbed the safety switch. Neither woman could know it, but Arya was actively keeping the boy calm. He shuffled to obey and wriggled an arm free to hold onto his Mopa's skirt.

Nicole stood just behind and slightly to the left of Jamie. pistol kept low but at the ready. "How real is this?" she asked into the waiting silence.

"Arya thinks this is a real threat," Jaime said as her spine turned into a rod of iron. A floorboard creaked in the hall. She slid her trigger finger into place. "I suppose we're about to find out."

*****

The sound was distant but unmistakable—a muffled boom from a small explosion. Arya's blast of fear hit a fraction of a second later. T'Rail entered the large room just as absolute chaos erupted. The multitude of security teams rushed from the walls where they'd all taken position and dragged their principles from the recently built conference room. Michelle's own detail shimmered into view as they rushed to surround her and Domaas, swords were half drawn and faced out.

"Arya! Arya and Jamie! Go! Now!" Michelle bellowed, but none of them moved.

"Cha'ol reports he is on the way to the residence. Regent, we need to get you to safety." Sheel responded coolly.

Michelle stood helplessly as she watched the room empty, taking her hope with it. "Sheel, what in the hell is going on?"

Michelle did not get an answer as the sentries began moving toward the exit behind the seats she and Domaas had been sitting in. Somehow Domaas had found her hand and was tugging her along as they accelerated. Behind her, P'alta had a hand at the small of her back, adding to the momentum.

She was just looking back at the room once more when there was a loud *crack!* And Michelle's vision was suddenly red as something hot and wet splattered across her face. P'alta's hand fell away, and his body collapsed to the floor behind her. It was then she realized it was gore that now coated her face and matted her hair. Her childhood best friend's mate had just died protecting her, and that was all the time she had before she noticed a bright beam of red light shining down from the high rafters of the room.

Sniper!

Michelle didn't have time to check the target. She dropped - hard, tightening her grip on Domaas' hand and pulling him down with her. As they fell, there was another crack, and the plaster from the wall was suddenly a cloud of dust raining down on them...exactly where Domaas' head had been. Time slowed as their eyes met on the floor for a fraction of a second. Long enough for Michelle to realize for a third time, Domaas had been right. Her enemies *had* been circling the entire time.

And she had invited them right in through the front door.

More distant automatic gunfire. *We need to get to Arya!* Michelle sent across the Bond as she was hauled to her feet, just barely managing to pull P'alta's sword free of its scabbard. This time, her guard had activated their shields, forming a nearly invisible wall to protect the Regent and Regis as they were bodily carried from the conference room. There were two more loud bangs from the hidden rifle as the forcefield pulsed from the impacts.

Chapter Thirty-One

Nicole gasped and roared in agony as she staggered backward, almost tripping over Brylie. Barely keeping her gun hand steady, she clutched at her chest with the other, searching for the connection that had just abruptly severed.

A gaping hole was all that she found. What had once been a glowing tether that had anchored her life for the last two years had suddenly and permanently ceased to exist. Nicole's pain was instant and absolute.

Jamie's machine gun chattered again, enough to damage hearing in the enclosed space and still keep their attackers at bay. From somewhere down below, she could hear fighting, but the Ceruleans wouldn't get to the top floor in time. The Humans were pushing hard and making excellent use of the exosuits they wore. Jamie had already felt several impacts herself, but nothing had punched through so far. She didn't have a ring on the unitard suit she wore, but neither did they seem to be using the shield function either.

They'd used a concussion grenade to blow the door off its hinges, but Jamie had expected that. Two warpings of light had entered and promptly retreated when they were greeted by automatic fire from Jamie's P90. Whoever they were had not anticipated the nanny to be armed. *Like an asp in the nursery.*

They were going to have to push back and force their way down. Two women with two kids in tow. They were on the third floor, and the hallway was the only way out. Behind her, Arya remained perfectly still and waiting. "Talk to me, Nicole. Are you hit?" Jamie dared not turn to check when she didn't get an answer. "Arya, is Nicole okay? Brylie?"

An image of a more-than-usual pale-faced Nicole flashed in Jamie's mind. A hand clutched to her chest, and pure agony etched across the woman's features as she looked down at her son with silent tears. Her mouth was locked open as if she couldn't pull a breath. *"Brylie's Popa is dead,"* came Arya's little mental voice.

She took in what Arya had said. Processed it and then set it aside. Now was not the time, especially with Nicole going into shock. "We need to get out of here, Arya. I need you to push Nicole into action, can you do that?" Jamie saw a glimmer of light and pulled her trigger, this time aiming for the space just above. Where the head should be. Red gore splattered against the hallway wall and Jamie knew she'd never forget the image, but processing that would have to wait. With practiced efficiency, Jamie pulled the spent clip and locked a fresh one into the top of her weapon.

"I'm here, Jamie," Nicole said, her voice small and wooden. "Let's go."

Because those Proctors weren't Cerulean either, that was why. Yet somehow, in the chaos, Rachel had managed to escape the manufacturing plant. She knew she was being hunted, but she knew this island better than her hunters and quickly left the path to dive into the jungle. Distantly, Rachel was glad to have worn flats instead of the low heels she'd intended to wear. *If I get out of this, I'll have to thank Michelle for convincing me otherwise,* Rachel thought while kneeling in a thicket of giant ferns. Whether or not she knew the island, there was no way she'd outrun them while five months pregnant with twins.

She had heard two loud shots from the conference hall and could hear sporadic gunfire from the primary residence, followed by more rifle fire from the conference hall. Rachel had no way of knowing how prescient her comments to Pitor had been just days before. Cha'ol had put an evacuation plan together just in case, and by now male Ceruleans should have been ushering the guests to safety. Helicopters from various countries' naval ships were now passing overhead and could be heard landing down at the landing pad. Hopefully, ferrying the world leaders off the island and probably taking Michelle's hope with them.

The security personnel had quickly and efficiently secured their principles and swept them out of the manufacturing plant. Luckily, none of them had been targeted. Fortunately, they seemed more interested in getting away than getting into the gunfight Rachel had predicted.

No, *they* had wanted her and almost succeeded. Rachel had only escaped by allowing herself to get swept up in the panicked rush. However, if they were after her, they were certainly after the Regen "I need a fucking tablet-" Pain exploded at the crown of Rachel's head as a fist was suddenly clutching her hair.

"There you are, you stupid bitch! You didn't really think you could escape us?" Human, Rachel realized. The Ceruleans did not use conjunctions in either language. "You are very much needed," the male voice said as he pulled her to her feet. As she rose, Rachel saw that she was surrounded by four Human males, all of their faces pointlessly covered with camo makeup and wearing ill-fitting exosuits. Each carried a submachine gun wrapped in the black exosuit material. *Crude, but obviously effective.*

One of them stepped forward, pressing his earpiece as he did. "Team three to lead. Tertiary target secured." There was a pause and then he said, "Understood." Looking at Rachel he asked, "You the one who controls the computers?"

"I don't know what you're talking about." The hand holding her hair suddenly tightened and she hissed in pain. There was a pulse across the Bond in response. Pitor was close.

The leader huffed as he lifted his gun and pointed the barrel at Rachel's swollen stomach. "Your capture is strongly desired. I'm confident we can get you back to the ship before *you* die, anyway."

Rachel's chest throbbed as blind fury came blazing across the Bond. Pitor was *very* close and at least within earshot. Looking the leader in the eyes more confidently than she felt, "You just signed your own death warrant."

He smiled, showing bright white teeth against his painted skin. "What mak-" The blade of a Cerulean sword appeared in the man's throat, extending like an over-starched necktie. Blood spurted from the wound as the Seal gargled and uselessly grasped at the blade. He lost fingers against the laser-etched edge for the effort. The man holding her hair released her as he raised his gun. The blade was pulled free as an unseen force shoved the now-dead body forward. His compatriots watched silently as the man fell, traversing their barrels across the jungle, looking for the now-vanished assailant.

Rachel lowered herself back to the ground, fighting back the bile from seeing such a gruesome death and having no desire to see the carnage her furious mate was about to deliver. "Oh no you don't!" The Seal behind her reached for her arm, but his hand suddenly fell away in a gush of blood. He didn't have a chance to scream as the blade sliced diagonally through his body. Rachel couldn't fight it this time, and vomit erupted from her mouth as the three pieces of Human fell around her.

A gun was fired, wildly it sounded like, and then it too went silent, followed by the thud of another body falling to the jungle floor. More silence, then; "Okay! Okay!" A gun clattered from being dropped, and Rachel finally raised her eyes. The remains of three Human bodies littered the ground around her - only one of them still whole. Dead, but whole.

Pitor stood, visible, in his exosuit. Yellow eyes blazing with an intensity that nearly stole her breath. "Are you well, *Flower?*" The gentleness of his voice belied the fury etched on his face.

"Yes."

"They did not hurt you?"

"No."

Rachel looked to the Human male Pitor held at swordpoint. The edge of the blade pressed across and into the man's neck just enough that a rivulet of blood was running down its length. "We keep this one alive, yes?" He asked in English.

"Yes, and I need a tablet." Pitor crooked his sword arm and slammed his elbow into the human's temple, leaving him to drop unconscious to the earth.

"Put me down!" Sheel obeyed, but only because he'd felt a static energy pulse that made his vision swim. Michelle kicked off her heels as soon as she was standing, and turned in a slow circle as she watched a German helicopter roar low and fast overhead. From this vantage point, she could watch the helicopter flare into a hard landing on the wide-open landing pad that had been cleared of shuttles for the conference. Guided by security, people ran up its already lowered ramp, and the helo lifted off again before the last person was fully inside the cargo hold. Commander Cha'ol had built an efficient evacuation plan.

Her throat was dry as she said, "Someone, please tell me this is not happening."

"Heartbeat..." Domaas went to grasp her elbow - they had to keep moving; they were much too exposed - he snatched his hand back when a tiny bolt of energy lanced out and zapped his fingers. She numbly handed him P'alta's sword, blade down, and he took it gingerly, searching her eyes and waiting for that wonderful mind to process-

Gunfire echoed from the top of the hill. Michelle and Domaas spun in unison at the sound to look up at the mansion. *Arya.* Without a word, Michelle burst into a sprint as bolts of energy began crackling down her arms; her bare feet leaving shattered and charred concrete with every step.

Michelle's vision tunneled as she ran up the sloping path. Sound muted to nothing more than the rasp of her breathing and the repeating bursts of gunfire. The wood of the front veranda splintered and scorched under her feet as she flew up the steps and through the open front doors. Her eyes took in the scene of the opulent foyer in a fraction of a second.

Two bodies lay sprawled at the bottom of the grand staircase. One was the body of a Human male, his face was obscured with camo paint, and was wearing an ill-fitting exosuit. His chest appeared to have been caved in deep enough to hold water, and a short barreled automatic rifle lay discarded at his side. Near him was Cha'ol liying across the carpeted stairs. His eyes were open, and he blinked when he saw Michelle staring at him. He clutched at his shoulder, where blood seeped through his fingers.

"Your Grace will forgive me if I do not get up. Those *guns* are nasty things, indeed."

"Will you live, Colonel?"

"I will die under the Cerulean sky, if it pleases your Grace."

Despite the brevity of the moment, Michelle gave the old soldier a small smile. "It does please me." Behind her, Michelle heard boots thudding heavily on the wooden deck of the veranda and she stepped forward to look up the staircase cautiously. Energy still crackled up and down her arms. "Arya? Jamie, Nicolette and Brylie?"

Cha'ol coughed and pointed toward the door to the rear of the house. "Gone. I got here just as they were fighting their way down. You chose well for a Nanny. I have never seen eyes so...hard." He angrily kicked the dead body near him. "This *pl'isha* surprised me. We fought, he lost."

Sheel was suddenly kneeling at the Colonel's side and went to pull the older Cerulean's hand away, but he snarled. "It is not fatal. Protect the Regent, Major."

Michelle turned away and locked eyes with Domaas as she sent a quiet thought to Arya. A feat in itself as her mind raced. *Baby, where are you and Jamie? We'll come to get you.*

The image came back hard, fast, and clear. They were in the jungle, low in the bushes. She and Brylie were squatting between the opposing backs of Jamie and Nicole. Both of them were armed and vigilant. *Does Jamie have a translator?* Another image, this one the back of Jamie's head and showing both ears, naked. *Okay, tell Jamie I said to stay put until I call for you.*

Arya didn't respond, but she knew the child would relay the message. "Your Grace?"

Michelle shook her head and turned to Sheel; Kato was now tending to Colonel Cha'ol while the others had spread out into defensive positions. The Major kept his distance as he gestured up the staircase. "There are three more bodies upstairs. One just outside the nursery. The body was cloaked, and I only found it by accident. When I deactivated the suit the head was missing, but he was also carrying this." Sheel handed the Regent a syringe. It was filled with a thin pinkish fluid. "I do not know what it is."

"It's a sedative, most likely," Michelle whispered in English as blood pounded behind her eyes and her vision narrowed on the plastic and steel item in her hand.

"What?" Domaas' voice was cold, lethally so. He had heard her just fine.

Sheel stiffened but shifted his gaze between the Regent and Regis. "It appears that they were attempting to capture the Princess." He settled his gaze on the Regent, who had nothing but abject fury on her face and eyes that were now glowing a bright purple. The same color they'd been before she had leaped from the *Folded Fist*. "It would be safe to assume you were also a target. I think the Regis was the target in the Conference room, not Colonel Bil'tun."

"Where are Rachel and Pitor?" Michelle nearly whispered.

"Here, your Grace." Michelle spun to see Rachel and her mate walking into the foyer from the back of the mansion, followed by her father and Ka'al with Makayla. A glance told her all of them were whole.

Albeit brief, a sense of relief passed through Michelle that was quickly swallowed back up by the fury she was barely keeping contained. Then she noticed the Human male Pitor was carrying over his shoulder like a bag of rice. Michelle barely noticed the Cerulean males wordlessly moving into a protective ring around her or the force field bubble that appeared around them with her and Domaas in the center.

"Is he alive?" Michelle demanded as she moved to meet them. Her guard matched her step for step, keeping her in the center of the force field bubble.

"Yes," Pitor answered, dropping the body to the floor. "This one and three others were attempting to take Rachel hostage. They failed." The dried blood spatter on Pitor and Rachel's green gills told the story. "My Flower thought one should be kept alive."

Looking at Rachel, Michelle asked, "Are you okay?"

A protective hand rested on her swollen stomach as she nodded, "As could be expected. I need a tablet, though. I can disable the stolen exosuits. They didn't sync the rings to their nervous systems." Rachel pointed to the quietly groaning body on the floor. "They can only cloak nothing else. There was the tearing of velcro, and Proctor Kato stepped forward as he pulled a tablet from where he had stored it on his back. Remaining silent, he handed it to Rachel and stepped back into position. The woman turned it on, activated the holographic display then quickly got to work.

Michelle turned toward the doors "I'm going to go get Arya-"

"No." Domaas stepped into her path. "Kato and Hal'isso, Major Ka'al, please retrieve the Princess, Jamie, Brylie, and Colonel Bil'tun's mate. Escort them to the Regent's Solarium. It is hardened against attack." Domaas held his mate's gaze in silent question.

"They're on the south side of the island. Arya thinks it's near the old swimming pool," Michelle said softly. "Arya says Jamie will be expecting you." The guards peeled away and quickly made their way out the door.

Domaas mouth was set in a thin line as he nodded. The only sign that he appreciated Michelle not fighting him at this moment. She understood. She had been wrong, again. Hal'isso was Ka'al's replacement, and Michelle knew Kato was capable enough. If Jamie had been able to hold the mansion by herself, then her guards certainly could make Arya's defense impenetrable. Sheel was giving orders to the rest of the Regent's Guard, and they vanished from sight to set up a perimeter. Michelle barely made a note of her protection cloaking as she focused on reeling her power back into herself. The adrenaline dump was ending, and she needed every drop of energy she had.

Looking around at those remaining, then down at the Human male still heaped on the floor, she stalked toward him. Pitor took one step back and unsheathed his sword, pressing the blade's tip directly over his heart as she approached. He must have been playing possum because his eyes snapped open as she came to stand over him.

Chapter Thirty-Two

"Do you speak English?" He didn't answer, but even under his thick camouflage grease paint, Michelle could tell he understood her just fine. She stood over him close enough that she knew he could see up the skirt of her dress, and she did not care. "If you so much as twitch a finger, the angry blonde Cerulean will stab you in the heart before I have a chance to tell him to stop. Do you understand that?" The man blinked once. "Name and rank?"

He still didn't answer. The coiled beast that had just been soothed raised its head and growled. "Step back, Commander," Michelle said as bolts of purple energy started crackling around her fist. Pitor obeyed but kept his sword near the man's head. Michelle stooped and placed her charged hand on the man's chest. "If I'm being honest, I actually don't know how powerful I am, but I'm feeling very confident. You know what I did to Captain Turney. I've wondered if he even survived, especially since that was before I learned how to control this." Michelle was speaking much more calmly than she felt. "I promised myself I'd never use this power to kill intentionally, but you will make a liar of me if you don't start answering my questions."

The man blinked, russet eyes blown wide open, as he took in the frighteningly calm demeanor on the Regent's face. She smiled and reached to his ear to remove the radio earpiece with her free hand. "You won't be needing this, either."

"John R. Gorsch, Chief Petty Officer, United States Navy, service number 555 54 6509."

Michelle cocked her head, "Navy Seals? They didn't send their best, did they? If I told you your sniper killed the mate of Captain Delroy Royce's daughter, would that mean anything to you?" The Navy Seal seemed to stop breathing at his recognition of the name. "I'm sure he'd love to hear the story of how my Nanny managed to fight your buddies off. What was your mission, Chief?"

"John R. Gor-" Michelle let a fraction of the energy slip, and Chief Gorsch's mouth locked open as his body seized and his back bowed off the floor. She reeled the power back in, and the man collapsed, suddenly gasping for air.

"Perhaps I was not clear. How did you get your hands on the exosuits?"

"Heartbeat-" Michelle hit the Navy Seal again, watching impassively, as every muscle in his body locked and only his eyes screamed in pain.

"*Heartbeat.*"

"Michelle-"

"No, Domaas," Michelle snarled in Cerulean, choosing to ignore her father. "They came into my *home,* attacked my friend, tried to kidnap my daughter, *and* tried to kill *you*! Colonel Bil'tun is dead, and I *will* know why they just ruined the only chance for a peace treaty with Earth!"

"Your Grace?" With a growl in her throat, Michelle snapped her head up to Pitor but managed to catch it. "T'Rail had received a flash message from Colonel Su'tok of the *Gifted Silence.*" Michelle's eyes narrowed, and she could feel Domaas go still behind her. "He was racing for the conference hall when I intercepted him. The Council Lords have escaped the ship. Upon further investigation, two crates of exosuits had also gone missing. Colonel Su'tok is certain they had help - both inside and outside."

Slowly, oh so slowly, Michelle turned her head to look back down at the human male she kept pinned to the floor - let him see the cold fury raging in her eyes. "Rachel?"

"The last helicopter just crossed the shield line, and the carrier has almost cleared the bay." It was a statement, but everyone present understood the question.

"No," Michelle said as she suddenly stood. "Raise the shield and lock down the island."

"To be clear, your Grace, not letting the carrier leave will be considered an act of aggression." Even though Rachel attempted to keep her voice calm and even, it still shook.

Michelle glanced down at the Navy Seal as she answered. "Better they had been happy with the gifts they had been given." They all watched in silence as the Regent began to twist the cuff around her right wrist slowly; the one Rachel had made to replace the one that had been vaporized. "Lock it down, Rachel. When the carrier makes contact, let them know I will only speak with th-"

Klaxons began blaring across the island. A two-tone sound that set Michelle's teeth on edge. "It's a bit late for alarms, is it not?" Michelle asked as she turned to Rachel...and saw abject terror on the Cerulean faces. The lights went out next, casting them into the dim afternoon light from the windows. Rachel's tablet flickered and then shut down. There was a brighter flicker, and the force field dropped, soon followed by her guards becoming visible. The blue threads of their suits had gone dark.

"What in the hell is this?" She asked to a room of frightened faces.

Domaas could barely contain the tremor that had taken over his body as he looked his Regent in the eyes. "They are here," he said over a thick tongue. "The Kesta are here."

All across the island, power failed. Or rather, it shut down. Every piece of Cerulean technology went inert as even the klaxons became silent. Looking up, Ka'al watched the *Regent's Mercy* fade from view, then blink away in a bright flash and streak of light. "That is bad, isn't it?" Was asked in a small voice using a mix of Cerulean and English.

Ka'al looked down at the little boy who stood next to him. They had been on the way to the Solarium when Ka'al had felt his suit power down, and the klaxons had started. The boy's mother was nearly catatonic, barely aware of her surroundings to the point that Jamie had collected the pistol she had carried. "Yes, Brylie," Ka'al answered. "It is very bad."

"But that was my Popa's ship. He would not leave me and Mopa, would he?"

"There are still people hunting us, Ka'al," Jamie interjected. "We need to get back to the mansion, especially if this is what I think it is." Ka'al swallowed as he looked at Jamie and confirmed her suspicions with his eyes. He turned to resume forging a path through the jungle when a shaft of blue light encompassed their group, and they vanished.

"Okay," Michelle said as she squared up on the remaining members of her Defense Council. "There's a hostile force on the island, and the most feared enemy of the Impire has shown up. What is the plan?"

"The evacuation has already started."

"How?"

"The power outage is intentional and is built into all Cerulean technology. It is the same subroutine Rachel exploited to trigger the mass transports before the *Rising Star* was destroyed. There are narrow-band passive sensors constantly scanning for Kesta energy signatures. Any sign they are approaching, and nearly all energy sources are powered down except for the core systems of the ships and transporters. Right now, the ships will automatically power up and lift off to prepare for transit out of the atmosphere and then jump to FTL. I had Lieutenant Bilson write a subroutine so that anyone in range with Cerulean DNA will be transported to a ship...any moment now," Domaas finished as he stepped closer to Michelle.

Michelle looked around at those gathered. "We can't leave."

"Michelle-"

"No, Domaas! We cannot leave! Not now! Rachel, cancel it! Abort, whatever! Do your magic!"

Rachel helplessly held up her dark tablet, no better than a paperweight. Michelle whirled her gaze on her mate. "Is this what you three planned when I asked you to-"

"Michelle Et'Kuraul!"

She had been building a heavy head of steam, and as always, her father was the only one who could bank her temper. The daughter dutifully turned to face her father and waited silently to hear what he had to say.

Roger closed the distance between them as he asked, "Who are you?"

"A Mizzi," she answered without hesitation.

"Our ancestors crossed a vast ocean to a new world to begin a legacy that is our family name, correct?"

"Yes, Dad."

"Your mother's grandfather led his family across deserts and oceans, did he not?"

"Yes, Dad."

"*Why* did your great-great grandparents leave Greece?"

"To escape harassment by the local crime lords."

Everyone watched in silence and mild shock as the indomitable Regent bowed to her father. Michelle bent to no one. Yield, maybe, but not allow herself to be spoken to as...as a child would for a parent. Even so, Domaas' understanding of what made Michelle who she was became even more apparent.

"And when our ancestors arrived in America, what did they do?"

Michelle swallowed and spoke quietly as she realized the point her father was making, "They made a home and reached back to those they had been forced to leave behind. Sent money for them to make the crossing themselves or to make it easier for others to stay. They didn't abandon their people." She nodded her head as she absorbed the lesson.

"Sorry for yelling," she said to everyone around her.

Roger smiled and pulled Michelle into a hug. "What is our family motto?" He asked into her hair.

In Greek, she recited, "Merikés forés prépei na to peráseis gia na to xeperáseis." *Sometimes you gotta go through it to get over it."*

"Never forget it."

Michelle blew a stream of air between her lips. "Thanks, Dad. I needed that."

There was a flash of blue light nearby, and Michelle pulled away and then turned to see who had vanished.

"Fuck."

Everyone was gone. Michelle stood alone with her father and the Navy Seal, who was now getting to his feet.

They were all gone.

"Fuuuuuuuuuuuck..."

*****

The transporter deposited them in the cavernous cargo hold of one of the ships. Instantly, he felt his exosuit power back on around him, and he visually searched for a member of the crew. A Proctor stood near the main doors giving directions to the others the emergency transport had deposited on the ship. "You!"

The Proctor's eyes shifted at the commanding boom of Domaas' approaching voice, and he quickly saluted. "Sir?"

"What ship is this?"

"The *Promised Sanctum,* sir."

"Inform your Colonel that the Regent is aboard his ship. Tell him to prepare appropriate quarters, understood?"

"Yes..." The Proctor's eyes shifted over Domaas' shoulders, then around the hold. "Sir? Are you sure the Regent transported with you?" It was such a simple question, yet it seemed to suck all sound from the hold.

Domaas felt time slowing as he whirled to see Rachel and Pitor, Colonel Cha'ol now standing, and the present members of the Regent Guard...but no Michelle. *Oh Gods,* Domaas thought as all sound slammed back into him at once. Rachel was already in motion as she lifted her tablet and tapped the screen. Her face had a flicker of relief as the screen illuminated but she didn't stop as her fingers began dancing over the tablet. "Rachel..."

"I am trying!"

There was a beep in Domaas' ear, and he tapped the now-working translator. "Regis Et'kuraul, this is Colonel S'aqui. Passive scans show the Kesta ship has just crossed the outer boundary of the solar system-"

"Reverse course!" Domaas roared at the ship's colonel. "The transporter failed to transport the Regent!" Domaas kept his eyes bored on

Rachel. *That* was panic on her face. Rachel never showed panic. Silence pushed in on him again as he waited for the colonel's response.

"Sir, we cannot override the system. You know as well as I, it is hard-wired into the ship itself."

Rachel looked up then and locked eyes with him as she shook her head. "I cannot abort the program!"

"What about the transporter?" Rachel didn't look hopeful but tried anyway.

"The FTL drive is nearly at full charge. If we jump while transport is in progress, it will kill her. There would be nothing to bury." The look of helplessness on her face could only begin to match the depths of despair taking root in Domaas' chest. Silence had fallen in the cargo hold as a deep vibration could be felt through the deck plates. Any second now the ship would jump to FTL, and they would not be able to regain nav control until they made it back to Cerul.

"The Regent is alone and surrounded by her enemies," Pitor muttered quietly.

Domaas buried his emotions for the moment and straightened his spine. Now, more than ever, she needed his - their unfailing support. Looking at the present members of the Regent's Council and her Guard, Domaas said with a clear voice, "Our Regent is indeed surrounded by her enemies. There is no one I would pity more. When we return to Earth, Kesta or not, we will find our Regent standing triumphant. There is no other alternative."

The rescue fleet blinked away into the depths of space.

Chapter Thirty-Three

A spinning kick to the chin had the Seal staggering back until he collided with the staircase's banister and collapsed unconscious. He had been weak from the shocks he had received before, but he'd tried nonetheless. Michelle counted three deep breaths to steady herself and listen to what was happening outside. Helicopters could be heard overhead again, and a glance down the hallway and out the open back doors showed the *USS Rickover* had slowed or stopped its exit from the bay. They had no way of knowing she was still there.

Michelle looked to her father, who had wisely backed away as Michelle fought with the Seal. "Dad, I have to get out of here," she said as she picked up P'alta's sword. Domaas had laid it across a nearby credenza. She thought about handing it to her father for a fraction of a second but decided to hold on to it instead.

"Where are you going?"

"I don't know, but I can't stay here. Not alone. I was wrong, so, so wrong. They'd be here in force already if they knew it was just you and I. Knowing Rachel, there's probably some security failsafe that triggered when the power went out, so I'm not worried about all the technology. The UN recognized the island, and you're still my ambassador. You *should* be safe, I hope." Michelle started moving toward the foot of the grand staircase.

Roger nodded as he followed his daughter, "Diplomacy is sacrosanct, they may question me, but they won't harm us. I'm on speaking terms with the German ambassador. I'll contact her before they get here." By *They*, he meant the United States military. *Us* meant her sisters and mother as well. The fact that he made the distinction would be chilling if Michelle gave herself a chance to consider it. "What about Domaas? Are you still connected?"

"The Bond still exists, stretching impossibly thin, but I can feel him. He says they'll be back and expects me to be waiting for him." Roger looked down at Michelle's right arm as purple lightning began to arc and dance, coalescing around the cuff that encircled her wrist. "I'll figure out how to let you know I'm okay."

Roger smiled as he said, "*This* is what I trained you for."

The cuff beeped as it came back to a full charge. Rachel had hinted at the function, but Michelle was not sure it would work with all other Cerulean technology rendered inert. "Time to go." She went to step away but stopped. Looking back at her father, she said, "Tell *them* about the Kesta. If you have a chance to speak with the Kesta, tell *them* the whole story. Especially what I have done and what I tried to do." Michelle turned and raced up the grand staircase.

*****

"Madame President?" President Willow looked away from the wall screen covering the CIC's rear bulkhead. Her security moved her here when the alien ships had begun lifting from their watery births without warning. As aboard every vessel of the United States Navy, the Combat Information Center is one of three hardened zones of the ship. The others were the nuclear power plant buried in the belly of the ship, along with ammunition and fuel storage.

"The island has been deserted. It appears every Cerulean was transported onto their ships before they departed. Ambassador Mizzi was found alone in the mansion, currently en route to being brought aboard." The president turned back to the wall screen and took in the live satellite feed of the island.

"The Seal team?"

From behind her, "The surviving members are aboard the same helo, ma'am."

Surviving. The word rang like a bell in the President's brain. They had held the element of surprise - her security carried swords! And the entire operation had gone completely belly up. She knew it would be hours before the details trickled up to her. But also knew there must have been an unexpected element; there *had to* be. How hard could it have been to capture a child and her *nanny*? The one thing that would have forced the young queen to surrender. "What about our...guests?"

"Vanished, like the others on the island."

So, she thought ruefully. *A complete shitshow, then.* The President also knew Christopher wouldn't be on that helicopter. He would know he'd fallen out of the President's favor for a while until the diplomatic fall-out lessened to a manageable degree, at least. She said over her shoulder, "Enough damage has been done to diplomacy today. Mr. Mizzi is the Ambassador of a recognized sovereign territory." *Of which we just attacked the sovereign of and his daughter*, she didn't add out loud. "Please see to it that he is given acceptable..."

President Willow's eyes focused on the center of the island; the mansion Regent Et'kuraul had been kind enough to give a tour of herself. Proudly showing off the Ceruleans' advancements to the structure and even inviting the President to a private lunch. The President had declined, and the Regent had not looked especially disappointed.

But it was the mansion's roof that her eyes focused on...and the tiny little speck moving across it. She stabbed her finger into the screen, causing the LEDs to warp and discolor. "Zoom in on the mansion, please, tight as it'll go!"

Somewhere behind her in the darkened room, a technician followed her order, and the image blinked once, twice, and then slowly pushed in until she was looking at the top of a head. A head with hair the color of copper. "She's alone...Somehow she got left behind! Do we have anything in the air?"

"Just the BARCAP, aside from the helios, ma'am."

"Get them on the radio, *right now!*"

How her mating bangle had survived her detonation months ago was still a mystery. However, Rachel had incorporated it into the cuff just like her last bracelet. With a click, it snapped into place along the small groove designed for it. There were several beeps and then a faint glimmer of blue light. Michelle's dress vanished, and for a fraction of a second, she wore nothing but her strapless bra and panties. In short order, an exosuit replaced it, fitting as if it had been tailored down to the millimeter. A ring appeared on her shoulders, and the transparent bubble flickered around Michelle's head.

A weight Michelle had not been aware of suddenly vanished from her scalp and neck. Curled strands of copper filament caught in the breeze and began drifting away. *My hair!* Never mind how she'd come into having long hair, Michelle had become quite vain about her copper tresses somewhere along the line. Especially the way her mate would drag his fingers through it during moments of intimacy. "Sorry, Domaas."

A flight HUD appeared before Michelle's eyes as a heavy weight settled on her back. *The thruster pack,* Michelle thought as she held her now gloved hands up and watched her specially designed control spheres appear in her palms. There was another series of beeps, and then:

FLIGHT CONTROLS READY

THRUSTER POWER 100%

FLIGHT PLAYLIST LOADED: BEGIN PLAYBACK

YES / NO

Began flashing in the lower right corner of the HUD. "Rachel, you mad genius, I'm going to name a planet after you."

How she had stuffed a powered flight-capable exosuit into a cuff three inches wide and less than half an inch thick was nothing short of incredible. Using the tracking reticle over her eye, Michelle selected YES and winked. The opening strains of *Flight of the Valkyries* filled Michelle's ears, and she laughed out loud until a roar overhead caused the music to pause. Two F-37s arced by on the edge of their wings, with the lead pilot looking up through his canopy directly at her. Michelle's grin turned wolfish as she reached behind her and carefully slipped the sword's blade down the valley of her spine beneath the thruster pack.

Turning to track the passing F-37 and its lead pilot, Michelle hoped the pilot could read the challenge in the gesture she sent his way, then sprinted toward the edge of the roof.

The two jets were starting to break and circle as Michelle leaped into the air. Gravity opened its arms to her once again, but this time there was a flight computer that instantly sensed her position and deployed wings made of an invisible force field. The thruster pack came alive, and Michelle was airborne. Rolling her left hand forward over the sphere was like pouring gas on a barrel fire, and Michelle broke the sound barrier before she even crossed the beach for open water.

Flight of the Valkyries came back up at full volume.

"Come and fucking get me."

Michelle's vision zeroed in on the island, the bulbous super structure of the supercarrier at the edge of the bay, and she reefed her craft into a high G turn. Keeping the throttle wide open, she lowered her altitude, intending to *buzz the tower.* The sonic boom over the flat top drove the flight deck crew to their knees, and the shock wave was strong enough to send an ancient F-35 over the edge to splash into the ocean.

She was just preparing to set course for the North American continent when a loud beeping cut through the crashing strains of the music filling the bubble around her head. The beeping suddenly turned to a steady tone, and Michelle instinctively banked hard to the left. A long white cylinder with a cone of flame at the tail shot through the space she had been in a mere second before.

She watched it continue for another few hundred yards before exploding harmlessly. Deep in her gut, that beast roared its fury as it seized control of her being.

"Alright then..." Michelle did not have a baby Arya strapped to her back this time, nor three other people to keep alive. It was time to figure out just how capable of a pilot she was.

She pulled back hard and put herself into a vertical climb, leaving her tail wide open and inviting the two jets to continue their pursuit. They'd see the challenge for what it was.

If she had been trying to escape, low and full throttle was the way to go. A pilot only sought altitude when they intended to fight. So the two fighters remained in attack formation and followed her up through twenty-thousand feet in only a few seconds. The entire climb up, Michelle was visualizing her plan of attack with no way of knowing if she could actually pull it off. No way of knowing if the exosuit would respond to her body's commands as it was supposed to. "Let's find out."

Michelle angled into the sun, blinding the heat-seeking sensors on her pursuer's missiles and, more importantly, blinding the pilots. The force-field flashed and sparkled as 20mm bullets impacted hard enough that Michelle felt the craft around her shudder. She backed off the throttle and glanced back, down, over her shoulder. *Almost...*

She let them gain on her through the ballistic climb as she counted down from five. At zero, she cut thrust to idle and deactivated the forcefield. Freezing cold wind whipped at her as she rapidly slowed, and then she felt the iron embrace of gravity one more time. Michelle had a brief moment of clarity to think, *Domaas would fucking kill me if he was watching.*

Michelle kicked hard and fell into a backflip as she pulled P'alta's sword from where it had been stowed against her spine. Time seemed to slow as she braced both hands around the grip of the blade and pivoted into an upright position. Tears ripped from her eyes, but she focused her vision anyway. The lead jet was too close to maneuver away, and with a grit of her teeth, she thrust and dragged the blade through the belly of the aircraft as it passed her. There was the sound of metal shredding apart, and Michelle felt the heat of a fireball as she continued her fall and pivoted for the second fighter. The pilot snap rolled away as it streaked passed, much too far out of reach, and Michelle lost sight of it for the moment.

The ocean, vast and blue, was rushing up to meet her. The island and naval ships, including the *USS Rickover,* were off to the left and growing in size as well. Michelle willed the suit flight systems to activate...

And got nothing.

It was still active, and the bubble returned, but as the HUD re-activated, it flashed red. "Not now, not now, not now..." She tried again and she was rewarded by a loud buzzer, then a diagram of her body appeared, the object in her hand flashing brightly. *Oh.*

Michelle didn't dare look down again as she did her best to quickly stow the sword into its previous position. The Hud flashed green, her control spheres materialized and the forcefield deployed. That was when Michelle finally visually checked her altitude and threw the throttle wide open. The thruster pack ignited at full force and flashed the saltwater mere feet beneath her into a column of steam that boiled away with enough force to simulate an explosion. What water didn't flash to steam became a fountain of erupting water. The G-forces gripped her body, and Michelle barely remembered to tighten her core muscles as the blood was pulled from her brain.

But the *Arya Express* rocketed up from the conflagration and transited back to level flight in a straight line back toward the *Rickover*. The other fighter was still up there somewhere, but there was no way the pilot would fire in the vicinity of his or her ship.

The flight deck was still in chaos from her low-altitude, high-speed flyby. This was compounded by the display she had just put on taking out the first fighter and their need to launch a rescue helo to fish the pilot out of the ocean. By the time any of the crew noticed her approach, she was already descending to land on the bow of the ship.

A crew was preparing a third fighter for take-off, and they were suddenly in a panic as alarm klaxons sounded off from the ship's island. Michelle paid them no mind as she allowed energy to build up in her arm and let it flow down into her clenched fist. A squad of Marines disgorged from the island and began running toward her, rifles raised at the ready. They were yelling commands, but she ignored them as well. Even without the forcefield, she knew her exosuit would protect her from small arms fire. Kneeling down at the very end of the starboard catapult, she slipped her hand into the trench and released her ire.

Sparks erupted down the lengths of all four launch catapults. The sound of powerful magnets shattering and a high voltage powerline shorting out greeted her ears over the din of the flight deck. The rumbling pulse of a minor explosion came from somewhere deep in the ship.

She was surrounded by the squad of Marines, with more rushing to the bow. A thrown lighting bolt to the feet of one of them was enough to freeze them in position as Michelle turned her back and jumped off the bow. She vanished momentarily and then accelerated away at incredible speeds heading for the F-37 orbiting overhead.

*****

"Where in the hell is she going?" President Willow demanded of the quiet CIC behind her. The feed from the satellite had pulled back to encompass the broad expanse of the South Pacific Ocean. Michelle had toyed with the remaining BARCAP fighter for a while until it was obvious even to the President that she was punishing the pilot for trying to engage her.

Eventually, the second fighter had to break off due to low fuel. Despite the President's demands, the *Rickover's* captain had to explain that his ship had been turned into not much more than an oversized barge until further notice.

Initial reports from damage control teams were grim. All four cata-pults had been utterly destroyed along with the primary power coupling to the secondary reactor. Whatever she had used to deliver that charge, it had been more than enough to knock the US Navy's flagship out of commission. The *USS Rickover* had a date with the dry dock in Pearl Harbor

After the F-37 pilot had disengaged, even wagging his wings as if to beg for mercy, the Regent had settled into level flight mere yards above the waves. The white line caused by her wake was easily visible as she raced over the ocean at twice the speed of sound. Something no sane pilot would do just *tens* of feet from immolation. Almost like she knew she was being watched and wanted them to see.

"If she remains on her current course and speed...she'll be feet dry in Southern California by tomorrow morning," the Captain finally an-swered. "I don't see how she'll have enough fuel to make it, though. That's a sixteen-hour subsonic flight. There's no way that little jet pack could remain supersonic for much longer." President Willow turned slowly to look at the Captain with abject ire in her eyes. They had just watched her use a goddamned *sword* to take out one pilot, somehow disable flight operations aboard a United States Supercarrier, and outfly a fighter pilot until he had to break off; that she had let him in an act of mercy, was as equal a slap in the face as the rest of it! What she could and could not do was a subjective notion at this point.

The Captain shifted on his feet under the President's gaze, but he did not look away. "If you order it, ma'am, I can contact Continental Defense and have them get some birds in the air to meet her."

"Do it." The Captain stepped to the crewman operating the comms console.

"From the time my daughter turned ten," Roger said quietly. "I and her uncle trained her with everything we could about self-defense, survival, and evasion...among other things." The President turned on her heel, nearly an about-face, to look Ambassador Mizzi in the eye. Her face soured when she saw he wasn't even trying to hide the pride on his face. He'd watched almost the entire display standing right next to the woman. "Once she reaches the US, you will not find her. You won't even hear from her until she decides. If you see her, it will be because she chooses to be seen." Roger's chest swelled. "And if her pattern holds, it will be in grand fashion."

President Willow bit her tongue and began to turn back to the screen, but Ambassador Mizzi spoke again. "We should speak in private, Madame President."

"About what? Did your daughter have some parting shots for me on the way out the door?"

Roger's face turned serious as he said, "She wants me to brief you about the Kesta - the reason why every Cerulean on the island evacuated and the fleet left in such a hurry. Their arrival is imminent."